Masquerade

Gayle Lynds

Masquerade

DOUBLEDAY

New York
London
Toronto
Sydney
Auckland

PUBLISHED BY DOUBLEDAY
a division of Bantam Doubleday Dell Publishing Group, Inc.
1540 Broadway, New York, New York 10036

DOUBLEDAY and the portrayal of an anchor with a dolphin are trademarks of
Doubleday, a division of Bantam Doubleday Dell Publishing Group, Inc.

Library of Congress Cataloging-in-Publication Data

Lynds, Gayle.
    Masquerade / Gayle Lynds. — 1st ed.
      p.   cm.
    1. Intelligence service—United States—Fiction. 2. Women spies—United States—
Fiction. 3. Amnesia—Fiction. I. Title.
    PS3562.Y442M37 1996
    813'.54—dc20   95-37569
                                                          CIP

ISBN 0-385-47961-1

Printed in the United States of America
February 1996
First Edition
10 9 8 7 6 5 4 3 2 1

For Dennis,
with love

For advice and assistance, I am especially grateful to former intelligence agent Philip Shelton; speech and language pathologist Karyn Lewis Searcy, M.A. C.C.C.; espionage specialist and author Michael Kurland; editor Fred Klein; and Linda Tesar, Ph.D., Department of Economics, University of California at Santa Barbara.

For all their generous analysis and help, I am indebted to Julia Cunningham, Nancy Fisher, Bina Garfield, Brian Garfield, Gary Gulbransen, Susan Miles Gulbransen, Sheila Johnson, Ken Kuhlken, Dennis Lynds, Christine McNaught, and Katy Peake.

In the often perilous journey to publication, I deeply appreciate the high professional standards and many courtesies of Arlene Friedman, Ellen Archer, Russell Gordon, Tammy Blake, Peter Block-Garcia, Brandon Saltz, and Gabrielle Brooks.

Finally, a heartfelt thank you to Danny Baror for believing so early, to Judy Kern for her unerring editorial eye, and to the extraordinary Henry Morrison for his insight and ideas, his patience and kindness.

Certainty is based on flimsier evidence than most of us realize.

—ELLEN J. LANGER, Ph.D.,
Harvard psychologist,
author of *Mindfulness*

Part One

Liz Sansborough

One

Her past was slipping away. One morning she awoke to find strange furniture in her room. The man told her, "It's all yours. Don't you remember?" She didn't remember, but it was too much effort to say so. She was exhausted and hurt and confused. Her head felt as if it would explode. After a while she no longer knew where she was. Then she no longer knew her name.

"You don't know your name?" he said.

"No." Pain pounded relentlessly behind her eyes.

"You will," he said. "Soon, I promise. Just rest, my beautiful darling."

As her suffering ebbed away, so did her strength. Her hands shook. Her lips trembled. She never answered the door or the telephone. She never sat beside the window or behind the desk. She'd come to distrust the world. Except for the man's voice, she lived in silence. Tried to hear in it who she was.

The man gave her medicine. He fed her like a baby. He undressed and showered her. She was helpless. All she had was the man, and a sense of loss so deep it shook her soul.

Sleep was her salvation. She stayed in bed. Time stopped.

The man gave her different pills.

She felt better. Stronger.

He told her his name was Gordon. "Don't you remember me yet, Liz, darling?"

"I wish—" She paused, the words lost, the idea forgotten.

Sunlight streamed through the windows. A fresh salt breeze fluttered her nightgown. She held onto furniture and pulled herself around the living room.

"You're Gordon?"

"Yes, darling."

"You said my name was Liz."

"Liz Sansborough." He grinned, pleased. "You'll be back to your old self soon now."

Liz Sansborough. The name repeated itself in her mind. She seemed to hear it at all hours, throbbing like a heartbeat.

The day she dressed herself, she asked, "Gordon, what's happened to me?"

"It was eight, nine weeks ago," he told her. "You slipped and fell down a cliff. You landed on the rocks just above the surf. It was terrible, darling. You didn't break anything, but you hit your head."

She grimaced.

"It gave you a concussion, and then sort of a brain fever. The doctor says that can happen. Inflamed brain tissue after a head injury, I mean. The inflammation caused your amnesia."

"I have amnesia," she said numbly. "Of course. Amnesia."

A stranger was in her room. She awoke sweating, panicked.

"Do you remember me, Liz?" He approached through the morning shadows, carrying what looked like a small suitcase.

"I . . . think so. Who—?"

"I'm your doctor. My name is Allan Levine." He was tall and cadaverous, but his voice was friendly. He set down his bag and smiled. "I haven't been here for a few days." He took her blood pressure and her pulse. "All your signs are normal again. The fact that you awoke while I was here shows how much more alert you are." He listened to her heart. He smiled but worked with the focus of a microscope. She wasn't sure she liked that.

"When will I be able to remember my life?"

"I don't know. Try not to worry about it." He took off his stethoscope. "I have some news you're going to like. First, you're so much better that I'll come only once a week from now on. And second, I'm reducing your medication to a pill a day."

"Which pill?" She hated taking so many of them.

"Your antidepressant. It'll help keep you on track."

"But I don't feel depressed."

"Of course you don't. But if you quit it, your brain chemicals will go out of control—wild—like before. You'll risk a relapse, and I can't guarantee you'll come out of it next time. Stop the antidepressants if you like, but I don't advise it."

The memory of the relentless pain in her mind, the horrifying chaos returned. "I never want to feel that again."

She and Gordon took walks. She grew stronger.

She dreamed and awoke with visions of other lives, other people, never herself. She looked around the dark bedroom. A room she had no memory of.

She arose and went to the living room. "Where are we?"

Gordon sat up on the sofa in the morning gloom, rubbing sleep from his eyes. "Liz? Is something wrong?" He turned on the lamp and looked at his watch. "It's only five o'clock!"

"Where are we?" she demanded again.

He studied her. "Santa Barbara. That's in California."

She turned, surveying the Danish-modern furniture, the stacks of books, the Venetian blinds closed against the dawn. This was the living room. There were three more rooms—kitchen, bathroom, and the bedroom, where she slept. Gordon slept on the sofa out here in the living room.

She swung her arms, gestured at it all. "I know, you told me that. But what's this place?"

"Your condo. We've been living here a couple of years. You and I." He paused, asked softly, "Do you remember, darling?"

She sat heavily in the rocking chair. "We were lovers?"

He smiled. "Do you mind?"

Her gaze swept his long frame, rumpled from sleep, and came to rest on his beaming face. He was muscular, tall, with wavy brown hair and a square jaw. Handsome and solid, like the cowboys she watched in old TV Westerns. All that was good, but far more appealing was his constancy. She hungered for that. She had no past, and he was her lifeline to an unremembered, unknown world.

"Of course I don't mind." She smiled back. Suddenly she felt better. "But everything's so new. You. Me. This condo. Everything. What woke me was I realized something funny about my memory. I can't remember where I've been living, but I can remember how to tie my shoes and cook and even how to program the VCR. How can I know all that but nothing about my life?"

"Good question. Come on, let's have one of our walks."

"At this hour?"

"I'll explain it to you."

The summer air was fragrant and quiet. Santa Barbara's early morning streets were shadowy. Palm trees stood tall and black against the pastel sky. Gordon and Liz took a winding path through Alice Keck Park.

"So?" she prompted.

"Ah, I see you haven't forgotten."

"Not likely. Not if it has to do with what's wrong with me."

"Of course. But all I know is what Dr. Levine told me."

"And that is . . . ?"

"There are two kinds of memory—task memory and fact memory. Task memory is just what it says: Tasks. Doing things. What you can do. Like cooking, or driving a car, or tying your shoes, or programming the VCR. Fact memory is the details around it—who, what, where, when, and why. Your identity. What's happened to you is typical of amnesiacs. You've lost all your fact memory and maybe some of your task memory. We may not know exactly what for a while."

"So that's why I know how to read, but I can't remember any of the books I read before. Or why I wanted to. Or my accident."

She lifted her face into the sea wind and increased her speed. She felt driven by some mysterious force deep within, a strange force that compelled her to race ahead as if by physical insistence alone she could heal her mind and recapture her soul.

Gordon kept pace. A fresh wind blew north across Santa Barbara's red-tiled roofs, rustling hibiscus and palms. The air tasted of salt and summer. Gordon told her the month was July.

The next afternoon her questions coalesced.

Who was she really? Not just a name, an identity. Where did she come from? How long had she lived in Santa Barbara? Was she married? Did she have children? Who were her parents? What kind of work did she do?

Who? Where?

What *kind* of person was she?

She asked Gordon, and he brought out a faded photo album. They sat together at the dining-room table. She smiled eagerly, nervously, as he told her, "Your name, as you know, is Elizabeth Sansborough. 'Liz,' right? You were born in London and grew up on Shawfield Street in Chelsea. Does that sound familiar?"

"England?" She shook her head. "No, dammit."

"Take it easy, darling."

Something was wrong. "Why don't I have a British accent?"

"All I know is what you told me—that you imitated your father, and his accent was, as you'll see in a minute, American."

He opened the album, pointed to a snapshot on the first page. In it picturesque row houses lined a narrow street. The white houses rose three stories, with chimney pots on top and black wrought-iron fences in front. Standing before one of the houses was a little girl in patent-leather Mary Janes and a tailored wool coat. She held the hand of a smiling man in an overcoat.

"That's you and your father, Harold Sansborough," Gordon said. "And that's the house where you grew up. Your father was an American salesman, but he moved to London after he married your mother. Her name was Melanie Childs, and she was English. He worked for U.S. companies there. See, that next picture's your mother. Quite a beauty."

From a large portrait, Melanie Childs Sansborough, somewhere in her early twenties, stared off into the future. Liz looked nothing like her. Melanie had delicate features, a slender nose, and moist blue eyes that spoke of a protected upbringing. A pearl hung on a chain from her neck.

Liz smiled, relieved. She was looking at her parents. Real people, a real past, tangible and promising.

"What did my mother do?"

"She was just a housewife." He turned more pages, pointed to snapshots of Liz as a child—riding a pony in Hyde Park, boating with her parents on the lake in Battersea Park, flying kites along the Embankment. Other photos showed family vacations in France and summer visits to New York, where her father had gone for annual sales meetings.

The last snapshot was of her, suddenly a young, leggy adult, standing between her proud parents. She resembled her father.

She glanced up, breathed deeply.

Then she looked down again at herself, a teenager, in the old photo. It was she, all right, but it was also a person she didn't know.

She took the album to the bedroom and stared into the mirror, then she studied the young woman on the album page. Tall and lanky. A high forehead, flared nose, and wide mouth. Distinct cheekbones. She looked closely at the photo: Yes, there it was. The little finger on her left hand was crooked.

She held up her left hand and looked at the finger. It was crooked in the same way.

"You broke it when you were a child," Gordon told her from the doorway. "A skating accident. It never mended right."

"Yes. It still aches sometimes."

In the photo she noted the young woman's thick auburn hair and the black mole just above the right corner of her mouth. She looked into the mirror and touched the striking mole on her face.

She and the young woman were the same.

One person. Her.

Dramatic, not delicate. With an odd sense of distance, she realized she was beautiful, and that for some reason being beautiful was important.

He told her, "You were eighteen then and headed for Cambridge."

"The university? Was I a student?"

"That's enough for now."

"But I need to know—"

"You'll know everything soon. Very soon."

It wasn't good enough. "But what kind of person am I? *Who* am I? Do I teach school, rob banks, what have I become?"

He shook his head. "We're going to do this right, darling. The doctor warned me. I'm supposed to wait until you ask for information and then feed it to you slowly so you don't get overwhelmed. Remember, you almost died from the brain fever. Your mind's healing, but we can't rush it. Your past has to evolve. With time everything's going to come back to you." He gave her a confident thumb's-up and headed to the kitchen.

She turned pages, studied the pictures. And suddenly another question struck her. If Gordon was supposed to wait until she wanted information, why had he just refused to tell her any more when she'd asked? Why was he afraid she'd be "overwhelmed" . . . unless there was something he was worried about, something *she* should worry about?

"Liz! What are you doing?" He strode across the cluttered living room to the desk where she sat. *Her* desk, or so he'd led her to believe.

"Who's Sarah Walker?" She waved a sheaf of correspondence at him.

Fury fought with worry on his square face. "The doctor said—"

"I don't give a damn what the doctor said! This is my life. I've got a right to know who—and what—I am!"

He leaned across the desk, his jaw jutting. "Dammit, Liz! It's too soon!"

"For what, Gordon? For what?"

He leaned forward another inch. His square face was red. His brown eyes snapped. She'd never seen him angry. His furious worry softened something hard and lonely inside her. But she had to *know.* She slammed the correspondence down onto the desk.

"I'm sorry I've upset you, Gordon, but Sarah Walker . . . I've got to know. Who is she? See, I found these magazine articles in the drawer." She dumped them onto the desk, too. " 'Tear sheets,' I think they're called. Articles published in some magazine called *Talk,* and they have Sarah Walker's byline on them. It seems to me, from looking through the files on the computer, that both the computer and desk must be hers. There's nothing in the drawers or files with my name. Nothing!"

Gordon inhaled, calming himself. He stood back. "I was warned this wouldn't be easy. But dammit, couldn't you have waited a while?"

"No. One way or another, I'm going to find out."

"I've got to call Dr. Levine first. Once he approves, I'm off the hook. Be fair, Liz. He saved your life. He cares about you."

"Even if he says no, I won't stop. I can't. I need to fill this empty hole that used to be my life. What will I find next you won't explain? Letters, more photos, mementoes—"

Before she could finish, he was at the telephone, dialing. She stood beside him as he talked to the doctor. At last he nodded and hung up. "He says if you're so determined, you can probably handle it."

"Of course, I can." She followed him to the hall closet, relieved to no longer be angry with him. As far as she was concerned, he, more than the doctor, had saved her life.

"Yes, but he still wants me to lead you through it." From the closet's top shelf Gordon slid a stack of thick file folders, another photo album, and two video cassettes.

"Thanks." Trembling, she took the materials and headed for the sofa. He sat beside her, and she opened the new album to the first page. A photo showed her and her parents standing before a majestic ancient church with buttresses and spires.

"Recognize it?" he asked. "That's King's College Chapel in Cambridge."

But before she could answer, a deafening burst of sharp, erratic explosions filled the room. At the same instant, a window shattered inward. The table next to her exploded. A lamp cartwheeled and crashed. She recognized the sounds in some deep recess of her mind. Gunshots!

"Liz! Down!"

She dove to the carpet and crawled behind the sofa. A second fusillade ripped through the condo, smashing wood, glass, plaster. Then Gordon was beside her. He pulled a pistol from inside his shirt and another from beneath the sofa. He shoved one into her hand. It was huge. An automatic, she thought.

How did she know it was an automatic?

"Take it!" he ordered.

She stared. "I don't know how to—"

"Yes, you do. Take it!"

She grabbed the gun. It felt . . . familiar.

Who was she?

Two

Suddenly there was silence. Plaster dust rained down from the ceiling. A shard of window glass shattered to the floor. Tension was electric.

Then another fusillade blasted through the broken windows.

Gordon's voice was tight. "They're shooting from across the street, keeping us down. They—"

"Why, Gordon? Who are they? Who are we? Who—"

An explosion rocked the condominium.

"Liz! Watch—"

The front door blew across the room, splintering chairs and a table. Three men burst through the gaping door frame. Gordon rose to a crouch, firing. One man fell back through the doorway. The two others dove right and left into the room, returned fire with a burst of bullets that ripped the couch.

"Liz!"

She held the big automatic, watched as the man on the right crawled rapidly out of view. He was on his elbows, a stubby black weapon with a short barrel and a hand-hold sticking out its side cradled in the crook of his arm. She turned as he came around the couch. He looked straight into her eyes. His face was bland, expressionless, topped by slicked-back brown hair.

He raised to his knees, the black weapon aimed directly at her heart. In seconds she'd be dead—

She pulled her trigger.

The gun bucked in her hands and she felt pain inside her. She was dead . . . she was . . . staring at the man on his knees as his chest turned red and his mouth poured red and he was thrown backward like a rag doll into the wall and—

Other men swarmed into the room and knocked over the third gunman.

"Look after Gordon!" someone shouted.

Liz turned again. Gordon lay collapsed on the floor behind her. Blood covered him. Hands lifted her up, pulled her toward the doorway.

"Gordon!"

"We'll take care of him. Come on. Quick! Now!"

She was in the hall and being half-pulled, half-carried to the service stairs at the rear. She resisted, fought.

"Christ, we're friends, Sansborough!"

"No time to explain it. Just bring her!"

Three of them wrestled her down the stairs and out to a waiting car. They shoved her in. Two new men pinned her there. The door closed, and the car screeched off in a stink of burning rubber. It turned up Micheltorena Street.

Another car was slewed across the street as they passed. Bullet holes riddled it.

Men ran to a third car as sirens blared. Police cars raced up Garden Street, heading toward her condo.

The car in which she was a passenger dove into the maze of small streets on the Riviera, climbed steep hills, and plunged across a long ridge and then down into a valley. She had no idea where she was. She and Gordon had never come this way.

Finally they stopped at a house hidden up a deserted canyon. The men hustled her inside to a room with a bed and desk. The door closed, and she heard it lock. There were bars on the windows.

Shadows spread long and inky across the small room. She had been sitting there for what seemed hours, her stomach roiling. How badly was Gordon hurt?

What about the bland-faced man with the slicked-back brown hair and the bloodied chest and mouth? Had she killed him?

And who were they, these men who said they were friends?

Did "friends" lock you in a room alone?

They had saved her from the attackers in the condo, and they knew Gordon. Or at least his name. But—

She heard the door being unlocked and a man came in. He was older, thin, with graying hair and a kindly face. He carried a tray of sandwiches and milk.

"Why am I locked in?"

"We're sorry, but there just hasn't been time to explain everything, Liz. You wouldn't understand yet. We were afraid you'd try to run away. But you're safe here, you need to eat, and we've sent for—"

"Where's Gordon? Is he hurt badly?"

"He's in the hospital. I don't know how serious it is, but I'll find out as soon as I can."

"What about the man I shot?"

"Dead. A clean kill."

She closed her eyes, nauseated.

"You had to shoot him, Liz. He would've killed you."

She steadied her stomach, forced her eyes open. "Are you the police?"

"In a way. We've sent for your doctor. He'll be here soon. Now eat, okay?"

She didn't want to. She thought of Gordon and of the dead man. She bit into the first sandwich.

"Liz, are you all right?" Dr. Levine hurried in, his long, gaunt face clouded. He turned on the overhead light, took a stethoscope from his bag, and checked her. "They tell me it was a close call."

"Who were those men? Why did they want to kill us?"

"Not Gordon. You, I'm afraid. And yes, you're certainly entitled to know why. But I warn you, finding out about your whole life in what amounts to a relative instant can be a shock, traumatic. If you begin to feel overwhelmed, stop. Finish tomorrow."

He left and returned with the photo album, the file folders, and the two video cassettes she'd begun to examine at the condo. She took them gratefully, and the thin man with graying hair rolled in a television set and VCR.

"Is there any word about Gordon?"

"Sorry, Liz." The doctor paused in the doorway. "I've given your medication to your security detail. They'll get you some clothes, fix you up. You can trust them. Do they have to lock you in anymore?"

She looked at the album, the cassettes, and the dossiers on her lap and shook her head. The doctor left. There was no sound of the door locking after him.

Outside her window, stars sparkled across the black sky. She went to the desk and turned on the lamp. She opened the first file folder and began reading about her life.

She'd studied international relations at Cambridge and moved in with a lover. The album contained dozens of photos, with typed lines of description, showing her with a dark-complected young man —in a tea shop, standing before the red-brick library, hiking along hedgerows, watching punters on the Cam. He had a serious face, smooth-cheeked, with coal-black eyes and hair. In almost every snapshot the hair tumbled over his forehead as if no force could control it or him. A dossier said his name was Huseyn Shaheed Noon, and he was a member of a prominent Pakistani family. He had returned home to tell his family about her, and while he was there he'd taken up his little plane for a recreational flight. The engine failed. He crashed and died.

In the silent room she tried to recognize the solemn youth with the earnest eyes, but she couldn't. She'd loved him. She must have been devastated to lose him. But what was love? She loved Gordon, still . . . she had no remembered experience of romantic love, and the concept, the hugeness and newness of it, was more than she wanted to deal with.

Her parents had died, too, while she was at Cambridge. Killed by a mugger in New York City during one of her father's annual sales meetings. She felt a jolt of pain for this unremembered couple. Her parents.

What would it take to retrieve her memory, to again feel their passing as the personal loss she knew it must have been?

For a few moments she sat and thought of those two unknown people who had been her parents. With a long sigh she returned to her reading and received another emotional jolt.

The year after her parents died she'd married a blond young man with freckles, muscles, and a look of easy confidence. Garrick Richmond, an American on a Fulbright scholarship at Cambridge. There were even more photos of her and the blond American. He was always smiling, radiating happy-go-lucky charm. Twenty-one that year, she had also chosen U.S. citizenship. Later she and Garrick had moved to Virginia, where he worked for the Central Intelligence Agency. It was dangerous work, and Garrick Richmond had been killed while on assignment in Lebanon.

She closed the album and the file folder. A dark, suffocating cloak fell over her. Another death of someone she'd loved. Had everyone she'd loved died? Was there something about her, some curse she couldn't remember? Without her memory she could only speculate and be afraid. Without her memory it seemed as if they'd never lived. Without her memory *she'd* never lived.

She walked to the bed. When the memory is blank, you can't be yourself because you don't know who you are. You have no identity. No past that shaped you. No experiences to make judgments from. No old emotions to test new ones against.

You're simply a face in the mirror. The taste of toothpaste. The square of sunlight that warms you. The feel of cotton soft against your skin.

You grieve and rage and speculate endlessly, fruitlessly.

Her name was Liz Sansborough. She was thirty-two years old. Widowed. Except for Gordon, everyone she had loved was dead. She lay on the bed in the strange room and cried for all those thirty-two years, for all those she had lost and didn't remember.

She had worked for the CIA. She was a spy.

Her complete CIA dossier was in the next file folder. She'd joined after Garrick Richmond was killed. She'd trained at Camp Peary, Virginia, "the Farm." The dossier listed the instruments and machines she'd checked out on. Her cipher and judo skills. Marksmen tests. She was a good shot . . . or had been. No wonder Gordon had insisted she take the automatic.

She put a cassette into the VCR. According to the label, it showed her London flat, filmed by a friend five years ago. The flat was small, with the same Danish-modern furniture that now decorated her Santa Barbara condo. A close-up showed her holding a book, the little finger on her left hand crooked.

She remembered none of it.

The second cassette had been made by the Company. It showed her on surveillance in Potsdam . . . picking up a drop in Salzburg . . . trailing someone through a murky alley in Vienna. At the end of the film, she looked up from the Vienna darkness, and yellow lamplight illuminated her in a haloed glow. That face was hers, right down to the dramatic beauty mark above her mouth.

According to her dossier, she'd been stationed in London because she knew it so well, and she'd worked throughout western Europe. Then, three years ago, she'd been sent to meet a courier in Lisbon. When she got there, the courier was dead. An assassin who called himself the Carnivore had just shot him. The Carnivore then shot her. Shot her and left her for dead.

It had been a long haul, but CIA medical people had pulled her through. Then they'd retired her and set her up in Santa Barbara as a journalist with the cover name Sarah Walker.

Sarah Walker!

So the desk in the condo was hers after all. She contemplated being someone named Sarah Walker. A magazine journalist. There was something familiar about the name, but it was more an emotion than a memory.

Then she thought about being shot and left for dead. In a way, she had died. Only the dead remembered as little as she.

Was all this really her?

The last item in the file folder was a photograph of her and Gordon, arms wrapped around each other, standing on the beach. They were wearing swimsuits, and behind them white surf pounded the golden sand. She studied the photo, turned it over. The inscription said the picture had been taken the year before at Hendry's beach.

They looked happy.

As she stared at the photo, she heard the door open. She turned. Gordon stood there, his face pale, his shoulder heavily bandaged, his arm in a sling.

She ran to hold him.

They were sitting side by side on the bed in the small room. She said, "I worked for the CIA. You knew that?"

"Yes, Liz."

"Then you must be with the CIA, too."

"That's how we met, you and I. We call it the Company, or the Agency, or simply Langley."

"And the men who rescued us, this house?"

Gordon smiled. "They're CIA, too. This is one of our safe houses."

"But how could you and I have been living together in Santa Barbara? What about your work? Your assignments?"

"Even agents have private lives, darling. I was in and out, but Santa Barbara became 'home.' *You* were home. See this?" He held up his left hand. On the ring finger was a wide gold band.

She remembered seeing it, but hadn't really thought about it. "We're married?"

"Not officially. Not our style."

He took a smaller band from his shirt pocket, studied it solemnly, then smiled into her eyes. "This one is yours."

"You gave it to me . . . before?" She glanced at her left hand, the ring finger, so smooth and empty.

"Yes. We gave the rings to each other when I moved in. But the nurse took yours off in the hospital. They worry about theft, especially when the patient is unconscious. Then, when we found out you had amnesia, I figured I didn't have the right to put it back on. Take it, darling."

The gold band was heavy on her palm.

"When you fell and got the concussion," he told her softly, "I couldn't leave you. You became my assignment. Making you well."

She sensed he wanted her to put on the ring, but she couldn't. It was too full of meaning she didn't yet understand.

She slipped it into her pocket and changed the subject. " 'The Carnivore' is an ugly name, vicious sounding. Who is he, Gordon?"

He acknowledged her decision with a disappointed flicker of his eyes. "An international assassin, with a code name to match his reputation. No one knows who he really is, and there are no photos of him. He supposedly kills anyone who sees him. That's what happened to you in Lisbon. He believed you had seen him, so he had to kill you."

She looked into his ashen face and said, "Tell me everything about him. The Carnivore."

Gordon stood, paced across the room to the barred windows. He gazed out at the night as if he could see not only the past, but the future.

"For thirty years, give or take, Langley's tried everything to neutralize him." He turned, his face grim. "And we're not the only ones. Every other intelligence agency on both sides of the old Iron Curtain would like to take him out, now more than ever. He's a loose cannon in an increasingly volatile world. Ruthless. Efficient.

Totally independent. His only allegiance is to money. We've heard his real name is Alex Bosa, but we haven't been able to confirm it. When and where he was born, his parents' nationalities, his schooling, if he even had any, his age, are also big unknowns. We don't know what he looks like, because, as I explained, he kills anyone who spots him."

"If I saw him, why didn't I give you a description?"

"Apparently, all you saw was a silhouette, but he thought you saw a lot more. He fired. His bullet knocked you unconscious and left one hell of a lot of fatal-looking blood."

Fear clenched her heart. "I was lucky."

"Very. If a police patrol hadn't turned into the alley just as he was heading toward you—his back was to them—probably to make sure he'd finished you off, he'd have realized you were alive. Fortunately he ran. We figured right away it was him, and the next day we got confirmation from covert ops."

Liz shivered. Then she realized Gordon was staring at her. He was intense, gloomy. She studied his pallid face, his bandaged shoulder, his arm in the sling. She thought about the sudden, violent attack on her condo and the CIA's swift rescue.

The pieces began to fit together with chilling logic. "Obviously the CIA's been watching me," she said. "Those men who attacked us! Who were they?"

"We're not sure. The one we caught hasn't talked and probably won't. But we know what they wanted."

She waited, her heart pounding.

He said, "We've had a leak. The Carnivore's heard you survived, Liz, and he says your claim that you didn't see his face is too convenient to be believable. He's spread the word he'll pay top dollar to your killer. He's taking no chances, so he's personally looking for you, too. One way or another, he's going to make sure . . . this time . . . you die."

Three

In a working-class area of Paris, a man wearing soiled jeans and a tight T-shirt fought his way through a pack of striking bus drivers and entered a tough bar. He needed the maintenance van that had been parked outside. He intended to steal the van and its driver.

The man had a light gait and an uncanny ability to blend into his surroundings. He was about sixty years old, but he looked at least a decade younger. In Zurich, cosmetic surgery had erased his wrinkles, flattened his nose, and decreased his chin. In Rome, a doctor had capped his teeth and destroyed the records, making the new teeth impossible to trace. In Berlin, a special acid had burned off his fingerprints. Now he was taking steroids again and working out daily. His mind was clear, and his heart was as cool and ruthless as it had ever been. He was a businessman. He had returned to Paris yesterday.

He kept his gray hair in a crew cut, and for that reason in some French circles he was called Plume. In English, he was Quill.

Quill moved straight to the bar, caught the bartender's eye, and jerked his head. As the bartender approached, scowling and wiping a glass, Quill scanned the patrons lined up as if at a trough. Better here than outside in the noise and chaos.

The bartender stood before him. *"Qu'est-ce que?"*

"Bock. Miller.'' Quill laid a few coins on the bar.

As the bartender scooped them into his white apron and headed for the tap, Quill spotted the man he needed. The driver. On the back of his tan jump suit was the name of the maintenance company, which was also stenciled on the van outside.

Quill picked up his beer and headed toward him. The man was drinking beer, too. It was early afternoon, and a hard-working Frenchman grew dry.

Far south of Paris, on the green banks of the Rhone, the *citoyens* of the ancient city of Avignon stepped from shops, offices, and homes into the sparkling summer sunshine. Gay calliope music was ringing in the distance, calling forth the city's excited children, who knew from colorful posters pasted to twelfth-century walls and twentieth-century lampposts that a circus would parade through that day. As the country spiraled deeper into yet another recession, people hungered for any respite from their troubles.

In the back of a petrol stop, a young woman in bicycling clothes locked herself into a primitive stall. There was no toilet, only a hole in the ground and two worn spots in the stone where she was to place her feet.

But she wasn't there to use the facilities.

With smooth, practiced skill she stripped off her cap, sunglasses, backpack, and biking clothes. From the backpack she took out a cheap, formless dress, put it on, and stuffed the bicycling outfit into the backpack.

She did not rush. Nor did she waste motion. Consequently she was very fast.

From a side pocket she removed a compact mirror and makeup. She rubbed on makeup base until her natural rosiness turned to leather. She drew furrow lines around her mouth and across her forehead. She smoothed the lines. With a scarf, thick-lensed eyeglasses, and a sun-dried face, she would turn no heads in bustling Avignon.

She felt a welcome rush of adrenaline. For three years she hadn't worked. She'd missed it, although she'd be glad—no, "euphoric" was more accurate—when this operation was finished.

Satisfied with her new appearance, she went outside. The calliope music was coming closer, which meant she had little time. She bicycled to an *épicerie*, where she filled the wicker basket on her handlebars with fresh carrots, strings of garlic, onions, and radishes. She paid with francs.

She pedaled away again, this time heading up the avenue to a spot she knew the circus would pass. She established herself on a corner and called her wares like any good French countrywoman.

"Ciboules grand! Carottes! Radises! Ail!" She held up a garlic rope in her right hand, and a bunch of plump red radishes in the other. *"Ail grand! Radises grands!"*

As the parade appeared down the avenue, a housewife bought garlic and onions. An office clerk looked over. He bought red radishes, dusted one off, and took a bite just as the first circus ponies pranced past.

Then came the clowns, tumbling, playing tag, and stopping for exaggerated handshakes among the crowd. Clowns were always the best advertisement for a circus, and the watching throng seemed to swell with excitement as they rollicked past.

The countrywoman was excited, too, and she rolled her bicycle closer so she was right on the curb. One of the clowns spotted her. Roly-poly and dressed like a Napoleonic sailor, the clown paused to juggle colored balls before her.

The countrywoman laughed and clapped her hands. But as she did, her bicycle dropped off the curb and crashed forward into the grease-painted clown.

The crowd gasped.

The clown snatched the juggling balls from the air and fell.

The woman grabbed her bicycle and dropped beside the clown.

"My apologies!" she cried loudly in French. "What have I done! Are you all right?" And then she whispered in rapid English, "How is everything?"

"Going as planned. And you?"

She smiled. "We're off to a good start then."

There was time for no more. The clown rocked back and bounced quickly forward onto huge buffoon feet.

The crowd clapped.

With a deep bow, the clown presented the blue juggling ball to the leather-faced countrywoman. She took it with a loud *merci*, and the clown raced back to join the jaunty procession.

Although she was impatient to be on her way, the young woman stayed on the curb, remaining in character. At last, after the entire circus had paraded past, she pedaled off.

In a different petrol station, she cleaned her face and changed back into her bicycling clothes. She cut open the rubber ball and removed a single rolled sheet of paper. She rolled the paper tighter and slipped it inside a ballpoint pen. Then she cut up the ball and dropped the pieces down the toilet.

She emerged, studied her surroundings carefully, and rode away in the French sunshine, south toward Marseille, where she'd change identities again and fly to Paris. She was a very pretty woman, and she was smiling.

In the smoky bar in working-class Paris, Quill bought beer for the French maintenance man until at last he staggered outside. Quill let another patron leave, and then *he* followed.

The maintenance man climbed behind the wheel of his van and fumbled for his keys. Quill glanced up and down the street, now quiet in the aftermath of the demonstration. He took a small black case from his pocket, opened it, and slipped out the loaded hypodermic. He opened the driver's side door.

The maintenance man turned, his bleary eyes suddenly alert. He saw the hypodermic, gathered himself in an instant, and swung a powerful fist at Quill's head.

Quill ducked, closed in, and injected the man's hip. The man lunged again, but his power was abruptly gone. Quill shoved him across the seat, and the Frenchman slumped back, eyes closed. When he awoke in the morning, he'd have a painful hangover and no memory of how he and his van had spent the rest of the day.

Quill got behind the wheel and started the engine. He kept four safe houses throughout Paris. No one knew about any of them, and he intended to keep it that way. He'd stayed in one last night. Now, with the maintenance man unconscious, he visited the three others, disguised with his new face and the maintenance company's jump suit and cap. He checked utilities, security systems, and exit routes. He carried in food, medical supplies, and disguises.

Quill could have hired people to do this, but he'd learned long ago even the most reliable "friend" could be persuaded to turn, if the price were right. He preferred to work alone.

At four o'clock he returned to the Left Bank and parked down the boulevard from a massive steel-and-glass skyscraper, a multimillion-dollar piece of Paris real estate called Le Tour Languedoc.

He turned off the van's motor, crossed his arms over his muscled chest, and nodded forward, as if dozing. This was the only time he felt nervous, but it was a peculiar nervousness, muted by the weight of years. It manifested itself simply as a heavy sense of expectation.

At last he saw her, striding down the street through the sunshine. He stared up through his eyelashes, still apparently dozing, and watched. He adored her lanky stride, tall height, glossy auburn hair, the way she looked in the skin-tight, black-sheath dress. He allowed himself only a minute to savor her.

His gaze expertly swept the boulevard, spotting the obvious tail: a woman one hundred meters back, in a boutique business suit, an artist's portfolio under one arm, the other hand free to pull a pistol from the thick portfolio, for he had no doubt she carried one in there.

Then he spotted the two other tails. They were ahead, waiting on the far side of the Languedoc. One was in a car, the other watering plants. He scrutinized them. And again moved his gaze. There was a fourth tail! Which signaled the high regard in which the Languedoc held this operation.

At last his long-striding beauty reached Le Tour Languedoc.

Quill checked the four who were surveilling her. She swung through the double glass doors and headed to the most distant elevator. Only the "artist" followed, and she stopped at the first elevator.

Quill nodded. Good. It was all going as planned.

He'd continue his own preparations only after she reemerged, after he'd followed her to make certain she lost her tails safely, and after he was certain she'd vanished safely. A lump ached in his throat. She was his weakness.

Four

A crescent moon rose silver and glowing above the CIA safe house in the secluded Santa Barbara canyon. Liz Sansborough was standing at the kitchen window when two heavily armed men emerged from the chaparral. Her heart pounded against her ribs.

"Gordon?" she said softly.

He came to stand behind her. "Sentries."

They wore camouflage and carried rifles. Grenades swung from their belts. They melted like shadows through the moonlight, their heads turning as they watched for the Carnivore's hired killers. For the Carnivore himself.

Abruptly she was chilled. "How did the Carnivore find me?"

"We're not certain. We knew he'd try. That's why Langley kept agents stationed outside your condo." Gordon filled two mugs with coffee and carried them to the kitchen table.

Her eyes narrowed. This was all too tidy, too neat. "It's time to tell me what's going on, Gordon. I don't want any more surprises."

He sat at the table, glanced at his coffee mug, but made no move to pick it up. He smiled reassuringly. "Langley's positioning itself to take the Carnivore. Alive. They want to get out of him everything he knows. All the political secrets. Where the skeletons are buried."

"That's great. Then I won't have to worry about him anymore." She paused, eyes suddenly aware. "Somehow taking the Carnivore involves me. A healthy me. How?"

"Langley needs you for the operation."

"You've got to be joking."

"No joke. Langley believes you can be an enormous help. Besides, they figure you've got a vested interest."

She paced across the room. "I don't remember how to do the work! All I've got is a list of dates and places, summaries of operations I was on. Only what you gave me to *read*. I could get killed. I could get someone else killed!"

His calm voice grew earnest. "Langley believes with proper preparation the risk would be minimal. It makes sense, Liz. You're already involved with the Carnivore, and Langley needs you because of that. They want to send you to our elite training camp in Colorado. You'll get back your endurance and strength, and a decent working knowledge of the world . . . current events, celebrities, politics, that sort of thing. They want you to be able to hold conversations and not draw attention to yourself. And, of course, you'll also need to get back your old intelligence skills."

She sat heavily at the table. She glanced at her coffee, but had no taste for it. From what she'd read, Langley's secret training camps were thorough and turned out highly successful agents. Still—

"I'll be with you, coaching you all the way." He gave her an encouraging smile.

"You said Langley needed me because of my connection to the Carnivore." She stared into his brown eyes, trying to see the truth in them. "Is Langley planning to take the Carnivore by using me . . . as *bait?*"

He broke eye contact. "Sorry, Liz. I honestly don't know. In fact, I don't even know my own assignment. Probably neither of us will until it's absolutely necessary. Security's paramount. This operation is higher than top secret. It's blue-code, need-to-know. It's not just that Langley's worried about the Carnivore. They're concerned some other country will try to grab him first. Obviously we want him —and what he knows—all to ourselves." At last he looked up at her, his square face steady, grave. "If you're the lure, you'll be trained and prepared for it, and you can believe Langley will cover all angles to protect you. They know exactly what to do."

He drank coffee. "You're under no obligation, darling. You can forget everything I've just said. Langley can't use you if you're not committed. If you don't want to do this, you can take a new cover somewhere else. Hide in a different city."

His words said one thing, his expression another. He—and Langley—wanted her.

She said, "Tell me what Langley has in mind."

He recited details. When he'd finished, she leaned forward, head in hands, thinking: She'd been terribly ill, but now her mind seemed perfectly sharp. Her body grew stronger every day. She considered her past. According to the records, she'd been a top agent. Langley believed in her so much they were willing to go to a lot of trouble and expense to back their bet she could help end their three-decade search for a major international killer.

The Carnivore would never stop searching for her, and she hated the thought of spending the rest of her life looking over her shoulder.

Then, too, going through the training might help her get back her memory.

She took a deep breath, picked up her mug of cold coffee. "I'll do it."

The next day Liz and Gordon flew across the dun-colored deserts of California and Utah and up into the green mountains of northern Colorado, where Camp William Donovan spread across twenty thousand remote, timbered acres. Named for OSS leader "Wild Bill" Donovan, the camp was so secret not even Langley's telephone directory was allowed to list it. To hide its purpose, signs on the high-security entrance and along the perimeter wall announced:

No Trespassing. Four-Rock Ranch—Property U.S. Forest Service

For this reason, insiders called Camp Donovan the Ranch.

The heart of the Ranch was a flag circle three miles in from the entrance. Around the circle stood quonset huts housing labs, offices, classrooms, and equipment. A sense of authority and precision showed in the exact angling of buildings, the fresh paint, the gleaming metals. All week, hour after hour, men and women strode around the flag circle going to and from classes and labs. Some double-timed. The air was electric, intense. The Ranch packed students' schedules because there was much to master and being able to perform expertly under stress was part of the curriculum.

Most of the trainees and some of the staff used cover names. Like Liz, most trainees were on their way to assignments. One of the Ranch's rules was no friendships, not even casual ones. This was because reacting like a friend outside the safety of the Ranch could, at best, blow a cover. At worst, it could get someone killed.

There were perhaps two other trainees who had their own personal handlers, but none was more attentive than Gordon. He brought her magazines, the *New York Times,* and health shakes from the PX. He accompanied her to the library and classes on small arms, surveillance, judo, and bugging and debugging. He sat patiently by during her long nights of study. Often he made notes in a spiral notebook with his favorite silver Cross pen. Gordon wanted her to succeed. She saw it in his watchful brown eyes, his anticipation of her needs, his positive, upbeat, encouraging words.

Could anyone be more devoted?

She wished she could remember the love they'd shared. He'd told her, "I've put us on hold. At first the most important thing was getting you healthy again. Now, of course, there's the Carnivore operation. I'll wait until you remember, or until you fall in love with me again. You're worth waiting for, darling."

She felt guilty and confused. He was parent, brother, friend, mentor, and lifeline. She'd had dreams of sex, and realized sex was part of the task memory she'd never lost. She literally remembered how sex worked, but not anyone with whom she'd been in love or had sex. Most importantly, she had no memory of Gordon.

Sometimes when he wasn't looking, she watched him, a muscular man with lionlike grace. She engraved in her brain the sound of his voice, the polish of his movements. Realized with a shock she could lose him. He could go away. He could die.

Was this love?

She asked him about himself.

"I was recruited into the Company when I was in college," he told her. "University of Michigan, early '70s. A history professor invited me into his office one day, and a recruiter was waiting. It sounded good, so I didn't bother to graduate."

"You knew that quickly you wanted to join?"

"I'd always wanted to fight for my country. It was the cold war. Sure, I wanted to join up."

"No regrets?"

"None." His face hardened. It was a ridiculous question.

But she wondered whether he was telling the whole truth. There was a tiny difference in his voice, something . . . grim and angry. It was so slight she couldn't be sure. But if she were right, it was one of the rare cracks she'd spotted in the cool, professional face he showed her and the world.

He sensed her appraisal. "Hey, don't get me wrong. Sure, I've had down days, but I don't sit around examining my navel. You can't do that and survive in our business. Remember that."

Everywhere they went at the Ranch, she secretly scanned faces. What did the Carnivore look like? Where was he? What would she have to do to survive when she met him?

To save her sanity, she focused on one single task—preparing for the operation, whatever her part in it would be. Gordon seemed equally obsessed. She excelled quickly, and she could see his pride. Despite her long, exhausting days, she became stronger and healthier. She had no sense of depression or inadequacy. As her confidence grew, she became increasingly irritated with her daily antidepressant.

One morning at breakfast she asked, "Why do I have to keep taking this?" She looked at the pill he'd just handed her. "I feel terrific. Yesterday I did a ten-mile hike with full pack, for God's sake."

"That's your body, not your brain," he answered mildly.

"But it's my brain *chemicals* Dr. Levine said were out of whack. Brain chemicals sound like 'body' to me. Certainly they're physical."

He returned his spoon to his cereal bowl and his brown-eyed gaze locked onto her. "Dr. Levine is a brain specialist. Without him, you'd be dead. We don't have time for you to get sick and crazy again. We have an assignment!"

"I seriously doubt skipping one pill as an experiment—"

Something snapped behind his eyes. A flash of fury, perhaps outrage, maybe fear. "Liz, you have your orders. We're almost at the end. I won't let you blow it! Take your pill!"

She blinked. Slowly she put the pill into her mouth, drank her water, and swallowed. His reaction had been a revelation: He blindly revered authority. She recalled the only other time she'd seen him angry. That had been when she'd insisted he tell her the rest of her life story. He'd wanted to follow Dr. Levine's directions then, too, to make certain she wasn't overwhelmed by too much bad news too soon.

He'd been wrong then, and he could be wrong now.

During the rest of the day she considered the situation. The next morning she decided to experiment on her own. At breakfast she pretended to swallow the antidepressant. Instead she spit it into her paper napkin, sneaked it into a pocket, and an hour later flushed it down the toilet.

She had no symptoms of depression all day, and the next morning she again secretly spit out her pill. By the end of the week she was sure her analysis was correct. For whatever reason, her brain chemicals had righted themselves. She took no more pills, and she saw no reason to tell Gordon about it.

The next week she began cipher class. The instructor told them, "I'm going to show you how to use one of the oldest encryption methods—the Playfair cipher."

Liz spoke up, "But what I read about is electronic espionage. Why bother with something as old-fashioned and slow as a cipher?"

The instructor, a balding man with wire-rimmed glasses, raised his eyebrows at her ignorance.

"Phone and radio transmissions can be tapped," he lectured. "Electronic signals can be tracked. The NSA spends billions a year doing just that. Those methods are sometimes good, but often they're much too risky. Which brings us back to basics. You'll want to avoid giving a message in person, because you might be overheard, or being seen with your contact might be dangerous. So what do you do? You leave a note at some neutral spot—a dead drop—to be picked up. And to make sure no one else can read it, you use a cipher."

"I see."

"Choose a word, any word."

Without hesitation, she said, "Hamilton." And immediately wondered where it had come from.

The instructor had her print it on the blackboard. "Five letters across, then start the next line underneath with the rest of the letters." As the small class watched and took notes, she did as she was told. "Fill out the columns with the rest of the alphabet. Remember, the I and J share the same slot."

When she finished, she had five letters across and five letters down:

H	A	M	I/J	L
T	O	N	B	C
D	E	F	G	K
P	Q	R	S	U
V	W	X	Y	Z

She printed *Got key. Must meet at five.* She returned to her seat.

He showed the class how to break the letters into pairs, eliminating punctuation and spaces between words:

go   tk   ey   mu   st   me   et   at   fi   ve

Then he used the first pair of letters to form the corners of a rectangle on the Playfair square. He chose the replacement letters from the rectangle's opposite corners, taking the one on the same line as the first letter first. The first pair, GO, became EB.

H	A	M	I/J	L
T	O	N	B	C
D	E	F	G	K
P	Q	R	S	U
V	W	X	Y	Z

"After you've encrypted the message," he instructed, "put the letters into five-letter groups."

Following his formula, *Got key. Must meet at five* became EBCDG WLRPB AFDOH OGMWD.

She stared at the letters. My God, it worked.

As the class manipulated ciphers, Liz paused. She had an odd feeling in the pit of her stomach. She forced herself back to work, but her gaze kept returning to the blackboard and the word Hamilton.

It was a peculiar choice for an exercise in ciphers, she decided. A person's name, like American statesman Alexander Hamilton, or Lord Nelson's mistress, Lady Emma Hamilton. It was odd how the mind made connections. Those historic figures were part of her recent memory; she'd read about them in history books she'd checked out of the Ranch library.

But she had a feeling the word on the blackboard referred to someone—or something—else. It lingered in her brain, beckoning like a half-remembered song. She stared at the name again and felt strangely, dangerously happy.

Five

A white August moon glared hot and naked over Washington, D.C. At short intervals after midnight, four men wearing business suits despite the oppressive heat and late hour arrived on the deserted street outside a large neoclassical building a few blocks from the Potomac River. Their cars were ordinary American sedans of the kind driven by almost everyone in the Federal bureaucracy, but each had a driver who stepped out to survey the dark street, then nodded to his passenger, who hurried into the building.

The four men were in their early sixties. Inside, each took an elevator down six levels into the bowels of the building. There they entered a boardroom and sat at a polished conference table. The room was bomb proof, climate controlled, and had cutting-edge video and audio equipment. It had been swept for bugs and isolated against electronic intrusion.

Out in the corridor a security guard pressed a button. But a few seconds before the sound-proof door swung shut, a fifth man entered and strode to his seat at the head of the long table. His erect bearing radiated power and authority. His face was patrician, with hollow cheeks and a prominent, thin nose. His flat gaze was fixed in its usual unreadable lines. He was Hughes Bremner, board chairman.

"Gentlemen," he said, "MASQUERADE will soon enter its final phase."

The faces of the other four showed no emotion, but tension

hovered in the secret boardroom like an uninvited sixth member. MASQUERADE's success was essential. Its failure would destroy them.

"Is the operation any less risky?" the oldest asked.

"We *are* still trying to eliminate him before he comes in?" It was mandatory the assassin never surface alive in any country.

"Of course," Bremner said in his detached voice. "But he's gone to ground, and our contacts are coming up empty. There's little chance of neutralizing him while he's out there now. More than ever we need MASQUERADE."

Lucas Maynard was a heavy man, the group's number one. He sat on Bremner's right and considered the situation: Three months ago the Carnivore had sent word to four nations that he was tired, he wanted out of the post–cold war world of new faces and rules. In exchange for protected retirement, he promised to reveal the details of every assassination and subversion he knew anything about. He was auctioning a priceless cache of the globe's most-secret secrets, and Britain, France, Germany, and the United States were invited to bid.

Hughes Bremner had arranged to represent the United States with the Carnivore's go-between. Immediately he'd run into a problem: The President was reluctant to participate. He'd said he hadn't become President to repeat the lousy ethics of his predecessors, and he'd be damned if he gave sanctuary to an assassin, terrorist, or anyone with that kind of blood on his hands.

With the director of Central Intelligence, Bremner had convinced the President of the Carnivore's value, and the President had given his reluctant permission—as long as the asylum were kept absolutely secret.

The number one, Lucas Maynard, said, "Good thing we won the bidding war, Hughes."

Hughes Bremner's smile was inside. This was a game few played as well as he. "Yes. Britain and France's recessions have weakened their ability to compete, and Germany has so many problems with neo-Nazis and the East, it has little energy for anything else. We gave the Carnivore everything he asked." He paused to see the minute signs from his fellow board members that indicated their relief. "The standard protocols to test his sincerity and intent are in place, and MASQUERADE is fully on schedule." He looked at each in turn, cool and imperious. "I'll run through the final steps to be sure we all know what we're doing."

For nearly an hour, Bremner described the groundwork, risks, precautions, and timetable. He showed a video interview with one of the world's foremost brain scientists. When he finished, they sat in the sealed room far below the sweltering streets, each evaluating what he'd heard. Bremner watched them.

"Let's get any doubts out in the open," Bremner encouraged. "Our lives are at stake."

The five men talked for another two hours, but in the end they made no substantial changes to the plan. Seldom did any Bremner operation require serious alteration.

It was 4:00 A.M. when they left the clandestine room one at a time. Lucas Maynard rode up in the elevator alone. He touched the playback button of the ultra-miniature recorder under his suit and conservative tie. He listened to the taped voices of his colleagues, and he smiled.

It was still hot in Washington, D.C., the next morning when veteran CIA agent Lucas Maynard, stout and pink-faced, arrived at the swank Hay-Adams Hotel for breakfast with his old friend, Undersecretary of State Clarence ("Clare") Edward. Maynard was purposefully early, and for a man of his long experience in covert operations, he was nervous. But he'd been out of the field many years, and he'd never had to worry about his own side before.

Maynard had chosen the Hay-Adams, just a block from the White House, because the restaurant's tables were far enough apart for private conversation. And he'd asked for this meeting because, after more than thirty years, he was about to call in the undersecretary's IOU.

The undersecretary didn't know this. Maynard would have found the situation amusing, if it weren't so damn dangerous.

Mindful of his diabetes, Maynard ordered fruit, oatmeal, and milk. He surveyed the room, checking for anyone from Langley. He recognized no one, saw no signs of listening devices, and spotted no one casually looking in his direction. There was no reason for anyone in the Company to suspect what he planned to do. His motive was known only to him, he was sure of that.

Maynard's food arrived, and so did the undersecretary. Clare Edward sat, and they exchanged the usual pleasantries. As soon as the waiter left, the undersecretary got down to business. Already he looked rushed and tired, and it was only 8:00 A.M.

"What's this about, Lucas?"

"Up all night again?" Maynard smiled.

Undersecretary Clare Edward liked the ladies, especially the ones who worked for him. He'd learned it was a simple matter to transfer their idolization from office to bed. The challenge was less, but the variety plentiful, and the physical results the same. If they protested, he transferred them to another department, with a little bonus or promotion to keep them quiet. He was a damn fool, Maynard reflected, but then his ego had always been bigger than even Bob Packwood's.

The undersecretary grinned and straightened his rep tie. "You know how it is."

Maynard tried the oatmeal. It was blazing hot. "How's everything at State?"

"The same." Undersecretary Edward had silver hair, lively blue eyes, and a Cabo San Lucas tan. He was in his late fifties, looked in his forties, and ate and rutted like a dysfunctional teenager. He ordered black coffee, prune juice, and danish.

Maynard tried his steaming oatmeal again. He said casually, "Anything new on the college girl missing in Guatemala?"

Undersecretary Edward looked suspicious. "The senator from Virginia's adventurous daughter? No, she seems to have simply disappeared. The current Guatemalan dictator—our friend, politically speaking, of course—denies knowing anything about it. Why?"

The oatmeal was still too damn hot. Well, Maynard would eat just the fruit. With this diet, he'd be down another ten pounds in a month. That was good. Once thin and wiry, he'd grown heavy with the years, and that extra weight had contributed to his diabetes.

"I was remembering another senator's missing daughter." Maynard watched with pleasure as the undersecretary grimaced.

He and Clare had been assigned to West Berlin right after the wall went up in 1961. In those days, Clare had been a Langley agent, too. True to form, he'd spent the summer chasing a senator's teenage daughter. Desperate to impress her, he'd invited her along to photograph an arms plant in East Berlin. The Soviets had caught them. One of Maynard's people had spotted the "arrest." Because of Maynard's intervention, the pair had been merely tossed into cells, where they'd spent the night listening to the screams of the tortured.

As the new station chief, Maynard had gone straight to the top.

He'd called the girl's father and the White House. President Kennedy had picked up his red telephone and spoken directly to Nikita Khrushchev. The next day, the couple had been exchanged on Glienicker Bridge for two KGB spooks.

"East Berlin. Yes." The undersecretary looked balefully at Maynard. "That was a long time ago, Lucas, but I haven't forgotten. I owe you. What do you want?"

The waiter arrived with the undersecretary's breakfast. Maynard studied the elegant room once more for Company tagalongs. It still looked clean. Maynard spoke quietly, with the measured tones of someone who thought before he opened his mouth:

"Do you also recall the surprising turnaround of OMNI-American Savings & Loan a few years ago?" In 1990 the S&L giant had been collapsing under the weight of junk bonds and too many shaky real estate loans. Then a sudden infusion of cash had skyrocketed it back into the black.

The undersecretary toyed with his danish. "*Surprising* is hardly the word. Astonishing, I'd say. Not to mention totally unexpected and impossible."

Since liberal Texas and Arizona real estate laws had allowed risky S&L lending practices, OMNI-American had offered loans without down payments, financed precarious development schemes, and bought junk bonds and preferred stock in troubled real estate investment firms like Southmark Corporation of Dallas.

Maynard lowered his voice and dropped his bomb. "The turnaround was funded by old Iran-contra money. Illegal, and some would say immoral, as all hell."

The undersecretary bit into his danish. He dusted his mouth with his linen napkin. He adjusted his tie. He stared off as if he'd just spotted Shangri-la. He smiled, and Maynard knew the undersecretary was considering the power of such information, if he played it right, and he always played it right. That's why Clare Edward had risen to be an Undersecretary of State.

"You have documentary evidence, Lucas?" the undersecretary asked quietly.

"Of course."

The undersecretary studied Maynard's plain linen banker's suit, white cotton shirt, simple blue tie. Maynard wore no rings. His watch was a Timex. He looked far from rich. Still, looks were deceiving, especially among Company officers after Aldrich ("Rick")

Ames's activities for the KGB were uncovered, and the undersecretary was well aware of this.

"You've been digging into this on your own?" the undersecretary probed.

"You could say that."

Clare leaned forward. "I need something to give the secretary and the President. Something concrete. You've got to give me something, or they'll laugh in my face."

"I know. Here's a beginning: BCCI."

The undersecretary blanched even through his tan. BCCI—Bank of Credit and Commerce International—had been the globe's largest, most reliable vehicle for the no-questions-asked movement of capital. It had merely been following in the tradition of a few freewheeling predecessors, notably Schroder Trust and Nugan Hand Bank. But even in the most pragmatic circles, BCCI still evoked embarrassment for its excesses and for the colleagues who'd helped it, both intentionally and inadvertently.

Maynard said, "You know, of course, Langley deposited tens of millions in the contras' BCCI accounts."

"That was against the law. Criminal behavior."

Maynard continued in his low voice, "Just to make sure we both understand what we're talking about, I'll remind you BCCI accepted without question sacks of our cash—Langley cash—and transferred the money wherever we asked."

"Which laundered it."

"And BCCI had no tax men or currency export-control officers looking over our shoulders. Under those conditions, would you be surprised if a few agents, while they were sending covert tens of millions around the world, skimmed off a million here and there, and then opened numbered accounts for themselves?"

The undersecretary exhaled and sat back.

Maynard allowed himself a smile. "I also have direct information about the sudden expansion of another U.S.-based corporation— Nonpareil International Insurance."

The undersecretary checked the room. At last his gaze returned to Maynard. "Funded by stolen Iran-contra money?"

"Yes."

Avarice darkened the undersecretary's tan face. For money and for power. "What's it going to cost me, Lucas?"

"My immunity, that's all. What I've told you is just the tip of an iceberg. I have enough evidence to explode the filthiest scandal the United States has ever seen. Compared to this, BCCI, Irangate, Iraqgate, and Watergate were trial balloons."

Undersecretary Edward drank his black coffee, and Maynard sat back and let him turn the proposition over in his mind, looking for hidden dangers, unspoken angles. It was all a matter of balancing risk against potential gain.

At last the equation seemed to come out in Lucas Maynard's favor, not that the undersecretary would let him see that too clearly.

"You've got to give me more," the undersecretary demanded. "Something to prove to the secretary and the President you've got the goods. That's the only way you'll get immunity."

"Check out a BCCI account under the name *Samuel Trooper*. It's in the investigation files. Follow the account long enough one way, and you'll see the initial deposits came from missile sales to Iran. Follow it the other way—I warn you, it won't be easy—and you'll find the account grew to $50 million, more or less, which was cashed out in November 1990."

"And?" Clare Edward prompted.

"The money dropped out of sight. What can you buy with $50 million without someone asking questions?"

"What?"

"The health of a loser S&L like OMNI-American. And I have the paper trail that proves it."

Again the undersecretary surveyed the room. He lowered his head and contemplated Maynard, who gazed steadily back.

"Tell me, Lucas," the undersecretary said, "why is it you need immunity? You didn't skim a few million here and there for yourself, did you, my old friend?"

Maynard showed no emotion. "What I did or didn't do won't help you. If you want the goods, you've got to play my game. If you try to go around me, I'll go somewhere else. I'm the only one with documentation. The only one. This is a steal for you, you know that. If you turn over what I have, you get to be a hero."

"And you, my clever friend, get to while away your retirement years on some tropical isle with your cash and no one breathing down your neck. Hell, you'll probably even get to keep your pension."

"Do you want to play, Clare?"

"Wouldn't miss it for the world," the undersecretary said.

"Then follow up the Samuel Trooper information I've given you, check out anything else you think you need to."

"Where do I contact you?" the undersecretary asked.

"You don't. I'll contact you."

Across the elegant dining room, a young woman in a gray business suit studied the *Wall Street Journal* while she finished her breakfast. She appeared not to notice the departure of the two older men who'd been talking so intently.

About five minutes later, she signaled the waiter. He brought her bill on a silver tray. As she turned over the bill, she palmed the tiny recording device he'd hidden underneath. She paid with cash and left.

Six

Eight miles northwest of the Hay-Adams Hotel where Lucas Maynard and Undersecretary Clare Edward had breakfasted, Hughes
Bremner spoke heatedly into his specially encrypted telephone.

"No! Not too fast! You buy francs too fast, and everyone from
Tokyo to London will get suspicious. Stick to the plan or you'll blow
the transaction!" He listened. When he spoke again, his voice was
quiet and cold. "You'll get your $5 million, Crowther. But for now,
go slow and steady. Monday we blitz them. Remember your $5 mil-
lion. It'll steady your nerve!"

Hughes Bremner hung up and glanced down at the papers on his
desk. His austere office was on the choice seventh floor of the great,
sprawling CIA complex in Langley, Virginia. He should do some
work, but instead he paced across the room. He was distracted and
irritated. He gazed out his windows to the sea of green forest that
covered Virginia's undulating hills. Contemplating the virgin countryside usually soothed him.

Hughes Bremner was a powerful man—the head of Mustang, the
CIA's most secret, most elite team. Under earlier code names, Mustang's directive had been to contain and destroy the forces of com-
munism. Now that the political world had turned upside down, the
team had two new directives: First, to keep the lid on the transi-
tional, post–cold war world, and second, to stop any superpower
from emerging to rival the United States.

Being chief of Mustang and its predecessors was a prized career spot, and Hughes Bremner, who had held the position for nearly fifteen years, never underrated it. Yet he'd once had higher ambitions. He'd hungered to be Deputy Director for Operations, the DDO: To lead the CIA's entire espionage division, direct all spy stations abroad, oversee the gathering of all foreign and domestic intelligence, and orchestrate its myriad covert actions, particularly in this exciting era when new allegiances, even countries, died and were reborn overnight.

Back in the 1950s at the beginning of his CIA career, Hughes Bremner's rise to DDO and ultimately to the top slot itself—DCI, Director of Central Intelligence—had seemed inevitable. This was due not only to his excellent record and to his having the right kind of character, but also because he came from the right stock. He and his wife, Barbara ("Bunny") Hartford Bremner, both did.

In the old days that had mattered.

In fact, according to a painting in his den at home, Bremner looked very much like the founder of his family's fortune—his great-great-great grandfather, the first Hughes Bremner. Both had gray, wispy hair and aristocratic English faces with hollow cheeks, pale blue eyes, and long, thin noses. Their gazes were remarkably alike, too—impenetrable and chilly as a coastal fog.

Hughes Bremner took pride in his lineage, but he kept his great-great-great grandfather's source of wealth to himself. The old man had been a "blackbirder," importing Africans as slaves to the New World. Bunny Bremner, too, had a so-called colorful forebear—a gold manipulator, who'd grown rich wiping out the savings of early nineteenth-century Americans, much like the corporate raiders and junk-bond salesmen of the late twentieth century.

A knock at the door interrupted his thoughts. He turned, but nothing in his stern demeanor showed his eagerness.

"Come."

Yes, it was the young woman he'd sent to the Hay-Adams Hotel. She was new to the Company and anxious to prove her worth. She'd jumped at the chance to impress the mighty Bremner by bugging the meeting Lucas Maynard had arranged with Undersecretary Clare Edward.

"I paid one of the waiters fifty dollars to attach the recorder to Mr. Maynard's oatmeal bowl." She was cool, calm, impeccably trained. "Said I was a private investigator. Showed him my cover license. He asked no questions."

"Good. Did you listen to the tape?"

She straightened indignantly. "Of course not, sir."

Bremner smiled graciously and praised her. Once she was out the door, he touched the recorder's tiny play-back button.

In his opulent office at the Department of State, Undersecretary Clare Edward sat down in his high-backed, wine-colored leather chair and dialed the head of the State Department's Bureau of Intelligence and Research.

He said, "I want a routine check on OMNI-American Savings & Loan, Nonpareil International Insurance, and an old BCCI account in the name of Samuel Trooper."

"Am I looking for anything in particular, sir?"

"I want the beginning and end of the Samuel Trooper account at BCCI and any cross-referencing among it, the S&L, and the insurance company."

The undersecretary hung up, buzzed his redheaded secretary, and told her to interrupt him as soon as an envelope arrived from their intelligence unit. Then he went to work on a pile of special congressional requests, a burdensome but politically necessary task. Sometimes something worthwhile, like an IOU from a grateful congressman, came out of it.

At 11:45 A.M., as usual, he left for lunch at his club, where he used the tanning machines to maintain the natural golden color he'd acquired in Cabo San Lucas. He returned to his office at 1:15 P.M. to face a long list of appointments. As the afternoon wore on, he found himself listening for his secretary's voice over the intercom.

At four o'clock his last appointment left. He'd hoped to be gone by now. Instead he phoned down to public information to send his new inamorata—an eighteen-year-old clerk—on to his Georgetown home ahead of him.

As the hour grew later he comforted himself with the thought she was there waiting—soft, eager, pretty, and nervous.

Finally at 5:45 P.M. as the huge old building grew somber with silence, he heard the messenger arrive at his secretary's desk. He signed for the large sealed envelope himself.

Controlling his excitement, he returned to his office, locked his door, and studied the reports and Xeroxes. The information on OMNI-American Savings & Loan and Nonpareil International Insurance was standard—dates formed, board members, chairmen, presidents, CEOs, other top staff, clients, branch locations. Both businesses were owned by the same international corporation, Sterling-O'Keefe Enterprises.

Nothing suspicious.

No Iran-contra money. No mention of the CIA. No cross-referencing.

Hell and damnation.

According to the reports, OMNI-American had saved itself by the surgical selling-off of big real estate developments while attracting solvent new customers. The report explained Nonpareil International had expanded dramatically by buying small money-losing insurance companies and turning them around with sound business practices and floods of new clients. As for the Samuel Trooper account, it was opened in London by an Austrian businessman in 1984 and closed out in October, not November, 1990.

Nothing.

Standard bunk, whitewashed to save somebody's powerful ass.

Fuming, he dialed the head of State intelligence. The son of a bitch had gone for the day. He left a message, demanding a detailed search for the source of the Samuel Trooper account. If the account had originated in Iran-contra money, it was the most direct link to CIA malfeasance, and he intended to have it.

At six o'clock Hughes Bremner was pacing his Langley office. Something was wrong with the bug, and he'd sent it downstairs for the R&D geniuses to fix. It'd been there all day, and so far no one had been able to get to its contents. Which meant he had suspicions, but no confirmation of why Lucas Maynard had asked to meet Undersecretary Clare Edward that morning.

At last someone knocked. It was a technician, with a lean, worried face.

"Sorry, sir." The technician started to hand the little recorder to Bremner, then seemed to think better of it. He put it on the big desk. Bremner merely nodded. In the Company, inexpressiveness had been raised to an art form. The technician backed toward the door, seeming to sense the fury that roiled Bremner's gut.

"Tell me what happened." Bremner's voice was low and cool.

"The recorder used very thin recording tape, sir."

"Yes. Go on."

"When it's that thin, it jams easily. Somebody must've left it in the sun or stuck it to something hot—"

"Like a bowl of hot oatmeal?" Bremner asked.

"If it was hot enough, yeah, that'd do it. Anyway, the tape warped and stopped moving. There's no conversation on it. We checked the whole thing to make sure."

"It never recorded anything?"

"Sorry, sir."

Bremner turned his back. As soon as he heard the door close, he knotted his fists, leaned over his desk, and swore.

He needed that conversation.

What in hell was Lucas Maynard up to?

Bremner called Sid Williams, the man he'd put in charge of monitoring Maynard's home and office phones.

"Nothing new, sir," Williams assured him. "Maynard's on the street now. Matt's tailing him."

"No more of these weekly reports. I want *daily* accounts of whom he talks to, whom he sees, where he goes, and all his phone calls. On my desk. Seven A.M. sharp, unless something looks important, and I want that instantly. Anything else going on?"

Sid Williams hesitated.

Hughes Bremner heard it. "What is it?"

"Well, Maynard disappears every once in a while. We think he still hasn't made us. But it's like he goes into routine antisurveillance, like he's keeping his hand in. We pick him up three, four hours later at his house or at Langley."

"Jesus Christ! I want to know what that bastard is up to twenty-four hours a day! Put on extra men."

"Yessir."

"Put people on Undersecretary Edward, too. Tails and monitors for his phone calls. Office and home, just like Maynard. The undersecretary and Maynard both, got that?"

"Yessir. No problem."

"There'd damn well better not be!"

Seven

The next afternoon Undersecretary Clare Edward gloomily considered the fresh batch of papers that had just arrived from intelligence. They described the BCCI account of Samuel Trooper, but they contained nothing useful.

Later, when Lucas Maynard called, Undersecretary Edward told him, "I'm not going to be able to help you, Lucas, my old friend. Can't seem to find what I need to move on this."

The CIA man's voice was tired. "I told you it wouldn't be easy."

"Intelligence here claims there's nothing to find."

"Christ, you'd think they'd figure out how to run their damn computers!"

"They say they've got nothing about your, ah, 'suggestion' in the data bank. They've searched thoroughly. It's a dead end. You've got to come up with something else."

"I'll think about it," Maynard snapped.

The phone went dead in the undersecretary's ear. Maynard's curt irritation said it was an explosive case all right, and he was disgusted he wasn't instantly getting his due. With a smile, the undersecretary hung up. His friend, the CIA man, was hooked. He wanted immunity, and one way or another, no matter how offended he might pretend to be, he'd do what was necessary.

The undersecretary leaned forward, elbows on his antique walnut desk, and raised his fingers in the shape of a temple. He rested his chin on the tops of his fingers, contemplating the future with genuine pleasure.

· He'd heard rumors the Secretary of State was considering retirement. With the kind of positive publicity he could now anticipate, there was no reason he shouldn't be appointed to that illustrious spot.

Unless Lucas Maynard changed his mind. . . .

No, the undersecretary knew Maynard wouldn't have risked revealing so much without evidence. Something had happened to Lucas Maynard, something that had knocked him off his CIA pedestal and brought him back down to the rough, uncertain terrain of ordinary mortals.

At the remote Ranch high in the Rocky Mountains, Liz Sansborough began to have sensations of familiarity, especially about sounds and odors. She described them to herself as near-memories. Each new one fueled a drive deep inside that was making her increasingly restless.

How could she know herself, understand herself, trust herself, if her personal history came only from reports and photographs?

Then one morning she was assigned to design a mock handler/asset operation. She opened her notebook to the Playfair cipher on the first page, and she saw the code word *Hamilton*.

Like a lightning bolt a full name hit her: Hamilton *Walker!*

She inhaled sharply. Where did that come from? She probed her mind for clues. She recalled how oddly happy she'd felt looking at "Hamilton" that first day in cipher class. Had she known a Hamilton Walker?

Damn! She needed more information to help her struggling memory. The logical place to start was with herself. Had Langley told her everything? She could ask Gordon—

But he was totally focused on the Carnivore operation. Those were Langley's orders, and he followed orders zealously. And she had to admit—although she didn't believe—her desire to explore her past again might be a sign of the "craziness" about which he'd warned her. What was it about that name, Hamilton Walker?—

Walker! She smiled. Of course. Her cover name back in Santa Barbara had been Sarah Walker, so the two might somehow be connected.

Encouraged, she rushed to finish the mock handler/asset assignment and then used her extra time and new tradecraft skills to design a plan to tap into personnel's computer base.

She told Gordon she wanted extra time on the pistol range. He authorized the ammunition, and when he went on an errand she put one of his camo shirts over her own. While the supply sergeant went for her ammo, she managed to swipe and conceal an infrared flashlight and goggles and a new laser lock picker.

After dinner she and Gordon went to a Ranch motivational lecture. She caught snatches of it as she mentally walked herself once more through her plan.

". . . A good case officer must be not only a master spy, but a psychologist and a father or mother confessor as well."

". . . In this politically chaotic world, the CIA is the one stable force for freedom."

". . . Although you're leaving your old life, you're on the verge of a better one. You can be of real service."

She felt a stab of guilt. Then pushed it away. What she planned would in no way interfere with capturing the Carnivore.

Liz and Gordon shared a cabin under the pines south of the flag circle. It was a single room with matching iron cots, small closets, pine desks, built-in bureaus, and a bathroom, shower only. It was utilitarian, rustic. Late that night, as Gordon snored on his cot, Liz dressed silently in her camos and gathered her infrared flashlight, infrared goggles, and laser lock picker.

She slipped out into the night, scanned the sleeping camp, then moved swiftly north across the damp grass, from building to building, staying close as she'd been taught. She ran around the flag circle and pressed against the log wall of the officers' club. A sprinkling of lights showed in the billeting cabins behind her. It was nearly 1:00 A.M.

She dashed across the lawn to the Quonset hut that housed personnel. She'd have to disarm the sensors and alarm on the door. This could be a problem. If she didn't succeed, the alarm's shriek would be piercing, loud enough to awake even a narcoleptic. She knew; she'd heard it tested.

At personnel's door she rested the lock picker against the keyhole opening to the mortise lock. She pressed a button on the lock picker, and a beam circulated within the lock's core. She held her breath.

Then she heard the soft clicks that told her the tumblers had rearranged themselves.

This was where speed counted. She'd have only fifteen seconds to reach inside and enter a code to turn off the sensors. She and Gordon had each received private codes their first day at camp. If hers didn't work, or if she was one second too slow, the alarm would sound.

She inhaled, twisted the knob, opened the door, slipped her hand inside to the number pad, and tapped in her code.

She waited.

She heard only silence. After a full minute, she allowed herself a brief sense of triumph. She'd succeeded!

She slipped inside the shadowy hut, closed the door, put on the infrared goggles, and turned on the infrared flashlight. She played the green beam, invisible to anyone without infrared eye gear, around the room. She strode around the visitors' rail, past a row of desks, and through another door into the computer room—an office with file cabinets, desks, and computers.

She removed her goggles, sat, and switched on a computer. When its screen asked, she keyboarded in her code. Once she had clearance, she called up the personnel file of "Elizabeth Alice Sansborough." In the unearthly glow of the monitor, she scrolled through the now-familiar data. Suddenly she stopped. Sarah Walker was listed as her first cousin, living in Santa Barbara, California.

That made no sense. "Sarah Walker" had been her cover name, assigned when she'd retired and Langley had set her up as a magazine journalist in Santa Barbara.

Why would someone list her cover as her cousin?

She read on, and then she saw it: Hamilton Walker.

According to the file, there was an entire Walker family—Sarah's father, mother, and brother. And the father's name was Hamilton Walker. This had to be more than a coincidence, especially considering all the near-memories she was having. She paused, hoping more information would pop into her mind.

But there was nothing.

Disappointed, she resumed reading. The Walker mother was supposedly her aunt, the sister of Harold Sansborough, Liz's father. But her dossier back in Santa Barbara had said she had no living family. Shouldn't it have mentioned the invented family of her "cousin?" It was damned confusing.

The remaining data was the same as what she'd studied in the Santa Barbara safe house—everything from her birth date, broken little finger, and mole above the right corner of her mouth, to Cambridge and joining the CIA. The file ended three years ago. That was when the Carnivore had almost killed her, when she'd retired and taken the cover name Sarah Walker.

She reread the material about the Walker family.

Father, Hamilton Walker.

Mother, Jane Sansborough Walker.

Brother, Michael Walker.

She switched off the computer and sat back in the dark. The names and relationships swirled in her mind, and neither memory nor logic could make sense of them. Frustrated, baffled, she left. At the outside door, she tapped in her code, reactivating the alarm. She turned the knob and opened the door a few inches.

And stopped. There was someone outside.

Heart pounding, she swiftly deactivated the alarm. It was a man, shorter and thinner than Gordon, and he strolled in a lazy slouch, hands stuffed into jacket pockets as he gazed up at the night sky. He was just taking a stroll, she decided with relief. But at this hour? She felt a flash of kinship with him, two strangers alone in the night, where neither was supposed to be.

Abruptly he stopped.

He turned to stare in her direction. The clouds parted and moonlight illuminated his face. It was angular, with bushy black brows and wide lips. He was the new personnel director. He'd arrived a few days after she and Gordon. He was younger than she, in his late twenties, a hotshot with a swagger. He was known around camp for his increasingly strange behavior.

The charcoal clouds floated together, cutting off her view of his features. He seemed to stare longer at the door of the personnel hut. At last he moved toward it.

Fear knotted her chest. She reactivated the alarm, closed the cracked door, ran softly behind the rail that defined the reception area, and then to the farthest corner.

But she'd forgotten to lock the door.

Stupid, stupid!

Too late, the doorknob turned!

She had no choice. She dropped under a desk, touching her lock picker and infrared flashlight to make sure she'd left neither behind. Her goggles hung from her neck. She silently pulled the desk chair in behind her. Thank God its wheels were well oiled.

She sweated.

When the door opened, he swore.

She held her breath, making no sound, encouraged: The quality of his swearing told her he thought he'd been the one who'd left the door unlocked, a breach of security.

Grumbling, he punched in his code, stepped inside, and closed the door. He turned on a small desk lamp.

His feet moved from desk to desk. He stopped directly in front of where she was crouched. She held her breath. The waiting seemed endless. His feet made a circle as he surveyed the room. Probably looking for something left out of place.

Sweat dripped from her forehead. Again she touched her lock picker, and then the infrared flashlight. But in her nervousness she bumped the flashlight. She could feel it topple.

Her hand lunged, caught it, and froze.

At last he headed toward the other room—the computer room. He stopped in the doorway to turn on the overhead light. He was going to check in there, too. Probably to make certain the computers were undisturbed.

As he stalked inside, she carefully rolled back the chair. She crawled out and raised her eyes above the desk. He started to turn. She dropped back down.

She strained, listening.

He was moving again, away from her. She had to take the risk, so she looked out again. He was walking toward the first computer in the distant room, and his back was solidly toward her.

Relieved, she crouched, moved lightly, swiftly, around the rail to the outside door. Low to the floor, she glanced back. He was nowhere in sight, probably sitting at a computer.

Out in the crisp mountain air, she silently closed the door and forced herself to calm down, furious about her two errors: Leaving the door unlocked and knocking over her flashlight.

Praying for luck to cover your mistakes was for suckers and losers. She'd have to do a hell of a lot better if she planned to succeed—and survive—whatever lay ahead with the Carnivore.

As she retraced her circuitous path to her cabin, a name reverberated in her mind. Hamilton Walker.

Now she was sure: She'd had a memory, but with a confusing

twist. She'd remembered the name of someone who didn't exist. How could that be? How could a nonexistent person be important enough to make her recall him, when she had no memories of anyone or anything else?

Unless, of course, Hamilton Walker was real.

Eight

Just a few miles from Washington's beltway, Lucas Maynard wandered through the underground boutiques at the Crystal City Metro stop in Arlington. He was practicing routine antisurveillance maneuvers. He'd also begun to carry a pistol—a Walther TPH, Taschen Pistole Mit Hahn. Easy to handle and conceal, the pistol was a lightweight, scaled-down version of the famed Walther PP/PPK series.

He crossed and recrossed streets, used plate-glass store fronts as mirrors, and paused to admire window displays.

In these ways he was able to check whether anyone followed.

After an hour, when at last he was sure he was clean, he reemerged onto the street. He took off his suit jacket and strode briskly through the August heat.

He turned down a side street and walked another three blocks to a red-brick apartment building. He was sweating, which annoyed him. He didn't like to arrive sweaty. He used his key to enter, climbed the stairs, and on the second floor unlocked the door to the front apartment.

"What smells so good?" he asked.

Hot meat-and-gravy odors filled the modest, air-conditioned apartment with a welcoming aroma. Suddenly he was a boy again, back in Terre Haute, Indiana. But then, Leslee always made him feel like a boy of seventeen with his future still ahead. This for a long-divorced man in his sixties with diabetes, a weight problem, and three alienated, adult kids.

As he locked the door behind him, Leslee Pousho emerged from the kitchen, flushed beneath her pale-blond hair, small and compact, and so happy to see him her blue eyes danced.

"Darling, you're early!"

He held her and his heart pounded against her small, hard body. He kissed her oven-warm cheeks and thanked God again for this second chance.

She gripped his face and kissed him on the lips, hungry, teasing. He started to pick her up, carry her to the bedroom, but she pushed him away.

"Look what I have for you."

She stepped back and pulled her halter dress up over her head. She stood there in a black-and-pink lace teddy. Shiny satin insets covered her nipples and pubic hair for modesty. But it wasn't modest, it was teasing. She knew it and spun on her heels, her short legs long in black net stockings, her small feet arched daintily in teetering heels.

She laughed because this was so unlike her.

"Christ, Les." His voice was husky as if they were in some trashy movie. He didn't give a damn. He grabbed for her. She ran into the bedroom. He followed, a boy eager and in love.

Afterward, Lucas and Leslee lay naked on the bed, the air conditioner bathing them in a cool stream. He was in awe of her body, so taut and smooth, her small breasts tight against her rib cage. She was thirty-two, he was sixty-two, covered with sags, bulges, and wrinkles, especially now that he was losing weight. But Leslee seemed to think he was beautiful.

"Have I made you burn dinner?" he asked.

"Nope. It's beef burgundy, slow-cooking on the stove. Too hot for this weather, but I was in the mood. Do you care?"

He smiled. "I'm always in the mood for whatever you're in the mood for."

She was a writer and editor at the *Washington Independent,* an alternative newspaper that had survived twenty-five years of shoestring budgets, conservative attacks, police inquiries, and an underpaid revolving-door staff.

And she'd changed his life.

"I wish I'd known you were this easy." She laughed.

She'd changed his life by changing his focus from past mistakes to future possibilities. He had made careful plans. To be with Leslee, he intended to get out from under his past.

Yes, what he and his colleagues had done was wrong. In fact, Iran-contra and Bill Casey, head of Central Intelligence during the go-go '80s, had been wrong. Reagan and Bush had been double wrong. It shamed Maynard that he himself had falsified records, stolen money, and aided killers.

Tiredly he closed his eyes and saw Leslee plainly in his mind. If he listened carefully, he could hear her voice in the silence of the room, even though she was drifting off to sleep in his arms. His new understanding came from Leslee Pousho with her little, compact body and her biting intelligence. He longed to tell her everything, but not until he had a deal for immunity.

Then he'd tell Leslee and marry her, if she'd have him.

"My God," she murmured. "The food."

"Let me. You're tired." He stood, held onto the bedpost, dizzy. Damn his diabetes. Why in hell hadn't he met her before he was old, sick, and in trouble?

"Are you all right?" She sat up, her breasts so small and perfect they hardly jiggled.

The teddy and black net hose were in a tangle with his clothes on the floor. He had no idea where her pumps were. In the hall, maybe.

"I'm fine." He put on his robe. "What do I do about dinner? Do you think it's burning?"

She chuckled. "No. It's just ready. Are you hungry?"

They ate as usual at her kitchen table on a red-checked oilcloth. Again, like Terre Haute. And she a career woman from Manhattan.

"I'm working on a story about your industry," she said between mouthfuls. "Want to comment?"

"Probably not. But go ahead and try me."

At first they'd fought about the responsibilities of government intelligence, its place in a democracy, whether its very existence was antidemocratic. Then they'd fought about the excesses of the Reagan and Bush years, and finally about the Company's role in today's post–cold war world.

She said, "The junior senator from Utah has submitted another bill to allow the CIA to engage officially in economic espionage."

"You act surprised."

"This time it may pass."

"That's what I hear." He chewed and watched her heart-shaped face.

She was getting angry, because he wasn't responding.

He said, "Look, I understand it. We Americans are afraid. We're sliding down a slick hill of our own greedy shit. We're the biggest financial power in the world, and now we want guarantees we'll stay there. But everything seems to work against us. Foreign intelligence agencies plant moles in our companies. They photograph and steal the papers and high-tech samples of our businessmen when they travel abroad. French espionage even bugs Air France's business class. Look at all the American consultants here in Washington on the Japanese, British, Russian, German, and Chinese payrolls. No wonder our businesses want us to recruit agents in the finance ministries of foreign countries. If we're in danger of falling behind, why not?"

"But when we steal a foreign business secret, how do we choose whom to give it to—IBM or Apple? Delco or G.E.?"

"Maybe we just publish it in the *Wall Street Journal* and give everyone a shot."

"If the bill goes through, we'll end up spying on our allies. And you know our corporations will try to bribe our agents every chance they get. Each one wants information first, so they'll have a competitive edge not only over other nations' corporations, but their U.S. competitors as well. Then there's the problem of the world's multinationals. How do we figure out which are even U.S. corporations?"

"Trade talks are more important these days to national security than arms talks, Les."

"We're a democracy, goddammit." She shook her blond head angrily. "Democracy mandates separation of private corporations from government, just as it does church from government. We'd need basic changes in our culture and laws to hand over CIA-acquired economic intelligence to businesses. Actually, if you take the idea of the feds mucking around in private industry to its logical conclusion, we could end up where the government and industry were one, a totalitarian, Communist state. Now that'd be a severe shock for knee-jerk right-wingers."

Maynard chewed thoughtfully. "Americans have always had a hard time resolving the conflict between an open democracy and the secrecy that gathering intelligence requires. I go along with

George Washington. He thought intelligence was vital, but only to
stop violence against our nation and our people. No matter how you
slice it, making money isn't violent. It *causes* violence when one
greedy son of a bitch goes after another greedy son of a bitch, or the
bastard tries to take food from starving people. But in itself, financial competition isn't violent. So I figure Langley's got no business
doing industrial spying."

Leslee put down her fork. "You're serious? I've made a dent in
that stubborn skull of yours?"

"A near-fatal dent that's caused a rebirth of sorts. You're right.
Our political system—democracy—has been polluted by our economic system—capitalism. In fact, we run the United States as if
capitalism *were* our political system. Profit is everything. The only
real measure of success is money."

She nodded. "When people ask what you do, they're really asking
how much you make."

"Langley wasn't intended for that," he said. "Its mission is simply
to give useful intelligence in a timely manner to government policy
makers so they can make decisions. That's all, and that's critical.
That's what our new DCI wants, and she's been working to put in
reforms that'll stop other activities. But it's hard. Langley's gone off
half-cocked for fifty years. Now if we bow to pressure and start spying
on foreign companies, we'll be turning our backs on what democracy stands for again, and that means we weaken our nation's ethical
base even more."

Her smile was radiant. "May I quote you?"

"You can quote me as an unidentified government source." He
frowned. "But soon, Les, very soon, I'll go public."

Nine

"Gordon, do I have family in Santa Barbara, real or imagined?" Liz said. "The Walkers? Aunt Jane, Uncle Hamilton, cousin Michael?"

They were alone at a long table in an empty classroom. He sat across from her, his spiral notebook closed at his elbow. She was hunched over her Beretta 92-F pistol, cleaning it.

Gordon said, "Walker was a cover name we made up for you."

"Yes, Sarah Walker. You didn't create a Santa Barbara family for me, too?"

"Where are you getting such bizarre ideas?"

She oiled the Beretta. "Is there something I should know? Something about me and my cover?"

"Where'd you get all this crap about a fictitious Walker family?"

"My CIA file."

"Not in the file I gave you."

"In personnel's. Here at the Ranch. I used the computer."

"When?"

She looked up. His face was red and growing thick.

She said, "Does it matter?"

Swift and sure as a jackal, he lunged, grabbed her wrist, and twisted back her arm. The violence stunned her.

"Listen to me, Liz Sansborough." His words were clipped, his eyes slits. "I've shown you everything that's relevant for you to know. What's in personnel's file is none of your damned business. It's *top secret.*"

Her belly churned, but her mind felt strangely calm.

His face was close to hers. "You're in the Company. You follow orders. Your orders are to stay out of government files you have no clearance to see. Do you understand?"

She could slam her fingertips into his eyes. Go for his balls under the table. Her Beretta wasn't loaded, but she could bash it against his head . . . but why did she think those things? That was the way she'd been taught to treat an enemy.

"Yes." Her tone was brittle.

He released her and inhaled deeply. "I didn't want to hurt you, darling." His voice was completely different again: Smooth, composed, the voice of the man she admired. "Being in the Company isn't a game. The rules are serious. Life and death. What made you even want to look in your file?" He stared as if trying to probe her brain. "I don't want you to get hurt in the field, or, God forbid, killed."

"Of course not."

A hot tide of anger rose in her throat. Who *were* Jane, Hamilton, Sarah, and Michael Walker? If they were real, did she know them? Were their identities lost in her past?

And why had the mere mention of them made Gordon lose control? What else didn't he want her to see . . . or know?

Dinner that night was spaghetti. The hot scents of oregano, thyme, and garlic filled the cafeteria. Liz sensed she'd had this meal many times with an elderly white-haired lady who spoke Italian and smelled of just-baked bread. The lady had a sideboard with ugly scrollwork in her living room, and when Liz was a little girl she'd loved to hide inside it.

Who was that white-haired woman?

A neighbor? A grandmother?

Later that night Liz studied Gordon's sleep patterns—the periods of restlessness, the periods of immobility. When he entered another phase of deep sleep, she again prowled across the camp and broke into the personnel building. Again she used her access code to enter the computer. But this time the computer refused it:

CANNOT READ. EXIT OR TRY AGAIN.

Gordon had blocked her code.

□ □ □ □

The early morning sky was pristine blue and cloudless over the Rockies. Lying on her cot, Liz stared out at it and thought of the photo of Gordon and herself on the beach in Santa Barbara. There was something about it—

"You're awake. Good." Gordon stood over her. As always, his smile was warm. "Put on your jogging clothes. We're going for a drive."

"Why?"

"Your endurance test. A twenty-mile run."

As she dressed, she eyed him suspiciously. He acted as if nothing had happened, as if he'd never exploded and twisted her arm, as if he'd not blocked her access to the computer. Instead, he chatted amiably about the day's classes, and when she was ready, he drove them in a green Ford Explorer out onto one of the dirt roads that wound through the Ranch.

At last he stopped, and they got out next to a mass of wild roses whose yellow heads dipped in the light mountain wind. The road stretched behind them, a dusty, narrow ribbon curving back through the timbered mountainside. The sun was pleasantly warm, but she knew that after half an hour of running its heat would blister as if she were in the Mojave.

"What's this endurance test for?" She stretched, preparing her muscles.

"Your physical conditioning. I'll be waiting for you."

"Then what happens?"

"I'll buy you a beer at the officers' club."

"Gordon, dammit. What's this all about?"

"When you pass, we'll talk." He got into the car.

He'd said "when," an important vote of confidence, because she didn't know whether she could do twenty miles, especially at this altitude. Her longest single run so far had been eight.

She took off at a slow pace, and he drove past, waving, and disappeared around a curve.

She kept up a steady jog. But as the miles disappeared behind, energy drained from her limbs. Occasional pebbles jarred her to the teeth. She knew she was approaching "the wall." She wanted to drop from exhaustion.

But her pride was involved. She had to do it.

Sweat plastered her running clothes to her skin. Her joints ached with every footfall.

Then, with an abrupt downshift in pain, she passed through the demoralizing wall. She could breathe again.

Vigor flowed to her muscles.

Triumphant, she ran on. At last she spotted Gordon, who was waiting in the car as he'd said. This must be the end of the twenty miles. Relief flooded her.

She slowed.

Her mind and body began to shut down, prepare to rest. But he leaned out the driver's window and pointed away, farther down the hot mountain road.

"Keep going!" he yelled. "One more mile to camp!"

She frowned. He must've stopped the car too soon. She ached everywhere. She was trembling. Did she have another mile in her?

She plowed ahead, swearing.

He drove past, not even looking back. She fought the urge to quit. She weaved, forced herself to concentrate on the dusty road when all she wanted was to collapse in the shade of the cool ponderosa pines.

At last she saw him again, waiting in the car at the edge of the flag circle. She ached everywhere. Her head was reeling. Then the gentle mountain air suddenly split with the noise of a baseball game.

Gordon leaned out the window again.

The loud baseball game was blasting from the camp's garbage truck, which was lumbering around the circle with a boom box blaring from the cab. It was a Dodgers-Braves game, and the driver was the new personnel director who'd nearly caught her the first night she'd sneaked into personnel.

When she reached Gordon, she refused to let herself fall. She staggered in circles, willing her muscles to cool.

"That guy's finally gone nuts." He nodded at the garbage truck.

"What happened?" she panted at last. "Did you misjudge the mileage?"

"No. I wanted you to do the full twenty-one miles."

"You bastard. You should've told me."

"So you could plan for the extra distance? Pace yourself? No, that's the point. In our business, it's a mistake to ever believe you've achieved your goal, because that signals you psychologically and physically to quit."

She was awed by the simple logic. "Just like I wanted to quit a mile back."

"You understand the real test?" He studied her.

She nodded. "Handling the physical demands was important, but the critical test was whether I could make myself go on."

"Exactly. Determination, tenacity, courage. Whatever you want to call it. There are times when all of us in the business have to achieve beyond our initial goals. But when our bodies and minds resist, we increase the odds we can't."

"Or that we'll make a mistake."

He smiled, and she saw his intense pride in her. "Well, darling, you had the guts and stamina to go that extra mile, and you have the brains to figure out what it meant. I could do a pop quiz on history, culture, and current events, but that seems silly. The way you devour information, you ought to be able to carry on a conversation with anyone."

Her breath caught in her throat. "What are you saying, Gordon? Am I finished here? Are we—?"

"I'll talk to Hughes Bremner, tell him as far as I'm concerned he can set a date. He'll be pleased." Gordon had told her Bremner was a very important Langley official who'd taken a special interest in her. It was to Bremner that Gordon faxed his notes each day. "The final phase will be training for the actual operation. Congratulations, darling. You've passed."

While Gordon went into administration to call Hughes Bremner, Liz returned to their cabin. She felt guilty.

Maybe she was wrong. Maybe she'd misjudged Gordon.

She stripped off her clothes and showered, thinking about it all, trying to find a fresh perspective. Then, as she put on her camos, the memory of her awaking came back to her. She recalled the odd feeling and gnawing doubt. There was something about the photo of her and Gordon—

She found it in her dresser drawer with the gold band she didn't feel right wearing. She examined their smiling, radiant faces. She could see neither of her hands, but Gordon's left hand was visible. And on the ring finger there was . . . no gold ring. None.

Her breath caught in her throat. That was what had bothered her. She stared at the hand for some time. At last she turned over the photo. The writing she remembered was there: Hendry's beach and a date.

The date was less than a year ago. But he'd told her he hadn't taken off the ring in *two years*. It could be a simple mistake, but she doubted it. He'd made too big a point of what the ring meant to him. He must have lied. But why?

He'd lost control, flown into a violent rage when she'd looked into her official personnel file. He'd blocked her access to the computer. Now she believed he'd be equally furious if he knew she'd stopped taking her pills.

She could no longer dismiss her doubts. Despite his lecture today about the seriousness of their purpose, and his congratulations for her going the extra mile, something was very wrong.

What other lies had Gordon told her? And why?

And what did they have to do with the Carnivore?

That evening before dinner, Liz accompanied Gordon as he stopped at the busy administration office to fax the day's notes back to Hughes Bremner at Langley. As usual, he hunched over the small fax form, covering it with one hand as he wrote with his favorite silver Cross ballpoint pen. There was no way she could see his personal code. He finished, tore off the top form, paper-clipped it to his report, and handed the sheets to the secretary. She said she'd fax them immediately. As Gordon turned and headed for the door, Liz glanced around. Everyone was occupied. She palmed the pad and followed Gordon out.

That night in their bathroom she rubbed soft lead over the top fax form. To the eye, the sheet looked blank. But Gordon wrote with an intensity that matched his commitment to Langley, and she hoped that meant he'd left impressions in the paper.

Slowly, patiently she worked, until a few letters, then words, and at last numbers became visible. She gave a silent cheer. She had it. Gordon's personal code!

Much later Liz again analyzed Gordon's sleeping. At 3:00 A.M. he fell into a deep sleep, and she broke into personnel. She sat at a computer and punched in his code. Would it work?

When the menu appeared, she exhaled, relieved.

She typed in a request for the file of her cover, Sarah Walker. In a few seconds the screen showed a face identified as Sarah Walker.

The face wasn't hers!

Instead she saw a pleasant woman with a small chin, slightly crooked nose, and no mole above the mouth. She studied the computer image as if she could make it talk.

Was it familiar? Maybe—

She read the file. Sarah Jane Walker, magazine writer and celebrity profiler, born the same year as Liz. Their height was a quarter inch different; their weight within three pounds. An entry said Sarah's mother had a brother living in England—Harold ("Hal") Sansborough. He'd married Melanie Childs, and they'd had a daughter, Liz. Hal and Melanie Sansborough had been killed in New York City.

How does one know, she wondered, the difference between memory and what one's been told is memory?

If Liz Sansborough and Sarah Walker were the same person, why were there variations in their physical descriptions? Was that operator error? But at her height—five foot nine, give or take—a quarter inch could be explained by posture or the measurer's instruments, and the three pounds could be normal weight fluctuation. When she thought about it, either physical description could be hers.

But if she were Sarah Walker *and* Liz Sansborough, why wasn't Sarah Walker's data simply copied from Liz Sansborough's?

And how could the face with the small chin and no mole be explained, particularly since it was identified as belonging to Sarah Walker?

Then she saw an entry about a Great-grandmother Firenze, who was both Sarah and Liz's great-grandmother, which meant she was also the grandmother of Jane Sansborough Walker and Hal Sansborough. As she read, an image of an energetic, white-haired woman appeared in her mind, and she smelled spicy spaghetti and freshly baked bread flavored with rosemary.

Her heart hammered with excitement. She closed her eyes and tried to hold onto the image, but it was like trying to grasp soft butter.

Damn. The vision vanished as quickly as it had come.

Another real memory?

Yes! It must have been! Great-grandmother Firenze!

She read on. Sarah had attended the University of California at Santa Barbara, edited the university newspaper, the *Daily Nexus*, graduated, and done a stint on the *Santa Barbara Independent*. Living on money inherited from Great-grandma Firenze, Sarah at last had broken into magazine free-lancing.

How could she explain what seemed to be her own personal "memory" of Great-grandma Firenze, when it appeared her family —the Sansboroughs—had never visited Santa Barbara?

Maybe Great-grandma Firenze had visited them in England, and she'd made up the rest of the memory.

Was there a real Sarah Walker out there somewhere? Someone who looked like the woman on the computer screen? If so, what had happened to her?

Thinking about it gave Liz chills. She sat for a long time in the glow of the computer in the dark room.

At last she scrolled back to the beginning of the file. She memorized the Santa Barbara telephone numbers of Sarah Walker, Hamilton and Jane Walker, and Michael Walker.

And then she turned off the computer and headed for the door. This time no one waited outside. She thought of the strange spectacle yesterday of the personnel director driving around the circle in the camp garbage truck, listening to the baseball game at full blast.

As she crossed toward her cabin, she noticed a cluster of pinpoint lights to the southwest—a mountain village that wasn't on the road she and Gordon had used to drive to the Ranch; they had come in from the southeast. The lights were only a few miles away but seemed a different universe.

On their way to her first class the next morning, Liz stopped at the women's john. Gordon headed around the corner toward the men's side. Once he was out of sight, she double-timed to the administration building where a public telephone stood outside. She dropped in coins and dialed Sarah Walker's number in Santa Barbara. After four rings, a computerized voice told her the number had been disconnected. She tried Sarah's parents' number in Santa Barbara. A woman answered.

"Mrs. Walker?"

"No. What number are you dialing?"

When Liz told her, the woman explained she'd had the number only three months.

Disappointed, Liz glanced at the men's room door from which Gordon would have to exit. He'd have his back to her. She dropped in more coins and dialed the number of Sarah Walker's brother,

Michael. The telephone rang and rang. No one answered. She hung up but was reluctant to leave. Why? It took her a moment . . . and then she knew what it was.

She'd heard two almost inaudible clicks just before she'd hung up. She double-timed back to meet Gordon, feeling a sinking fear. The camp's only public telephone was bugged. Now someone would know she was still investigating Sarah Walker.

Ten

As Washington's beltway began to swelter from the hot morning sun, Lucas Maynard arrived at the bench under the cherry trees where undersecretary Clare Edward waited impatiently.

Maynard had a plain manilla envelope tucked under his arm.

Inside the envelope were documents he'd copied the night before from a fireproof safe he kept locked under Leslee Pousho's bed. Leslee had slept on unaware as he'd slipped out and then returned from an all-night copy shop. The safe was his, and she had no idea what was in it. He'd promised to show her soon, and she trusted him enough to wait. As a precaution he'd given her Clare Edward's office and home phone numbers. If anything happened to him, she was to turn the safe over to the undersecretary.

She hadn't liked the thought of something "happening" to him. But he knew eventually she'd grow disenchanted with all the problems that came from having an overaged, reformed spy for a lover. She'd want to move on to a relationship where there were no secrets.

If he didn't want to lose her, he'd have to get out of his messy life as soon as possible.

The documents he was delivering to the undersecretary gave the secret points of origin of some $10 million in Iran-contra money he and the others had skimmed off drug profits and dumped into no-questions-asked numbered accounts at BCCI. Once the money was in the BCCI system, it was anonymous. But he had a paper trail that proved the accounts had later been cashed out and invested in OMNI-American and Nonpareil International Insurance.

Neither man spoke.

They carefully studied everything around them.

Maynard casually laid the envelope on the bench. He got up, walked away, and disappeared among the trees.

When Clare Edward arrived at State, the ordinary manilla envelope under his arm, he hurried into his private office without giving more than a glance to the man with a stiff face and roaming eyes who was talking to his redheaded secretary. She waited until the undersecretary had passed, then smiled up at the young man who had been dropping by often lately. She found him amusing, a brother, not a potential boyfriend, which was a refreshing change.

He handed her a bouquet of roses.

"They're beautiful."

"How about a bite of late breakfast?" he suggested.

"Now the boss is in, I've got tons of work to do. Sorry."

Undersecretary Clare Edward sat grinning behind his antique walnut desk in his walnut-paneled office. His blood raced with excitement because he was reading Lucas Maynard's documentation.

It was everything he'd hoped for and more.

He recognized no names on the list. Probably dummies, but they'd be traceable. And the account numbers and descriptions of arms and drug sales were more complete than any the Iran-contra prosecutors had been able to confirm.

He telephoned the Secretary of State's office, reached his top assistant, and pleaded urgency. The assistant gave him an appointment for 10:10 the next morning.

For the rest of the day the undersecretary worked with only half his mind on what he was doing. When Maynard finally called that afternoon, Edward's cultured voice reverberated with bonhomie.

"This is the real stuff, Lucas. I've made an appointment with Warren in the morning. Get the rest of your information ready. If it's as hot as this, we're going to have some fun."

Lucas Maynard's voice was bristly. "Nothing more until I have a deal. Full immunity."

□   □   □   □

"Excellent." Hughes Bremner was at his desk at Langley, and Gordon had just telephoned to relate the good news about the woman's twenty-one-mile test. "You've done a fine job bringing her along. How'd she take the extra mile?"

"Furious about being tricked, then extremely proud she'd pulled it off."

Bremner chuckled. Pride. Her undoing. But the vanity that would destroy her would also make him successful beyond anyone's wildest dreams.

"How is her behavior overall, Gordon?"

"She's calmed down, sir. All she ever found was dead ends. No way she'll ever break into the database again."

"She's no hotshot hacker."

"No, sir," Gordon agreed over the long-distance wire. "When do you want me to start her on the next stage?"

Bremner considered. "I'll be in Paris tomorrow. Back home the next day. Start then. I want to be here to stay on top of this. Meanwhile, remember, we can't afford to have anything go wrong. Especially when we're so close."

At noon a transcript of the telephone conversation between Lucas Maynard and the undersecretary arrived in Bremner's office. Bremner read it with growing anger and alarm.

Lucas Maynard was demanding immunity, and the undersecretary was taking Maynard's information to the Secretary of State!

Bremner felt a sudden chill.

What exactly did Maynard know? What was he trying to sell that required immunity? It couldn't be the French operation. Not even Bremner's board knew about what would be the greatest operation of his career—GRANDEUR. He'd already given them so much, he saw no reason to cut them in on this, too, and GRANDEUR would be his ultimate triumph. It would shake Europe to its smug foundations and leave the United States reeling. But Lucas Maynard knew enough. The details of Sterling-O'Keefe alone would destroy them all, and GRANDEUR with them.

Again he studied the transcript and its short appended report. One of Bremner's agents, whose assigned territory included State, had been keeping an eye on Undersecretary Edward. He'd reported the undersecretary's hurried arrival at his office with the manilla envelope, and the transcript of the phone call had confirmed its significance.

But neither surveillance nor Bremner's agent at State had been able to determine where Maynard disappeared for hours at a time. Bremner could delay no longer. He was going to have to take care of this himself.

Years ago he'd begun holding afternoon coffees in his austere seventh-floor office. Invitations to these gatherings were coveted by ambitious underlings. He was near the top, and he doled out news and career suggestions with the precision of a Las Vegas odds maker. Everyone knew wooing Bremner paid off.

He telephoned Maynard and invited him up for coffee. "Just us, Lucas," he said smoothly.

Maynard agreed. A refusal would have made Bremner wary. They both knew that.

In ten minutes Maynard was at his door. "We haven't talked in a long time, Lucas," Bremner greeted him, gesturing graciously toward the sofa and chairs grouped around a slate-topped coffee table at the far end of his office. Beyond the grouping, through the office windows, spread the sea of Virginia woods.

"You've been busy, Hughes. We both have." Maynard sat in a chair with its back to the timbered landscape, not the door.

"You've lost weight." Bremner poured coffee into Haviland cups.

"Twenty pounds so far. For the diabetes."

"Ah, yes." Bremner set the full cups on the slate table. He laid a linen napkin beside each. Halfway between them he put out cream and sugar, in matching Haviland china, and a sterling tray of sandwiches. He'd arranged everything himself, having found the personal attention made his guests feel more important and amenable to suggestion.

"I've been thinking about Sterling-O'Keefe and MASQUERADE." Bremner sat across from Maynard, where he could look through the windows to the world. "Do you have any misgivings?"

An alarm went off in Maynard's head. They never discussed Sterling-O'Keefe at Langley. Never. Was something else going on? Something Bremner wanted to keep quiet? Or had he discovered what Maynard was up to with the undersecretary?

But the veteran agent sipped his coffee quietly. "That's an odd question, coming from you. Sterling-O'Keefe is your baby. You've made us rich as Midas. Why would I have misgivings?"

Bremner smiled. "You tell me."

Maynard put down his cup and crossed his arms over his heavy chest. "No misgivings, Hughes. Except about myself. Getting old. Maybe it's time to hang it up."

"Retire?"

"It happens to us all."

"Except the stars in the lobby." Hughes Bremner never forgot the simple, five-pointed stars carved into the wall down in the entrance lobby. Each of the nearly sixty stars symbolized an operative who'd died in the line of duty, but only half were listed in the honor book nearby. The other heroes' names remained as secret as their fatal missions. The words carved into the marble above the stars said it all: "In honor of those Americans who gave their lives in the service of their country."

Service. Country. That's why Hughes Bremner—and all the men who'd come aboard in the '50s—had joined Langley. They'd been idealists. As for himself, Bremner would have given anything to become one of those stars. In those early cold war days, he'd longed for it. Not death but glory, heroism. Back then the United States had known her enemies, and she'd had the guts to pursue them. Relentlessly.

The 1980s were different. When Bremner organized arms sales to Iran and drug sales to the United States to finance the contras— *contrarevolucionarios*—in Nicaragua, new U.S. laws made him a criminal. That's when he'd finally acknowledged his once-glorious country had been on a three-decade trip into the dumper.

The grand United States of America had been ruined, made pussy-weak by radicals, do-gooders, and liberal Congresses.

He'd come to a painful realization: No point in his going down, too. It wasn't *his* country anymore. It was time to take care of himself. For the split second of that final decision, he'd felt what it must have been to be that blackbirding forebear of his, a renegade. In that instant, too, a new, soul-altering conviction had given final shape to his destiny: If he was going to do it, he'd go all the way. Make himself so rich, so powerful, no one would ever be able to touch him again.

As head of Mustang, Hughes Bremner was a CIA division chief, a feudal king with a fiefdom. The top people—the director of Central Intelligence and her three deputy directors—had too much to supervise. They blessed division chiefs like Bremner with their confidence and expected them to operate independently, with no one looking over their shoulders. It was a prescription for personal profit, and Bremner and his four deputies were no fools. The notorious case of KGB mole Aldrich Ames had simply made them more careful. Every problem had a solution; every rule had a loophole.

"We won't die behind a desk," Lucas Maynard said.

"I sure as hell hope not." Bremner gazed past Maynard and out his windows. Now was the time to set his trap. "We do go back a long way, Lucas. Tell me, do you miss the cold war?"

Maynard seemed to feel the question deep in his gut. "God, yes. We knew the good guys from the bad then. All this fuss now about intelligence not being reported accurately to the top makes me laugh. They think it's a new thing. Remember in '57 and '58 when we were running that covert operation to topple Sukarno? We reported only what Langley wanted Washington to hear. We lied to the ambassadors who tried to stop us, and then we got them reassigned when they wouldn't butt out. We didn't think a thing of it. And that was just one incident. Do I miss the cold war? Hell, yes. It was so much simpler. So exciting. We could do something. We were united for freedom. Democracy."

"The cold war gave the United States purpose." Bremner lifted his patrician face and smiled. "We were everything the other side wasn't. Remember when Ike had to drum up support to build the interstate highway system? He said it was to evacuate cities in case of nuclear war. And when Kennedy decided we needed better science and physical education classes, he said it was to whip the Soviets. Now we accomplish so little."

Lucas Maynard's gaze grew misty. Bremner saw he'd established the rapport he was seeking. Maynard had stepped into his trap.

Now Bremner would wait. This was the trick: Make the other fellow comfortable and beholden, find a common ground, and say nothing. Soon the silence would demand to be filled, and more often than not the guest spoke into it what was on his troubled . . . or guilty . . . mind.

At last Maynard said, "Did you ever stop to think, Hughes, for fifty years Langley's been ordered to work with humanity's underbelly. The mafia. The drug lords from Miami to Hong Kong. The generals who raped their countries for money and power. We were expected to mingle with the scum, ally ourselves when we had to, but we weren't supposed to get into bed with them."

"A different world, Lucas. Not a pretty one."

Maynard's heavy face was tense. What was bothering him? Bremner was tempted to encourage him to be candid, but that wouldn't work. Maynard had seen too many interrogations, conducted too many himself. He'd be suspicious.

Bremner breathed evenly, slowly. Would Maynard go on?

Maynard set down his coffee cup as if he were setting down a burden. He looked straight into Bremner's eyes, and for a moment Bremner sensed he was about to spill his most profound secrets.

Instead, Maynard glanced down at his watch.

"A meeting?" Bremner experienced a rare emotion: Surprise.

"Sorry, Hughes. You called late, and I couldn't cancel it."

"It must be important." He spoke mildly, but he wanted to squash Maynard's fat, diabetic face between his hands.

Maynard seemed to know an unimpeachable excuse was expected. He gave it without missing a beat. "My ex-Stasi snitch. You know how frightened he is. If I ditch him, we could lose one of our most reliable sources inside the German government."

"Of course," Bremner said coolly. "Very important."

"Is there anything else you wanted to tell me, Hughes?" Maynard stood. "I'm not quite clear why you asked me here."

Bremner stood, too. He smiled inwardly. The bastard had just tried to turn the tables on him. "I like to keep up with my friends. You know that, Lucas."

"True. Well, this has been like old times. The good old times. Not that many of us remember them anymore."

"Yes. Most unfortunate."

Bremner lingered in the doorway as his longtime ally walked away toward the elevators, his shoulders square. Dignified. For the first time in many years, Hughes Bremner was nervous.

Eleven

Hughes Bremner waited thirty minutes, plenty of time for Maynard to reach his office, check in, and leave for his meeting.

If he had one. If he hadn't invented it at the last moment to save his lying ass, because he'd sensed a trap.

Bremner dialed Maynard's line. The secretary answered. He asked to speak to Maynard.

"I'm sorry, sir. He's gone for the day."

"Ah, yes. What was it? I've forgotten—"

"A meeting with his German informer, sir."

So Maynard had been telling the truth after all. Bremner was in no better position than before. Disgust welled up in his throat, sour as bile. He was about to make a polite, empty comment and hang up, when a final question occurred to him.

"He told you about the meeting before he came up to see me?" Bremner asked. "Or after?"

"Oh, before, sir. He asked me to call him if it looked like your meeting was going on too long for him to see the German."

Damn. Bremner had been sure the whole story was cooked up to give Maynard a legitimate reason to leave. He tried one last question: "When did the German arrange the meeting?"

"I believe Mr. Maynard did. It must have been sudden."

"Sudden?"

"Uh-huh. After he left I realized he was going to miss a doctor's appointment. He never misses them. His diabetes, you know. So I suppose he must have talked to the German only a few minutes before his meeting with you, or—"

Bremner smiled. Maynard was still good, but this time not quite good enough. Maynard had arranged the appointment himself, suspecting he might need an excuse to exit Bremner's office.

The woman's voice faltered. "Sir . . . is anything wrong? I mean, all these questions about Mr. Maynard's schedule?"

Bremner knew enough. It all added up: Maynard's breakfast with the undersecretary, the demand for immunity, and the manilla envelope that had excited the undersecretary so much. There was only one logical conclusion: Lucas Maynard had kept records.

"Actually there *is* something wrong, Mildred," Bremner said, his voice sincere, concerned. "I've been worried about Lucas's diabetes. Do you think he's working too hard?"

"Oh, Mr. Bremner, you're so right—"

He listened absently as she recited a litany of concerns about Maynard's health. His mind was busy making plans.

There was nothing worse than a traitor, and Lucas Maynard was a traitor. At another time, Bremner might have had the luxury of continuing to watch Maynard, of trying to find the reason for his betrayal. There was always a reason, and it could be used to turn the enemy. But not now. Now there could be no unnecessary risks, no mistakes, no chances taken with MASQUERADE or his private French operation, GRANDEUR.

As soon as he got rid of Maynard's secretary, Hughes Bremner called Sid Williams on his secure line.

"Maynard has stolen critical top-secret government documents," Bremner told his subordinate. "It's a grave breach of national security and MASQUERADE. We've got to have the documents, and he's got to be silenced. Do whatever you have to do. And that includes taking care of the undersecretary. Immediately."

At four o'clock the usual limo picked up Undersecretary Clare Edward at State for the drive to his classic Georgetown home. He carried Lucas Maynard's manilla envelope safely locked in his briefcase. He'd debated whether to leave it in his safe at State, but too many people had access to the safe.

In fact, too damn many people had access to his office. Just this evening there'd been a new security man standing in the doorway, chatting up his secretary, while he had been packing his briefcase for home. He'd ordered the man away. The fellow had been genuinely apologetic, but still—

No way would he leave Maynard's explosive documents in the office. He wanted this bombshell all for himself.

He'd sleep with the papers under his pillow.

As his limo pulled up in front of his brownstone, he decided to ring up the new file clerk and invite her over for the evening. She was a delectable little morsel, hardly out of high school. Very young. Very tiny. He liked tiny women. They were so safe.

As the limo rolled away, he started across the sidewalk. He had a spring to his step just thinking about the little girl.

Then he heard a sound and turned.

A blond youth on Rollerblades skated recklessly toward him. The undersecretary caught a brief glimpse of a silvery knife blade. Fear crunched his chest. He opened a hand, ineffectual and too late. The knife slashed up across his palm and lodged itself under his rib cage. The skater toppled onto him.

Pain and shock rocked the undersecretary. He couldn't move.

The mugger rifled his pockets and took his wallet, Rolex watch, and two diamond rings. Then he jammed the knife in farther, pulled it out, and pushed himself back up onto his Rollerblades.

The undersecretary raised a feeble hand. He wanted to call out, tell the thug to stop. But he couldn't. The pain receded to a dull nausea. Hot blood covered him. He was dying. With a surge of clarity he decided it was all right. Life had become meaningless. Imagine, he'd actually been looking forward to an evening with a barely literate teenager. He closed his eyes as the thief raced away. His last image was of his brown leather briefcase tight against the youth's chest.

At the same time that afternoon, Lucas Maynard stalked the floor of Leslee Pousho's apartment in Arlington. He'd been a fool. He'd underestimated Hughes Bremner. He'd sensed it in Bremner's office, and it was confirmed when he'd arrived home.

Sid Williams and Matt Lister had been waiting. They had used the new laser lock picker to break in. If it hadn't been for his years of automatic caution and his Walther, he'd never have escaped.

As he'd walked from the garage toward his front door, he'd spotted the faint movement of the drapes at the window. The old outdoor cat, who never sat at the front door unless someone was in the house, was parked there. He'd turned instantly and raced back to his car. They'd come running out as he backed away. He'd knocked Lister down with a leg shot and forced Williams to dive for cover. Then he was gone.

He smiled gloomily. None of the Sterling-O'Keefe or MASQUERADE papers was in the house. Everything was here, in the safe under Leslee's bed. Now he had to call Clare Edward. The undersecretary would have to arrange protection and a State safe house for him and Leslee. Thank God for Clare Edward. Without the undersecretary, how would he and Leslee get out of this mess?

Lucas Maynard picked up the phone and dialed.

At 4:45 P.M. at a busy Georgetown intersection, Hughes Bremner watched the side-view mirror from the back seat of his black government limo. The powerful engine idled. The limo had full, high-security accessories—armor plating, antimine flooring, and bulletproof windows blackened against the world.

At precisely 4:50 P.M., a young blond man on Rollerblades sped up the street with traffic, coming up on the limo's rear.

Bremner lowered his window. As the racer flew by, he flung inside an expensive, brown-leather briefcase.

A good shot, it landed almost on Bremner's lap.

"Dulles, Tommy." Bremner pulled out Lucas Maynard's manilla envelope and opened it.

The skater disappeared around a corner, and the limo entered traffic, heading for the airport. Bremner had a reservation on an overnight flight to Paris.

He flipped quickly through Maynard's documents and saw instantly what had made the undersecretary salivate and Maynard expect immunity. Maynard had provided a paper trail of laundered greenbacks detailed enough to convict all of them, destroy everything they'd built, and scuttle the entire French operation as well. And Maynard had promised a hell of a lot more documents where these came from.

But there was no hint of GRANDEUR. Bremner smiled, relieved. That at least was still secure.

He relaxed as the limo fought its way through heavy five o'clock traffic, and his mind moved on to his most crucial quest. In a few hours his best surveillance teams would try again to follow the Carnivore's intermediary to the assassin's lair.

Twelve

It was lunchtime in the Ranch cafeteria. Liz Sansborough pretended she had nothing on her mind but her meal. Then she gave a startled jerk, sat upright, and looked at Gordon.

"I forgot the notes for my next class." She stood. "They're in my locker. I'll be right back."

He arose to go with her, but she raised her voice slightly to remind him operating independently was one of the skills she'd learned. Sitting nearby were three trainees and an instructor. They looked up. Gordon noticed they'd noticed. He smiled at her, nodded, and sat back down. She could feel his questioning gaze hot on her back as she strode from the cafeteria.

She checked her watch—12:06. She ran. She had to make the most of every minute. But when she rounded the corner of the officers' club, she collided with the personnel director.

"Sorry."

He grinned. "Dodgers ahead three to two."

He wore a Walkman on his belt and headphones on his ears. Dressed in T-shirt, shorts, and jogging shoes, he was listening to baseball in the middle of the workday. He *was* crazy. And she had no time to waste. She mumbled an apology and ran on, straight for her locker.

If she were right, the public phone she'd used early this morning had been bugged. There were no phones in billeting. Private phones were located only in offices and staff huts. The phone she'd used in front of administration was the single public one at the Ranch.

Since trainees were discouraged from outside contacts, she doubted the only public phone was being monitored just for her. The bug had probably been installed for general, all-purpose fishing. What would be more natural than for a foreign intelligence agency—enemy or friend—to try to infiltrate this top-secret birthplace of U.S. spies?

But no matter its purpose, the bug had recorded her attempts to contact the Walker family in Santa Barbara.

At her locker she grabbed her supplies, already neatly bundled. She ran across the lawn to the personnel hut. It was locked as usual, everyone at lunch or exercising. Which was what she wanted.

She looked carefully around, then used her lock picker and Gordon's code to break in. She locked the door behind her and hurried to the computer room. There she removed the face plate from the light switch and installed a radio-triggered device she'd taken from electronics. The device bypassed the on-off toggle without affecting regular use.

Far back under the top of the first computer desk, she hid a miniature recorder-player. About the size of a matchbook, the recorder-player could be triggered by remote. Its tape contained a half hour of office noises—footsteps on the floor, file drawers opening and closing, a desk chair dragged out, the clicking of someone at work on a keyboard, muted voices. She'd taken the recorder-player from electronics, too, and made the tape while studying in the Ranch's library.

Finished, she checked her watch. She'd been gone just eight minutes. She grabbed her notes and raced back to Gordon.

That night after Gordon was apparently again deep in sleep, Liz silently left their cabin and hid in the shadows beneath a fir tree across from personnel. The air was cool and damp with the scents of pine and earth. Off to the southeast, pinpricks of light reminded her of the village strung out to the southwest.

Time passed slowly.

She reviewed each step of her preparation. She could think of nothing she'd left out. Perhaps she was wrong. Perhaps there was no reason to set this trap.

Then something moved between the trees.

She stared, all her senses alert. Someone was coming around the corner of the officers' club!

She dropped low beneath the pine branches. The figure unlocked personnel's door. From her control pad she triggered the devices in the computer room that turned on the overhead fluorescent light and started the tape of office sounds.

When the figure slipped indoors, she closed in. At a window she put on her infrared goggles, turned on her infrared flashlight, and shot the green beam into the dark room.

She located him, a man, leaning against the computer room door, beneath which a line of yellow light showed. He was listening to the sounds that indicated someone was inside, working. But still, she couldn't see his face.

Then he turned around, and her suspicions were confirmed.

Gordon!

Furious, disgusted, she watched as he moved to one of the computers in the reception area and flicked it on. She knew what he'd do next: Feed in his override code so he could check what she was doing in the next room. She had to move before he discovered the room was empty.

She ran, scanning the sleeping camp, feeling a deep sense of betrayal. In the beginning the camp had been a source of hope. Now she felt differently. Whoever had been monitoring the public telephone must have told Gordon about her calls to Santa Barbara. The Ranch had deceived her, too.

What didn't he want her to know?

Why couldn't he be straight with her?

She had trusted him, but he hadn't trusted her.

In her heart she still dreamed of innocence and the Gordon she'd grown to trust and admire in Santa Barbara. Now she doubted their love affair had been real. The gold rings had been a beautiful idea— romantic, touching. More important, they'd cemented her faith in him.

Then there was the Carnivore himself—

Because of her training at the Ranch, she now knew how devious Langley could be. Gordon could have staged the attack at her condo back in Santa Barbara and fabricated the dossiers that claimed the Carnivore was searching for her. The bland-faced attacker she'd supposedly killed could have used fake blood. Gordon could have been shot in the arm to confirm the reality . . . because, without the attack and the dossiers, she had no evidence the Carnivore even existed. For all she knew, no assassin had ever tried to kill her!

She was entitled to know who she was. Everyone had that right. It wasn't earned. It wasn't given. All you had to do was be born. And now more than ever she needed to know, because, judging by the way Gordon was acting, her lost memory must contain clues to what he, and perhaps Langley, were really planning.

Inside their dark cabin she moved swiftly. She snapped her survival knife and canteen to her belt, grabbed her day pack, and threw into it her infrared flashlight, compass, wire clippers, 9mm Beretta, and Gordon's billfold with its money and credit cards. Her infrared goggles still hung from her neck.

She checked the window for signs of Gordon. She saw and heard nothing. She cracked open the door.

A fist reached in. She slammed the door against it.

Gordon grunted and blasted open the door. "Get back in! You're not going anywhere!" He shoved her, and she stumbled. Rage swelled his face. His words snapped like a steel trap. She'd broken the rules again, and—worse—she'd fooled him.

She'd fooled God.

Loathing rose in her throat, but she had no time for it. She headed around him to the door. If memory was the foundation of knowing, then she was definitely having memories. She *knew* she had to leave the Ranch.

"I'm going, Gordon."

"Like hell you are!" He grabbed her arm and turned her. "You'll do as you're told!"

"You've blown it. I don't believe you anymore." She tried to pull free. "I want no part of whatever you're doing here!"

"You bitch. You stupid, arrogant bitch!" He grabbed her day pack's shoulder straps, shoved, started to yank them down.

She responded instantly, seized the upper sleeves of his shirt, clipped the inside of his right foot with her right foot, and using his momentum, threw him off-balance. He crashed down onto his back in a *ko-uchi gari.*

"Liz!"

"Fuck off, Gordon."

Before he could get to his feet, she slammed through the door and tore away.

"Liz, darling!" he called behind her, his voice once more kind, concerned. "Come back. You've got to have your medicine!"

"Fuck my medicine."

She raced away through the night, heading southwest toward the lights of the village, where there would be a road to civilization and to identity.

Thirteen

The new, temporary director of Ranch personnel, Asher Flores, was asleep in his cabin. He dreamed of choir-boy robes flapping at his heels as he escaped Sunday morning mass, baseball games where the Dodgers always won, and the funny stories his uncles told as his mother's family gathered for Rosh Hashanah.

Then something shook his shoulder.

He tried to return to the safety of the dreams, but the shaking got harder. He opened his eyes.

Gordon Taite stood over his bed in the glow of a flashlight.

"Lay off." Asher rolled away.

"Get up, Flores." Taite shook him again.

"I've got $2,000 in dental work. You going to pay for new bridges? Get lost."

"Up! That's an order!"

Asher opened his eyes again. "We're not in the army, Taite. Give me a break."

But groaning and swearing, he got up anyway. Gordon Taite was one notch higher on Langley's pecking pole. At another time he would have enforced his recommendation Taite get lost, but not now. He was so sick of the Ranch he could puke. It was driving him nuts. It was worse than boring. Hell, even the Dodgers were losing. If Bremner was going to punish him by keeping him in the United States, at least the Dodgers could have a winning season.

Asher tucked in his shirt, zipped his pants, and fastened his belt.

He had a strong, wiry body that his camos covered like a rumpled bed. To him, style was zero priority.

"Okay, what's up?" He tried to use his most captivating voice. Then he saw blood in Taite's hair, an ugly wound on his head. "What happened? Wake up a less-obliging person?"

"I'll tell you when we get to security." Gordon Taite had no sense of humor.

"Which is it—hiking boots or tennis shoes?"

"Hiking boots."

"Terrific," Asher grumbled. "Just what I wanted. A midnight stroll." He put on the boots and did up the laces.

"You could use some action, Flores. People are beginning to talk."

That made him grin. His black bushy eyebrows beetled. Gordon Taite was referring to his forays with the camp trash truck, his boom box turned up full volume so everyone could hear when the Dodgers were ahead, and his general inattention to his job as interim personnel director. Of course, he'd accomplished other carefully planned misdemeanors, too, but he couldn't immediately recall them. In any case, maybe the word would get back to Hughes Bremner, and Hughes Bremner would start to worry about the damage he'd do to the Ranch.

"So they're talking, eh?" Asher led the way toward security. "What are they saying?"

"That you've lost it."

Asher grinned wider. He knew Gordon Taite was disgusted with him. But then, Taite was a tight ass. He'd never liked Taite. Taite was the kind who kissed up and shat down. All charm on the outside, zero quality on the inside. You could never trust weasels like Gordon Taite.

"I hope you reported me to Bremner," Asher said.

"Of course."

Inside, Asher chuckled. Maybe he had a future again. "Where's your protégée—the beautiful one with the long legs? She ran into me today, in a manner of speaking. If I'm going to be up all night, I'd rather look at her than at you."

Gordon Taite's voice turned brittle. "Liz has gone over the wall. I need you to get her back."

□   □   □   □

Asher Flores had run field ops his own way once too often and, as punishment, Hughes Bremner had reassigned him to this tiresome little training camp in the middle of nowhere. Asher didn't take to discipline easily. In fact, he tolerated it only by maximizing the few pleasures and dodging the drudgery. Eventually some new emergency would erupt, and Asher figured Bremner would have to throw him back into the field.

Maybe this was it. "So tell me about Liz . . . Sansborough, right?" Asher pushed into security, where rows of wall monitors showed various camp locations in infrared.

"See that?" Gordon Taite pointed to a flashing blip on the radar screen. The blip was moving southwest. "That's her. She was once a good operator, then she had some psychiatric problems. We need her for a special operation. Our doctor thought she'd be okay. If not, we'd find out in training. Well, we've found out, dammit. I've called the doctor. He's flying in now."

"She cracked?"

Gordon Taite nodded. "Tonight for sure. Couldn't take it. It's too bad. Anyway, we've got to get her back so we can get her medicated again."

Asher studied the blip. "Looks like she's heading for Ten Scalps. That's the little burg southwest of here."

As Gordon watched, Asher pulled out a chair, sat, and propped his feet up on a desk. He'd keep his eye on the radar screen from here. He ignored Taite's black look, and when Taite opened his mouth, Asher spoke quickly: "No sense stumbling around in the dark. We'll pick her up when she lands. Anybody got some coffee? Tonight's drug of choice is caffeine."

As Liz ran through the night, she wondered about Gordon. Surely he'd alerted security. But if he had, why was there no alarm? She didn't understand it. Unless Gordon was protecting his pride . . . or had some other way to catch her—

Worried, she slowed to a fast walk, trying to figure it out. She was breathing hard, more from contemplating Gordon's treachery than from the run. Still, she had hours of tough hiking ahead, and she needed to conserve energy.

She moved cross country, watching for sensors and cameras, wondering when the alarm would sound. And when it didn't, wondering what that meant. The moon gave good illumination in the open places. She hiked down slopes and across meadows. She jumped narrow summer streams, fed by snow melting high in the Rockies. Occasionally she heard animals scurrying away. Once she saw a herd of deer silhouetted in the moonlight. She drank from her water bottle frequently and stopped only to pee.

She saw one Ranch structure, a parachute tower. She circled widely around it. She spotted no devices that could track or view her. Maybe security was only at the camp's perimeter.

At last she arrived at the towering, concrete-block, perimeter wall. It loomed black and enormous in the night. Concertina wire was rolled across its top. She put on her goggles and shone her infrared light along the walls and through the trees, searching for cameras, sensors, sentries.

Then she found a closed-circuit camera, and a second. Both were located high in fir trees where they could observe overlapping segments of the wall but would be impossible to spot in aerial photographs.

She squatted in the pine needles, considering her situation. At last a solution occurred to her. She reached under the needles to the moist dirt beneath. There'd been a rain this week, and here, where the earth was protected by the duff, the dirt was still mud.

She grabbed a handful and climbed the first tree. She smeared mud on the camera's lens, making a brown film. Then she did the same on the next two cameras. With luck the film would look like a normal dirt coating, and when someone came to clean them—or to look for her—they'd have more than a hundred yards of wall to investigate.

On the ground again, she leaped up on the part of the wall surveilled by the second camera and, without touching the concertina wire, balanced precariously on the edge.

She trained her infrared beam along the length of the wall.

Then she saw them: Small metal boxes attached to rods from which the concertina wire was strung. Vibration detectors. If someone pulled the wire, an alarm would instantly warn security.

She took a deep breath and snipped through one thick wire. She watched her watch and, at sixty seconds, she snipped the wire two feet to the right. The time interval was long enough that, with the absence of bad luck, security would think the tiny quivers were normal—wind, birds, or some adventurous squirrel.

Her hands steady, she dropped the clippers into her backpack, picked up the section of cut rolled wire, crawled through, and returned the wire to its previous spot.

She dropped down the other side of the wall. Someone would eventually find the wire had been cut, but by then she expected to be far away. She double-timed off across a long ridge and down a valley toward the little town whose lights she'd spotted. As dawn rose pink and marigold on the horizon, she entered its outskirts. She longed to shower and sleep at the only motel, but that would be an invitation for Gordon to find her.

She was sweaty and exhausted, but she breathed deeply, savoring her freedom. Savoring the knowledge that she'd learned the Ranch's—and Gordon's—lessons well. Now she had two goals: Find out not only what her memories meant, but what Gordon had done to her, and—perhaps most important—why.

She wasn't going to let the bastard get away with whatever the hell he was up to, no matter what she had to do.

Part Two

Asher Flores

Fourteen

Liz moved swiftly through the mountain village and followed the narrow, two-lane blacktop out the other side. She slowed again, pacing herself. After a quarter mile she heard the engine of some vehicle approaching from the south. She stepped off the road and into the trees. She crouched, making herself small. Sweat dripped off her forehead. She waited.

Then she saw it—a Jeep, dammit. It could be from the Ranch. She moved swiftly back through the trees, staying low.

The Jeep skidded to a stop.

Her temples throbbing, she dropped, belly on the ground, and slithered into the underbrush. Branches tore her clothes and skin. She could hear male voices behind her and a great clumping and thrashing. They seemed not to care about the noise. That worried her more.

Sweat pasted her shirt and pants to her skin. Her breathing came in painful rasps. Fear had an iron grip on her chest. She'd escaped a hundred feet from the road when she heard someone ahead of her. Then someone to her left, a third on her right.

Swiftly she reversed direction. If she could get back to the road, she could hot-wire the Jeep.

There was abrupt silence. Not even the insects and birds sang. The shadowy forest was eerie, oppressive. Predatory.

She froze, sweated more. A twig snapped ahead of her. She resumed slithering backward. Quickly. Away from the sound.

That's when Gordon lunged from the timber to her right and landed flat on her back, knocking the wind from her. At the same time, but from the left, a second man—the personnel director—shot from the timber, too.

She struggled, gasping for air.

The men were fast and perfectly coordinated. They rolled her over. The personnel director sat on her legs. Gordon straddled her chest.

"Dammit, Gordon! Let me up!" She tried to break her arms free.

"Just relax, Liz," Dr. Levine commanded as he emerged from the forest ahead of her.

"What are *you* doing here!"

"You're not yourself, Liz." The doctor set down his black bag and removed a hypodermic syringe.

"Jesus Christ! What have you been doing to me!" She looked wildly at the syringe and then at the doctor.

"You need some time out, darling, to compose yourself." It was Gordon's most soothing voice. He smiled gently.

"Let me go!" She kicked and struggled, but Gordon and Flores had her pinned.

"Hold her still! I can't get close enough to inject her!" The doctor circled.

"Take it easy, lady. There's three of us. No way you can get free." It was Asher Flores with his angular face and black bushy hair and eyebrows. He was the one who'd almost caught her the first time she'd broken into personnel.

"You son of a bitch!" she yelled. "They've got to have been drugging me—"

Gordon clamped a hand over her mouth. "Now, Doctor!"

Doctor Levine injected her hip through her camos.

Within seconds she felt the potent chemicals. She willed her body to reject the poison, but drowsiness swept over her like a warm, liquid bath. She heard the doctor's voice. She turned to look at him, to remember . . . something . . . but her lids refused to lift.

"That's a hell of a crooked finger," someone said. Asher Flores, the personnel director. "What happened?"

Gordon breathed hard, angry, distracted. "She broke it a few weeks ago. Is she unconscious yet, Doctor? The sun's up. We've got to get out of here."

She felt somebody take her pulse.

Through the murky haze of her mind, Doctor Levine sounded pleased. "You can relax, boys. She's in dreamland."

Asher Flores ate breakfast in the camp cafeteria, contemplating what to do. For him, the big issues—like Life with a capital "L"— were taken care of. That left the little stuff, like what to do with the day.

It was the little stuff that drove him nuts.

Now twenty-nine, he was the son of a Polish-American mother, who was Jewish, and a Mexican-American father, who was Catholic. He grew up eating matzos and tortillas, knishes and burritos. He went to both church and temple until he was eight, when he refused to go to either again. He'd realized he'd be expected to choose between them someday.

That's when his family still lived in volcanic South-Central Los Angeles, where drive-by shootings and hate crimes were the week-end entertainment. In elementary school he'd hung out with a group of tough Vietnamese kids, so his parents had moved to con-servative, upwardly mobile Mission Viejo in Orange County. There he'd made friends with three boys from French families who'd flown the French tricolor every day except the Fourth of July, when they'd hoisted the Stars and Stripes in homage to their new land. He'd thought that was wonderful. He'd helped them start a soccer team at school, and they'd awarded him a T-shirt decorated with the Eif-fel Tower in glitter.

In high school his new best friend had been a boy from West Germany. And in college, at the University of California at San Diego, he'd studied international studies so he could get to know people from as many nations as possible. That's where the Company had recruited him. He'd liked their pitch: Help us spread democ-racy around the world.

He'd been stationed in Europe during the scandals of the 1980s, and so he'd missed Iran-contra. It was mostly over by the time he'd joined anyway. Like everyone, he'd followed the hearings and trials in the newspapers, and he'd picked up some juicy gossip from other agents, but he'd never really understood why anyone in the Com-pany would do anything so criminal, so dumb.

Asher took pride in being one of Hughes Bremner's top field operators. He even liked the idea that the new director of Central Intelligence was female. He figured it was time. He believed in Langley. The purpose of covert ops was to enlighten the uninformed, give people a new way to see things, back up faltering democracies, and make sure evil intentions failed.

What was wrong with that?

Asher kept his goals and his heart simple.

But there was another side to him, too, the side that craved the excitement of South-Central L.A., where a short, half-Jewish/half-Catholic kid had to fight his way to school and fight his way home. Where allies were brothers for life.

Where you never knew when you woke up what the day would bring.

He was a rule breaker. It was not only guaranteed to make life more exciting, it also ensured he had to live by his wits. The best field operators were the ones who used not only brains but "gut." Asher was blessed with gut. Too much, according to Hughes Bremner. Which was why Asher had ended up pushing a computer keyboard at the godforsaken Ranch.

The KGB wasn't the only one with a Gulag.

Now he ate breakfast with a hundred eager rookies. He'd not had enough sleep because of Gordon Taite's sunrise adventure, but still he toyed with the idea of jogging. After that he could try out the new earth-moving equipment Uncle Sam had delivered yesterday to clear land for a new Ranch gymnasium.

He could also check in at personnel. After all, he *was* acting director.

He left the cafeteria and strolled around the flag circle, trying to decide. It was too early for the Dodgers game, so he couldn't do that. As he passed the small infirmary, he thought about Liz Sansborough.

What a good-looking broad. Too bad she was bonkers.

On his second lap around the flag circle he decided he really, *really* disliked Taite. There was something slimy about him anyway, but the way he hovered over Sansborough all the way to the infirmary was enough to turn even a rag-picker's stomach. He was probably in there right now, drooling, even though the doctor had said she'd be out cold for a couple of hours.

Gordon Taite was probably a necrophiliac.

Yeah, Asher could believe that.

On his third circle around the flagpole, Asher spun off and

headed into his office. His intuition had kicked in with a wallop. He had a sudden feeling Gordon Taite was up to something.

As an expert in maverick field ops, Asher had a sixth-sense for such things. Was old Taite dealing a little private business? If true, Asher would enjoy causing the prick some trouble. He sat at his computer and considered. Might as well start at the beginning. It had to be something that involved the woman.

He asked for Elizabeth Sansborough's file. It came up promptly. After all the preliminary stuff, which looked standard, the file did a nice narrative on her childhood. He read it. Very traditional. Then he found a gem: According to a medical affidavit, the little finger on her left hand had been broken and healed crooked during a childhood accident.

Not a few weeks ago, as Taite had told him when they'd captured Sansborough.

Asher grinned. He was on to something. With luck, it would fry the hell out of Gordon Taite.

Fifteen

The regular three-person staff in personnel worked around Asher Flores. They updated files, figured vacations and sick times, shuffled in marine replacements, and examined applications for a teacher of Farsi. In the time he'd been there, they'd learned to ignore him. At worst he was negligent; at best he at least let them do their jobs. Obviously he had no idea what a director did and had no interest in learning. If this was Langley's idea of a joke, they found nothing amusing in it.

They eagerly awaited a real personnel director.

Still, Asher Flores knew his way around a computer. The only time they grew upset was when he played games on it—Hammurabi, Harpoon, and his favorite, Jet Flight Simulator. He lacked respect. So this morning when one of them slipped behind and saw he was reviewing a personnel file, the staff member spread the word with relief. Maybe there was hope.

Asher was vaguely aware a wave of optimism had swept the usually taciturn personnel office, but his mind was on the file before him. Other than the inconsistency about when the finger had been broken, he'd found nothing unusual. But then, Sansborough was a stranger to him, so finding other inconsistencies would be next to impossible, unless they were within the file itself.

There was one oddity: The entries ended three years ago. Nothing since. Maybe that's when she'd become unstable.

Just to make sure, Asher accessed Langley's multimillion-dollar Connection Machine 5, a massively parallel computer that could out-crunch and out-run most supercomputers. On his last trip to Langley, Asher had visited it—a severe black cube studded with red blinking lights. Now he argued with it over whether it would let him see Sansborough's file. Finally he realized he had to use the new ultra-high, blue-clearance code bestowed on him as Ranch personnel director.

With the blue code, the CM-5 coughed up Sansborough's file. It was identical to the one at the Ranch, except there were two additional paragraphs at the end.

Asher leaned forward as he read the first one. He thought he'd seen it all, but this blew him away: Some three years ago, CIA agent Liz Sansborough had fallen in love with the deadly international assassin known as the Carnivore and crossed over to him.

Asher let the news sink in, then read it twice more. He leaned back in his chair and whistled tunelessly to himself. That beautiful broad was a traitor. She'd fallen for the world's highest-paid killer. And then she'd abandoned everything she'd believed in so she could play house with him.

He rubbed his chin. He hadn't shaved, and his skin was grade-six sandpaper.

So what in hell was Liz Sansborough doing *here*? Gordon Taite had said she had psychiatric problems. With the Carnivore as a lover, that wasn't surprising. She must have crossed back. Apparently she wanted to help Langley. But if she'd cracked, there was no way they'd trust her now.

Then Asher read the last paragraph: Last month Liz Sansborough had sent word she and the Carnivore were applying to four countries for sanctuary: the United States, Germany, France, and Britain. In exchange for new identities and luxurious retirements, the Carnivore would tell all.

After that was a terse sentence: "The Carnivore accepts U.S. offer." A series of dates followed. The most recent was today's. Sansborough was acting as go-between in Paris, delivering the Carnivore's "proof" of sincerity on those dates.

Which meant Liz Sansborough couldn't be here at the Ranch, too. Or could she?

□   □   □   □

The Ranch infirmary smelled of chemicals and antiseptic. It was in a long Quonset hut behind personnel and had a six-bed ward, a private room, an examination room, and a lab.

Asher sat politely but impatiently in the tiny waiting room. When the doctor from last night, Allan Levine, came in from the back somewhere, Asher asked to see Liz Sansborough.

"I'm afraid not. She's unconscious. We're going to keep her that way a while."

"Why?"

In his mid-fifties, Dr. Levine had a long, bony face, a concave chest, and a gruff manner. He stopped writing on his clipboard long enough to wave one of his little hands irritably at Asher.

"Young man, I'm the doctor. I'll say when she can have visitors."

"I have to ask her something. It'll take only a minute. It's important."

"Her health is far more important." Dr. Levine turned on his heel and headed for the door.

"Nice talking to you," Asher grumbled at the white-coated back as it disappeared down the corridor.

If she was that bad off, Asher decided, she must be in the private room. He checked the hall, listened at the door, and opened it.

Gordon Taite was sitting at the window, writing in a notebook. He scowled. "What in hell—"

"Good," Asher improvised. "I've been looking for you. What's all this about Liz Sansborough?"

"What are you talking about?" The scowl deepened.

"I've been told she's asking for me. Where is she?"

Gordon Taite blinked. "That's ridiculous. She doesn't even know you. What're you trying to do—jump her in bed? Get the hell out of here, Flores!"

Asher smiled. It had been worth the try. At least he now knew she was in the ward. It was the only place left. He decided to try being straight with Taite:

"Look, old buddy. What's really going on with Sansborough? She doesn't look like any nutbar to me. She seemed to be doing real well in training. I've just been reading her file, and—"

Gordon Taite stood up. He strode across the room. Unconsciously Asher backed up. Taite was pissed. He was actually very menacing when he was a hair out of control.

"She's on a top-secret, need-to-know operation. Got that? It's none of your damn business. Now get out of my face before I report you to Langley!'' Taite breathed heavily. He'd really worked himself up.

"Guess that's good enough for me.''

Asher retreated to personnel. He sat again at his desk. At noon, when everyone left, he phoned Hughes Bremner at Langley. But Bremner wasn't there. He was in Paris on something need-to-know and wasn't expected back until much later. Hell.

Asher scratched his grade-six beard, which was growing in as black as the black curly hair on his head. Bremner was in Paris, and according to Sansborough's Langley file, Paris was also where the messages came in from the Carnivore. In fact, one was coming in today. It didn't take an Einstein to figure Bremner had probably gone to Paris to see some doll who was calling herself Liz Sansborough and to pick up the Carnivore's newest tidbit.

While he ate lunch in the cafeteria, Asher put on his earphones and listened to the Dodgers. They were losing to Houston, three-to-one. He ate two tuna-fish sandwiches, a bag of potato chips, a kiwi, and drank two iced teas with lime. When he finished, the Dodgers were still losing, three-to-one. It was the bottom of the eighth. He decided to see how the game turned out. He polished off three brownies. The Dodgers lost, four-to-one.

What a shitty day.

He headed for the infirmary. Maybe this time he'd get in to see Sansborough. But as he was rounding the flag circle, Gordon Taite was leaving administration, sporting a huge Cheshire-cat grin.

"Flores, I've got something for you. It just arrived.''

Taite handed him a sheet of paper. It was faxed orders from Langley telling Asher to report immediately to Spitsbergen, an island in the Arctic Ocean so far north it was even north of Norway. Its greatest claim to espionage fame was its boredom, flash-in-the-pan summers, and freezing, suicidal winters. It was Langley's ultimate version of the Gulag.

"Your new assignment. *Bon voyage*, Flores.'' Gordon Taite had used his one notch of superiority to pull a fast one. He crossed his arms. His Cheshire-cat grin was really disgusting.

"Thanks, Gordon. May I kiss you?''

□ □ □ □

Back in personnel again, Asher convinced Langley's CM-5 to show him the Carnivore's file. He read it rapidly. Nothing much of interest, just the standard speculation about the Carnivore's mysterious identity and the wet jobs he was suspected of doing.

One interesting note: The Carnivore apparently had done no contract work in the last three years. Three years ago was supposedly when Sansborough moved in with him. That was too much of a coincidence. There had to be a connection.

As Asher printed out the Carnivore's file, he watched the door. Gordon Taite could show up at any moment with the marines, toss him into a truck, and order him shipped the hell out of here. Speed was of the essence. So, as the computer printed out the stuff on Sansborough, he told it also to print the files of any of the people named in Sansborough's file who appeared in the Langley super-computer as well.

The personnel staff looked at the printer, then they looked at Asher. They looked back at the printer. Asher couldn't tell whether they were impressed or worried.

"A little assignment Langley shot me," he explained.

They smiled. Since they returned to work as usual, he decided word he was on Langley's shit list must not have reached them yet. As the printer hummed away, he contemplated the "top-secret, need-to-know operation" for which Langley wanted Liz Sansborough. Obviously some woman in Paris who claimed to be Sansborough was already involved with bringing in the Carnivore. But what did the one in Paris have to do with the one here?

It seemed to Asher the Sansborough in Paris must have the Carnivore's confidence, since she was his chosen go-between. The Carnivore must believe she was real. And Langley must believe it, or else it wouldn't be in her file.

But what if the woman here in Colorado was the actual Sansborough? Did that mean the Parisienne had been posing as her for the last three years, while she was unstable? He supposed it was possible. Yet Sansborough's file definitely said she had fallen in love with the Carnivore and crossed over to him three years ago. The Carnivore ought to know his own lover. Unless it hadn't been the real Liz Sansborough in the first place.

Asher shook his head. The puzzle pieced together wrong because there were too many pieces. Too many Liz Sansboroughs.

When printing finished, Asher tore off the tractor margins, stapled each file together, and tucked them into a folder.

What stuck in his mind was bugger-head Taite. Where Gordon Taite went, good seldom followed. Was it possible Taite was screwing up Langley's plan for Liz Sansborough? If so, and Asher could document it, Asher would be off the hook for Spitsbergen. And he might get a shot at bringing in the Carnivore himself. Now *that* was a challenge for a field operator.

Sixteen

That morning in Arlington, Virginia, Lucas Maynard was sweating like a glass of iced Jack Daniel's. He told himself it wasn't the terror. It was the shock and his damned diabetes.

But it was the terror.

He was in Leslee's kitchen. He'd just poured himself a cup of black coffee, sat at the table, and opened the *Washington Post*. Instantly his chest had contracted and the sweating had begun. There on the front page, above the fold, was a recent head-and-shoulders photo of Undersecretary of State Clarence Edward and the headline in huge block letters:

TOP GOVERNMENT OFFICIAL MUGGED AND KILLED

The night before, Maynard had tried for hours to reach Clare at his Georgetown home. Now he knew why he'd gotten only the answering machine. His stomach knotted. With Clare Edward had died his and Leslee's best chance to get out clean.

He wiped his face with a dish towel and read the story. According to the newspaper, there'd been no bystanders, but a few drive-by witnesses claimed to have seen a blond young man on Rollerblades knock down a well-dressed older gentleman as he headed up the sidewalk toward Clare Edward's address. The police said the murderer had stripped off the undersecretary's valuables and knifed him to death.

The story continued on page two, where a photo of the crime scene showed the undersecretary's splayed corpse.

Where was his fancy briefcase?

Fresh sweat covered Maynard. Surely Clare would have left the manilla envelope with the numbered accounts locked in his safe at State. He wouldn't have carried home such hot evidence in a simple briefcase with no precautions.

Or would he have worried someone in the office would see the list and cut himself in? That would've been like Clare. So would the cockiness that got the better of him sometimes. Just enough cockiness and lack of sense to bring the list home in his briefcase. If Clare had any real sense, he'd have given up thinking every pretty woman at State was his own personal toy.

For a moment Maynard was hopeful: Maybe one of the women's boyfriends had killed him. That would be poetic justice, and it would mean Hughes Bremner wasn't behind the undersecretary's death.

But Maynard knew better. Hughes Bremner had ordered the undersecretary killed. Bremner had the manilla envelope that contained the Sterling-O'Keefe paper trail. And Bremner would get Maynard next if he didn't move fast. Very fast.

In the bedroom Leslee was still asleep. Maynard looked down at her pale, tousled hair and heart-shaped face. It wasn't only his life, it was hers, too.

She'd arrived home from the newspaper at one o'clock in the morning, blue circles under her eyes, exhausted. But she'd finished her big investigative piece. Now she was taking the day off and would sleep late into the morning.

And she should wake up alone. As long as he was here, her life was in danger, too.

He studied her sweet face, and his love made a spot at the back of his throat ache. He'd found her after all the lonely years; he couldn't lose her now.

It was time to run. Forget exposing Sterling-O'Keefe and MAS-QUERADE. Forget immunity. Cut and run. Fast.

Since Leslee was planning to take the day off to catch up on groceries, laundry, lunch with a friend, the day-to-day details she ignored when wrapping up a big story, Maynard had told her he was taking comp time, too, to catch up on her, and that's why he was staying over. She hadn't believed him, but he knew she'd wait until he told her . . . or her impatience grew too great.

While Leslee slept on, Maynard made four trips to a phone booth to call "friends" in Liechtenstein to make arrangements for a safe, secret exit from Washington early the next morning. At least his security precautions had paid off. Her neighborhood was clean. Which meant they were both relatively safe for the moment.

Without the IOUs he'd collected over the last forty years, he couldn't have pulled it off. For the rest he'd paid big money. The results were official courier status for him and Leslee on Swissair. They'd fly into Zurich, which had the nearest airport to Liechtenstein, and drive into the tiny, mountainous principality above the Rhine River. This would be a simple matter, since there were no border-crossing formalities between Switzerland and Liechtenstein.

That evening he and Leslee ate dinner, talked, and made love in her bed. Briefly, the pleasure of it seemed to wipe away his dread. Except that he had to tell her what was going on, explain the plans he had made, and he was running out of time.

Her small, compact body was soft and flushed from sex, pliable as a kitten in his arms. The dim bedside lamp sent long shadows across her air-conditioned bedroom. The room was like her—small, well-furnished, intelligent, terribly alluring.

"Do you like Europe, Leslee?"

"Love it. Why, honey?"

"Would you like to fly over tomorrow morning?"

Her little hand uncurled on his naked chest. Her fingers were tiny, like a child's, but her mind was completely adult. Maynard had always found the contrast exhilarating. But now it unnerved him as she looked into his eyes.

"What's wrong, Lucas?"

"I hope you'll say yes." He squeezed her to him. "I need to leave the United States, and I'd like you to go with me. I'm getting out of the business. I'm past due, I guess. Anyway, I made all the arrangements today. I've got some money saved up in Liechtenstein, enough to take care of us. We'd be comfortable."

She was silent. "There are only two things for sale in Liechtenstein—scenery and secrecy. Do you have so much money that you had to set up one of their shell corporations with bank accounts managed by a local attorney who's really a front man?"

He ignored the outrage in her voice and plunged ahead. "I want to marry you, Leslee. I can't think of anything that would make me happier. I love you. Please say you'll marry me."

She sat up in bed and studied him. "Do you love me enough to tell me the truth?"

The question hung in the air.

The time had come at last. He'd known that, really, before he'd begun the conversation, known his greatest fear was not of what Hughes Bremner would do to him, but of losing Leslee. He couldn't live without her. There was nowhere left to hide.

His voice was low and passionate as he related the long story—his hopes of serving his country when he was young, the painful disillusionment of his middle years, the feeling of betrayal that had made so many fine, seasoned Langley officers grow lazy or quit, and finally the birth of Sterling-O'Keefe and MASQUERADE.

"Our division chief, Hughes Bremner, decided to stay on, make the Company pay for all the years he'd sacrificed. He recruited his four top deputies in Mustang—me, Adam Risley, Tad Gorman, and Ernie Pinkerton. We were all old cold warriors, we knew Washington's putrefaction firsthand, and we felt betrayed.

"It was so easy it seemed almost as if we had Langley's blessing. We skimmed millions from Iranian arms sales and U.S. drug sales. We called in IOUs from BCCI, the mafia, weapons traders, congressmen, several S&Ls, and some entrepreneurs we'd been keeping tabs on who'd been skating on some thin but profitable ice. From the beginning we had all the right contacts. Once we were bankrolled, we set up our corporation, Sterling-O'Keefe Enterprises. *Sterling* to give the sound of quality, and *O'Keefe* in honor of our old mentor at Langley, Red Jack O'Keefe. He's retired now, at least ten years." Maynard allowed himself a grim smile. "He used to tell us, 'The speed of the leader determines the speed of the pack.' "

He glanced at her. She said nothing. Her face was a mask.

"It was totally secret," he continued. "We bought up legitimate businesses. Eventually Sterling-O'Keefe owned OMNI-American Savings & Loan and the Presidents' Palace hotel-casinos in Las Vegas and Atlantic City. We got control of Gold Star Credit Resources, the nation's biggest credit-check company, and Gold Star Rent-a-Car, one of the biggest international car rental agencies. Nonpareil International Insurance—that's ours, too. Lots of our corporations own other companies. I don't even know all the holdings, maybe I didn't want to. Sterling-O'Keefe is one of the fastest-growing companies in the world."

Maynard waited, but Leslee's only response was silence in the dim light of the bedroom.

Uneasily he continued, "The company is fronted by one of Bremner's blue-blooded cousins, Leland Bremner Beaver, but it's owned and operated by our secret board of directors. Hughes is chairman. He owns fifty-one percent. Tad, Adam, Ernie, and I divide the remaining forty-nine percent."

"How nice," Leslee said. "A sweet deal for everyone."

"It was," he agreed. "But now there's trouble that could blow Sterling-O'Keefe and MASQUERADE out of the water."

He told her about the international assassin, the Carnivore, who could ruin it all, but who didn't know what he knew. Maynard didn't give her the details, he couldn't bring himself to go that far even now. He rationalized to himself it would be too dangerous for her to know.

"But I'd already decided to get out anyway, Les, because of you," he told her earnestly. "I fell in love with you, and you changed my life."

She reached for a cigarette and sat unmoving against the headboard. Her voice was frosty. "So I've made you see the error of your ways? Funny, but I don't see this so-called change you're so proud of. What I see is a criminal . . . a coward . . . running for his life."

He flinched, but she went on, her voice rising. "If you run away now, Sterling-O'Keefe will continue to rape the country, and you'll get out with a fortune and your girl friend, if you can talk her into it. And you say you've changed?" She clutched the sheet to her thin chest. "You sicken me!"

"I tried—"

"You got the undersecretary killed!"

"Maybe it was just a mugging."

"You'd like that, wouldn't you? You think it would let you off the hook!" Her small upper lip curled in disgust. "What are you keeping in that safe under my bed?"

"Papers and notes about Sterling-O'Keefe and MASQUERADE."

"That's where you got the information you copied for the under-secretary?" When he nodded, she continued, "This is where you've hidden the evidence that could destroy Sterling-O'Keefe and MAS-QUERADE?"

When he nodded again, she slapped his face. Hard.

The sound was like a thunderclap in the quiet bedroom. He didn't touch his face, although he wanted to. It didn't hurt all that much, but the pain he felt from her just rage slashed through him like a hot knife.

"You could get me killed!" Her eyes blazed. "If Bremner murdered an Undersecretary of State for a few account numbers, imagine what in hell he'd do to me for what's under my bed!"

Now Maynard was angry. "I protected you! No one knows my connection to you. No one ever followed me here. Unless you told someone, we're safe. I guarantee it!" He liked the firmness in his tone. He still knew a thing or two.

"You just don't get it, Lucas. Take your crap and get the hell out. I've been wasting my time."

She turned on her bedside lamp, flooding the room with light. She walked naked to her closet. Her small buttocks trembled as if from outrage. She took her white terry-cloth robe from the closet and wrapped herself up as if she were ice cold, as if this weren't a night so hot the air conditioner was up full blast and the bedroom was still too warm.

"What don't I get?" he asked faintly.

Her pale hair was almost white in the lamp light. With the white robe and her rosy-cheeked, heart-shaped face, she looked like one of the angels from his mother's Christmas tree back home in Terre Haute.

She lighted another cigarette and stood in the doorway. "You don't exist. You created some idea of who you thought I wanted you to be, and that's who you pretended to be, and that's who I fell in love with. But then, charm and empty values are your 'profession's' stock in trade, aren't they? How arrogant of me to think I could tell the difference!" She laughed bitterly. "And you say you've re-formed? What a joke. You couldn't even turn in your evidence without first cutting a deal, a golden parachute to immunity. And the poor undersecretary—your *friend!*—got killed for it." She headed down the hall. "You're a joke, Lucas. Take your shit and get the hell out."

Naked, he followed her to the kitchen. Without her, he had nothing to live for. "What else could I do?" he tried to reason. "Me against Bremner and the clout he's got? The network? Jesus Christ, Les, that man has people working for him privately all over the globe! I know enough to destroy him. Yesterday his goons were waiting at my house. He's already ordered me dead!"

Leslee measured Salvadoran beans into her coffee grinder and pushed the button. The noise was loud, jarring. She released the button, dumped the grounds into the percolator, and turned it on. The red light flickered, and soon the comforting smell of brewing coffee filled the kitchen.

She put out her cigarette, turned, and leaned back against the counter. She crossed her arms over her chest and said nothing, just looked at him and his nakedness, her pale blue eyes brimming with betrayal. There was no room for love in those wounded eyes.

"You want me to pull down Sterling-O'Keefe and MASQUERADE? In the open? Publicly?" His voice said it wasn't a question but a death sentence.

With two fingers she lifted another cigarette from the pack in her pocket. She smoked Pall Malls, unfiltered. She liked the taste, she'd told him, the polish on the big, rough tobacco. He'd told her the same thing a hundred times, and now it sounded as if he were telling himself, too: "Those things are going to kill you, Les."

She lit the cigarette, inhaled deeply, and blew out a stream of smoke. "With cigarettes at least I get a warning label."

They remained that way, staring at each other, through a long silence. He naked, defenseless; she wrapped tight in her angel robe, smoking.

At last he sat down, facing her. "I could go to State myself. I could take the secretary my documentation. That would mean you and I couldn't fly to Europe right away. I'd have to stick around to testify against the others, probably face charges myself. Prison. It could be years."

"Yes," she said.

"Is that what you want?"

"I want the truth to come out for all of us." Then she smiled. It seemed to him the harsh fluorescent kitchen lights turned soft and forgiving. "I'll wait for you," she said. "I love you."

He smiled, gazing into her eyes. The future was still within his grasp. Naked, he stood up, walked around the table, and crushed her to him. He smelled her face, her throat.

"I'll go to the Secretary of State tomorrow," he whispered.

Seventeen

Liz Sansborough felt trapped in a black pit. Her fingers bled as she scrambled up walls of ice. She sensed movement and flailed out. A voice ordered her down. She fought, tried to keep climbing. More noises assaulted her. There was terrible, blinding light, but she longed for it.

Something about the light meant safety.

Her eyes opened. White walls. Two rows of white cots with an aisle down the middle. A hospital? The air smelled of antiseptic and laundry soap. It took her a moment to realize she was in the Ranch infirmary. Her cot was beside a window. Outside, a ponderosa pine climbed toward the Colorado sun.

An orderly tried to push her back down onto the cot. "Quit fighting it, lady. You're going to be all happy again."

He turned and lifted his gaze as he worked to replace her IV bottle. He must be late changing it, because the drugs had worn off enough for her to awaken. The new bottle would contain more of the chemicals that poisoned her. He had a nice face, but it was also dog-dumb. He'd follow orders to the bitter end. She had no time to convince him differently.

While he was distracted, she summoned all her strength and moved awkwardly but swiftly up onto her knees. He turned to look at her.

"Hey! What are you—?"

With her right fist, she socked him square in the jaw. He stag-

gered back. Grasping the IV tubing attached to her left wrist, she
followed with a second punch. He crashed sideways against an
empty cot. A patient down the row of cots moaned.

She cradled her aching fist and listened. Silence again. She forced
the fogginess from her mind and pulled the IV from her wrist. Her
clothes had been tossed in a corner. She peeled off her hospital
gown and dressed in her camos, buckled her belt, put on her boots.
The orderly must have been the only attendant in the infirmary, or
the crash would have brought someone to investigate. Eventually a
doctor, a nurse, or another orderly would show up. By then she'd be
gone.

She tied and gagged the orderly. She found her day pack in a
locker next to her bed. Her Beretta and Gordon's wallet were gone.
Damn. She'd have to stop in the cabin to get Gordon's Beretta.

She opened the window, surveyed her surroundings, and
dropped down onto the grass.

Asher Flores headed out of personnel with the thick folder of dossiers under his arm. He debated whether to hijack a helicopter or
simply take his car. Then a sane voice warned him he was about to
go too far. The Carnivore was hot stuff all right, and Gordon Taite
was mastodon puke, but Hughes Bremner was his boss, and Bremner had always been a straight shooter.

Maybe Bremner and Taite had a fool-proof plan to grab the Carnivore, using the Colorado Sansborough and bypassing the assassin's offer to come in. If Asher screwed this up, then that remote
island in the Arctic might look like paradise. Langley had some
pretty strict ideas. It was okay to bend the rules a little, as long as you
produced. But if you broke the rules and failed to produce, you
could be out on your ass. Asher reminded himself to try to call
Bremner again. Maybe he could talk the chief into letting him in on
the Carnivore operation.

As he mulled this latest idea he noted the camp trash truck making its rounds. It was a great piece of equipment, and to Asher, its
very cumbersomeness was divine.

Then he saw shadowy movements to his right. Without turning his
head, his peripheral vision honed in. Stunned, he slowed to study
the figure more closely.

It was Sansborough!

She was dressed, had her day pack on, and was trying to reach the parking lot. She was one gutsy broad. Asher took ten seconds to absorb this latest development. It looked as if he was going to be in on Gordon Taite's big, secret deal by default.

Sansborough had escaped. Gordon Taite had screwed up. Asher grinned. This could be a way to get out of Bremner's doghouse—and stick a knife into Taite at the same time.

Asher trotted over to the trash truck.

"Hey, Asher." Bernie was Asher's pal. Bernie loved the trash truck as much as Asher did.

"Hey, Bernie. Ready for a break? How about I take her into town for you?"

"I don' know." Bernie wiped his forehead. "We're pretty full today. You got to mind the worst grades when she's full."

"You taught me. You know you did."

"You're right." Bernie beamed. "An' I sure could use a break. Okay, take her on in." Bernie patted the bulky truck's fender, and the deal was done.

Asher hopped behind the wheel, released the brake, and barreled away.

At the officers' club Asher unloaded the last dumpster into the garbage truck. Then he headed for his cabin. He threw his gun, ammo, clothes, money, credit cards, and several I.D.s into a gym bag. He had a hunch he might need to be someone Gordon Taite didn't know about before this was over. He tossed the bag into the truck's cab and thundered over to the parking lot.

Liz Sansborough was bent under the hood of a green Ford Explorer, hot-wiring the ignition. She saw him, slammed down the hood, and jumped into the driver's seat.

He stopped the garbage truck behind the Explorer, blocking her exit. He spoke softly. "Hey, Sansborough? Want a lift?"

She gripped the Ford's wheel so hard her fingers were white.

He said, "You'll never get out of here without me."

Her hot eyes fixed on him. Boy, was she mad.

"I'm sorry about this morning," he said. "I was following orders. Now Langley's blackballed me, too."

She slid out of the Ford, day pack in hand, and, from a crouch, surveyed the parking lot. No one was around. She ran to the passenger side of the truck and climbed in. He turned to grin at her, but his grin froze on his face.

He was looking straight into a 9mm Beretta.

"How did you find me?" she demanded.

"I saw you. But I don't think anyone else did. You've got a real talent for being sneaky."

"How'd you find me this morning, in the woods?"

He furrowed his brow, puzzled. Then he got it. "Your belt. Yeah. See, the buckle looks ordinary, but it's got a tracking device inside. Those special buckles are issued to all the trainees. Security doesn't trigger the device unless it needs to, like if someone gets lost."

"Lost. Yeah, sure," she said acidly as she unhooked her buckle with her free hand and heaved the belt out the window. It skidded under the rear bumper of the green Explorer.

"Nice shot," he observed.

"Why are you doing this?"

"Get down on the floor where no one can see you."

"No." She held the pistol steady. "Tell me." Her gaze scanned the sloped parking area and the line of trees that surrounded it. If anything moved she'd see it. She managed this while never letting him out of her sight.

"I want in on whatever's going down." My God, he was sitting next to the Carnivore's ex-girl friend. Or was she?

"What do you mean?"

"Like I said, I'm in the doghouse, and I want out."

"If you want to make yourself look good, just turn me in."

"I guess I could." But all at once Asher didn't want to. He liked this woman; she had guts. She was running from Gordon Taite, and Gordon Taite was terra firma's grossest turd. "But I don't like Taite, and there's something funny going on. I want to know more before I do anything."

She continued to watch him, the gun unwavering. "Then get me out of here."

He put the truck into gear, and they rumbled away.

She studied him with something more than hate or anger. Some curiosity. "Maybe we do have something in common. But if you give me away or turn me in, I'll shoot. Got that?"

He nodded. She slid to the floor, the Beretta pointed at his heart. She folded her long legs under her. It was amazing how small she could make herself. He liked that she could amaze him.

"I always thought Gordon was a jackass," he said.

"I didn't. I believed he'd saved my life. But I'm not going to take his damn drugs. Where are we now?"

"We're out of the central camp, heading toward the gate."

"What makes you think we can get past the gate? Security's got all kinds of cameras there."

"True. But they can't see through steel doors, and the angles aren't targeted to view down through the windows to the floor of a garbage truck. The floor of a car or Jeep, yeah. This truck's too high. Besides, you got a break. Today's the regular day to drive out the trash."

"You seem to have a weird thing for this truck. Have you driven it into town before?"

"Yup. Bernie taught me. Security won't blink when they see me at the wheel."

"Tell me when we get there."

The big truck lumbered past stands of ponderosa pine that grew so thick their trunks were toothpicks. Their frilly green tops swayed against the azure sky. At last they stopped.

"This is it." His lips made no movement, because the cameras would see. He was tense, waiting to hear the camp alarm sound. That would mean they'd discovered Sansborough was missing. He also worried word of his reassignment had reached security. If they knew that, they'd never let him drive into town.

He jumped out, and as he punched in his code a long mechanical screech suddenly shattered the tranquil mountain air. It was the alarm, and its horrible noise seemed to come from the forests all around.

God, he hoped the gate would still move!

He reached to punch in his code again. Then he saw the gate inch open. He took a deep breath and leaped back into the cab.

The gate gained momentum. The alarm wailed on.

"They know." Sansborough's voice was a parched whisper.

"Yup." He drove them through. They knew about her, but maybe not about him. Not yet.

Out on the potholed road he increased the truck's speed and considered the situation. One thing was certain: There was no turning back. He'd made his decision when he came to Sansborough's aid. Now he needed to win her confidence.

As the alarm's scream faded with distance, he told her what had happened because he'd read her file and questioned Taite about her.

"You expect me to believe they'd reassign you to an Arctic island just because you were nosey about me? I may have lost my memory, but I'm no fool."

"You lost your memory?" That wasn't in her file. "When?"

"Two months or so ago."

"You don't remember anything before that?"

"Don't look so surprised. It happens."

"Without a past how can you catch the Carnivore?"

"There really is an assassin named the Carnivore?"

He frowned. "Yeah, of course! Why?"

She was silent, then nodded. "Okay. Well, at least Gordon told the truth about that. Apparently the Carnivore's tried to kill me twice. Now I'm supposed to help Langley capture him."

Inwardly Asher smiled. The Carnivore *was* the point of Gordon's big, top-secret, need-to-know operation. But if the Carnivore *wanted* to come in, why create an operation to snatch him? And why did the Carnivore want to kill her?

"Let me get this straight. Your lover, the Carnivore—"

"Wait a minute!" She stared, shocked. "My *lover?*" The Beretta inched closer to his heart, her finger white on the trigger. "What are you talking about?"

He admired a woman with a wide range of emotions and a steady gun hand, but not when the gun was aimed at him. "You don't remember?"

"God, I hope there's nothing to remember!"

He said, "How about I tell you what Langley's most secret computer files say?"

The gun never lowered a hair. "I'm listening."

He took a breath. "The most recent three years of your file in Ranch personnel are blank."

"I've seen them. That's when I was in Santa Barbara, with a new identity. My cover was as a journalist, Sarah Walker."

"Langley's file isn't blank. It explains your relationship to the Carnivore."

"Does it tell you I was sent to Lisbon to pull a message, but was too late? That the Carnivore killed the messenger and left me for dead? An attempt to kill me doesn't sound like a love relationship. He thinks I've seen his face, and he knows I'm alive. If the attack in

Santa Barbara was real, he's looking for me." She described the assault on her condo.

Asher mulled the information. "That's nuts. He's cut a deal with Langley to come in. Quit the game. Why would he care if you'd seen him?"

She stared at him. "Come in? But Gordon told me—"

"Ah, gadfly Gordon. Asshole of the Universe." A lightning bolt flashed through Asher's mind—Jesus Christ, was Gordon Taite out to screw up the whole coming-in? A fast one on Langley, even a sell-out? Hughes Bremner would kiss Asher for exposing it.

He said, "Get one thing straight: Gordon's got no humanitarian streak. If he saved your life, it was for his own reasons. Remember Clair George? He used to be Deputy Director of Operations, before he retired under fire about Iran-contra. To outsiders, he looked like the consummate spy—witty, brave, impatient, and hugely successful. But one of our ambassadors had him figured. He said George had the remarkable combination Langley sought—he exuded friendliness and trust while being duplicitous as hell." He paused. "Sound familiar?"

She nodded. "Gordon."

"You can read your dossier yourself once things settle down, but according to Langley you fell in love with the Carnivore three years ago and crossed over to him."

"Okay, I absolutely agree about Gordon. He's a liar, a jerk, and God knows what else. Which makes me pay attention to what you claim my dossier says about the Carnivore and me. But I—" She grimaced. "Three years as the soul mate to one of the globe's worst killers? God!"

"There's more. According to the dossier, you're his courier to Langley. This very minute you're somewhere in or around Paris. You've been ferrying his revelations to our command center there. That's how he's buying you both a future."

"A nice piece of magic, considering I seem to be sitting right here. Someone else has to be in Paris with my name."

"Could be. And now let's discuss that crooked little finger on your left hand. When did you break it?"

"When I was a kid. A skating accident. It's in my file."

"Gordon told me you broke it a couple of months ago."

She blinked, thinking, and he studied her face. He decided he particularly liked the mole above the right corner of her mouth. Very sexy. He had a sudden desire to touch it.

She said, "Right after you caught me this morning, Doctor Levine injected me. I heard someone—you—ask Gordon about my finger. Yes. Gordon said . . ." She remembered.

"Yeah, you remember right. So someone's lying. Either the Langley master file or our dear pal Gordon."

Doubt battled doubt in her mind. Then she heard a distant buzz. She peered up above the pines. "A helicopter!"

"Two of them. Probably from the Ranch, looking for you."

She didn't ask what to do. She checked her Beretta, and she squeezed farther down against the truck's floor.

Asher watched the pale blue sky as the two big birds closed in.

Eighteen

One of the helicopters was an AH-64 Apache, and it looked as if it were loaded with enough rockets and missiles to blast the trash truck into Arizona. The Apache's loudspeaker blared out: "In the truck, stop! Asher Flores, your orders are to stop!"

Asher looked down at Sansborough. She lifted her chin. She had a very fine chin. "No way a garbage truck's going to outrun a couple of helicopters," he explained. He'd have to figure out another way. He obeyed the command and halted the truck.

The Apache hovered back over the trees where it could keep the truck in range. The second chopper, a spruced-up Huey—one of the UH-1B workhorses from the Vietnam War era—landed on the road ahead of them. Two marines sporting M-16s jumped out.

Asher got out of the truck and ambled over.

"Asher, what in hell are you doing?" shouted the first marine over his helicopter's roar.

"Well, to be truthful, I thought I was taking a load to the dump! Is there something I should know about?"

"We've got orders to search you!" yelled the second marine.

"For what? Something radioactive get out of the labs?"

They moved back to the garbage truck where it was quieter and they didn't have to shout. The first marine lighted a cigarette. Asher didn't smoke, but he asked for one anyway. It was a minor distraction, a gesture of friendliness. Psychology was important.

The first marine held a Bic under Asher's Marlboro. "Some trainee went berserk. Elizabeth Sansborough. Know her?"

"Seen her around." Asher inhaled. God, his mouth burned right down to his gullet.

"We've got to find her so the doc can put her back on her meds. That means we've got to search you."

"I understand. I can tell you for sure no one's in the cab. But I don't know about the bin. Come on, let's take a look."

The two marines raised their eyebrows, and Asher led them around to the back of the truck. He pulled the lever, and the maw growled open. The stench hit them like a flying curtain of ripe manure.

"Jeez," said the second marine.

"Good thing we're up so high," Asher said cheerfully. "Not many flies at this altitude."

"Yeah. Well, guess we'd better check it out."

"Would you like me to do it for you, boys?"

Gratitude was a powerful friend, maybe powerful enough for them to trust Asher and not look in the truck's cab. If the stench didn't make them run away so fast they forgot the cab.

The first marine smiled. "If you insist."

"Oh, I do." Asher crushed his cigarette, flicked it into the bin, and crawled in after it. He walked over black plastic sacks and sank to his hips in the mire. He pawed through beer bottles, kitchen scraps, wadded papers, smelly old tennis shoes, sticky microwave dishes, torn underwear, used tissues, and other flotsam and jetsam of the human condition.

"See anything?" asked the second marine.

Asher pawed more. "Nothing alive. Want me to go deeper?"

"Nah. That's enough, don't you think?"

The marines consulted. They agreed it was, and Asher crawled out. He stank as bad as the garbage. The marines took a step backward. They thanked him.

"You've got to go back to camp now, Asher." The first marine looked regretful. Everyone knew how much Asher loved the ungainly truck.

"How come?"

"Orders. I guess you know you've been transferred. They want to fly you out right away."

Asher nodded. Here it was. He stepped forward so they'd get a reminder of how bad he reeked. "It'll only take me an hour to dump my load. Don't you think that'd be better than making poor Bernie have to drive down here all over again? An hour's not so bad. Besides the longer the truck's full, the worse it's going to stink. Nobody'll want it back in camp until it's empty again. I can just hear the bitching."

Asher looked himself up and down. He wrinkled his nose. He'd done them a favor, and now he was asking one in return.

"No problem," the first marine decided. "I'll clear it when we get back. Hell, they can always fly you out tonight."

Every once in a while you got lucky. The marines climbed back into the Huey. Asher stood at the trash truck's fender and savored his success. He waved enthusiastically as the two helicopters flew off over the treetops.

Flores smelled disgusting, but Liz knew he'd saved her for the moment. The question was, why? She lowered her Beretta but didn't put it away. She thanked him. He acknowledged her words of gratitude with a dip of his curly black head.

He drove the truck off down the forest road. "Tell me what you think you've been doing the last three years."

As she talked, she felt almost as if she were relating a story that had happened to someone else, and in a sense it had, because she'd only read about it, not recalled the living of it. She clenched her Beretta until her hand hurt, angry and frustrated not to be sure of the truth of her life.

"And then the Carnivore heard I was alive," she finished. "That meant he had to kill me before I could identify him."

"Maybe you never saw him. Maybe it isn't Langley. Maybe Gordon made it all up. Remember, he did say you were a lunatic. Maybe you imagined everything. Maybe it's a good thing he put you on drugs."

She swung the Beretta up instantly, her finger tight again on the trigger. Her voice was arctic and hard. "Why didn't you turn me in if you think that? Stop this truck. Now!"

Flores slowed the mammoth vehicle, its brakes grinding and huffing air as it stopped at the side of the narrow, pocked road.

In the silence of the majestic pines and high blue sky, they watched each other.

Flores spoke in a steady voice. "Get out, if you want. I won't stop you. But you won't have much chance on foot, especially if you're

not a trained woodsman. Since you asked, the reason I didn't turn
you in is what I told you. I think Gordon's up to something. Maybe
against you. Maybe against Langley. Maybe against the country. I
want to know what it is . . . for you, for the country, and for myself." He smiled.

She was silent. At the very least, he could be useful in stopping
Gordon. As for her memory, that she'd have to work on alone.
Nothing would keep her from it now.

She said, "You think you can get us away from here?"

"I can try."

"Okay, let's go."

Flores put the truck into gear. It picked up speed on the winding
road.

After a while, he asked quietly, "So what are the drugs?"

She didn't answer at once, still not sure of him or his questions.
"The last pill was an antidepressant. One a day. Then, when we got
to the Ranch, I was feeling so well I stopped taking it. But Gordon
acted as if it were the end of the world whenever I suggested quitting my medication, so I never told him, and I felt terrific. I haven't
taken a pill since."

Flores said, "If it was an antidepressant, you should've got depressed when you went off it."

"I know, but I didn't. The stuff the doctor shot me up with this
morning was different, really strong. I vaguely remember having the
same woozy feeling back when I was on lots of pills. The pills
stopped my headaches, which were god-awful."

"Why did you have to take so many pills?"

"Gordon said the first were for the brain fever, and then the
doctor changed my medication when he realized I had amnesia.
The doctor was supposedly trying to help me get back my memory."

The truck rolled out of the pocked mountain road and made a
right turn onto a wider state road.

He said, "It's probably safe for you to come up on the seat now, if
you like."

Stiffly and warily she raised herself and looked around. She sat
next to Flores. He stank like a mule barn that hadn't been mucked
in a year. She stopped. A mule barn? How did she know about mule
barns? She tested her memory, but nothing more came. She sighed,
stretched, and rubbed her arms and legs.

He glanced at her. "So how'd you get amnesia?"

"Gordon said I hit my head, and then I got one of those mysterious brain fevers, the kind doctors aren't exactly sure about. The doctor said I was fortunate to have no brain damage. Memory loss was better. Sometimes memory comes back on its own."

"Spontaneously?"

"That's it. I figured I was lucky all around. Look what usually causes amnesia—hardening of the arteries, seizures, strokes, tumors, or metabolic or toxic problems like reactions to medicine. I had a little brain fever caused by an inflammation after an accident. That's apparently a lot easier to deal with."

"It must be crappy to lose your past. Personally, I'd just as soon lie down in a gutter and let Hortense roll over me. This is Hortense." He patted the dashboard. "Hortense, meet Sansborough. Sansborough, meet Hortense. So tell me, Sansborough, what are you without a past?"

"I wish I knew."

For a moment she allowed herself to feel the aching void next to her heart. Nothing but true memories could ever fill it. She found herself beginning to warm to Flores. In any case, she was stuck with him, and he with her. And now they had the same immediate problem—escaping Gordon.

"What will they do to you if they find out you helped me?"

He shrugged. "The worst would be to bring me up on charges and fire me. I suppose they could throw me into the joint, too."

She studied him again. "You love this work, don't you?"

"You could say that."

"Maybe you're the one who's crazy."

He laughed, reached down into the pocket on his door, and handed her a fat folder. "Check this out."

Inside were printouts of dossiers: Two for Liz Sansborough, one from the Ranch and the other from Langley. The others were for her cover, Sarah Walker; her first lover, Huseyn Shaheed Noon; her husband, Garrick Richmond; and the Carnivore himself.

"Thanks. Maybe there's something in here that will explain what's going on." And who—and what—she really was. She'd like to think of herself as a decent person, kind, even honorable, but now she had to wonder.

The truck bounced and yawed. The cab was warm from the mountain sunshine, the road stretched ahead in hypnotic curves, and Dr. Levine's drugs were still in her system. She tried to read but

dozed instead and awoke with a violent jerk, afraid she'd been medicated again. Often she had indistinct images of what might be her
past. Faces, houses, events. The impressions jumbled through her
mind like a television gone haywire. Flores looked at her but said
nothing. She was glad. What could he say? Fear was something you
had to work out yourself.

At the Ranch high in the Rockies, Gordon Taite paced the security
hut, hands locked in a death grip behind him. He wore fresh wood-
land camos and hiking boots polished to a high sheen. He stopped
to glare at the woman's belt, curled like a viper on the desk. Marines
watched the bank of monitors.

"Her belt was under your Explorer, sir," one marine explained.
"It looked like she was trying to hot-wire it."

Gordon's jaw jutted out. "Bitch. She didn't just vanish into thin
air. Where in hell is she?"

"We've got the Ranch on high-security alert, sir." The marine in
charge stepped forward smartly. "We'll find her!"

"You'll find her if she's here, yeah," Gordon said, "but what if
she's not?"

"Don't see how she could've got out without us knowing it."

"Yeah, asshole. But you don't know where she is either. Get your
people out on the roads. Cars and helicopters. We've got to find
her, *now.*"

Nineteen

In August as thermostats climbed, Paris emptied for the traditional vacation month. Aristocrats, industrialists, and couturiers left for the cool seashore at elegant Cannes and yacht-loving Saint-Tropez while bakers, stationers, florists, and shop girls and boys pinned their hopes on relatives who might take them in at industrial Marseille or Toulon, home of a major French naval base. Anywhere in the countryside—away from the narrow, winding back streets of the two-thousand-year-old city.

The oppressive heat seemed only to feed the discontent sweeping France. Demonstrations were increasing, spreading from Paris bus drivers to all transportation workers. Factory laborers were threatening to strike in solidarity. Everyone agreed the hideous *économie* was to blame. Tempers were short. *Les citoyens* were angry, depressed, agitated.

And so, when a traveling circus put up its billowing big top on a razed block in Seine-St-Denis, it did a brisk business selling distraction from the heat and *les troubles*. Who could resist the gaily costumed performers, the exotic animals, or the merry calliope music? Laughter and applause sang out from the tent, and even the most dubious lined up for tickets.

Among these was a work-worn, middle-aged Frenchwoman. She was gray haired, walked with a stoop, and had wrapped herself in a bulky sweater as if she were perpetually cold. She carried a shabby Samaritaine shopping bag. She bought a ticket and entered the big top, but instead of climbing the wood bleachers for a good view of the rings, she faded into the side shadows.

And waited.

In the center ring glamorous poodles in tutus and tall pink bows were finishing their act. They took deep bows and pranced out on long hind legs to thunderous applause.

A heartbeat later the next act began: A dozen clowns rolled and tumbled from the side exits toward the rings. By chance one bumped into the shabby Frenchwoman. The clown slipped her a small envelope, and they exchanged a few words in English.

"Why is this taking so long?" the clown demanded in a husky whisper.

"We haven't been able to find out. Quill says to force their hand, give Langley a take-it-or-leave-it deadline."

"We'll need time to make our own arrangements."

"Three days." The Frenchwoman watched the crowds. "Sunday night. Eight o'clock?"

"Good. Contact the Germans, and tell them to stand by. Their offer was almost as good." The clown glanced quickly around, did a back flip onto huge buffoon feet, and said loudly in French: *"Pardon, madame!* Enjoy the show!"

As the clown dashed off to the big ring, the gray-haired Frenchwoman wearily climbed the bleachers. She watched and clapped at the appropriate times. At intermission she walked off through St-Denis, watching to make sure no one followed. At last she boarded the *métro* and sat alone in a seat far at the back. As the *métro* raced along, she bent over her shopping bag.

With moist tissues, she wiped off her wrinkles and sallow complexion. It took many tissues, but at last her face was clean. For one brief stop, the entire back of the car emptied of other passengers. That's when she pulled off her gray wig and shook free her auburn hair. As the car filled again, she put on dark glasses and let her hair fall over her face. She stared out the window, willing everyone to ignore her.

She was unafraid. She loved her work.

At last she stood up to disembark. With one quick motion she peeled off her sweater and dropped it into the bag on top of the wig. As she stepped onto the sidewalk, she took out two Victor Hugo novels and tucked them under her arm, titles out.

With her cheap cotton dress in a muted floral pattern, she looked like any poor university student.

She entered the bustling, frenetic Gare du Nord on Rue de Dun-
querque. There she joined a huge crowd of tourists, uneasy about
transportation in a country where at any moment trains, taxis,
buses, and the *métro* could be shut down by strikes. The tourists
would offer the perfect diversion if a tail had picked her up. She
stayed with them until they swept past the women's room.

She slipped inside and locked herself into a stall.

She took a deep breath, her heart pounding. These last two
months had been very hard on her, but well worth it. Then, too,
there was the *frissonnement*, the thrill, to keep her going.

She kicked off her heavy work clogs and pulled her dark, sticky
nylons down off her tan legs. She took off the cheap floral dress and
put on a black linen sheath with a T back. Its simple designer lines
emphasized her slim figure and large breasts. She slipped into high-
heeled black sandals.

She applied makeup, brushed her glossy auburn hair until it flew
around her head, and dropped her discarded clothes into the shopping bag. She put on oversized black sunglasses and pulled one last
item from her bag—a black cloth purse lined in faded lavender.
Inside she put makeup, money, fake identification, a Walther pistol,
and the envelope from the clown. This was the outfit she always
wore for meetings at Le Tour Languedoc.

It was a very versatile outfit.

She dropped five francs onto the saucer for the attendant.

Last she locked the shopping bag into a public locker. Ridding
herself of it was the final act of her transformation.

A half hour later the young, beautiful Frenchwoman wearing oversized black sunglasses arrived at a cluster of stylish high-rises near
the Montparnasse railroad station on the Left Bank. Big air condi-
tioners hummed like mosquitoes in the August heat. Tall and lanky,
she strode through the long afternoon shadows. She ignored the
admiring stares of passing businessmen.

At last she entered the massive Tour Languedoc, an elite steel-
and-glass skyscraper that housed architects, doctors, lawyers, and accountants. She passed a bank of burnished-steel elevators and
stopped at the last one. It had no call button.

She used a key to open a hand-sized door next to it, and she
tapped in her code. She waited while hidden cameras examined her
to make sure she was whom her code claimed.

At last the elevator opened. It took her up to the top floor, higher than any listed on the building's register, higher than the blueprints filed with the city. Sheets of reflective glass on the outside hid the number of stories at the Languedoc. Few people knew this floor existed, but that was to be expected.

Langley owned the building, and it was Langley's floor.

It always went the same. First she handed over the envelope with the Carnivore's latest revelation. Then they invited her to sit with them in the designer sling chairs around the starkly modern, glass-block coffee table. The envelope lay on the table while they offered her coffee or a drink, and, as always, she refused. God knew what they might put into any food or drink. She never set down her purse. They might slip into it a bug hidden in a pen, a lipstick, or even a credit card.

She believed the room was wired for sound, and somewhere hidden cameras must whir. No doubt their meetings were being recorded in living color and relayed by satellite to the Lords of Langley.

She had seen some of the rest of this warehouse-sized floor. Before she defected from Langley to go over to the Carnivore, she'd sometimes worked out of this place. She'd been in the lab with its stench of formaldehyde, in the communications center with its walls of monitors and constantly blinking lights, and in the computer center where three-dimensional wireframe drawings were transformed into fully fleshed humans, weapons, and secret sites. There was also a modest conference room ringed with wall screens and maps. There were bedrooms for personnel who had to sleep over.

Now she was in the formal reception area, where two Company operatives made polite small talk, and she was polite in return. To them, she was a traitor. She'd betrayed her country and, far worse, Langley, by going over to the infamous assassin. She understood their view without animosity.

That irritated them. If she didn't feel guilty, she could at least pretend embarrassment.

She came to the point. "This is the last information you'll get from the Carnivore." She nodded at the lone envelope on the glass-block coffee table. "He's proved his value. Either we come in at eight o'clock Sunday night, or we go elsewhere."

"That's only three days."

"It's not enough time."

She shrugged. "This isn't negotiable."

"We don't make the decision," said the first agent. "Look how long it's taken Langley to bring in others. Arkady Shevchenko, for instance. Three years."

"It's been only a few weeks for you," the second agent reminded her.

Langley had a reputation for being careful, especially since international fugitives could turn out to be uncooperative, or to have overblown reputations, or to be full of disinformation. But Langley already knew the value of the Carnivore's information, and he'd made it obvious he was willing to hold nothing back.

Annoyed, she shrugged, and both men's gazes automatically went to her breasts. That annoyed her further.

She smiled coldly and lied: "Tell Hughes Bremner the game's over. Finished. We have an acceptable offer from a certain other country. We've notified them, and they're willing to bring us in on Sunday. This is your last chance. Sunday, or we go elsewhere." Today was Thursday. That gave the Americans a few days to resolve whatever bureaucratic entanglements a speeded-up schedule created.

"We'll pass your request on to Langley."

"I expect the answer by noon tomorrow." She stood and walked toward the elevator. "If it isn't affirmative, you'll never hear from the Carnivore again."

They jumped up and followed her.

One asked, "Where's the new drop?"

As the elevator door opened, she turned and named a bulletin pole in St-Germain-des-Prés, the message to be in a cipher disguised as a love note addressed to "Michelle." At each meeting she named a new dead drop. She distrusted electronic messages; they could be monitored too easily.

The agents nodded.

She studied them, then stepped into the elevator. "*Au revoir, messieurs.*" The elevator took her down, and she looked forward eagerly to losing herself among the *boulangers, bouchers, fruitiers,* and flower peddlers of summertime Paris.

Behind the painting that was a window on the unrelentingly modern reception area, Hughes Bremner watched the woman depart and considered what to do.

Last month, after several long sessions, he'd convinced Arlene Debo, Director of Central Intelligence, that the United States must be the one to acquire the atlas of dirty secrets in the Carnivore's brain. Then he'd gone with the DCI to calm the President's dangerous squeamishness. Ultimately the President had given his official consent to go ahead.

Until only a few minutes ago, Bremner had been in control, the protocols going smoothly, MASQUERADE going smoothly.

But now the Carnivore had turned the tables. The turncoat bitch had delivered his ultimatum.

But MASQUERADE wasn't ready! Close, but—

Bremner had to get the Carnivore, first and last!

From a hidden speaker, he told the operatives to bring him the envelope. There were two doors in the reception room. One led to the elevator, the other to the corridor that ran the length of the floor. Using their keys and then their personal codes, the two men opened the bullet-proof corridor door, handed over the envelope, and returned to other work.

Bremner gave the Carnivore's latest revelation to decoding and hurried into electronic surveillance. From there the courier would be monitored. He had his best teams tailing her. This time he was determined she'd lead them to the assassin. Once the Carnivore was dead, MASQUERADE would be irrelevant, and his new operation, the greatest of his career—GRANDEUR—would be safe.

He'd been running the traditional three-person team on the courier, plus an occasional fourth, but she'd always shaken them. This time he'd positioned two men and a woman on foot, one man and two women in cars, and two more men in a van loaded with equipment. He'd had the van painted to look like a delivery truck for a *pâtisserie*, a cake shop.

It aggravated him she'd never eat or drink here. But Langley had trained her well. R&D had just released a tasteless metallic substance to be put in food or drink and then tracked, as long as the tracker stayed within a half mile of the subject.

If he could just get that into her, she'd lead them to the Carnivore, and the Carnivore to his death.

As the woman left the building and his surveilling agents smoothly picked her up, he moved toward the door.

"I'll be in my office," he told the operators, whose gazes never left their monitors. "Call me instantly if you have the slightest suspicion our target has shown."

When she left the Languedoc, the courier spotted her tails immediately. She was astounded at the overkill. She walked along the sidewalk as if she hadn't noticed them. She also gave no sign she'd spotted Quill. His distant presence was assurance against the unknown, because no matter how good, how careful one was, there were always elements beyond one's control.

Later tonight she'd leave him a message at their private drop, reporting on today's meeting. One way or another, one country or another, she was determined they'd have asylum by Sunday night.

She strolled away along the busy rue de Vaugirard, past the street vendors and the saxophone player on the corner, and into the Jardins du Luxembourg. The Palais du Luxembourg had been built in the 1600s as a residence for Marie de Médicis. Today the grand palace housed the French Senate, while the lush gardens were a paradise for strollers. Inside the garden walls, she sauntered past elaborate fountains, paused at ornate flowerbeds, and stopped to buy a sausage and a Coca-Cola at the café.

She sat on a bench in the shade to enjoy her food.

After two more hours she was satisfied her tails were either lulled or frantic. In either case, they'd not be as sharp as before. She left the garden and retraced her steps as if she were returning to the Languedoc. Instead she ducked inside the Montparnasse railroad station. Now only those on foot could follow fast enough to have a hope of staying with her.

Even Quill couldn't keep up with her here.

She dashed between an immense pillar and a magazine vendor's stall where, five long steps later, she was sheltered on three sides by two other stalls and a wood-backed phone booth. To see her, someone would have to stare intently down the dark passage.

Still, she had no desire to test her luck.

Instantly she pulled off her high-heeled sandals, broke open the heels, and dusted her face, lower legs, feet, and hands with a filthy black powder. She shoved her feet back into the flattened shoes, pulled down black leggings from her crotch to her ankles, and broke away her skirt at the waist.

Twice she spotted Bremner's people passing by. They were frenzied, searching among the crowd.

Her rhythm never broke. She pulled out a ratty black-satin cape from beneath the magazine stand and put it on, along with a pair of hot-pink, heart-shaped sunglasses. She tied her black skirt around her head like a scarf. With a quick swipe, she applied fiery red lipstick and turned her purse inside out, revealing its faded lavender, grease-stained interior. Then, with her finger, she wiped brown stain onto her teeth.

With that, she assumed a cynical slouch and took out a long, brown cigarette. Lavender purse swinging, she rejoined the railway throngs.

The only agent who was nearby stared at her. She saw distaste in his eyes, but a certain curiosity, too. That made her tense. Professional curiosity was bad. She must convince him his distaste was the more accurate assessment.

She stuck the unlighted brown cigarette between her lips, swayed up to him, and spoke boldly, her dirty face so close she could smell the coffee on his breath, which meant he could smell the garlic on hers: *"S'il vous plaît, monsieur?"*

He hesitated, stared.

She exposed her stained teeth in a hideous grin and, with her free hand, firmly grabbed his balls.

He jumped back.

She followed. *"Oooh-la-la, monsieur!* So handsome! One light for a lady will pay you many dividends." She reached for his crotch again. "For a price, of course!"

He turned, disgusted, and strode away. He had no interest in venereal disease, armpit hair, a brain fried from drugs, and God knew what else. He resumed his search.

In his Languedoc office, Hughes Bremner's telephone rang at last. He reached for it.

"Sir, she . . . we can't find her."

"What!"

"We followed her into the Gare du Montparnasse. You know, sir, the transportation crisis is making people take their trips while they can, and the station was jammed. We lost her there—"

He listened to the excuses with cold fury. The Carnivore's courier had disappeared, and with her Bremner's last best chance to eliminate the assassin's threat before the coming-in.

"Keep your people posted around the station for the next twelve hours," Bremner ordered. "She may be inside, waiting until you're gone."

As he finished his instructions, his other line rang. He thought of Gordon. Now more than ever MASQUERADE was vital. He'd been trying to reach Gordon for hours.

"Gordon! Where in hell have you been!"

In the distance, Gordon hesitated.

"Goddammit, what's happened?"

"Sir, I have bad news." Another pause. "The woman's gone. Escaped. Asher Flores, too—"

Twenty

At the small mountain town where the dump was located, Asher Flores gave Liz a credit card and dropped her off at a gas station that also sold used cars. She picked out an old Chevrolet Caprice for $3,000 and handed over the card. She hoped Langley hadn't yet thought to put a hold on it.

The owner carried it back smiling. She signed *Mrs. Asher Flores* and thought with disgust how gullible she'd been about Gordon and his two gold "wedding" rings.

She considered driving away without Flores, but she still had neither money nor any credit cards but this one. It might get her close to Santa Barbara, which she figured would be the best place to resume her search for her memory, but Gordon would eventually attempt to track her through Flores's cards.

There was another problem: Where would she even begin to try to unravel the mess with Gordon, Langley, and the Carnivore?

And what about Sarah Walker? If there was a real Sarah Walker, she might need help urgently.

One of Flores's advantages was that he had the experience to untangle this mess. But what if Flores were somehow connected to Gordon? What if he turned on her, or if he were simply out for himself? If she decided to cast her lot with Asher Flores and she was wrong, she could lose more than her past.

She frowned and started the car. So far Flores had made no move against her. In fact, he'd helped her escape. He'd brought her the dossiers from Langley's ultra-secret database. He'd saved her from the marines in the helicopter. She herself had heard them talk about how he'd been ordered to Spitsbergen, and that made his story even more believable.

He'd never tried to take her Beretta.

She drove toward the highway, fingers drumming the steering wheel. He was a risk she'd have to take . . . for the time being. She'd keep her Beretta near her hand, and she'd stay on the alert.

He was waiting at the dump in clean jeans and shirt.

"Where'd you get the shower and clothes?" she asked suspiciously. Had he somehow arranged all this?

He lifted his bushy eyebrows at her, patted Hortense good-bye, threw his gym bag into the Chevy's trunk, and climbed in beside her. "The guy who runs the dump let me use his shower. And I'd packed a few things. I had a little more time and flexibility than you. You got a change of clothes?"

She drove off. "All I've got is what I'm wearing."

In the next town, they stopped at a dry goods store. He bought her jeans, T-shirts, and cowboy boots. No more skirts and blouses. No more camos for a while, although they were better than skirts and blouses. She turned in front of the mirror and admired the way the jeans fit—as if they'd been sprayed on. Her kind of clothes. Flores watched, his angular face amused. She had no idea what he was thinking, and she didn't care.

He was a strange man. About her height, he had a wiry body that radiated intensity. His black hair was wild and curly, his black eyebrows like Brillo, and his nose aristocratic. He wore clothes as if they were an irritation, and when he talked he often jabbed the air as if it were life's punching bag. She wondered what he'd done to end up in the Ranch job, which he obviously hated.

They stopped in another town and bought sunglasses. He chose Stetsons. She didn't want a hat, but he insisted: "We've got to fit in." He handed her black hair dye and scissors.

"You want me to cut my hair?"

"And dye it, too. I'm growing a beard." He rubbed his long chin. He already had plenty of black stubble.

He paid with cash this time. They stopped outside town, and he massaged forest duff into their hats and boots. He slapped the hats around. He showed her how to scuff her boots with a pine branch, and he did the same to his own. When they'd finished, the Stetsons and boots looked worn.

As they were about to return to the Chevy, they heard the distant buzz of a helicopter.

"Gordon?"

"Yeah, could be his people." Flores's gaze was instantly on the far-off bird.

They moved back under the trees and watched the helicopter draw closer, following the highway toward them. It patrolled a ridge-line and then swooped down over the highway again. For ten long minutes it approached, inspecting the vehicles beneath.

"Lucky we were out of the car," she murmured.

"Yeah."

"Glad you suggested the Stetsons."

"Thought you might be."

The helicopter hovered over the empty, parked Chevy, then passed on down the highway. She let out a long breath. "Nothing like a little more excitement to keep the adrenaline pumping."

In the next town they traded the Chevy for an old Ford pickup, which they'd noted was a particularly popular make and style in this part of the Colorado Rockies.

Flores took the wheel, and they headed east on Interstate 70. Liz opened the files on herself and Sarah Walker. There was nothing new in the Walker dossier, but the Sansborough dossier showed the last three years as Flores had said: She'd fallen in love with the Carnivore, gone over to him, and was now his go-between with Langley. She shivered. Who was lying? Gordon or Langley? And, for God's sake, why? Or was the Langley file some kind of trick to make her think she really was mad?

She glanced at Flores and wondered again how much she could trust him. Then she gazed out at the mountain scenery, and in her mind she saw silvery creeks and snow-crowned mountains. She had a sense of picnics, backpacking trips, and long mountain drives. This, when she'd grown up in England? But it could be true, she re-minded herself, thinking of family vacations in Europe.

She glanced at Flores, again suspicious.

"I didn't make up the Langley file, Sansborough. If it's a trick, they're using me, too." His eyes never stopped moving, surveying the interstate and the air overhead.

He had a quick mind. She hoped it was an honest one.

She opened the next dossier: Huseyn Shaheed Noon, her first lover. "Listen to this." She read aloud, remembering the photos she'd studied: He'd been a handsome youth with smooth dark skin, serious eyes, and black hair that tumbled over his forehead.

In Pakistan, a 1980s referendum endorsed the president's Islamic-law policies and extended his term six more years. With that security, President Zia called for elections to a civilian parliament. Huseyn Shaheed Noon's father, a popular statesman, announced his candidacy. But before the election, the father visited Shaheed at Cambridge and was killed in an automobile accident. There were no witnesses, and the father was driving alone. According to the police report, he ran his car into a ditch and broke his neck when he was ejected. According to the coroner, he'd been drinking heavily. Authorities found no reason to suspect foul play.

Shaheed never accepted his father's death as an accident. He claimed his father was a devout Muslim, and Muslims do not touch alcohol. From Cambridge, Shaheed charged President Zia with murder because of his father's outspoken support of the outlawed Pakistan People's Party.

Shaheed investigated the death himself, and later told friends he believed President Zia had hired the shadowy international assassin called the Carnivore for the job. When Shaheed next returned to Pakistan to visit his family, his single-engine plane went down not far from his ancestral home in West Pakistan and he died. He was alone. The Pakistani government investigated and found a faulty fuel line had broken, Shaheed had panicked, and the plane had crashed through pilot error.

"That stuff about his father being drunk—" Flores said. "Devout Muslims abstain. And I can believe old Zia would have both of them killed. Zia was a savage. He liked to strut around in a uniform covered with medals he'd awarded himself."

"Look at this about the Carnivore. The first file said nothing

about him. You'd think it would have had *something*, since so much
seems to revolve around the Carnivore."

"Maybe Gordon or someone else didn't want you to know the
Carnivore had been involved with Shaheed."

"But to what purpose?" As they drove through the deepening
afternoon shadows, she read Garrick Richmond's file. He'd been an
all-American boy—Presbyterian, Eagle Scout, captain of his high
school football team, and president of the senior class. He'd won a
full scholarship to college, where he'd played quarterback, graduated *summa cum laude* in economics, and won a Fulbright to Cambridge. With his blond good looks and happy-go-lucky charm, no
wonder she'd fallen in love with him.

"Oh, lord. Listen to this." She read:

```
Garrick Richmond's senior honors thesis dealt with
popular knowledge of the Carnivore, the international
assassin. Richmond compiled clippings, contacted
Langley's public information, interviewed spokesmen
for Interpol and intelligence agencies of the United
States, Britain, and West Germany. Because of his
initiative, he was offered a position with Central
Intelligence upon graduation. He accepted. He went
through training and then moved to Cambridge, where he
studied and worked for Central Intelligence. There he
met and married Elizabeth Sansborough.
```

"The Carnivore again." Flores scratched his head. "He do keep
poppin' up."

"Consider the odds. Both my lover and husband 'investigated'
the Carnivore. That can't be a coincidence. It's got to mean something, but neither Gordon nor my dossier ever mentioned any of
it."

"And of all people, *you* just happened to be seen and shot by the
Carnivore. Another coincidence, right? Jesus, maybe Gordon Taite
himself was involved with him!"

She pondered it all. Then she finished reading Garrick Richmond's file. According to the dossier, he'd died as she'd been told
—tortured and killed by the Shiite Jihad. It was a tragic end, but
somehow worse because his life had been so young and promising.

They filled the pickup's tank about an hour from Denver. When
they returned to the highway, Liz again opened Sarah Walker's file.

There was the computer-generated face the file claimed was Walker
—unremarkable, no mole, slightly crooked nose. She held the image of herself next to Walker's and studied the two portraits as if
they could not only give her the answers she sought, but the questions she didn't know enough to ask.

"She looks a little like you," Flores observed. "There's something
about her bone structure."

"She *is* me, idiot."

"Not Liz Sansborough. Sarah Walker."

Liz contemplated the picture of Walker. "Maybe someone at
Langley took my photo, made some cosmetic changes, including
getting rid of my mole, and *voilà*—Sarah Walker, an official portrait
for an official file for a nonexistent person."

"Langley tailors a cover to match the person being covered." He
poked his finger at her. "In other words, since Sarah Walker was
your cover, her photo should look exactly like you."

"Are you saying she really exists?"

"That would explain the different photo."

"I've been thinking the same thing. But if there's a real Sarah
Walker, where was she while I was pretending to be her?"

"Maybe in Paris, cozying up to the Carnivore?"

"That would explain a hell of a lot. But why would Langley give
me her name and life as a cover?" Liz shook her head, frustrated,
and her mind returned to the assassin. How could anyone cozy up
to him? She'd put it off until last. She opened the Carnivore's file.
Then she snapped to attention, suddenly aware something was
wrong.

"Oh, great," Flores breathed. "Down to the floor, fast!"

Without question or complaint she dropped to the floor of the
pickup and squeezed herself small. "Helicopter again?"

He pulled the brim of his Stetson low over his face. "No, an Olds
Cutlass. I remember seeing one like it at the Ranch. It's coming up
on us from behind."

Twenty-one

As the pickup sped along the Colorado interstate, Liz Sansborough began to sweat. Squeezed down on the floor, she felt helpless. She hated to have to rely on Flores.

"What's the Olds doing?" she demanded.

"Hell! It's Gordon himself!"

Her heart beat faster. "Where?"

"Coming up on the right. God, that guy's got a barber pole for a neck. His head never stops turning."

Flores pulled the brim of his Stetson down some more, and he adjusted his dark sunglasses. The brim and glasses almost touched. And then Liz saw a strange and awesome sight. While he'd made the two small motions with his hands, his face had somehow thickened itself. His features had grown heavier and broader, and the short black fuzz on his jaw and cheeks enhanced the new effect. He looked burly, black-bearded, and rough, not like wiry Asher Flores.

"Where's Gordon?" she asked.

"Almost on top of us. If he knew we were in this pickup, he'd have tried to stop us long ago. By the way he's acting, I figure he— and probably a squad from security, too—are fishing, hoping they'll spot us. He's going to pass us on the right. I think I'll inspire him to go look for another fishing hole."

She frowned. "Just don't mess up."

"Here we go!" He pressed the turn signal, indicating he wanted to move into the right lane. He pulled over abruptly.

"Are you crazy?" she said. "You're pulling right in front of him!"

"That's the idea."

"Flores!"

She listened for a horn's blare or the screech of wheels, but there were only normal traffic sounds.

"What's going on?" she demanded.

Flores was watching his rear-view mirror. "He's annoyed. I think I did it just right. Yup, here he comes. He's passing me on the left and speeding up. Make me eat his dirt."

"Gordon's ego. You were counting on it."

Flores was watching ahead. "There he goes. Gave me one real dirty look. He's still picking up speed. But you'd better stay down there on the floor, just in case. There may be others. Sorry."

"No problem." She was relieved. "The way you look, I wouldn't want to be seen with you anyway."

He was curious. "How do I look?" His eyes never stopped moving, watching for another threat from the Ranch.

She was honest. "Neanderthal."

"Thanks. It took me a long time to learn to let my real character come out." He grinned, and for a moment she felt oddly safe.

As the pickup continued along the Colorado interstate, Liz stayed on the floor and opened the Carnivore's file on the seat. She skimmed the Langley printout, then she reread the opening:

The international assassin who calls himself the Carnivore is believed to have been born in the late 1930s. He may have at least one U.S. parent, since reports from informants indicate he has an American accent when speaking English. He also speaks at least four other languages, most with no accent—German, French, Italian, and Spanish.

His real name is allegedly Alex Bosa. Bosa could be Hungarian, Italian, Portuguese, Spanish, or from any Central or South American nation, such as Cuba. He is believed, however, to be Italian.

She told Flores what she'd read. "It also says: 'He apparently began a monogamous liaison in the late 1950s.'"

"Married?"

"Doesn't say. Makes you wonder, though, what happened to her. And it also makes me wonder about this woman over in Paris who's calling herself Liz Sansborough. Whether she really knows what she's gotten herself into."

"Or whether she can get herself out of it."

"Good point."

She read aloud:

The Carnivore's fame began at Fidel Castro's overthrow of the Batista regime in Cuba on January 1, 1959. Afterward a CIA operator picked up a rumor that a new assassin called the Carnivore had eliminated one of Batista's top generals, thus paving the way for Castro's victory.

The Carnivore is also considered responsible for the December 1975 attack on a Vienna meeting of the Organization of Petroleum Exporting Countries in which three powerful oil ministers were killed.

He supposedly assassinated Hans Martin Schleyer, president of the Employer's Association of West Germany, in the late 1970s.

In 1978 he loaded a tiny metal pellet containing poison into the tip of an umbrella and bumped into renowned emigré writer Georgi Markov in London—

"I remember that," Flores said soberly. "A case I studied at the Farm. A near-perfect kill. Looked like a heart attack, not murder. But the pathologist was suspicious, thank God."

"How did the pathologist figure it out?"

"Checked the entire body. Finally he found the remains of a pinhead-sized pellet in Markov's thigh, and that's when somebody remembered a guy with an umbrella had bumped into Markov earlier. By the time the pathologist found the pellet, the poison had decomposed. It was ricin, highly toxic, made from castor-oil seeds. That assassination sent all kinds of nasty waves through intelligence circles, because it showed how vulnerable all of us really are. In the end, the Bulgarians got the blame. We only found out it was the Carnivore because he sent word after the pathologist figured it out but before anyone else knew."

"He's a real sweetheart, the Carnivore. No wonder his name stuck." She continued reading aloud:

In 1981 he bombed the offices of Radio Free Europe in
Munich, seriously injuring four persons.
    During the late 1980s he is believed to have taken
refuge in East Berlin. He is considered responsible for
the 1983 bombing of a French cultural center in West
Berlin in which one person was killed. According to
Stasi reports, the East German government and the Stasi
protected the Carnivore as if he were an official
visitor.

Flores whistled. "Jesus-God. The Carnivore was living in East Berlin in the '80s, and the East Germans knew it?"

"According to this, he was there until the wall fell. The report says, 'He pursued his affairs from East Berlin with no interference, lived in a Yemeni diplomat's flat, and used a chauffeur hired by the Syrians. His presence seems to have been known only to four top East German officials.'"

Asher ruminated. "Yeah. Obviously he's very valuable. So not only did the Stasi let him stay, they coddled him. Which made it even more difficult for us to find him, much less take or eliminate him. What I'm wondering now is why he went there in the first place, and then why he left?"

"And where did he go afterward?"

"Good question. Read on."

She did.

Perhaps most noteworthy about his *modus operandi* is
that he has been credited many times with nearly
simultaneous kills in different parts of the globe.
This has tended to create fear among more primitive
nations that he has supernatural powers. It is
believed, however, such closely spaced executions are
probably the work of a highly trained, loyal staff.

Flores snorted. "Yeah, real fun trying to catch a shadow when he's in two different hemispheres at the same time."

"You think he's trained other assassins to help him?"

"Could be. He's getting older. Although I think if it were me, I'd give up the reputation for wizardry and stick to solo hits. In his business, decisions are based on security first, money second. Once someone knows more than your code name, you're vulnerable."

"Maybe no one else does know. Maybe he really is in two different hemispheres at the same time, just like I'm here and in Paris at the same time."

"Yeah, right. Very funny."

She allowed herself a smile. She resumed reading:

Three years ago the Carnivore met CIA operative Elizabeth Sansborough while she was on assignment in Lisbon. She crossed over, and he apparently ceased his assassinations. What is not known is whether their relationship caused the assassinations to stop. It also could be due to injury or to his reluctance or inability to work in the political upheaval that has followed the end of the cold war. It's also possible he died.

She sighed, disgusted. "God, I'm getting tired of hearing I'm his girl friend."

"Well, at least you maybe got him to quit murdering people. Must give you a warm, cuddly sense of accomplishment."

She looked balefully at Flores. "You can be a real pain in the butt, Flores, you know that?"

He waggled his bushy black eyebrows at her. "Anything more in there?"

" 'A full list follows of his believed kills. Confirmations are being sought.' " She read the list. They discussed some of the wet jobs, and at last she closed the file.

During the next two hours, Liz dozed on the floor. Flores spotted three more cars driven by Ranch personnel. But as with Gordon, they apparently hadn't identified the pickup and thanks to the sunglasses, Stetson, and Flores's thickened features, they didn't recognize him. Which would have been reassuring to Flores, if his gut didn't tell him there was going to be one hell of a lot more trouble ahead.

It was twilight, and bright stars were blinking on in the charcoal sky. Liz asked, "Think it's safe for me to come up on the seat?"

"Yeah. Can you move?"

"I'd like to know that myself." She ached everywhere. She pulled herself up and stretched. Gratefully she massaged her legs and then her arms. She'd been thinking about the Carnivore as she dozed. She told Flores what she'd decided. "He's psychotic or amoral. A sociopath. In a symbolic sense, a flesh eater, just as his name implies. Why would someone like me have gone over to the butcher, much less fallen in love with him? There must be some basis for Langley to believe I did. It's in my dossier, and in his. But I don't want to believe it."

"It has to be in both, if they're trying to fool someone."

"But who are they trying to fool? Me? It reminds me of a poker saying I heard at the Ranch: If you look around the table and can't figure out who the pigeon is, it's you."

Behind them the sun set in vibrant reds and purples. Ahead, the sky had darkened into a starry indigo canopy. As they topped a ridge, the great metropolis of Denver spread out below. Looking down from I-70, the mountain city was a vast ocean of twinkling lights. It was a glorious sight, but they were tired and worried, and the visual pleasure of it registered only briefly.

In downtown Denver, Asher Flores pulled off the interstate at a drug-and-fuck motel between the stockyards and the coliseum. Gordon Taite was less likely to find them where rooms rented by the hour, and the man behind the counter asked no questions and looked no one in the eyes.

In this shabby area the streets were marked by flashing neon, eager prostitutes, and wailing cowboy music. The stench of animals, sweat, and thwarted ambition hung heavy in the humid night. It was just another August night, and metropolitan Denver sweltered in the success it had created.

Asher paid for the room with cash, and they carried in the gym bag, day pack, and thick dossier folder. There was no air conditioner. Liz opened the windows and went into the bathroom to shower, cut her hair, and dye it.

Asher drove away to buy takeout at a Chinese place they'd spotted near the interstate exit. Within a block he saw a phone booth. He stopped, pulled change from his pocket, and dialed. In a moment Langley was on the line. The operator reported Hughes Bremner had returned from Paris. It was after midnight in Washington, but

Bremner had left instructions for Asher to be patched through to his home.

Asher heard the phone ring once more.

Bremner picked it up instantly. "Where are you, Asher? I've been worried." The older man's voice was warm, concerned, reassuring.

Asher began to talk.

Twenty-two

Asher told Hughes Bremner, "I think you've got a major problem, chief. Gordon Taite."

"Ah, I was afraid of something like that." In the distance the CIA division chief sighed heavily. "When I got in tonight, Ernie Pinkerton phoned. He said Gordon had transferred you to Spitsbergen. I tried to reach you at the Ranch, but they said you'd disappeared. Tell me what's happened, Asher."

"Taite's gone off the deep end over Liz Sansborough. I don't know how she fits into the Carnivore's coming-in—"

"You've heard about that?"

"Sure." Asher's reputation for doing his homework was earned. "I tapped into the CM-5 and found she'd crossed over to him three years ago. Can you explain how in hell she can be in France and at the Ranch at the same time?"

"I can explain it, but I won't. It's need-to-know."

"Maybe I should be need-to-know, Chief. She won't be worth a plugged nickel if Taite turns her into a zombie."

"She needs medication."

"Yeah, well, she says she won't take it anymore."

"If you're telling me this, can I assume she's with you?"

Some deep instinct told Asher to lie. But his boss had always been straight with him. This recent punishment—banishing him to the godforsaken Ranch—was unavoidable, and both had known it wasn't forever.

"Yeah, she's with me."

"Bring her in, Asher. She's critical to national security."

"National security" was one of those catchphrases that came cheap. Richard Nixon had used it to try to cover Watergate. Ronald Reagan, George Bush, and former DCI Bill Casey used it for Iran-gate. Back in the days when Company murders were legal, it covered them like a shroud. In 1992 the Pentagon art museum even tried to use it to hide the fact some hit-and-run tagger had felt-tipped a mustache onto the dignified oil painting of Air Force Chief of Staff Tony McPeak.

The problem was, "national security" also had legitimate, vital uses. You should be suspicious when someone threw it at you, Asher had long ago decided, but you should also show respect. So he said, "A crazy woman's critical to national security? Kind of hard to believe."

"Have you fallen for her?" Bremner's cool reserve never cracked, but Asher heard worry behind it.

"Not yet. Think it's a good idea?"

"Knock it off, Asher. Obviously you doubt the woman's deranged. Believe me, she is. She'll act perfectly normal, and then she'll lose control and leave reality. If you don't bring her back you'll find out the hard way. We need her. Our medication will help her. Look, if she were sane, she'd go along with us. Because she's insane, we have to help her to help us."

As always Bremner was persuasive. Yet in his mind's eye, Asher saw Liz Sansborough's outraged struggle against the doctor's needle. Her determination as she escaped the Ranch infirmary. Her animal fear when the helicopters closed in. Her intelligent study of the dossiers. Her probing questions.

If she were insane, wouldn't so many emotional extremes have caused her to "leave reality," as Bremner had put it? "I'll think about it, Chief," Asher said. "But if I bring her in, it's to you. Not to Gordon Taite."

"Of course." Bremner was understanding. "It needs to be soon. Tomorrow at the latest. Call me. I'll meet you."

As they said good-bye, Hughes Bremner complimented Asher on his years with Langley, his contribution, his reliability, his fairness, his resourcefulness. He also promised to fix the Spitsbergen matter and give Asher a field assignment he'd like.

"Just get her to me, Asher."

Asher had never heard his reserved boss so effusive.

He drove two more blocks to the Chinese place, got food, and returned to the motel. Sansborough had showered and now wore a T-shirt and a towel around her waist. Her hair was short, straight, and black. He speculated about her, unsure what to do. He believed she was as sane as he was, probably a hell of a lot more than Gordon Taite. And he believed Bremner needed her.

"I hate it." She grimaced at herself in the dusty mirror that hung across from the two twin beds. She put on sunglasses, pulled her wet, short hair back behind her ears, and snapped on big shamrock-green plastic earrings. "I found them in the drawer. What do you think?"

She looked like a dimestore beauty—a girl from the wrong side of the tracks trying to look classy.

He chuckled. "You need three-inch fingernails, orange lipstick, and purple Naugahyde hot pants."

"I'm a success then."

"No one will recognize you. That's what we wanted."

She had a thin body anyway, but her despair made her look like a waif, all elbows, knees, and skinny ankles. Her neck had stretched long and flimsy. With her rounded shoulders, her beautiful breasts had disappeared flat against her rib cage. Her fingers were bony. Actors knew the effect emotion played on the body. Asher, who was proud of his ability to create characters in the field, was witnessing a fine example of this.

He told her what he saw. "The imagination is one of an agent's most vital tools. Actors know it. Ever see Paul Newman play the hobo in *Hemingway's Adventures of the Artist as a Young Man?* Newman was so believable no one recognized him, even though he was a huge box-office star."

She smiled a little. "It's an accident. I didn't learn it at the Ranch."

"They should put it in the curriculum." He smiled back.

They ate spring rolls, hot-and-sour soup, and a double order of beef in oyster sauce. There was no Chinese beer, just Coors. But then, they were in the empire of Adolph Coors. She drank two bottles; he drank three. It was okay beer if the weather was hot and you had nothing else.

"The real problem with losing your memory," she said at last, "is when you're rebuilding it you're never sure what's true enough to add and change."

She had nothing to sleep in, so she went to bed in her T-shirt and underpants. She slid her Beretta under her pillow.

From his gym bag Asher took out his Gunsite Service Pistol. It was a .45 that had begun life as a Springfield Armory 1911A1, all steel and forged to military specifications. Then Gunsite had altered it into a combat service pistol with a big sight, a short and dry trigger, a dehorned rear smooth against hands and clothing, and a bobbed hammer. Asher particularly liked the smaller grip. It felt natural in his small hands. He balanced the gun a moment, his friend, then slid it under his pillow.

"Got any ideas about tomorrow?" Her voice was normal again.

He liked that she bounced back quickly. She'd learn, or she'd get out, or she'd die.

"Depends on what our goal is." He turned his back, flipped off the light, and stripped to his shorts. He crawled into bed.

She said, "Can we go around Gordon? Get help from Langley?"

"It's a possibility."

"Where would we go?"

"My boss's name is Hughes Bremner. He's chief of Mustang. We'd go to him." She didn't realize it, Asher thought, but she was considering just what Bremner wanted. It'd save them all a lot of trouble. Still, there was a part of him that wanted to keep her and the Carnivore to himself.

The most beautiful woman. The most feared assassin.

She said from the distant bed, "I remember the name. *Hughes Bremner.* Gordon said he was watching my progress. That he took a special interest in me. Bremner's important. Gordon faxed him reports all the time about how my training was going."

Yes, he told himself, she must be vital to the Carnivore operation, "blue-code, need-to-know." But if the Carnivore already wanted to come in, why all this extra fuss? He lay there a few minutes, trying to hear her breathe. Then he fell asleep, one hand on the small grip of his big .45.

FRIDAY

She dreamed of unknown countries and harsh landscapes. Sometimes desert, sometimes ice and snow. In her dreams she was two Liz

Sansboroughs—one married to the Carnivore, the other to Gordon. Helpless, and as evil as they. She wanted to die.

She awoke in a cold sweat, terror racing through her veins.

Christ! Who was she? *What* was she?

The red-and-yellow neon motel sign blared in through the grimy windowpanes. It colored the room a dull, hazy rouge. Through the only window, still open, came the roar of the nearby interstate and the hot odors of manure and stockyard slaughter.

She breathed deeply, accepting her fear. Sleepiness washed over her. Her eyelids drooped. It must be near dawn.

She closed her eyes. Then she remembered the open window.

Had she seen movement around it?

Her eyes snapped open. Without turning her head, she used her peripheral vision to survey the room. At last she saw it. An aberration in the shadows near the dresser in the corner. It looked like a hand with a pistol and a long sound suppressor extending out into the still room.

Fear froze her. Then she remembered what to do.

What she'd been trained to do.

As if still dreaming, she sighed and moaned softly. She rolled onto her side. She moved her hand up under her pillow and gripped her Beretta. She slid it out.

Twenty-three

Liz fired the Beretta as she rolled off the bed. The room shook with the explosion. Instantly a shot from the intruder followed. Her mattress erupted. Tattered cloth and ticking sprayed the air, and another shot rang out.

Flores's bed exploded.

"Flores!"

She watched the darkness. A shot whined past, honing in on her voice. Wood splinters showered down. She dropped under the bed and slid across the cracked linoleum. It cut her thighs.

She raised herself just above the other side of the bed.

Two more shots exploded in the little motel room.

Flores was alive! One shot must be his, but which one? One had come from her left, the other from her right. The thick red darkness made it impossible to see.

She slid under Flores's bed. She heard sounds of movement, someone trying to be silent. Two more shots shattered the quiet. The men had relocated. Then she saw shadowy shoes near the door. It couldn't be Flores. He'd be barefoot. The intruder must be crouching, legs and torso lost in the shadow from a table. She aimed where she thought the legs would be. She wanted the guy alive. She wanted to ask questions.

She squeezed the Beretta's trigger. The jolt traveled up her arm and into her teeth. She heard a grunt and thud.

"Flores! Where are you?"

"I'm okay."

She heard him scrambling toward the lump by the door. She got up on her haunches, waiting. Soon the police would come. Even in this rotten section of town, where life was worth no more than a drink or a needle, someone eventually would call the cops. The habits of civilization die hard.

She rested the Beretta on her bare arm. Why was there no sound from the downed man? Not a groan or a curse. If he were alive, he'd make a sound.

"Sansborough, the window!"

She whirled in time to see a face and a gun in the harsh red glare of the motel sign. She shot instantly. It was as if she were back at the firing range, but instead of hitting the target, she hit the man's forehead. He was a blond young man with a muscular jawline and astonishment in his eyes.

Her bullet blasted through his forehead and took the top of his head off. Blood, tissue, and bone showered the carnival-colored air. There could be no doubt this time: She'd killed someone. Vomit surged up into her throat.

His gun went off spontaneously. Its bullet went wild.

"Check the window!" Flores was in trouble. His voice was strained. There were thuds.

The first intruder had been playing possum, and Flores was worried there were more.

Feeling ill, drenched in sudden sweat, she scrambled to the window. She heard another shot behind her. She whirled.

"It's okay." Flores's voice was gruff. "He was more alive than I thought, dammit."

"You killed him?"

"Had to." His voice was somber. Now he'd go through the corpse's pockets, try to find something that would tell them who he was and what he'd been after.

She raised her eyes over the windowsill. The window faced a weed-choked, trash-infested empty lot. She saw no signs of movement. She looked down and recognized the gun in the hand of the dead man. It was an Ingram M-11 machine pistol. Only ten inches long and under four pounds, it was lightweight and concealable, an automatic that could fire 850 rounds of .38 ammo a minute. A lot of power. This was no casual weapon.

The guy had been a pro. Without turning from her sentry post, she told Flores about the Ingram.

"Other than his gun, all this one's got is his cigarettes." He dragged the intruder by the heels toward the light of the window. "Nothing else in his pockets. Not even money. But I know him. His name's Matt Lister."

"I know him, too!"

She studied the dead face in the flashing red glare. It was the man she'd been told she'd killed in her Santa Barbara condo: The same bland features, the same slicked-back brown hair. She told Flores about the attack. "Gordon gave me a gun, and this guy came at me around the sofa and pointed his gun at me. I fired. It all happened so fast, and I was in a daze. Shocked, really. The next thing I knew, he flew back with blood—what I thought was blood—across his chest and coming out of his mouth!"

"Blanks and fake blood. Good staging of an old trick."

"And it worked, dammit! After that I believed everything they told me!"

"Of course, you did. They're damn good, and at that point even I'd be inclined to believe them. The important thing is you didn't let it convince you permanently." He leaned out the window and stared down at the blond youth. "I don't recognize him, do you?"

She shook her head, and he crouched beside her. He wore only his Jockey shorts, a slash of white in the ruby gloom. He had a good body, wiry, with long muscles. The legs had the long sexy lines of a runner. The shoulders were straight and wide, the kind a woman liked to run her hands across.

"Are there any more out there?" he asked.

"Not that I can see." She could smell him, sweat and intensity.

"Dress and pack. We've got to get out of here."

"No kidding."

He smiled briefly. She shimmied into her jeans. He dressed and threw things into his gym bag. Oddly, she no longer felt sick and shaky. She was damn angry.

She finished first. "Gordon sent them?"

"He wouldn't have the clout to order an assassination. They had to come from Bremner himself." Flores was grim. "My mentor. Your mentor. Not just Gordon Taite, it's Hughes Bremner, too.''

"How can you be sure?''

"No time for explanations. Come on.'' He opened the door. They surveyed the night. There was no traffic. Parked across the street was a Honda Accord, clean and new among the battered, rusty heaps that littered the street.

"They must've come in that,'' she said.

They jumped into their pickup. Flores started the engine.

Liz looked ahead at the silent Honda. "It's a rental car.'' On the back left bumper was a Gold Star Rent-a-Car sticker. Gold Star was the new number-one car-rental agency in the United States. No clue there.

In the distance, a siren wailed.

Flores spun the pickup out onto the street. "Too bad we don't have time to search their car. The way it looks to me, Matt Lister was going to kill me and grab you. He was right beside my bed, trying to decide which of us he had. If he'd wanted to kill us both, he would've shot from the window before we had a chance to wake up and fight back.''

"How do you know Bremner's part of it?'' She'd had high hopes the CIA division chief would help them. Gordon was out of the question, but Bremner, the head of Mustang, she'd hoped—

In the distance, the sirens stopped. The police had arrived at the motel. To the east, dawn was breaking over Denver's mile-high serrated skyline. In her mind she saw the blond youth's astonished face when her bullet had burst his skull.

She'd killed him. A human being.

She said quietly, "Tell me about Bremner.''

His jaw flexed with fury and betrayal. "I called him last night when I went for the food. I'd tried to reach him from the Ranch, but he was in Paris, 'unavailable.' He got back last night.''

"That's not so bad. You wanted him to help us.''

"I wanted information.'' He was silent, guilty.

Then she understood: Flores had made a mistake; he hated to make mistakes. "Bremner traced your call. Then he sent his people out to look for us. There aren't that many motels around here. Your phone call brought the killers to us.''

Flores's jaw was hard. "That's the way I figure it.''

□   □   □   □

Hughes Bremner stepped into the hall of his wife's Virginia mansion and found her, Bunny Hartford Bremner, the former belle of
Fifth Avenue, pounding toward him. It was early morning, and he
could smell the clean countryside calling to him. Instead he had to
deal with a broken-down drunk, old-looking beyond her sixty-one
years. She was angry because she had to appear for jury duty at
9:00 A.M. Civic obligations called to one and all, even to Bunny
Bremner.

She started appropriately enough: "Hughes, really. Must you look
like a thundercloud all the time?"

"That's a cliché, my dear."

"And you're a pompous jackass."

She presented her back to him. Beneath her too-youthful red
dress, she wore a red bra. The back and one shoulder strap were
twisted. She couldn't even dress correctly.

"Zip me," she demanded.

He zipped. He liked the viciousness of the sound. With satisfaction he noted the twisted bra made a bulge beneath her dress. Her
ineptitude grew more public each day.

"You used to like to dress me, Hughes," she continued. "And
undress me. Back in the Dark Ages when you were poor and I was a
love-sick fool."

"Aren't you going to remind me again your sweet papa was right?
That I was a nobody going nowhere with nothing in his head or his
pockets? My God, Bunny. You're losing it. The first sign of a Scotch-
boiled brain."

She returned to her bedroom and was back before he'd reached
the top of the stairs. She had on her hat and pumps now, and a prim
little purse in her hand. "At least you had an acceptable pedigree."
She went down the stairs first.

Even though he hadn't seen it, he knew she'd had her first drink
of the day. Her pores oozed alcohol. The odor followed her like a
hungry cat. He had a sudden urge to push her. It wouldn't take
much to topple her down the stairs. She was a fat old woman on tall,
teetering heels. She'd go ass over teakettle and break her pleated
neck. Her money would end up in a trust fund he couldn't touch,
but he no longer needed her money.

Alas, she had no knowledge of that.

"How about giving me a little shove, Hughes?" she sniped up over her shoulder as she descended. "You'd like to. We both know you would."

That's when he laughed. It was a huge, guttural laugh that shook him dangerously and made her stop and turn around. He wiped his eyes and grabbed the handrail while she watched in stony silence.

At last he was able to speak. "No, my dear. Killing you is the last thing I'd want. And it's not your money. No, dear Bunny. Without you, what in hell would I do for amusement?"

Her eyes narrowed with suspicion. Was she being ridiculed? She couldn't seem to make up her mind. Finally she tossed her head to indicate the unimportance of it all, and her little hat slipped precariously to the side. She didn't notice.

They continued down the stately staircase, two Eastern Seaboard blue bloods, each aware of a desperate bond to the other.

Bunny said, "Do be on time for dinner tonight, Hughes. The Coxes and Cabots will be here."

"I'll be late. As usual. Maybe I won't even come."

"Hughes!"

At last he'd worn her down to a one-word reply. Her inarticulateness was his victory.

At the front door, their cars were waiting at the top of the long, circular drive. Beyond, the lush countryside spread vivid and green in the morning light. Once he'd wanted to have this land developed. A shopping center, gas stations, and satellite stores. Around these would have spread a sea of tract houses, dotted with parks where the wild Virginia forests would be tamed and manicured. This land was too good to waste, and civilization should leave its imprint, control Mother Earth, and make her pay her way, just as he'd had to pay his.

"Good-bye, Bunny, dear," he said with mock affection. "Hope you have an awful day."

Tommy opened the driver's door to her fire-red Mercedes 450SL sports car, a classic she refused to give up. She scowled at Bremner, smiled at Tommy, and climbed in with a flash of flabby thigh. Bremner stared at the flaccid flesh, burned the image into his brain. If love and hate were two sides of the same coin, he must love Bunny very, very much. And she him.

At last Tommy opened the back door to the long, black, government limousine. Bremner stepped inside and sank into the familiar seat. He glanced out ahead, through the window. As Bunny burst off into the morning in her extravagant Mercedes, the limousine door closed softly next to Bremner, encasing him in the sound-proofed chrysalis of the back seat. The telephone rang. He picked it up, invigorated for the day. It was Sid Williams.

"Matt and Beno are dead, sir." Sid's voice was stone.

Damn! That'd be Matt Lister and Beno Durante, the two he'd sent to bring in Flores and the woman in Denver.

"What happened?"

"Flores shot them. Killed them at the motel."

Bremner leaned back in the hushed limo. "I'm sorry. They were good men." He meant it. He was loyal to those who were loyal to him. "What about Flores and the woman?"

"Got away. The police found nothing."

Bremner's mind worked quickly. "Contact our friend in the Denver police. Explain our situation—two renegade Langley operators have killed two others sent to negotiate with them. Give him photos and descriptions. He'll alert the interstate police network."

Back at Langley, Sid Williams chuckled coldly. "We'll have cops looking for them everywhere. They'll never get away."

"Yes. And make sure our private subsidiaries are alerted. We've got to get the woman back. *Today.*"

"And Flores?"

"He's turned. Kill him. Anything new on Lucas Maynard?"

"We haven't found him yet, sir, but we've got around-the-clock surveillance on his home as well as transportation centers in the D.C. area. And we just put taps on lines into the Secretary of State's office."

"Excellent."

The taps had been his idea. He figured Maynard, who was known for his tenacity but not his imagination, might decide to simply follow through on the dead undersecretary's plan.

"And we've told the area police Maynard's wanted for stealing a car from Langley." Sid Williams laughed at his lie.

"An excellent improvisation," Bremner said approvingly. If Maynard were stopped anywhere for any reason, the officer would run his driver's license through the computer. The police would automatically hold him until Sid got there. "Let's do it today, Sid. Get Maynard and his documents. Then neutralize him. A robbery or an accident, whatever appeals to you. But as soon as you get his papers, make sure he's dead.''

Twenty-four

In her Arlington apartment, Leslee asked Lucas to show her the Sterling-O'Keefe documents in the safe under the bed. He and she were in this together now, and it was time she knew what the fuss was all about. As she sorted through the stacks he'd gone to so much risk and trouble to Xerox, he prepared to leave.

"I've got to go to the office, honey," she told him. "I won't be long. Where are you off to?"

"To make phone calls. I don't want to take a chance they might be traced here to you."

She smiled her thanks, and he left to call the Secretary of State's office. He again used the telephone booth two blocks away. He endured the usual bureaucratic torture until at last he reached the secretary's personal assistant. He identified himself and explained, "Undersecretary Edward had an emergency appointment scheduled with the secretary yesterday morning."

"So?" The powerful personal assistant was busy and unimpressed.

"The appointment was about me. I have some—"

"Just a minute, Mr. Maynard. I must put you on hold."

Maynard swore as the phone went dead. He wanted to forget this madness, fly to Zurich and his money in Liechtenstein. But not without Leslee. He considered alternate plans. He could take the information to the DCI at Langley, but Bremner would be waiting for him one way or another. On the other hand, State had a historic rivalry with Langley, and he hoped the touchy relationship would keep Bremner and State safely distanced.

At last the assistant returned. "Please continue."

"I have information of critical importance. Clare was going to tell the secretary about it. That's why he was killed."

"If you know something about the murder, you should take it to the police."

The woman was an idiot! He growled, "I've got the details of an insider scandal that'll blast the beltway inside out!"

"It seems odd you don't handle this through Langley," she said sternly.

Maynard sweated in the stifling booth as the morning sun rose higher. He scanned the street outside for any hint of danger. He didn't need this goddamn bureaucratic power game.

He snarled, "You've got five seconds! Either give me an appointment or quit wasting my time. I'll take this somewhere else. Then you can explain to your boss how he almost had it, until you blew me off!"

There was a wintry pause. "Very well. I can squeeze you in at 11:50 this morning. But you'll have only ten minutes. The secretary has luncheon with three Saudi princes."

"I'll be there." Kiss my ass, Maynard thought and banged down the phone. When he got back to the apartment, Leslee was still gone. He sat in the kitchen with a cup of cold coffee, his gaze on the clock above the stove.

Just a few more hours. He thought about Clare's murder and toyed with the idea of calling the *Washington Post*. No, his documents were going to a more important place. An idea struck him. He'd become the epitome of civilized man, depending on the written word, not the sword, to stop grievous wrong.

Leslee would like that.

As he finished his coffee, he heard her key in the door. She came in with a quick kiss and her briefcase thick and heavy. He told her about his appointment at State.

She was delighted but worried, too. "I'll drive. If you don't have to park, you'll be exposed less time in the open. And we'll be together longer." She said nothing about how much time might elapse and what might happen before they were alone again.

"I'd like that." Maynard smiled.

She kissed him and went into the bedroom. In the kitchen he

poured coffee for her. When she came back she dropped into a chair, took her cup, and looked at the clock.

"Plenty of time," he said. "What did you think of the Xeroxes?" It made him feel peculiar and strangely violated to know she'd gone through them, even though he himself had opened the safe and had been pleased at her interest.

She smiled. "I appreciate your letting me see them. It's fascinating. The laundering and shifting of money. The buildup of the businesses. The false fronts Sterling-O'Keefe used to shield itself from the public all these years. And then there's the report on MASQUERADE." She bowed her blond head. When she looked up, her blue eyes were sad again. "MASQUERADE gave me insight into the fragility of the human psyche."

He shrugged, all his good feelings swept away on a tsunami of guilt. Leslee put a hand on his shoulder.

He said, "It always seemed so necessary. Whatever we were asked to do. Or decided had to be done. I guess after enough years of living lies and inventing self-serving excuses, a person's character gets eroded. That's what must've happened to a lot of us oldtimers, and that's why the five of us ended up starting Sterling-O'Keefe. And now MASQUERADE. I'd like to think we never would've started MASQUERADE back in the '50s."

"I'm sorry, Lucas. What you did was wrong. But what you're about to do is genuinely courageous. It's easy to be without sin when one's never tempted. You've been tempted, fallen, and are now about to resurrect yourself. The resurrected are the cream of our species. You make me proud and so very glad you're mine."

She stood and kissed him.

He wrapped his arms around her slim hips and pressed his cheek against her soft belly. She was life and hope.

At 11:00 A.M. Leslee drove them south on Twenty-first Street in her old blue Volkswagen Rabbit. The Department of State, the crown prince of U.S. government, would soon be on their right. Just ahead, on the other side of Constitution Avenue, spread West Potomac Park with its classic Reflecting Pool and polished black-granite Vietnam Veterans Memorial. To the west flowed the Potomac, lined with lush shoreline parks and crossed with congested bridges. The variegated cityscape with its noise and turmoil was an unconscious monument to and denouncement of the human species.

Traffic was lighter than usual, which made watching for Bremner's people easier. Between Maynard's feet, in a heavy shopping bag, were the Sterling-O'Keefe and MASQUERADE documents. He'd chosen a tourist profile. Binoculars and a camera hung from his neck. He wore a straw hat and a light summer sports jacket. Under the jacket, tucked in his armpit, was his streamlined Walther TPH. For a "civilized" man, he felt inordinately comforted by the pistol's presence.

Leslee kept up a light, engaging chatter as they closed in on State. He checked his watch. 11:04 A.M. Plenty of time. He asked her to drive around the enormous old building, and he surveyed vehicles, the building's doors, outdoor walls and walks, windows, everything and anything, looking for Bremner's people.

But was this necessary? How could Bremner possibly know he was coming here today, and at this time?

He couldn't. And yet, how had Bremner known about the documents and the undersecretary? No matter how thoroughly he'd gone back over his actions and precautions, he'd still not been able to figure out how Bremner had discovered what he was doing. But Bremner had a thousand ways to find out what anyone was doing. Maynard knew that now better than anyone.

He asked Leslee to drive around the building a second time. And then a third. There was no sign Bremner's people had staked out State. Maynard checked his watch. Still early. Good. A simple precaution, in case some miracle disclosed to Bremner at the last minute he should send his people here.

On Twenty-first Street, Maynard told Leslee to pull in before the wide paved area where an old WPA mural hearkened back to simpler times. A row of gleaming brass-and-glass doors stretched across the State building.

"Call me as soon as you can?" Leslee was anxious, and her usually bright blue eyes had a flattened look to them.

He kissed her lips, savoring the sweetness of her mouth.

"You taste wonderful." He gave her an encouraging smile and opened his door. "Don't worry." But he knew she would.

As he stepped up on the curb between concrete traffic posts, he looked up and his stomach went hollow.

In ten seconds he took it all in: At the top of the steps three men emerged from the shadows of State and walked briskly toward him. Their faces were hidden behind black sunglasses. There was an automaton air to them, a precision about their movements that chilled anyone who knew the training behind it. And Maynard knew. He recognized two of them—Bremner's operatives. They were directly between him and the doors he wanted to enter.

That bastard Bremner! Instantly Maynard went into action.

He tucked the shopping bag under his left arm, flung away the camera and binoculars, pulled out his gun, and spun around. He hurled a young man aside and tore back down the steps.

Twenty-five

Yes! She was there! Just as Maynard hoped, Leslee had waited to see him safely inside. Her car's engine was running while she stared up at him, her face chalky and strained.

"Maynard!" The voice boomed behind him. "Stop! Treasury!"

He ran faster, gravity pulling him as inexorably as his mistakes. ATF agents. It was almost funny. Even now Bremner covered his ass. He could do that so easily, because Tad Gorman, one of the secret board members, was now at Treasury, high up and powerful. The two would hide in each other's armpits.

But there was Leslee, waiting in her car. Her heart-shaped face grew larger and closer with each step. He was sweating terribly. It was his diabetes. His heart seemed to pound like a kettle drum. God, would it explode?

And then he was almost at the curb. Leslee leaned over and swung open the door. His head reeled.

"Hurry, Lucas!" Leslee beckoned.

He was shocked at how bloodless her little fingers were.

"Lucas, they're right behind you!" she cried.

Shots rang out. They bit into the concrete beside him and exploded chips up into the air. A bullet rammed through his left arm. The arm went numb. He dropped the documents.

He turned, squatted, and fired. It was as if he were back in the field again, a well-oiled machine.

Bremner's two men lurched back and fell, splattered blood-red.

The third man fired again. The shot hit Leslee's fender, a blistering sound so close it left Maynard momentarily deaf. He fired instantly, and the third man flew back as if in a movie stunt. Blood sprayed the air pink.

Were they all dead? Maynard didn't know, and he didn't care. Their bodies lay unmoving on the suddenly silent State department concrete. They were no more trouble to him.

Quickly he analyzed the situation. The Department of State. Should he try to go in now? Then he realized that was stupid.

Somewhere in the distance a siren wailed. He was in for it if he stayed. He had to find another way to get his information into hands that could keep him alive long enough to testify.

"Lucas!"

He ignored Leslee. His head swiveled as he made rapid decisions. No way was he going to get her involved. A car was pulling up behind hers. He'd take it.

He crouched and took a rapid step, the shopping bag and his gun in his right hand, his injured left arm dangling. That's when he heard two more shots and felt a terrible jolt, as if a truck had slammed into his back. Oddly, there was no pain. He looked around. Sid Williams was running toward him from across the street. Sid's pistol was raised in both hands, ready to fire again. Sid must've just arrived.

Damn fucking Bremner all to hell. He'd sent Sid Williams, and Williams had shot him in the back.

Maynard dropped to his knees, staring down at his own chest. The bullets had hit deep inside, making a pair of explosive rips. Red tissue and oozing blood formed a thick mat across his belly where the bullets had exited. He lifted his face to stare at Leslee. She was leaning toward him, trying to drag him into the car. Tears streamed down her cheeks.

He grunted out: "Go! They'll get your license plate number. I'm dead!"

He fell forward. His eyes closed, and he couldn't open them. Someone jerked away the shopping bag. Someone picked him up and dragged him back onto the sidewalk.

"Out of the car, lady!"

He heard sobs. Leslee. And then the squeal of tires and the stink of exhaust. But she was too late. They'd have her license number.

They'd find her. What a fool he was. He'd lost everything after all. The world was different, and he'd mislaid his place in it.

Hughes Bremner was called into the DCI's office at Langley only minutes after he'd received confirmation from Sid Williams of Lucas Maynard's death, which gave him no time to savor it. He had no doubt the DCI's summons was about Maynard; word traveled with ballistic speed in Washington, especially when the news was that ATF agents had publicly killed one of your own people in a drug bust right on the State department's steps.

He was sure the director knew nothing about why Maynard had died, or about Langley's connection to Sterling-O'Keefe, or about MASQUERADE, or about the imminent success of GRANDEUR on Monday. But Bremner was a prudent man, careful and cautious, and there was no hint of a smile on his patrician face as he entered Arlene Debo's office.

The first female director had been in office for a year, and the general consensus was she had bigger balls than most men. Her suite was on the elite seventh floor at Langley, the same floor as Bremner's, but her office had double the windows—two rows that met at a corner. Her view was so panoramic it seemed to extend all the way to the Lincoln Memorial. Of course, this was impossible, but the idea appealed to Hughes Bremner.

The two-room suite was decorated in antiques picked up as Debo had moved from office to office, rising in the National Security Agency and the Federal Bureau of Investigation. She was waiting for him behind her big mahogany desk, dressed in an expensive, tailored business suit. A square woman, smooth around the edges, she had gray hair, full cheeks, and an abundant chest. She gave the appearance of fluidity and solidity. A woman going places, but someone you could count on every step of the way.

When she gestured, Hughes Bremner took a seat in an armchair before her desk. Three large telephone consoles waited on a table beside her. Photos of her with the President, world leaders, and her family decorated the walls. On her desk stood stacks of striped folders with color-coded legends signifying the degree of sensitivity of the enclosed intelligence summaries from U.S. agents, assets, and satellites around the planet.

Arlene Debo's short forehead was wrinkled beneath her gray hair. "Can't you keep an eye on your people, Hughes?" she demanded.

"Good lord, Lucas Maynard was pushing dope! And we didn't even catch him ourselves. Embarrassing as all hell. What have you got to say about it?"

"Absolutely right, Arlene." Bremner nodded solemnly. "I put surveillance on Lucas a few days ago. I'd suspected something about him had changed." He never underestimated her. Not only was she occasionally liberal, she kept introducing reforms into Langley's well-greased wheels. She was dangerous.

The DCI said nothing. She glowered and drummed her fingers on her mahogany desk.

Bremner continued, "Lucas had a lonely life, and his diabetes depressed him. He was near retirement age. What did he have to look forward to? Our pensions are generous, but not enough for a man who spent money like water. We heard he used prostitutes. High-class, *very* expensive ones, for what he liked done. So he went into drugs. I sent out our men with the two from ATF to make sure the arrest was handled properly, but Lucas drew his weapon. Hell, he killed one of the Treasury people. It was almost as if he was begging to be killed himself."

The DCI pursed her lips. Again she said nothing. Bremner sensed she was trying to decide whether to discipline him for not overseeing his domain better.

But the DCI had more. She glowered again. "Why in hell haven't you contacted me about the Carnivore?"

"I have. There's nothing new. He and the woman have demanded to be brought in Sunday, and I've given orders to accommodate them."

Arlene Debo pushed a computer printout across her desk. It was the Carnivore's latest deciphered revelation: Five years ago the assassin had been hired to kill the president of Beni-Domo, a Japanese corporation that was also the world's dominant computer builder. The president's protégé had been Taru Mukogawa. It was he who had hired the Carnivore to kill the president, and when the president was dead, the younger man had taken over. Now Mukogawa was Beni-Domo president and chairman of the board. In Japan, where business was war, the cunning and ruthless Taru Mukogawa was considered the nation's most powerful businessman. Besides that, this week at his party caucus he'd announced his plans to run for Prime Minister.

Bremner had already read the deciphered message. It was good

intelligence but had no direct bearing on him, Mustang, MASQUER-
ADE, or GRANDEUR.

"Beni-Domo plays hardball," Arlene Debo rumbled. "For years
their executives have obstructed U.S. companies from going into
Japan. Every chance they get, they grab us by the short hairs." She
smiled, a crack in her stony exterior that revealed her savvy. "With
our balance of trade with Japan sucking big time, this information
was important for me to know instantly. It's leverage. When the
time's right, we'll tell Taru Mukogawa what we know, and you can
bet he'll make sure Beni-Domo—and Japan's Diet—give the United
States what we want."

What the DCI left unsaid, but Hughes Bremner realized, was she
could easily have overlooked this information in the intense activities of her day. It was Bremner's job to bring critical intelligence to
her attention, but he'd been distracted with MASQUERADE and Lucas
Maynard's disloyalty. Only by chance, because she'd spotted it herself, could she now take the information to the President and look
good. It gave the United States an edge, especially if Mukogawa
became Prime Minister. Someday it might even be leaked to the
press. A scandal to bring a competitor nation up short was sometimes just what the United States needed.

Bremner had made a mistake. The DCI leaned forward, and her
chin jutted. "Why in hell didn't you bring this to my attention? Are
you getting sloppy?" Her voice was icy, and Bremner sensed hazard-
ous shoals ahead. "I went out on a limb for you with the President
on the Carnivore business. He's still worried he'll hurt the ethical
tone of his administration by giving that murderous assassin sanctuary. He'd much rather the Carnivore go to one of the other bidding
countries. You know the agreement—"

"No leaks," Bremner said quickly and smoothly. "I guarantee it.
The press—the public—*no one* will ever know we're taking in the
Carnivore. It's all under control—"

"Is it? When you neglect to bring to my attention something as
basic as the Beni-Domo intelligence, I'm concerned. Don't give me
any reason to be unhappy, Hughes. Believe me, before I let you fuck
up the Carnivore's coming-in, I'll take it away from you, seniority or
not—"

"I get the picture, Arlene."

"Good. Memorize it."

□   □   □   □

Leslee Pousho could still see the scene in her mind, a slow-motion horror film: Lucas stumbling down the steps, the men in dark glasses relentless in pursuit, the shock of pedestrians and tourists.

The men firing.

Lucas firing in return, his bullets hitting them.

And then that other man shooting Lucas from across the street. Killing him.

Hot tears streamed down her face. She'd see that scene and hear those words the rest of her life. She'd never escape it, but she could stop the treachery that had corrupted Lucas and eventually killed him. Treachery that could still kill her.

She said his words aloud, "I'm dead . . . go. . . . I'm dead . . . go."

She hoped the sound would make her believe them. It had been no more than a half hour, and as she drove north from Washington she wanted him back with all the raw pain of fresh, appalling loss. Tomorrow when she'd begun to accept his death, she'd miss him even more. Next week, more than that.

But now she had to deal with the present, with what she had to do next. Lucas had told her to get out of there. Leave before they got her, too. He'd said they'd get her license number.

She passed a Gold Star Rent-a-Car outlet. She had to get rid of her car. As she gazed back at the rental agency in her rear-view mirror, she had a glimpse of her white, drained face and terrified eyes. She lit a Pall Mall and inhaled deeply.

She thought about Lucas. He'd been a man of contradictions, and that perhaps more than anything was what she'd found appealing about him. When she'd first met him, he'd been like a granite boulder—heavy, immovable, trapped beneath too much flesh and too many wasted years. Their relationship had started with a fight.

She'd told him the disease was our government. It operated on a premise of corruption. Trade-offs lined pockets. Deals served the deal makers first, the constituencies last, if at all. Our government lied to us, their willing, gullible public.

Lucas fought back, but he'd already begun to question his own life. She was a born reformer, and he wanted to be reformed. She had a fine mind, accustomed to short shrift from men, but he respected and was attracted to her intellect. He actually wanted to understand her.

This was all new, and she found herself drawn to him like a struggling flower to the spring sun. He showered her with tenderness and respect, and she forgot his age, his health problems, his career, and fell recklessly in love.

In the end, as he'd been dying, he'd worried more about her than himself. Dear Lucas.

A flood of tears streamed down her cheeks.

Angrily she wiped them away. She knew what she had to do.

She got off the George Washington Parkway and returned to it, heading in the opposite direction. She abandoned her car in long-term parking at Washington National Airport, rented a new Ford Taurus from the most convenient agency, Avis, and drove back to her apartment in Arlington. With luck, it would be days before Langley found her Volkswagen stored in the packed garage.

She patrolled up and down her street. She saw no one suspicious. She'd moved to this apartment only six months ago. She hoped a new address would be enough to delay Bremner from tracing her license plate immediately.

She parked behind the building and ran up the back stairs. Nervously she lit a cigarette. At last she unlocked the door. The apartment was empty, untouched. She pulled out a suitcase and threw in some clothes.

She wanted to scream. To run.

Instead she coolly put out her cigarette and closed the suitcase. She picked it up with one hand, and with the other she grabbed her briefcase. It was full from this morning. A morning that now seemed so long ago. A morning when Lucas had been alive. She'd kissed him and believed he'd soon be under the protection of State. Safe. Doing what needed to be done. And then they could be together forever.

Now he was dead, and she was running for her life. With her secret.

He'd had his secrets from her, and now she had one from him. She wished he knew: She'd been so appalled by Sterling-O'Keefe and MASQUERADE that early that morning, when Lucas had left to telephone State, she'd taken his secret documents to her office and Xeroxed them. All of them.

A copy was inside her briefcase. And no one knew.

She locked the briefcase and suitcase in the trunk of her rental car. Her eyes moved constantly, watching. She returned to the apartment for her laptop computer, portable printer, paper, pencils,

Rolodex, and groceries. She loaded everything into the Ford, got in, and nosed the car out of the parking lot.

Then she saw him. The man who'd killed Lucas. He was with another man, and they were cruising up the street in a worn Honda Accord.

She slid lower behind the steering wheel, grateful she'd had the sense to rent this car. They parked around the corner from her building and rolled out of the Accord. One headed up the building's front steps; the other strode down the walk toward the back.

She shook with a sudden palsy.

At last she got the car into gear and drove off, heading for Georgetown, where she stopped at a pay phone. She called her boss at the *Washington Independent* and set up a meeting in twenty minutes at a café near the National Gallery of Art. She knew the café slightly; her editor knew it not at all. That was best. It reduced the chances of either being seen by acquaintances.

"Why?" the editor demanded from the safety of her newspaper office.

Tears streamed down Leslee's cheeks as she thought once more of Lucas. Her voice shook. "I have a story we have to take public. It could get me killed."

Twenty-six

As morning light spread soft and pastel across Denver, Asher Flores drove and thought. Whom could he trust at Langley? He'd better stay away from anyone at covert ops. He wanted to help Sansborough find out what was going on with the Carnivore, and he wanted to warn Langley about Bremner. For a moment he felt the dreadfulness of Bremner's deceit. He'd admired Bremner and had affection for him. It wasn't easy to feel fondness for such a cold, intractable man. That made the treachery even worse.

"Who'd believe us if we took this to Justice or even to the President?" Sansborough was doing her own contemplating on the seat beside him. He liked the way she'd handled herself. She was a beginner, and killing was still a shock to her. He hated it himself. That's why he stayed out of black work. But this time he'd had no choice. Damn Hughes Bremner and Gordon Taite.

What in hell was Bremner up to?

"I doubt anyone at Langley, much less the President, would believe us," Asher said, watching traffic for tails. "Bremner's a long-time member of Langley's inner circle. He's got family connections up and down the East Coast. One of his cousins was Secretary of the Interior, and the last Vice-President is his wife's cousin. Then you figure Bremner's got medical proof you're loony. As for me, he's got my file under review because, as he said, I took field ops into my hands once too often."

"When are you going to tell me what you did that got you sent to the Ranch?"

"It was no big deal." He glanced at her from the corners of his eyes and returned to the subject at hand. "If you were in government, would you believe us?"

"We're hardly the most credible accusers."

"Exactly."

"I've got an idea, Flores. Let's go find the Carnivore and this extra 'Liz Sansborough' ourselves. Then we'll know what's really going on. There's something wrong about all this. You say Bremner's in charge of bringing in the Carnivore and me, yet Gordon said Bremner was grooming me to help capture him."

"True."

"So here I am, in Colorado, but I'm *not* in Colorado. I'm in Paris, an intermediary. It makes no sense. We need to know what Bremner's doing so we can give solid evidence to the DCI. . . . Or to the President. What do you say to Paris?"

Asher liked the way she thought. "I know a great artist here in Denver. Among her many talents, she does passports, driver's licenses, that sort of useful thing."

It would cost a fortune, $5,000 each, but the artist guaranteed secrecy and quality. She wanted the money up front, but Flores gave her what cash he had and told her she'd get the rest when they got the finished artwork. She snapped their photos and told them to come back at three o'clock.

Out in the pickup, Liz said, "From the look on your face, I assume you have a plan to finance this?"

"Absolutely. Let's switch places."

She drove around the block while he went into a janitorial supply shop. He came out wearing drab-green coveralls over his regular clothes. He carried a clipboard stacked with official-looking forms, and climbed back behind the wheel of the pickup.

"D'you still remember Taite's access code?"

She gave it to him. "What are you going to do?"

"Tell you later." He smiled mysteriously. "How about you?"

It was her turn to smile mysteriously. "Tell you later."

He dropped her at the public library at Broadway and West Thirteenth Avenue. The library was in the Denver Civic Center, where three square blocks of lawns and gardens also housed the Denver

Art Museum, the Greek Theater, and the Pioneer Monument. To
Liz, the parklike grounds and neoclassical architecture were refreshing reminders of humanity's accomplishments, especially important
after last night's motel of horrors.

Once inside the library, she went directly to periodicals. She got
copies of *Talk,* the magazine she'd written for under her cover
name, Sarah Walker. She paged through the previous eighteen
months. Sarah Walker's byline last appeared two months ago. Before that she'd had many bylines. At last Liz came to what she'd
hoped to find—a small, tasteful announcement of Sarah Walker's
promotion to senior contributing editor a year ago.

Liz closed her eyes and looked again.

Yes, there was Sarah Walker's photo. Not hers. There was the
small chin and the crooked nose. No beauty mark. She had not used
Sarah Walker as a cover, because if she had, *her* photo would be
there. Not Walker's.

With his computer-repair credentials and his official-looking green
coveralls, Asher Flores glanced at his clipboard and announced to
the sleek receptionist at the big branch bank on East Colfax he'd
come to make sure the bank's networking handshakes were working
properly. In a business where computers were constantly being
tinkered with and upgraded, the request was reasonable. The receptionist gave him permission to sit at the desk he'd indicated he
wanted—the one with not only a computer, but a check-writing machine.

While she took care of new customers, he used the computer to
create a fictitious account at the bank. Then he used Gordon Taite's
code to tap into the CIA slush fund Mustang maintained in Denver.
Last he transferred $47,500 from the slush fund into the fictitious
account. Going to Europe was expensive these days, especially if you
had to hide two sets of tracks.

He then ordered up five cashier's checks for $9,500 each from
the account, which cleaned it out. He slipped blank checks into the
machine on the desk, and it printed them out to the pseudonym on
one set of fake I.D.s he'd carried from the Ranch. He slipped the
checks beneath the forms on his clipboard, and he penciled some
boxes and made some notations on the top two forms as if he'd
accomplished something for the bank.

He reported to the helpful receptionist that all handshakes were now working properly, and he left. At the end of a deserted alley he stripped off his coveralls and buried them and the clipboard in a trash can. Once again in his boots, jeans, and Stetson, he was just a free-wheeling cowboy fresh off the range.

He went to five more banks, and at each he turned a cashier's check into $4,000 cash and the rest into traveler's checks, made out this time to the pseudonyms the artist was putting on his and Sansborough's passports and other I.D.s, in case Langley backtracked on the money withdrawals at the first bank. None of the banks challenged him; transactions under $10,000 didn't have to be reported to the federal government.

Next he visited a travel agency and bought two tickets, with seat assignments and boarding passes, for a flight that left early that evening for Paris. The tickets were also in the pseudonyms the artist was putting on his and Sansborough's passports and other I.D.s. He paid cash.

Then he repeated the entire transaction at a second travel agency for a flight to Copenhagen half an hour later.

He was feeling good. But then, anybody would feel mighty good with so much dough in his pocket. He shoved his thumbs down his waistband and whistled a little tune. Yup, a lot of dough and he was taking the most gorgeous female—emphasis on *female*—spy he'd ever met to Paris. He was feeling exceptionally good about that, too, until he walked past a newsstand.

There were huge three-column photos of him and Sansborough on the *Denver Tribune*'s front page. In color. At least five inches high. The headline seemed almost as high:

POLICE HUNT 2 MURDER SUSPECTS

He swallowed and pulled his Stetson lower over his face until it touched his sunglasses. His beard was scruffy, and he hoped it changed him enough that no one would connect him to the criminal on the front page of Denver's only afternoon daily. Flores bought the *Tribune* and turned to saunter away.

"Hey, mister."

His pulse pounding, Flores turned back. "Yeah?"

The old man at the cash register looked at the front page of the *Trib,* and then he looked at Flores. "Damned if you don't look like this guy. What is he—your brother?"

"What guy?" He played dumb, let the man explain about the

slaying of two out-of-town businessmen at dawn in one of Denver's more notorious "hell-tels." Other customers gathered around, discussed how much Flores resembled one of the murderers.

At last Flores glanced at his watch. "My wife! Now there's a real killer. I'll be dead in fifteen minutes if I don't get to where I'm supposed to meet her! Sorry, folks."

As he headed away, they laughed behind him. This time he'd escaped, but Bremner had lost no time making sure the local authorities knew who the killers were. Now not only Bremner, but the police and the state patrol were looking for him and Liz.

It was time to ditch the pickup. And that meant he'd need one of his other identities.

Fortunately he had a New York driver's license and a Gold Star Rent-a-Car credit card both in the same fake name, both created by private artists, not Langley's. That would take care of his immediate problems. With luck, he'd need no other I.D. Flores drove to an office of the huge car-rental agency, thinking grimly the airport would have been alerted, too, which meant getting past security and onto a jet would be next to impossible.

The young, ambitious assistant manager of downtown Denver's Gold Star Rent-a-Car outlet recognized Asher Flores immediately, despite his Don Johnson beard and sunglasses. This was because she had a nearly photographic memory and because she was acutely aware of her responsibilities now that she was to be promoted to manager of Gold Star in Littleton, a prosperous Denver suburb.

Of course, she expected him to have a fake I.D., because the central office had alerted her he would, although the pseudonym he was using hadn't appeared on their list. She guessed they'd probably told every Gold Star Rent-a-Car employee in the United States about him, and maybe in Europe and the Orient, too. The company was thorough.

In fact, they'd included the guy's photo and a warning he was dangerous. And since he was thought to be in the area, this morning the FBI had delivered tracking devices to every Gold Star agency in metropolitan Denver, requesting it be placed under the bumper of any car rented to Flores.

So as Flores filled out the rental contract, the assistant manager excused herself, went into the back to see to his car, handed over the tracking device to the service manager with an explanation, and returned to the front desk.

Her excitement only added to her natural enthusiasm. As soon as Flores left, she called the 800 number the FBI agent had given her. Such cooperation between the government and a private company impressed her greatly. She was proud to know she'd made a contribution to her country today.

Flores used the phone booth at the rear of the dark cocktail lounge to call the corporate headquarters of International A.M.-P.M. Catering, Inc., in New York. He asked for Abner Belden.

"This is Belden."

Asher said, "A lot bigger trucks in New York than in Sofia, aren't there, Pericles?"

"Asher? Jesus, where are you?"

"Denver, Abner. I need a favor."

"You've got it."

"This one you've got to trust me."

There was a pause. "Improvising in the field again?"

"Langley hasn't changed. Tightassed as ever."

Belden laughed softly. "Tell me what you want done."

Asher told him.

In the Denver library, Liz waited until the restroom was empty. Then she stood at the mirror and tried to see through the thick makeup to the face beneath.

Who was she? Who was she *really*?

Why had the dossier said Sarah Walker was her cover?

Her stomach churning, she tipped her face back and forth. Flores had said there was a resemblance between her and Walker, similar bone structure, but she didn't see it. Then she spotted something that made her chest tighten.

There was a narrow scar only an inch long beneath her chin.

She tilted her head far back to get a good look at it in the mirror. It was pale purple. White would have indicated she'd had it a long time. Purple meant more recent.

She dropped her chin and stared at herself in the mirror. There was something she should remember—

She returned to periodicals and found the *Talk* magazine in which Sarah Walker's last article had appeared. She flipped through the pages. Had she seen it? Yes, a quarter-page advertisement for the magazine. It heralded:

COMING ATTRACTIONS!
Facing the Future: To Cut or Not to Cut?
Our senior contributing editor, Sarah Walker, acquires a brand-new face with the help of cutting-edge cosmetic surgery. . . .

A brand-new face! Had she missed that article? She searched the issues up to the current one. No. The article had not been published, at least not in *Talk*. She turned to the front of the last magazine, found the telephone number, and memorized it.

She returned the magazines to the counter. Then she saw it: Her photo stared up from the front page of a newspaper. Fear turned her stomach upside down. She began to sweat. Next to her photo was one of Asher Flores. She glanced around. The periodicals librarian was on the telephone. One person stood at the desk, reading a magazine while waiting to ask a question.

She turned over the newspaper. Under it were two more papers, and each showed the same two mug shots. One reported:

> Elizabeth Sansborough, 32, and Asher Flores, 29, both of California, are sought as prime suspects in the robbery and brutal slayings of two out-of-town businessmen before dawn this morning in downtown Denver.
>
> Police say Sansborough and Flores are armed and dangerous. They report mounting a widespread effort to capture the two before more citizens are killed. . . .

Liz glanced at the librarian on the telephone and at the woman who was still reading her magazine. Liz picked up the newspapers and, as she strode out the door, she turned the photos inward, so her body hid them.

In the lobby she found a public telephone. She dialed *Talk* in Santa Barbara. The receptionist had a friendly voice. She transferred Liz to an editor.

Liz asked, "Can you tell me when Sarah Walker's article about her plastic surgery will appear?"

"Oh, that one. Sorry. It's been canceled."

"What happened?"

The editor sounded annoyed. "The writer got sick and couldn't fulfill the assignment. Terribly disappointing."

"I see. Did Sarah Walker go ahead and have the plastic surgery?"

"Of course."

"I'd like to get in touch with her."

"Sorry. She's away on family business. Besides we're not allowed to give out employees' addresses and phone numbers. Company policy."

She tried Santa Barbara information for a new phone listing for Sarah Walker. There was none. She hung up, her hand resting on the telephone receiver as she allowed herself to absorb the full impact of the news—

Sarah Walker had a new face.

Sarah Walker had dropped out of sight.

Liz Sansborough couldn't be both in France and in Colorado. Could the one acting as the Carnivore's intermediary be real, while the one in Colorado—she—was the fake?

The reluctant truth began to penetrate the opaque walls of disinformation that had imprisoned her. Liz Sansborough wasn't in two places at the same time.

Liz Sansborough was in Paris.

She wasn't Liz Sansborough.

She was Sarah Walker with a new face. The face of Liz Sansborough.

She was Sarah Walker.

She held onto the telephone, drenched in cold sweat. The dam to her past cracked open, and it swept over her in a powerful tide. Trembling, she recalled family trips to the Sierras . . . sunburned Aqua Camp at Santa Barbara beaches . . . sweaty bicycle rides with her brother, Michael . . . the aggravation of her father's help with math. She recalled the delicious aromas of the kitchen—Campbell's tomato soup, coffee brewing in the morning, bacon frying. Her mother's fingers, so gentle, as she stroked her face—

She leaned into the telephone booth where no one could see. She cried as her found heart grieved.

Part Three

Sarah Walker

Twenty-seven

Relieved, exhilarated, and furious, the tall, slender woman with the movie-star face and the lanky stride hurried through the Denver library to the entrance steps. Asher Flores was waiting in a rental car, a new Toyota Camry. She slid into the front passenger seat.

He said as he pulled into traffic, "Next stop is the forger's house. Don't pine for the old pickup, dearie. Time we changed our *modus operandi automobilius*. You know how it goes—" He glanced at her. His joking stopped. "Jesus. What happened?"

"I'm Sarah Walker."

"What?"

"You heard right."

He pulled to the curb, turned, and stared. He nodded once, and pulled back into traffic. "Okay. Let's have it."

"I'm not Liz Sansborough. She must be in Paris with the Carnivore. I don't know what I'm doing here, or why Gordon and Bremner need me so much. But I do know I'm definitely Sarah Walker, and those bastards have done one hell of a number on me."

"A journalist? You don't work for Langley?"

"Never. I do mostly celebrity profiles. Jimmy Stewart, Madonna, Jonas Salk, Hillary Rodham Clinton, Magic Johnson—"

Memories flooded her in an exciting bath of identity. She told Flores her first news job had been as a general-assignment reporter for the iconoclastic *Santa Barbara Independent*. Her big break had come three years later—show-biz pieces for *Los Angeles* and *California* magazines. Then Tina Brown, who'd been editing *Vanity Fair* at the time, had taken her on, a fresh voice from the wild and kooky West. That had led to assignments for *Talk*, one of the nation's two largest personality magazines. She'd become *Talk*'s top interviewer, and last year she'd been promoted to senior contributing editor, her fantasy job. At *Talk* her long-itchy fingers had found a home at last.

She'd never married or had children. Through the years she'd had several boyfriends and lived with one. Somehow her relationships seemed never to last. The men had blamed her, and perhaps they'd been right. The first serious one had been kind and simply told her she had a restless soul. In any case, she'd always felt the need to keep a suitcase packed.

She was born Sarah Jane Walker, the second child, the baby, which she'd minded only on occasion. Her older brother, Michael, was so interested in lizards, dinosaurs, Hot Wheels, football, and then girls, he'd given her little trouble.

Her father was Hamilton Walker, one of those warm, loving men all children need. Her mother was Jane Sansborough Walker, who'd grown up wanting to be a wonderful wife and mother—nurturing, encouraging, loving—and that's what she'd done.

There'd been only one problem in the Walker family, and that had been the unspoken history of each parent. It loomed over the children, a dark secret, casting uncertainty and insecurity.

Only when they'd grown did they learn Hamilton Walker had been put into foster care by his mother when he was four, and he'd never seen her again. He was shuttled from home to home, some good, some bad. He was physically abused in two, beaten and left to go hungry. Yet he'd put that rocky start behind him and made his own life. By the time Sarah was born, he was a respected professor of English at Santa Barbara City College, where he stayed until his retirement. Hamilton Walker loved his family, his students, and the life of an educator.

Jane Walker's father—Otto Sansborough—couldn't stand Hamilton, because he "lacked ambition," an abomination to Otto, whose entire life had been devoted to success and power. Otto was one of the West Coast's top litigators. A shark, Sarah had heard her grandfather called. A bandit, a thief, a swindler.

They were dead now, Sarah's grandparents. But her parents—
Jane and Hamilton Walker—were still alive, and her brother, too.

She had a family. She remembered telling Gordon—

They were in her condo in Santa Barbara. It was June, and Gordon
wasn't living with her. In fact, he'd just introduced himself. He'd
moved in downstairs the week before.

As she thought back she knew: Everything he'd told her about
their relationship had been a lie. They hadn't lived together two
years. They'd *never* lived together. But the story of their fictitious
coupling had cemented her bond to him.

On that June day she'd offered tea. He'd followed her into the
kitchen and insisted on making it himself. As he opened the new
Twinings can, she'd opened a letter from her parents. Return address: Cielo Tranquilo, Arizona.

As the kitchen air had filled with the tarry odor of the fresh black
tea, she'd told him, "They won an amazing retirement prize from
OMNI-American. So they cashed in their Santa Barbara real estate,
put most in the bank, and spent the rest on one of those lifetime-
care deals in a ritzy golf-club park in Arizona. The prize was they got
it for about ten percent of the usual price, which meant they could
afford it."

"They like it?"

"Love it. In fact, it's a kick for Mom. Her father was a high-
powered Beverly Hills lawyer, so she grew up rich. But then she
married Dad. He taught at city college, and her life-style plummeted
to real-folks level. So here she is, forty years later, making a come-
back at a tony retirement complex."

He laughed. "Ah, sweet revenge."

"Yes, and it's the only place I know where the average age and the
average temperature are the same." She smiled.

He laughed again, and she skimmed through the rest of her mail
—bills, junk, the usual invitations to "in" parties in Santa Barbara
and Los Angeles, common for a well-known profiler for a hot magazine, and a postcard from her brother, Michael.

"Michael's an anthropologist. He left last week for a big dig in the
Himalayas. He loves it. Everyone on the trip's Italian. He doesn't
have to talk English or bathe for months."

"Ugh. Better him than me. I like my showers, and only high-
school Italian teachers understand my Italian."

She'd noticed Gordon's eyes were brown. They matched his hair, a wavy mop. He'd needed a haircut, which she'd found endearing.

"Who else is in your family?" he asked.

"That's it. Well, I've got a cousin somewhere in England. I don't know much about her, and I've never met her." That was Liz Sansborough. The *real* Liz Sansborough.

Then the teakettle whistled. Gordon took the pot to the kettle, hotted the pot, added the tea leaves, filled the pot with boiling water, and topped it off with lid and cozy.

"Now, *I'm* impressed." She smiled. "You really do know how to make tea." Yes, he'd impressed her right from the beginning. He'd known exactly what to say and what to do. But that was the job of the secret agent. To ingratiate, to worm one's way in, to go covertly where it was impossible to go honestly.

"I don't know what happened after that," she told Flores as they drove through the Denver sunshine to the forger's studio. "I mean, I remember meeting Gordon, but that's all. He took me out to dinner, I think, and then—" She struggled, tried to recall, and said angrily, "I just don't know."

"We'll find out," he said. "What and why and who." He squeezed her hand. "What about your plastic surgery?"

"That was before Gordon. About six weeks before, I think—"

She had a new face, and it hadn't been what she'd expected. She'd stood before her bedroom mirror, studying herself. She was a stranger. Beautiful, but a stranger. The swelling had mostly disappeared, and she should resemble the sketches she and the surgeon had agreed upon.

She turned her stranger's face from side to side. The new nose was wrong. Instead of straight and narrow, which it was supposed to be, it sloped and flared. The chin and cheekbone implants were far more dramatic than she'd expected. There was no change in her mouth, of course. It was still too wide. Not a lot could be done about a mouth. Except the surgeon had put a black beauty mark just above the right corner. Very striking.

Dammit, she'd prepared herself for a quietly attractive face, not this flamboyant one. She looked like a goddamn movie star. Not the interview*er*, but the interview*ee*. Being the interviewer was far better; it gave the illusion of control.

Besides, after you've been considered on the plain side for three decades, you got used to it. Becoming attractive was rational. Gorgeous was dangerous. God knew where it might lead.

She turned from the mirror before she found more questions reflected in it. At her desk in the living room, she went to work on the article she was writing for *Talk* about her before-and-after face. What a deal. Free cosmetic surgery, and *Talk* paid her for the article, too. That's what happened when you had a name as a top writer for a top magazine: The famous, the infamous, and those wanting to be famous or infamous suddenly started stuffing unlisted phone numbers into your pocket.

She pushed all questions from her mind. It was time to be philosophical, because she sure as hell wasn't going to go through surgery again. She should consider this new face an opportunity, not a calamity. After all, what could be the harm in being beautiful?

Twenty-eight

As he drove east, Asher Flores nodded thoughtfully. "Hughes Bremner's gone to one hell of a lot of trouble to get you ready for whatever he's got in mind. It's got to be critical."

"That bastard. Could he have made me lose my memory?"

"Maybe you really did lose it. Accidentally, I mean. Maybe all this time you've had legitimate amnesia, and Bremner just took advantage of the situation. Or he somehow had to rewrite his plan to accommodate it."

"The fall down the cliff—or whatever—was after I met Gordon. Maybe that's why that part of my memory's still blank." She paused, thinking. "Could Bremner have set it up for me to get the free cosmetic surgery?"

"Sure."

"Obviously he wanted me because I'm Liz Sansborough's cousin, just as the Langley dossiers say. A few implants here and there, and I was her double. You know, I did a big cover story about survivalists for *Talk*. I spent a month training in one of their camps in Montana. That's why I knew how to fire the gun Gordon pushed at me, and probably why I adapted to the training at the Ranch so well. Plus I'm a work-out freak, which means I was in really good physical condition."

"Bremner would know all that. You can bet you were researched completely."

"But what does Bremner gain by having me a lookalike for the Carnivore's girl friend?"

"Good question. What do you know about Liz Sansborough? And I don't mean out of some file."

She considered. "Nothing. I mean, I know my mother had only one brother—Harold, 'Hal.' And I know he married, lived in London, and had a daughter my age. I never met any of them. And I don't remember letters from him, not even birthday cards. But he and Mom must've corresponded, or I wouldn't know what I do."

"Go on."

"Their mother, my grandmother Sansborough, was nice but sort of vacant. She used to bake cookies for Michael and me when Mom drove us down to visit her and Grandfather in Beverly Hills. She was Great-grandma Firenze's daughter. But, you see, Great-grandma Firenze lived in Santa Barbara, and she was the grandparent I saw all the time and really loved."

"And your Grandfather Sansborough, the Beverly Hills lawyer?"

"He was cruel, vicious. I remember once he took his shotgun and without a word shot the neighbor's Labrador retriever. No one knew the barking had bothered him. Later I got to thinking he must've chosen the shotgun because he'd wanted the dog to suffer a lot before it died. Mind you, he had perfectly fine rifles in his gun case, and he could've used any one of them for a clean kill. The police came, and the neighbors sued, but Grandfather knew where the skeletons were buried. Nothing came of it."

"Nice guy."

"Yeah," she said dryly. "Mom's a terrific person, and I got the feeling she still loved him. But she made it clear to Michael and me he wasn't the kind of adult to emulate. Maybe that's why she didn't keep up with her brother. Maybe Hal Sansborough turned out to be like his father."

"Could be. What happened to your Sansborough grandparents?"

"They died in a yachting accident. Their will left nothing to Uncle Hal or Mom. It all went to the University of Southern California. There's a chair at the USC law school in my grandfather's name."

"You're right. He did have dough."

"And no friends. He'd screwed them all. But his partners in the law firm 'loved' his clients and their whopping fees. I overheard Mom tell a neighbor the will made clear Grandfather was getting even with her for marrying beneath the family."

"Your father?"

"Mom got something better than money when she married him."
She grinned. "Now it makes sense why I thought of 'Hamilton'
when I had to come up with a word for cipher class, and why I felt so
happy afterward. What a great guy. But Mom and Dad have moved
to Arizona. That was about the same time my brother left for his big
dig in the Himalayas. He won't be back for months."

Flores said, "Could've been Bremner."

"What?"

"Removing your support system. Isolating you. Making you vulnerable to needing a new friend, like Gordon."

She grimaced. "Well, at least one good thing came out of this—
Mom and Dad are happy in their new place. It must be great to be
in love. I don't know how they do it after so many years."

"You consider love the better choice? Over money?"

"Don't you?" A wave of unexpected loneliness swept over her.

Flores said mildly, "Romantics don't live long in our business."

"Your business is *not* my business. Get that straight. I'm no spy.
I'm here only because I've been used."

"Yup. But you'd better start thinking of yourself as a tough, well-
trained spy, if you want to get out of this mess."

She pursed her lips, flooded with fury. She wanted to grab the
wheel from Flores and ram the car into the nearest building. She
wanted to smash her fist through the dashboard and rip out the
engine. She wanted to put a bullet through Gordon's head and
Bremner's heart. She wanted—

She stopped, shocked at the rage that boiled just beneath her
modulated voice and quietly folded hands.

Damn Hughes Bremner and his black heart for what he'd done.

She inhaled sharply. "Cynics lead lonely lives, Flores. I'd like to be
happy someday." She stared ahead, willing the fury to subside.
"Anyway, that's what I remember about my family, the clean and the
dirty linen. Let's try looking at it from the other end again. What
does Hughes Bremner gain by having me look like the Carnivore's
girl friend?"

"Maybe Liz Sansborough's shaky or wants to quit being his intermediary. Maybe she's sick and can't hold on."

"Maybe Bremner—or Langley—doesn't trust her."

"Whatever it is, the stakes have to be sky high for Bremner to try
to murder us, and to use Langley resources to do it."

She paused. "We know Gordon's in on it. And Bremner, and the two we killed. Is all of Langley after us?"

"Looks like it," he said somberly. They drove past western restaurants and tall office buildings. "So, Sansborough—"

He stopped, glanced at her.

"That's okay, Flores. It's going to be tough for a while, but you've got to start calling me by my real name."

Sarah Walker. She played with it in her mind. With sudden clarity she remembered writing it on school papers. Schools, yes! Monte Vista Elementary, La Colina Junior High, Santa Barbara High, UCSB. She could name most of her teachers and old friends. Thiel Rivers! What had happened to her best friend, Thiel? There was something she should remember about Thiel. . . . Something recent—

"Okay," Flores said. "Walker, we've got trouble. Bremner's thorough. He'll alert every agency from the FBI on down."

"We have to move fast."

"We will." He handed her $5,000 in cash.

"Hey! Did you rob a bank?"

"You could say that." He described his work with the bank computer.

"That's why you needed Gordon's code."

"Couldn't use my own." He glanced at her from the corners of his eyes. It was a look both shy and sly. "A few months ago I requisitioned a lot of dough to cover an operation I'd set up in Monte Carlo. The dough was casino bait for two Korean entrepreneurs who'd stolen specs to one of our breakthroughs—an antenna so small it's the size of a grain of sand. Problem was, the Koreans won big at the tables. In fact, they won $4 million, and all of it was Langley's. I collected enough evidence to send them to the slammer forever, but they skipped to Korea and took their goddamn winnings with them."

She laughed. "So Bremner exiled you to the Ranch."

"Yeah. And my code won't transfer funds anymore. I'm supposed to get his approval first." He laughed, and the car filled with his exuberance. He'd outwitted Hughes Bremner.

She was amazed he could be so lighthearted with the police, FBI, and CIA all breathing down their necks. He was like one of those old outlaws of the Wild West. But then, that's what she was now, too, whether she liked it or not. An outlaw.

He drove around the artist's studio several times. At last they decided it was safe.

He went in and she slid behind the wheel, motor running, on guard, her senses sharply tuned as she watched pedestrians and vehicles. Why had Bremner given her Liz Sansborough's face? Why had he sent her to the Ranch to be trained? Was he really trying to capture the Carnivore, or was the Langley dossier correct when it said the assassin wanted to come in?

All roads in this entangled, violent mess seemed to lead back to Hughes Bremner. Whatever he planned, the stakes were so high he was willing to risk everything to make it work.

She stiffened behind the Toyota's wheel. Flores was right, to survive she'd have to integrate Liz Sansborough's training into Sarah Walker's personality. But she resisted. Keeping the two separate seemed somehow vital. She not only desperately wanted to resolve this mess, she wanted to return to her old life, pick up the pieces, and figure out what to do so she—Sarah Walker, not Liz Sansborough—could find some happiness.

At last Asher Flores reappeared on the steps of the artist's studio. He gazed around and sauntered across the street. He got into the passenger side of the front seat, and she drove away.

"She did a good job," he told her. "This should see us through most anything."

He showed her passports, driver's licenses, and VISA cards. The passports not only looked real, they were real. The artist had bought stolen ones and used her fine hand to make the necessary changes. Both the Colorado driver's licenses and the VISA cards were fake. Although they looked perfect, the VISA cards would be unusable anywhere a clerk checked for charge approval. But they looked real and so confirmed the rest of the new identification. Flores was now Eric Hoffman, and Sarah was Julia Fasick.

As Flores directed, she turned the Toyota northeast toward Denver International Airport. As they approached the mammoth airfield, one big jet after another roared in low for a landing.

"Airport security must know about us, Flores." She glanced at him. "How in hell are we going to get past them?"

"We're covered." With a flourish, he slapped an employee identification sticker onto the car's front window and directed her to pull into an employee lot.

She parked, and they got out. He opened the trunk and took out navy chino trousers, navy caps, and loose white shirts.

"Put 'em on," he said. "And here's your employee I.D. badge. We'll leave our Stetsons here. If we wore 'em in Paris, we'd stick out like the dumb Yanks we are. But in jeans and shirts, we'll fit right in."

"Uniforms? Where did you get these?"

"Made a little stop on the way to pick you up. The uniforms are real, and we're now employees on the books of International A.M.-P.M. Catering, Inc."

As they quickly stepped into the big trousers, she asked, "How'd you ever manage that?"

"The pal I told you about is a V.P. in the head office. At Langley we teamed a lot, and I saved his ass once in Sofia. So I called him in New York, and he called the manager here, told him to do whatever I asked. CIA, national security."

"Will your V.P. friend check with Langley?"

They pulled on the loose white shirts and snapped on their matching navy-blue caps and their badges.

"Not Abner. He's no fan of Langley, and he knows me."

"We're not going through the terminal?" She took off her plastic earrings and tugged her short black hair out from under her cap until it straggled over her face and sunglasses.

"Nope. Don't have to."

"The badges will get us past security on the field?"

"Like ghosts. The FAA treats employees different from passengers. Employees don't have to be searched or pass through metal detectors. So only the ones who go through the terminals to get to the airfields have to be checked."

"You're amazing, Flores." She was impressed and relieved.

They surveyed the parking lot. He grabbed his gym bag, and she took her day pack. Her Beretta was heavy inside. He slid the thick folder into his gym bag and zipped it up.

"There's a nice maintenance field ahead," she said. "Is that for us?"

"You bet. Our badges have magnetic strips that get us through the gate's mechanical scanner. The badges are our key to restricted areas. The airport department issues 'em. Come on."

They walked briskly, and Sarah shook her head. "If I were a passenger, I'd be worried. How does the airport protect the public from crazy employees bringing in guns? Like us?"

"In the first place, lots of employees don't work for the airport authority. They're like my friend, employed by private contractors. They handle bags, clean planes, do all kinds of things. To require 'em all, especially the ones who have to run around a lot, to go through magnetometers or be searched every time they pass check-points would bring airport operations to a screeching halt. So to protect the public, the FAA conducts spot-checks. Likewise, security agents for the airport department patrol with portable computers that verify employees' badges. But since you and I are registered with International A.M.-P.M., we'll pass all badge tests with flying colors."

"You have an amazing amount of information floating around in that brain of yours."

"Yeah. And I'm modest about it, too."

She chuckled as they approached the unmanned gate built into the perimeter fencing. Then a car squealed to a stop behind them. She and Flores whirled. It was Gordon. Armed, and with three more agents.

"Let's go!" Flores snapped. Instantly they pivoted and raced toward the airport gate. Behind them they heard shouts and pounding feet.

Twenty-nine

Asher Flores reached the gate first and squatted down with his gun drawn, covering Sarah as she pushed her badge through the scanner. Gordon, a woman, and two other men were closing in. Her heart pounded as she pulled out her Beretta. Then the gate clicked open, she jumped through, and Asher slid after her.

Gordon shouted, "Liz, wait!"

It was one of his typical self-assured commands.

She leveled her weapon through the steel-mesh fence. The late-afternoon sun shone down, hard and flinty. Gordon and his people froze, impressed by her Beretta and Flores's Gunsite Service Pistol. In the parking lot, some startled airport employees gathered, frowning, unsure.

Gordon stepped toward the gate, smiling. "Come back with me, Liz, and we'll forget all this crap. Both of you. We've all made mistakes, but we can straighten them out at the Ranch."

He stopped when she cocked her Beretta. She liked the idea Gordon was afraid of her.

"You've got an important date with the Carnivore, Liz," he continued, his voice serious. "We haven't finished getting you ready for it."

Flores spoke low. "We've got to get out of here."

"I know."

Behind them were maintenance and storage buildings, and beyond those big jets taxied in and out of the terminal. But before they made a run for the one that would fly them to Paris, there was something she had to understand.

She made her voice small and needy. "I don't know what to do, Gordon."

"Come back, Liz. Finish your training. Resume your career with the Agency." He stood there like a sexy gun advertisement—long sturdy legs, muscular chest, wind-blown hair, face as honest as the Fourth of July, gun firm as he faced the enemy. Her.

She asked, "What about the Carnivore?"

"You'll be ready for him, Liz. I promise."

"But Gordon, I'm not Liz Sansborough. She's in Paris. I'm Sarah Walker." She waited for him to deny it, but he said nothing. The expression on his face remained unchanged, an impenetrable mask. She said, "Why would the Carnivore want me?"

"Because he thinks you saw him. I told you about that."

"That was Liz Sansborough. Why would he want to kill *me?*"

"Jesus Christ, Liz! You've got it backward. You're remembering your *cover* story. That background about Walker was made up to protect you from the Carnivore, and you *memorized* it. You're Liz Sansborough! Come back to me, darling. Together, we'll get that assassin." His voice softened. "Besides, I miss you." No wonder he'd fooled her so long. He was damn good.

Flores moved closer to her. "I'm gonna be sick right here. I'm gonna puke on the tarmac, on you, and definitely on Gordon. Can't you hurry this up?"

"Shut up!" she snapped. Then, to Gordon, "How will we find the Carnivore?" She wanted a clue, a hint to take with them.

"There's a place—" He was interrupted by one of his men.

"Damn!" she muttered.

Gordon and the man spoke intently. In the parking lot one of the distant airport employees was hurrying back to an office building, probably to call airport security or the police. One way or another the authorities would converge soon, and they'd believe Gordon and his credentials, not her and Flores.

Gordon stepped closer to the gate. "My colleague's just reminded me we're on a tight schedule. You don't want to shoot me, darling. Come with us. This is your last chance. I've never failed you, and I won't this time." He swung his pistol nonchalantly from her to Flores and back again. Gordon wanted them alive, especially her, and he was pushing her, forcing her to make a choice he believed must be in his favor.

His entreaty was so earnest, she actually felt herself weaken. With sudden insight she realized there was a fragile part of her that wanted to trust him, wanted to do whatever he asked, just as before. How comforting to have someone else guarantee her future, her life.

"Nice try, kid," Flores told her, "but it's no go. You aren't going to find out a damn thing."

She nodded. "We'll make a break for that first shed. They don't want to kill us, not yet anyway, but they'll wing us if they have to. We better make lousy targets. Ready?"

"Ready, Walker." Flores grinned.

She yelled through the wire-mesh fence, "Gordon, you're a lying son of a bitch! Someday somebody's going to shut you up with a stake through your mouth!"

She and Flores tore off in an erratic zigzag pattern. Gunshots sprayed the tarmac. Chips of asphalt sliced through the hot, humid air, stung their legs, and blasted high against their hands and faces.

They dove into the cover of the shed, rolled, and returned fire. Gordon and his people took cover behind the fence. Sarah and Flores ran again, to the next building. Suddenly she realized there were only three guns firing at them.

"Flores, where's the fourth?—"

They turned. Behind them the fourth gun—the woman—ran out from between two gasoline trucks. She spread her legs for balance and pointed an ugly Uzi at Flores's heart.

"My orders say I can kill you, Flores." Her voice was frosty. "Go ahead. Take another step. Try me. Please."

Around them rows of gas trucks and irregularly placed sheds and warehouses dotted the airport tarmac. The roar of many jets hummed in the distance. A lone driver, close enough to see what was happening, slid from his big gas truck and tore away.

Flores looked as if he was going to try to jump the woman. Already Gordon and the two other men had come through the fence and were on top of them. Fear churned Sarah's belly. She wasn't going back with Gordon.

"Bitch!" Gordon knocked her Beretta away, grabbed her arm, and, lightning fast, palm-slapped her on one cheek and back-handed her on the other. Her face blazed with pain. She refused to touch it.

"Charming as always, Gordon."

His actor's mask dissolved in violent and irrational rage. He yanked back her arm. "I understand you, whore. You're fucking Flores. Round-heeled bitch. *I* made you. You're *mine.* I won't let you screw up the operation. Whores like you are always coming between men!"

Gordon spun on his heel, fury overwhelming his judgment, and shot an elbow at Flores's belly. But Flores was fast. He slid back, grabbed the elbow, and threw Gordon back. The other male agents jumped in to help, and for an instant the woman watched.

It was the opening Sarah wanted. She slammed her fist into the woman's belly and, when she doubled over, karate chopped the back of her neck. The woman dropped motionless.

Flores kicked high into the face of one of the men, and he toppled backward.

"Get her out of here!" Gordon ordered the last standing man.

Gordon tackled Flores, and the third man grabbed Sarah's arm to drag her back to the gate. She jammed her foot behind his knee and used his momentum to throw him sideways. Astonished, he hit the ground hard with a loud grunt that emptied his lungs.

Sarah scrambled to retrieve her Beretta. She covered the downed woman and two downed men, while Flores and Gordon rolled on the blacktop. Flores shook free enough to dislodge an arm. He crashed his fist into Gordon's jaw. Gordon lay dazed, and Flores slammed a fist into him again. Gordon lay still.

Sarah continued to cover as Flores gathered weapons.

"Fucking traitors," one of the men growled.

"The only traitors are Gordon and Bremner," Sarah said.

"Tell that to Beno and Matt!" the woman snapped. "Gordon and Bremner didn't kill them at that crummy motel. *You* did."

Flores shook his head at Sarah. "All they know is the party line." He made the two men carry Gordon into a hot, dim shed and then he had them take off their belts and shirts. As Sarah covered, Flores used the belts to tie the two men's hands behind them. He ripped off one shirt sleeve and tied the woman's hands, too, while Sarah ripped up the rest of the shirts. Then Flores used the strips to tie Gordon's hands and the feet of everyone, and he gagged them.

Sarah emptied their pockets into her day pack. She took everything, unwilling to leave behind even the most remote clue to what
was really going on in Washington and Paris.

At last he stood and rubbed the muzzle of his pistol under his
scraggly jaw. He was studying Gordon. "We should get rid of him,
Walker. He's a killer, a loose cannon. That was a revealing temper
tantrum back there. He's fixated on you, and he's not going to quit
until he catches you . . . or kills you."

"Could be."

"If you can't do it, I will."

Gordon's eyes fluttered. He was waking up. She studied his square
face beneath the tousled brown hair. Unconscious, his emotions
were free to reshape his features. The slight realignment was like a
shift in the earth, and what she saw in the fissure was brutality and
guile.

She could let Flores kill him. Gordon had harmed her terribly,
perhaps more than she'd ever know, because she recalled nothing
of her transformation to Liz Sansborough. And what about the
barely controlled anger she'd just discovered boiling inside her? It
was for him, for Bremner, and for what they'd done to her. Killing
Gordon would be revenge, satisfying—

She became aware Flores was waiting. The shed was stifling. She
was dripping sweat. She looked at the two other men and the
woman, who lay like trussed mannequins. They glared back, silent
behind their gags. They would have killed Flores and maybe her,
too, but that was different, because they knew they were right. Certainty made choices simple . . . inevitable.

In the distance a siren began to scream.

"No," she decided. "I don't have a crystal ball. I can't kill someone just because he might kill me."

"It's a mistake, Walker."

"Maybe. But it's a mistake I'm going to make because I can't live
with the other choice. Liz Sansborough would probably kill him.
Sarah Walker can't. Let's get out of here."

Gordon's eyes opened at last. He'd heard and understood. His
gaze shot hatred at her. It reminded her of an old Chinese proverb:
Do someone a favor, and they'll never forgive you.

She and Flores dragged the trussed agents into a corner of the
storage shed, checked their knots, and stacked a wall of heavy boxes

in front of them to hide them from the door and anyone who wandered into the shed.

Out on the tarmac, Flores padlocked the door. The siren grew into a screech. They paused, located the sound, and sprinted toward the long rows of giant jets.

Thirty

Sarah and Asher Flores ducked behind a garage. The siren blared toward them, but if they tried to run, they'd expose themselves. She pressed back into the wall, Beretta tight in her hands. Her face ached from Gordon's vicious slaps.

The ear-deafening wail passed in a sudden downshift of intensity. "It's going to the perimeter gate," she decided.

"Yeah." Flores wiped an arm across his sweaty forehead.

They dashed toward a warehouse. High on its front was painted in navy-blue letters, the same color as their trousers, jackets, and caps: INTERNATIONAL A.M.-P.M., INC. They paused in the doorway of the cavernous building. Employees dressed in similar uniforms pushed dollies filled with canned goods and baking supplies toward a stainless-steel kitchen, visible through two open doors near the back.

A short, heavy man swore at them. "Jesus, where the hell you been? I thought I heard shootin'—"

He was the local manager who'd been instructed by Abner Belden to ask no questions, help them board the Paris jet, and then keep his mouth shut. National security.

"Never mind," Flores said quietly. "Get us to the plane."

"Hell, I already had to send the provisioning truck out. Otherwise the goddamn planes don't get loaded. The next—"

"All right. We'll take another. Do it."

The man scratched his head and led them to a large truck whose empty van lay on a collapsed scissor lift. He got behind the wheel,

Sarah and Flores climbed in, and they were off. As the thunder of jets grew louder, the manager handed out ear protectors. They passed rows of 747s and DC-10s.

"This is the 747 for Paris," the manager shouted.

"Second change in plan," Flores yelled back. "The Copenhagen plane."

"Flores—" Sarah began.

He shook his head.

The manager studied them, curious. Then he shrugged. "Your rules." He stopped at another 747. "Copenhagen plane." The trio rode the scissor lift up to the galley. The manager held out his hand. "This is it. I'll give the attendants the story. Good luck on whatever the hell you're up to."

Flores said, "Third change. You're coming with us."

The manager's heavy-lidded eyes widened.

Flores stepped close. "This is for your own protection. That shooting you heard was from assholes who won't give up, and they'll find you. They won't be nice. Tell the attendants there's an emergency in Copenhagen, and you have to deadhead over. You've done that before, right?"

The manager swallowed. His eyes were suddenly scared. He stepped inside and explained he was briefing two new subordinates who were flying to Copenhagen to see how A.M.-P.M. operated from the other end.

Sarah spoke in Flores's ear. "What the hell's going on?"

"One way or another, Gordon and his pals are going to get free, and then they'll be all over the airport," he whispered. "Gordon saw our uniforms. He'll figure my trick, follow us through A.M.-P.M., and have Bremner's people waiting for us at the Paris airport. Our only chance is to throw 'em off now."

She smiled. "There are lots more ways to enter Paris by land than by air."

"Yup." He grinned. "That's the backup plan."

As the manager convinced the attendants of his need to go to Copenhagen, she told Flores, "I'll park the truck. There's an employee staircase outside I can use to come back up through the terminal." She slipped her Beretta into her shirt and rode the scissor lift down. She drove the truck to an empty spot near a different jet and nonchalantly inspected the tarmac and the windows of the terminal above as she moved up the stairs and through a door into the boarding area.

Across the waiting room, two Denver police officers were studying the crowds, perhaps looking for the two rogue CIA agents who'd killed the two men at the downtown motel. She walked on, efficient, businesslike in her catering-employee disguise. But as she closed in on the door that led to her jet, she had a horrifying vision: She could lure the two police officers back into one of the deserted service hallways or a supply closet, and she could put bullets through their heads.

It would be a simple matter. An ambush. Two police officers dead. She knew how to do it.

Her temples pounded, and a wave of nausea engulfed her. Murder was unthinkable, and yet she'd thought it, found herself automatically planning it. What was happening to her?

Neither officer paid particular attention as she passed by the flight attendant and entered the long passageway to the Copenhagen jet. In the galley, she stepped out of her uniform. Then she found Flores and fell into the empty seat beside him. He was back in his regular clothes, too. The manager was sitting just ahead, where they could watch him.

As the great jet at last roared down the runway and its wings caught the air, he took her hand and squeezed it.

"Why?" He looked closely into her face.

She knew he was asking why she'd refused to kill Gordon Taite.

She gazed out the small windows of the big jet as it gained altitude. "Ever read Abraham Maslow?"

"Don't think so."

"He was a groundbreaking psychologist and educator," she said. "I studied him in college. His book *Toward a Psychology of Being* gave me some insights into our nature, we human beings, and it helped me understand what kind of person I wanted to be."

"So what did Maslow say?"

"That the science of psychology traditionally studies neurotic and psychotic people. In other words, sick people. So he and some colleagues set out to study happy, productive people. What they found was fascinating and very different from the thinking of a lot of modern-day psychology."

"And that was?"

"The search for values is a crucial part of our nature. After our basic needs for food, water, and shelter are met, we want excellence, justice, beauty, truth, compassion, fulfilling work, that sort of thing."

"The crud I deal with, truth and compassion are the last things they think of. Fulfilling work? Forget it. All they want to fill is their pockets."

"I know. Maslow says that's what happens when people deny, or are forced to deny, their true inner natures. Karen Horney, another psychologist, says every time we do something wrong, something we feel guilty about, it 'registers' inside us, and every time we do something good and honest, it 'registers,' too. In other words, each of us unconsciously keeps our own private scale of justice. It eventually weights itself in one direction or the other, for good or for evil, and as a result we either like and admire ourselves, or we despise ourselves and feel worthless and unlovable. Then we behave accordingly. You know, a self-fulfilling prophecy."

"Gosh, criminals feel unlovable. Gee whiz."

"Go ahead and sneer, Flores. You can spot the disease, but I'll bet you haven't a clue what the world would be like if we were all living fulfilling lives."

"Can't happen to Homo sapiens. We're a warrior species."

"Wrong. That's ancient history, our primitive past. The search for excellence and altruism *is* our nature, and if we survive long enough, it'll be our future."

"Tell that to Langley and the people at the Ranch. Tell it to yourself. Now, with what's happened to you."

She frowned. "We're still psychologically evolving, so it's tough for us to envision the kind of remarkable world we could create. But even though we can't see it, we have to trust that it's possible. We have to keep trying. For me, that means because I look like Liz Sansborough, I've got to protect myself. That's a basic instinct, too, idiot. Self-preservation."

But it wasn't self-preservation she'd felt a few minutes ago. It was as if a thunderbolt had struck and forced her to face how easily she could use her new skills: Entice. Kill. Escape. And that she might enjoy it.

She'd always lived a safe existence. Despite her many interviewing trips to major cities around the world, she'd never had even her purse stolen. Her words to Flores said one thing, while her mind recoiled at *her* potential.

Flores smiled. "Glad to hear it. I think you, Maslow, and Horney are batty. However, I'll offer one little observation. You've been worried about what kind of person you are. In a sense, Gordon raised you. You should be like Gordon, but you're not. If the situation had been reversed, he'd have shot us at once. Doesn't that tell you a lot about who you really are?"

"Maybe I'm a lot more like Gordon than you think."

He laughed. "Not likely."

Yesterday she would have found solace in his words. But this morning she'd killed a young man, shattered his cranium with a perfect bull's-eye shot, and then this afternoon she'd looked at the two policemen in the terminal and known she had the skill and perhaps the will to execute them, too.

She closed her eyes. No. She couldn't be that kind of person. She wouldn't allow it!

She looked into Flores's warm black eyes. In them she saw something rare—genuine kindness. Crazy Flores was a kind man. And yet he was a complete professional, hard, ruthless when he had to be. And he'd probably been right about killing Gordon. But for her, that would have been like leaping off a cliff into a wretched, bottomless void. She was proud she'd resisted. In the end, it was not what you felt but whether you acted on it that mattered. She hoped the difference between Gordon and her was the difference between those who believed in the future and those who wanted to despoil it. Now she must be wary of herself, wary that she could follow in Gordon's toxic footsteps.

"Flores, are you a typical Langley operative?"

He grinned. Then he saw she was serious. "One of the tests I had to take was the old square-peg-in-a-round-hole routine. They thought they had me. Most of the pegs were too big."

"So what did you do?"

He pulled out his pocket knife. "They were wood. I shaved the damn things until they fit."

She laughed. His black eyes danced.

The seat-belt light flicked off overhead, and passengers unsnapped themselves and moved around the cabin.

"At last." She reached for her day pack, which she'd slid under the seat ahead of her.

"Good. Let's see if we got anything useful."

She'd put each of the four agents' belongings in separate places in the pack. None had carried much, a tradecraft rule when on a job. She took Gordon's things, while Flores took the woman's.

There was Gordon's billfold with $521 cash, a Virginia driver's license, and one VISA card. He also had car keys for the Buick in which he'd arrived at the airport; a coin purse with 79 cents; his favorite Cross ballpoint pen, which he'd been using as long as she remembered knowing him; and a bag of peanuts.

"Not much here." She was disappointed. She made a small pile of the items next to her feet where it was less likely to attract attention and reached for one of the other men's belongings.

"Nothing here either." Flores sounded equally disappointed. He collected the last man's things to inspect.

When they'd finished, they had four small piles that included the usual fake driver's licenses and credit cards, plus a pack of Rolaids, a Brian Garfield paperback, an opened pack of Winston cigarettes, and the woman's small makeup kit.

Flores sighed. "Guess it's time to get down to the nitty gritty."

He opened an airline vomit bag on his lap and shredded the first cigarette. As loose tobacco and tattered white paper fell into the bag, Sarah reached for the makeup kit to examine it more closely, then stopped.

Instead she picked up Gordon's car keys. "I suppose this could be a coincidence, but look where he rented his Buick." She held out the keys with their Gold Star Rent-a-Car tag. "Remember the car Matt Lister and Beno Durante had at our motel? It was from Gold Star, too. And—" She struggled. "I know, somehow another Gold Star car figured in with Gordon and me back in Santa Barbara before I lost my memory." She grappled more, but the memory wouldn't come to her. Stymied, she looked at Flores.

He was frowning. "Jesus. Maybe that's how he found us."

"What?"

"He could've ordered tracking devices and our photos passed to the Gold Star agencies in Denver, figuring we'd have to switch cars and that renting was safer than stealing."

"There are Gold Star agencies everywhere. He just plain out-thought us. And then he got lucky."

"Not us. *Me.*" He was angry. "Why didn't I leave well enough alone?"

"It was the right decision, just the wrong agency. Look, by then they probably had an all-points bulletin out on our pickup."

His black, disturbed gaze turned on her, and she smiled.

"Yeah," he said. "First thing in Paris, I'll check out Gold Star, see if there might be a connection to Bremner."

"Good." She picked up Gordon's silver Cross pen. In Santa Barbara and at the Ranch, he'd written everything with it. She could see him in her mind bent over his spiral notebook, recording intently, preparing yet another report to be faxed back to Hughes Bremner. Inwardly she shuddered.

What was it about this pen? She examined it. There was tiny lettering engraved on the side.

Asher asked, "Does it say something?"

"Je Suis Chez Moi."

"Your accent stinks. Let me." He read quickly. "It means, 'I am at home.' "

She repeated the translation. "What is it, a code?"

"Could be." He scrutinized the pen, took it apart, put it back together, and returned it to her. "It's an expensive pen. Maybe it was a gift from one of Gordon's lovers. You know, dahling—" He rolled his eyes and waggled his bushy black eyebrows. " '*Ah am at home.*' Come up and see me sometime!"

She smiled, but stuck to business. "This pen is very expensive, and the lettering is discreet. It's engraved, which means the phrase is intended to be permanent. And the first letter of each word is capitalized, like a title."

"So what do *you* think it means?"

"You've got me. But for something French and secretive, especially if it involves scandal, I know just the guy to ask."

"In Paris?"

"Yes, a colleague."

They were over Canada now, and turbulence rocked the jet. She wondered whether Gordon was free yet. It was only a matter of time. Despite all Flores's work and skill, Gordon—and Bremner—would eventually trace them to Paris. Like a past that haunted, Gordon would follow. In fact, he *was* her past, one she desperately wished she'd never lived.

She looked down at her day pack, once again under the seat before her. In it was her Beretta, her lethal friend. Now she had three killers to fear: The Carnivore, Gordon, and herself. She was unsure whether the Carnivore really wanted her—"Liz Sansborough"—dead, but he might. She knew Gordon wanted her, one way or another. Who would find her first?

And what would she do when he—or they—did?

She held Gordon's pen tight in her fist. She had to stop him and Bremner from whatever plan they had that was causing so many deaths. She refused to feed the grim, outraged part of herself that yearned for revenge. No, she believed in redemption, even though she knew there were those who could never reform, would never change, who would wallow forever in their personal cesspools of injuries and sick dreams.

To heal that empty place next to her heart, she had to go on. She had to know what had happened and why. And then she had to stop Bremner and Gordon.

Thirty-one

Chantelle Joyeaux massaged exotic eucalyptus oil into Prime Minister Vincent Vauban's shoulders and chest, lingering over the well-developed trapezius and pectoral muscles. The poor man was exhausted from *les troubles,* which had cursed France almost from the moment of his swearing-in last March. She felt deep sympathy for him. Also a great deal of respect for his fine body.

The Prime Minister was fifty-five years old and beset by rising unemployment and a worsening recession, but he maintained the robust physique and vigorous attitude of a man in his thirties. Only his hair showed the stress; it was snow white, which to Chantelle's eyes made him look even more distinguished. He must please Madame Vauban very much.

"Chantelle." It was the whisper of Maurice.

"Oui. I am almost finished."

The doctor stood in the doorway in his long white coat, and tiny Maurice hovered behind in his white T-shirt and trousers, the uniform worn by all staff members including herself at this private health spa in the heart of Paris. The tall, skeletal doctor and Maurice came into the room like that, the doctor followed by The Mouse. Chantelle repressed a chuckle.

The doctor checked the nutrients dripping into the unconscious politician's leg. "Another five minutes, Maurice. Remove the IV. Let me know when he awakes."

As soon as the doctor left, Maurice sat on a stool and watched her hands move down to the Prime Minister's abdominal muscles. Just below them, the white towel across his naked hips bounced and jerked upward.

"Ah, Chantelle, you naughty girl. You have given our great statesman a hard-on."

"Shhh, Maurice. Someone will hear you."

"He is a lucky man. How many years have I begged you to give me a hard-on?"

It was their usual banter, and although she'd never found it nearly as amusing as he, she didn't stop him. She liked The Mouse. He was a gentle man who never said a cross word and showed great understanding for the spa's clients. The banter was his way of forgetting who and what he was, and of dreaming.

"The Banque de France is getting his massage next door and snoring like a thousand grasshoppers," he informed her. That would be Henri le Petit, governor of the Banque. The Mouse was a great source of gossip. "The Banque was supposed to come at noon, but there was some huge meeting, and he was delayed."

Chantelle took a soft jelled cold pack from the refrigerator and draped it over the thick towel that covered the Prime Minister's heaving cock. She rubbed her hands to warm them. The Prime Minister shivered, and the ice pack lay quiet.

"You are a cruel woman, Chantelle."

She took away the pack and laughed. "No. It's just that the real thing is far superior to the fantasy."

"Cruel! You are shattering my heart!"

She laughed again and rubbed eucalyptus oil into the Prime Minister's quadriceps as she admired his long, handsome legs.

The Mouse checked his watch, turned off the drip system, and removed the IV. He started to return to his stool, then thought better of it. First he closed the door. He sat again and caressed her with his gaze.

"Chantelle, shall we be serious a moment?"

She looked up. "Of course. What is it?"

"You are a medical student. Tell me, should I worry?"

She didn't understand. "About what?"

"Our clients seem to change more than their physiques after they have been with us a while. Have you noticed? Their minds seem to alter as well."

"Of course," she said. "The doctor has explained that our clients grow more fit in all ways, and their attitudes improve. That is the advantage of our health spa. Everyone comes back day after day. What is the problem with that?''

He nodded thoughtfully. ''I wonder whether you would do me a favor. I have copied some reports from the doctor's office that you will understand better than I.''

''Maurice!''

''Shhh. I know, I know.'' He raised his hands and shrugged. ''They are not for myself. If I am wrong, I will say confession for the first time in twenty-three years.''

She smiled. ''What are the papers about?''

''Some kind of research on our clients. The files are in a drawer labeled MK-ULTRA in the doctor's very elegant office. After your shift, I can meet you at Café Justine and give you my copies. You will meet me, *si'l vous plaît,* Chantelle *cherie?*''

For a moment she wondered whether this was a trick to seduce her. But the small Mouse's eyes were worried, not lustful.

''Of course,'' she told him. ''I will meet you, *mon ami.*''

It was midnight in Henri le Petit's nineteenth-century mansion on the rue de Grenelle. The *cuisine classique* dinner was finished, and his wife, Madame le Petit, Prime Minister Vincent Vauban, Madame Vauban, and the two other guests followed Henri into the library for brandy and coffee. Henri was the powerful governor of France's central bank, the Banque de France. He was rich, conservative, and full of unquenchable vitality.

''Non, non!'' he argued good-naturedly. ''The human body is like government, a system of checks and balances. Or should I say *banque cheques* and balances?'' He chuckled at his little joke and listened happily as his guests joined in. He was in a rare mood, confident, less and less feeling burdened by the responsibilities of his sober position.

''This new spa then is the source of all your youthful vigor?'' asked Gigi Devant, the founder of Paris's toniest fashion salon. ''If you have been going daily for nearly a year, you must know what you are talking about. How do I join?''

Henri exchanged a look with Prime Minister Vauban. The spa discouraged members from suggesting new members.

''Ah, dear Gigi.'' The Prime Minister took his brandy snifter to the huge ornate fireplace and stood before it. ''Alas, the spa is by invitation only, although certainly you should join, if that is your wish. We will give your name to the doctor who runs the establishment and insist he take you in. How would that be?''

Gigi, with her close-cropped platinum hair, glowing pink skin, and shining, curious eyes, was only thirty-five years old, and, in Henri le Petit's opinion, hardly needed to be reinvigorated or relieved from the stress of life.

"I suppose you would like to join, too, Charles?" Henri asked, to be polite.

Charles la Marie owned controlling interest in an engineering firm that built dams, bridges, and power plants around the world. He shook his head and raised his snifter. "I find plenty of energy in my glass, *merci*. But Gigi, of course, is on her last legs—although they are very lovely legs, I assure you—and needs every bit of professional help she can get."

Gigi slapped his arm, and again the group laughed, mellowed by the fine dinner and congenial company.

"Too bad Phillipe Paquin did not join your miracle spa," Gigi said mischievously. "He would no doubt be alive today."

"And Prime Minister," added Charles, grinning wickedly.

"Ah, but that would not be good for France!" Madame Celeste Vauban said quickly.

The Prime Minister stared into his empty glass, then went to the Napoleon III table to refill it. Henri le Petit knew the Prime Minister felt some kind of odd guilt about his youthful rival's death, and so he glared at Gigi and Charles and said, "Thank heaven Vincent has sense enough to take care of himself. He began at the spa even before Phillipe's heart attack, which at last drove less visionary leaders, such as myself, to better health care. See how fortunate we are? Our new Prime Minister doesn't wait for problems to make themselves known, he takes care before there are problems!"

"Speaking of problems, Vincent. I have waited long enough." Gigi fixed her guiltless eyes on the Prime Minister as he resumed his spot before the fireplace. "My salon is in an uproar. Between the higher taxes, the recession, and the general *malaise,* my business has plummeted."

"*Alors!* No wonder you are worried!" Madame le Petit raised her perfectly lined brows in mock horror. "A yearly profit of a million francs is never enough!"

Gigi looked around the room for sympathy, but found none. "It could be so much more, if my clientele felt secure!"

Shaking his head, Henri again exchanged a look with Vincent. They had a daring plan to set France back on her financial feet and make her the economic giant of all Europe. Of course, some would be hurt, but there were always costs for bold action. In the long run, the nation—and Europe—would thank them.

"On Monday, dear Gigi, just three days from now," the Prime Minister said with a calm, knowing smile, "many of these economic problems will begin to end. You can be assured Henri and I are going to restore *La Grandeur* to France!"

Outside, across from the *banque* governor's mansion on the rue de Grenelle, a man sat in a parked van, his gnarled hands aiming a rifle microphone. Next to him was a video camera on a tripod, aimed at the library. His grizzled partner leaned forward, constantly adjusting gauges to maximize the quality of sound. They were excited. They'd been here three hours unable to record anything because the dining room was out of sight. But since the party had moved to the library at the front, they'd been able to chronicle it all. They were back in harness, and life was worth living again.

On the other side of the Seine, Chantelle Joyeaux had no trouble ignoring the students still carousing outside her Left Bank rooms as she read Maurice Arl's stolen reports. She was sweating and feeling faint. At one o'clock she forced herself to lay aside the clinical studies and prepare for bed. She took a sedative because otherwise she'd never sleep with so many questions and suspicions rampaging through her brain.

In bed, as she tried to compose herself, she planned the next day. In the morning she had a four-hour anatomy lab, and after that she would put on her white T-shirt and trousers and go to work, as she did each Saturday. But this time instead of looking forward to massaging the handsome Prime Minister, who came daily for rejuvenation, she planned how to slip into the doctor's office. She must learn more about this MK-ULTRA.

Unnoticed by the noisy students on the street in front of Chantelle Joyeaux's rooms on the rue de la Harpe, a man of medium height and weight, his body hidden in the dark shadows of a recessed doorway, stared up at her windows. When her lights went out, he left to make a phone call. He walked stiffly, his face constantly in shadows.

"Good work, *compadre*," his chief told him. "Think you can get a copy of the clinical reports?"

He returned to continue his vigil another two hours. When at last the streets emptied, he limped up the stairs to her door and listened. He moved with quiet deliberation, each footstep an act of planning. He used skeleton keys to enter, listened to her breathing in the bedroom, and then saw the papers on the desk. Using infrared light, he scanned enough to know they were what he was seeking. He photographed them, then left as silently as he'd entered. He disappeared with ease into the narrow streets of the ancient city.

Thirty-two

About ten o'clock that night in Virginia, Hughes and Bunny Bremner sat in their leather-lined den, apparently watching a new film by Bunny's nephew, the producer. Bunny was engrossed in her usual Scotch on the rocks, the sixth since cocktail hour, and Hughes had more to worry about than a drunken wife and some stupid goddamn film.

He stretched the tension from his arms under his Chinese silk lounging coat and continued to read Sid Williams's report on Lucas Maynard and Leslee Pousho. Maynard was dead, and his documents safely shredded. That was the good part. The girl friend was another matter. By the time Sid and his men had traced her license plate to her apartment in Arlington, all they'd found was an empty safe under the bed.

But she'd clearly been there not long before, since a cigarette stub still smoldered in an ashtray. Why had she risked returning after Maynard's death?

Sid had found the answer—a single Xeroxed page from a secret Sterling-O'Keefe report with that morning's time stamp. It must have fallen out of what she was carrying, and she hadn't seen it. A journalist's reflex: Always date your source material. The bitch had copied Maynard's documents.

One of Sid's men still watched outside, a female operative was staked out at the *Washington Independent*, and Sid himself led a team combing Washington, Virginia, and Maryland. They'd entered

Pousho's name and driver's license into the Langley computer, the interstate police bank, and Sterling-O'Keefe's private corporate network. With luck she'd do them the favor of renting a car from their company, Gold Star. That way they'd have both her business and her corpse. One way or the other, they would eliminate her and the documents.

Bremner glanced over at Bunny, calming his mind as he reflected that, after all these wretched years, he could at last sit with her in their den, the picture of matrimonial harmony.

Once he'd wanted her money. The Bremners' wealth had been only a memory by the time he'd been born. Once the thought of his being evicted from this fifty-room mansion had seemed the end of the world. His family had owned it for nearly a century before hers. Once he'd believed marriage and time would win her over and she would tear up the prenuptial agreement that doomed him to a life of relative poverty after her death.

They'd had no children, and Bunny had willed everything to her nephews and nieces. Nothing had softened her. She was still connected at the hip to her money, her father's daughter.

When he'd complained and she'd still loved him, she'd made good-natured vows. "Next year, sugar. When Grandfather's estate is settled." But when next year had come, she'd said, "I'll talk to my accountants. Promise." She never had.

When she'd at last begun to hate him, she'd waved his bills in his face: "You spendthrift! I've given you plenty. Why should I keep supporting you when you put me through such hell?"

"Because, dear Bunny, you need our hell as much as I do."

Such clarity had given him an odd sort of peace. The half-billion hidden in tax havens in Luxembourg and the Cayman Islands gave him even more. Now GRANDEUR would give him everything.

He rubbed his eyes and felt the sharpness of his cheekbones against the heels of his hands. He was tired. When he was tired, his resemblance to his blackbirding ancestor increased—the hollowed cheeks, the thin, prominent nose, the chilly gaze. He leaned back and let his eyelids droop.

Until he was suddenly aware of Bunny watching him. His eyes snapped open. Her pink pig eyes stared from her fat face with hatred so open he saw the vulnerability behind it.

"Close your mouth, Bunny. You'll drool."

"You bastard. What're you hidin'?"

He chuckled. "Amazing your brain works at all. Alas, I hate to disappoint you, but I'm not 'hiding' anything. I do appreciate the vote of confidence though. Perhaps it will motivate me."

"Asshole." She drank long and deep.

The phone rang. It would be for him. Bunny's few remaining friends knew not to call after cocktail hour. He picked it up.

"Sorry, sir." It was Gordon Taite in Denver, cool and professional as always. "Flores and Walker got away again."

Inwardly Bremner groaned. "What happened?"

Gordon reported quickly and succinctly. Then, "The team found us five hours later in the shed. We traced Asher and the woman to a catering company. An employee told us the manager drove them away. They must've boarded one of the jets, but we don't know which. Thirty-six were loaded while we were tied up, and we can't ask the manager because he's missing."

"Continue." Where in hell had Walker and Flores gone?

"The homer we had planted in Flores's rental car led us to a forger. They had passports made, so they must have taken some international flight. We've got the artist. She told us the cover names they're using."

"That had to have cost cash. Where'd they get it?"

"Flores tapped one of our emergency slush funds."

"Impossible. I cut him off. Whose number did he use?"

A brief silence. "Mine, sir."

Bremner swore inside, but his voice was calm as he asked his next question. "The woman stole it from you?"

"She must have, sir."

He sighed and considered what Flores had discovered in the Langley computer base. That's when he knew. He didn't want to know, but he knew. The pair had to have gone after the truth about the Carnivore and Liz Sansborough.

"All right, it's got to be Paris," he told Gordon. "I'll notify our people to cover De Gaulle International, but I doubt that will do it. Flores will have some other way to get into the city. You'll need a jet to go after them. Arrange it."

"Yessir." Gordon hesitated. The silence stretched. "She knows she's Sarah Walker."

"Jesus Christ!" This time, Bremner couldn't stop the curse. For MASQUERADE to work . . . for the Carnivore to be eliminated . . .

for Sterling-O'Keefe to be saved . . . and—most especially—for
GRANDEUR to succeed, she had to believe she was Liz Sansborough!

Bunny turned in her stupor to stare at him. He seldom swore in
front of her, and he knew his face was blotched with anger. He
composed himself as his mind fought panic.

He lowered his voice. "How?"

"Hughes, she must've fooled me. She could've stopped taking her
pills. I know she wanted to."

Bremner said, "That's why she kept snooping in personnel. Okay,
I'll talk to the doctor to see what else he's got in that lab. Now
you've got a real job: Get her back alive, quickly!"

Gordon's voice was low and furiously controlled. "I will, Hughes.
Believe me, I will."

"I'm going to authorize a new access code for you. Call the section in fifteen minutes." Bremner hung up and dialed his personal
shift operator at the computer center. He described Asher's use of
Gordon's code. "Keep both codes open. I want to know if either is
used anywhere—bank accounts, slush funds, whatever. Be sure to let
him in so we can trace where he's accessing from. Also, input his
credit cards."

"Yessir. Anything else?" The voice was almost mechanical, trained
to dispassion. But the operator had worked with Bremner for nearly
twenty years, and Bremner knew he could trust him.

"Sarah Walker and Asher Flores are probably on their way to
Paris. Inform all our special people they're likely to arrive shortly."
Bremner hung up and sat back to think.

Bunny was staring at him, looking almost frightened. He was accustomed to anger and hate, but not fright. What had scared her?
With Scotch regularly flooding her blood, her brain had to be more
a pickled lab specimen than an operating mind. Yet she seemed to
be suddenly afraid of . . . what?

"Hughes!" Bunny glared at him. "Who is Sarah Walker?"

He was startled. She must have heard him use the woman's name
over the telephone, but why would that bother her? Then it struck
him. She was jealous. She thought he was going to Paris to meet a
woman. He hadn't thought she was capable of even that much ratio-
nality. The ridiculousness of it pleased him.

"No one you know, my dear," he said soberly. "No one you need
to know."

Thirty-three

It was early morning and the Virginia countryside glowed with dew and vigor. The timbered shoulders of the Blue Ridge Mountains stood sharp against the cloudless sky. Leslee Pousho stared out through the window of a small market as she waited for the clerk to fax the first Sarah Walker story to Washington.

She'd been up all night writing it, and she was tired. But she was also elated at what she felt was a good beginning to the series she and her editor envisioned about the rise, decline, and ruthless transformation of Sarah Walker into Liz Sansborough. Tonight she'd write the second part and fax it off tomorrow morning. But now she wanted to sleep, and she would be able to do that once she returned to the isolated cabin she'd rented in the mountains some ten miles above here. She felt moderately safe in this backwater of vineyards, horse farms, and hunt clubs.

She'd chosen the area not only for safety, but also because Hughes Bremner and his socialite wife lived somewhere among these thoroughbred estates. Lucas had told her they owned a landmark manor and a thousand acres of pristine forest.

For Lucas, she'd do a series on Hughes Bremner, a man without a shadow. A professional spy who managed a secret global corporation from the bureaucratic safety of Langley with the adroitness of a Lee Iacocca and the ruthlessness of an Idi Amin.

It was a dangerous idea. If they realized who she was or what she was doing, they'd kill her. But they'd kill her if they found her now anyway. She wanted to kill them first, if only metaphorically. Reveal them. Ruin them. Destroy them.

It was dangerous, yes, but the only way she knew to survive was to fight back. Besides, where would a criminal be safer than across the street from the police station? The last place Hughes Bremner would look was under his nose.

"I'm finished." The young man offered Leslee Pousho a nervous smile. "Sorry it took so long. My first time."

As she slid her originals back into their folder, she noticed a classic red Mercedes 450 SL pull up to the market. A sixtyish woman with bleached platinum hair, too much makeup, and a silk Town-and-Country dress emerged from the Mercedes with a flash of thigh. She teetered up the stairs on too-high heels.

Pousho thanked the clerk, paid him, and accidentally brushed past the woman. The air of the chic market was heavy with olive oil and fragrant potpourri, but she could still smell last night's liquor on the woman's breath.

"Cup of coffee, Buddy. Black." The woman's voice was faint and wavery, like an old, worn 78 rpm record.

"Trial still going on, Mrs. Bremner?" the boy asked.

Leslee Pousho looked back.

The perfectly coiffed platinum head nodded. "There's a special session today." She paid and headed toward the door.

Pousho held it open for her.

"Thanks, dear." Bunny Hartford Bremner smiled her capped teeth in Pousho's direction, held her big Styrofoam cup in both hands, and stepped outside. She headed across the town square toward the Federalist-style county courthouse.

Pousho hurried after her. "Mrs. Bremner?"

The woman looked at her pleasantly, but her high heels kept up their resolute march. "Not now, dear. I have jury duty."

"May I buy you lunch when you break?"

Bunny Bremner looked startled, like a cat disturbed from a nap. It appeared to Pousho few people asked the alcoholic socialite out to lunch, much less offered to pay.

"Well, I don't really know you—"

"I'm a newspaper reporter doing a series about this area. I was hoping you'd let me interview you. I've been told you're one of the county's most respected citizens."

Bunny Bremner perked up at the idea of being respected. She agreed, set a time and place, and traipsed on into the courthouse without spilling a drop.

Leslee smiled for the first time since Lucas was killed. One way or another, no matter what it cost, she'd expose Hughes Bremner— not to avenge Lucas's death, but to vindicate his life. Few of us walk through the valley of the shadow and emerge triumphant on the other side. Lucas nearly had.

"I don't know, dear. Hughes is like most husbands, I suppose. He wanted my money. You won't put that in your article, will you?" Bunny Bremner nervously fingered her egg-salad sandwich and glanced around the café. Many of the diners still wore their leather-and-felt riding clothes.

As Leslee Pousho had expected, the café was small and modish, with blue-checked tablecloths, fresh carnations, and bottles of wine from local Meredyth and Piedmont vineyards.

"Of course not," Leslee said. "This is just background. But what I don't understand is why Mr. Bremner bothered to take a job at all."

She ordered Bunny Bremner's water glass refilled.

The older woman shot her a weak smile and drank the water. "Partly it was because he loved the work. I can't reveal which agency he's in, but you don't need that for 'background,' I'm sure. He never could get himself promoted to the top though. He's good, you know. So three years ago I pulled a few strings. I'd never done that, but I thought, well, if he becomes head of the agency, that's better than inheriting my money, isn't it? But there was nothing I could do. Either they didn't like him, or he did his job so well they wanted to keep him in it."

She picked up her sandwich and put it down again. She had an alcoholic's meager appetite. What surprised Leslee was that she ignored the bar in the corner, which was already doing a brisk business. Obviously, she still had some control over her drinking.

"It must be hard to see him so unhappy." Leslee ate her sandwich, Swiss cheese on rye, although a combination of fear and excitement had stolen her appetite, too. This woman could be a gold mine of information.

Bunny frowned, and her sun-weathered face spread in a pond of wrinkles beneath her platinum hair. "That's what bothers me most. He's not miserable. In fact, he seems happy most of the time. But he's got no reason for it. We have a . . . less-than-perfect marriage. Sometimes I wonder whether he's planning to run away. I shouldn't be telling you this, should I?"

"Of course you should. You need to talk, and I'm not taking a single note. Women understand these things." It was sexist and simplistic, and she regretted using such low-down tactics, but she felt Bunny Bremner would connect this way in a world dominated by unspeaking, unfeeling, insensitive males.

"Yes, we do." Bunny's pink-rimmed little blue eyes grew moist. "Last night I ignored most of the conversation he was having on the phone. Well, actually, I'd been drinking a tiny bit. Anyway, at the end I couldn't help hearing him mention some friends' going to Paris. A Sarah Walker and an Asher something. What kind of name is Asher? Anyway, I could tell Hughes wanted to go with them. I think he may meet them there. He's been flying to Paris an awful lot lately. He wouldn't tell me who Sarah Walker was. Do you know them? Sarah Walker and this Asher person? Are they rich? Glamorous? Is she young and beautiful?"

Leslee Pousho forced herself to chew normally. "At this point, if he's happy as you say, I doubt he'll run away. And I don't know any Sarah Walker. Asher is a biblical name."

Her mind grabbed the information and worked it over. Sarah Walker was going to Paris! But who was "Asher?" Nowhere had that name appeared in Lucas's files. If "Liz Sansborough" was taken to Paris, it would be by her handler, Gordon Taite. Something must have happened at the Ranch to change MASQUERADE.

The older woman continued, "You have to understand, once the Bremners were as wealthy as my family. There's this silly secret about their money coming from some blackbirder. That's a sea captain who imported slaves. This was back in the early 1700s—"

Leslee listened with half attention as the older woman detailed the Bremners' and Hartfords' ancestry. Then she rattled off the genealogy of the rest of the county's prominent families. By the time Bunny needed to return to the courthouse, her wan cheeks had flushed and she'd eaten most of her sandwich. There was something about her that was forlorn, Leslee decided. She was like a piece of fine china brought out only to impress others, never to be enjoyed or used for herself.

As Leslee paid the bill, Bunny Bremner said, "Well, I have a little secret, too, don't I? You. What's your name, dear?"

"Marilyn Michaels."

It was the pseudonym she'd put on her Sarah Walker article. But when she said the name, an idea struck her. Could Sarah Walker, aka Liz Sansborough, have escaped? Is that why she was headed to Paris?

As they walked out, Bunny Bremner said, "Because it's a special Saturday session, we're going to be let out early. Maybe we'll even come to a decision. Anyway, would you like to meet for coffee at three o'clock? It's been so pleasant chatting with you."

Leslee eagerly accepted, and the older woman smiled and teetered back to the courthouse. As Leslee watched, she had a sudden insight: Bunny Bremner was greatly underrated, not only by her husband, but by herself. She wondered what it would take for Bunny to be who she really was.

Leslee returned to the market and faxed her editor a note making a few changes in her article to reflect Sarah's possible escape. She also asked her to fax the Sarah Walker series on to a friend at the *International Herald Tribune,* a global newspaper written and edited mostly in Paris.

At lunchtime Hughes Bremner was eating from a plate of Brie, Gala apples, and water crackers at his Langley desk when his telephone rang. It was a trusted computer operator at Sterling-O'Keefe headquarters in downtown Washington.

"Sir, we have an entry on that woman—Leslee Pousho?"

"Yes. What is it?" Good. Progress at last!

"Gold Star Credit Resources okayed her credit last night to use her card to rent a cabin in Virginia for a month."

Bremner smiled. "Exactly where in Virginia?"

"We're having a bit of a problem with that, sir. We've been unable to reach the realtor. He's supposed to be back soon."

"What's his name?"

Bremner recognized it: James Carr. How strange. Mentally he shrugged. The location was immaterial. Leslee Pousho's freedom—and her life—were as good as over.

Thirty-four

Sarah Walker crossed the tree-lined Boulevard St.-Germain under the hot Paris sun and pushed through a crowd of noisy students protesting yesterday's Banque de France announcement of higher interest rates. The students carried signs and shouted for everyone to join them. Towering overhead were the regal eighteenth-century homes of European nobility. Only in France did the two extremes meet with such regularity: A heritage of aristocracy and an enthusiasm for revolution.

Sarah stopped at a newsstand and bought an *International Herald Tribune.* She flipped through the English-language paper, looking for her and Flores's photos. But they appeared nowhere, and neither did a headline heralding the arrival in Paris of two killers from Denver. Relieved, she walked off, just another Parisian in jeans, Western shirt, and day pack. For a city notoriously snobbish about *couture,* she found it amusing that American Western clothes remained a perennial favorite.

Neither she nor Flores had changed since their arrival an hour ago. After two nights of little rest, they'd slept heavily on the jet to Copenhagen. By the time they'd taken high-speed trains, rental cars, and had finally arrived in Paris, it was 5:00 P.M. Checking into a hotel under the names on their fake passports was risky, since a tracking device had likely been planted on the Gold Star car Flores had rented in Denver, which meant the car would also have been tracked to the forger. If so, Gordon knew their cover identities.

Asher had a backup passport, but Sarah didn't, so he was checking himself into a hotel he'd used once before when he was undercover, but of which Langley had no knowledge. He'd have to sneak
her in. Meanwhile, he planned to dig into Gold Star.

Sarah had her own quest. She stepped into a phone booth and
dialed her old friend Blount McCaw, who free-lanced for U.S. and
European magazines and who had published kiss-and-sell blockbust-
ers on everyone from Princess Grace's gossip-plagued children to
the licentious Count of Paris, pretender to the French throne. As a
result of these successes, he'd earned a reputation as Europe's Sul-
tan of Scandal.

"Allo? Allo? Allo?" he answered.

"I'd recognize your sweet-talking voice anywhere, Blount."

"Sarah? Good lord, is it you? Where are you calling from?"

"Los Angeles." A useful lie to avoid showing him her face.

"Get out of that hellhole right now. How can you stand all those
tiresome palms?"

Outside the phone booth the students stripped off their clothes.
A demonstration, Paris style. For a moment Sarah smiled, thinking
what a great piece this would make for *Talk*. She knotted her fist and
pressed it into the telephone, but her voice showed none of her
frustration:

"Blount, I'm calling because I have an esoteric question only you
can answer."

"Esoterica, erotica, whatever."

"Ah, but maybe you won't know the answer."

"I *always* know the answer."

"Always?"

"Well, if I don't, I'll find out."

"That's what I needed to hear. Okay, here it is: What does *Je Suis
Chez Moi* mean?"

" 'I am at home.' "

"That's the translation. What I need is what it *means*. The phrase
is engraved on a very expensive Cross pen, and each of the words
has initial caps. The lettering's very small, very discreet, as if given to
a secret lover, but I have a hunch it's some kind of memento. Maybe
from an event or an organization."

"You expect me to find out something that obscure and probably
private?" Doubt was in his voice.

"I always believe everything you tell me, Blount, and you just told me if you didn't know you'd find out."

He grumbled, and she said she'd call back.

At the same time, on the rue St.-Honoré, Asher Flores checked through the *Herald Tribune* for news of his and Walker's arrival, and then, encouraged by its absence, he found the baseball scores. Yes! The Dodgers had won the double header yesterday. They'd beaten the Padres 5-2 and 13-11. And they were away games, in San Diego, Padre territory. His boys were picking up speed!

Savoring the victories, he tucked the newspaper under his arm and slouched down the street. He was thinking about Sarah Walker. A damned puzzling woman. He sensed she was going through a period of questioning, that she wasn't sure she was up to what she was facing. He hoped she was. He liked that she thought about what she did—and whether it was worth it.

As he turned into a computer shop, he could see her in his mind. There she was in the shed at the airport, sweating like crazy and mad as hell at Gordon, but refusing to kill him. The woman had ethics. Also extremely good legs and a knock-out face. He thought about it a while longer and decided he liked her. Yup. He'd been distracted by her dynamite looks, but once you got beyond that, there was a lot of other good stuff there, too.

The manager of the computer shop greeted him warmly: *"Bon soir! Comment ça va?* It has been months, Asher!" Gray-haired and steely faced, Christine Robitaille eyed him up and down as if he were a fine Charolais steak.

Because of his boyhood French friends, Asher spoke the language with no accent. He said in French, "Months, Christine? No. I've stayed away too long. I must be losing my mind."

She laughed heartily, her gold-tipped cigarette dangling precariously from the corner of her well-lipsticked mouth. "You are my favorite liar, *petit* Asher. Oh, how I adore you! Now you must tell me we will have dinner tonight. *Poisson cru marine au citron vert!"* Seafood marinated in lime juice.

"Sounds delicious. But I can't, Christine. I'm working."

She frowned around her cigarette and glanced at the quiet store. *"Zut! Zut! Alors, qu'est-ce vous voulez?"* She wanted no one to overhear.

He dropped his voice. "May I use one of your computers?"

She was a stringer for Interpol, and she'd saved his life once. That gave her a proprietary interest in him. If she could help, he knew she would.

"What about the Languedoc's computers?" she demanded.

"What I have to do is much too secret for the Languedoc."

"Ah?" She smoked thoughtfully. "Very well." And led him to a terminal with a modem. On the wall above, overlooking the entire store, was a hand-lettered sign: *De par le roi, defense a Dieu, de faire miracle en ce lieu.* By order of the king, even God isn't allowed to work any miracles here.

Using Gordon's code, Asher ran Gold Star Rent-a-Car through Langley's behemoth CM-5. He hoped to find a link between Gold Star and Hughes Bremner, Gordon Taite, and/or Langley.

On the Boulevard St.-Germain, Sarah Walker made three more telephone calls. Between each one she dialed her colleague Blount McCaw, but each time his line was busy. The students were growing more enthusiastic, singing and dancing and making speeches. Some were selling *delire,* "delirium," which she knew to be an illegal drug composed of half LSD and half ecstasy.

At last she got through to Blount, who picked up instantly. "Jesus, darling!" He was impressed. "How did you find out about that restricted little spa-club? Do you know the Prime Minister goes there? And the governor of the Banque de France, and the Archbishop of Paris, not to mention the *crème de la crème* of Paris business and government? It's by invitation only. If you have to apply, you're not good enough to get in!"

"I'm not following you, Blount. 'Je Suis Chez Moi' is a club?"

"An inordinately exclusive, exceptionally expensive, very, *very* secret health club."

"Why is it so secret? What exactly happens there?"

Over the phone line, Blount cleared his throat. "You have no idea how impossible this information was to come by. I think you'd better fill in old Uncle Blount with what *you've* got."

"The phrase was on a pen owned by somebody I used to know. A nobody, as far as you're concerned. Neither you nor I would bother to do a profile on him." How had Gordon come to possess a pen from such a select club?

"You're researching something, Sarah. I know you. Fill me in, if you want me to fill you in."

She hesitated, then: "I can't. My life's in danger. I can't say any-more than that."

"Your *life?* Give me a break."

"Do you remember the Italian godfather—what was his name, the Beast?—who put out a murder contract on you for researching the revered *Catholic* actress who was the mother of his six illegitimate children?"

"Five illegitimate children." Blount sighed. "What a marvelous, juicy scandal, and no one will ever read a word of it. One of my most glorious exposés! To die for . . . almost." He'd withdrawn the article and mailed it and all his research to the Beast's lawyer in Rome. It would never be published, but at least the Beast had canceled the contract on his life. "All right, Sarah, I suppose I'll have to take pity and share what I've got, but you have to promise to tell me what happens. If you drop the ball, I'll want to write about this place myself."

Blount McCaw told her the spa's address and phone number. He warned her there was nothing outside the building to identify it, only a street number. The club was open seven days a week, 5:00 A.M. to midnight, to accommodate clients' busy schedules. It was a private health spa that ran a full regimen of stretch, aerobic, and resistance classes, plus the usual massage, vitamin and nutrition therapy, and cosmology. At the same time, the doctor treated mild psychological disorders, particularly depression and anxiety brought on by the stress of high-powered life-styles.

"The clients love this place," Blount finished. "People who hate exercise, or who maybe were sunk in depression, have found they never miss a day of workouts and treatments. Think of a designer drug like Prozac. It sounds to me like this health spa does what Prozac's alleged to do—help clients design their ideal personalities as well as their bodies. People arrive a mess, and a few months later they're fit, energetic, and have a strong sense of well-being. No won-der they keep going. Who'd want to lose results like those?" He paused. "I'm talking myself into this. I may have to pull a few strings and join."

The demonstrators outside Sarah's phone booth were painting slogans on one another's naked bodies. TV cameras had arrived. She turned into the stuffy air at the back of the booth where no one could record her face. A plan was forming in her mind—

"Sarah, are you daydreaming?" Blount's voice was stern.

"I've got to go. Thanks, Blount. When things settle down, I'll get back to you. Promise."

"Sarah! Wait a minute. What are you up to?"

"Can't talk. Sorry. Cross your fingers for me."

She hung up and slipped out of the booth. At the edge of the crowd, she stopped and watched the drugs changing hands right out in the open. She approached one of the peddlers of delirium. Beyond the view of the television cameras, for US$500 she bought a tiny vial wrapped in a wad of paper towel. She put the vial and its protective towel carefully in her backpack.

The address for Je Suis Chez Moi was on rue Vivienne near the Bourse, the Paris stock exchange. Blount had been right: The spa's only identification was a tiny gold street number on a massive double door enameled in black. The gray stone building resembled others on the block, most modeled on ancient Greco-Roman architecture and dating from the time of Napoleon.

Sarah passed the facility once, noting it extended deep into the block with a cobbled drive on the right. It was stately and enormous, probably a private mansion in earlier days, an *hôtel parh'culier*. She glanced up at the sky. It was nearly 7:30 P.M., and the sun was low, but night was still an hour or more away. She saw a café—Café Justine—went in, ordered *café glace* to refresh her from the August heat, and returned outside to sit at a small table. From here she could watch Je Suis Chez Moi.

What an odd name—"I Am At Home." But it fulfilled an interesting objective: It was deceptive. Who would guess it was really an elite health spa?

She drank her iced coffee and glanced around. An older man was the only other patron at the outdoor tables. He was wearing a straw Panama hat with a red tartan band, reading *Le Monde*, and smoking a pipe. Just as she looked at him, he lifted his gaze, and their eyes accidentally met. Both were unguarded, and the experience was too intimate. They looked away.

Over the next hour two limousines turned down the spa's narrow drive and stopped to let passengers out directly at a side entrance. Some half-dozen clients left during the same time, out through the same side door straight into taxis or sedans. No one had used the massive front entrance doors.

Sarah ordered a seafood salad. A young couple arrived in light summer clothes, holding hands, in love. They ordered *vin ordinaire.* The older fellow finished his newspaper, got up, and left. Sarah settled in to continue watching Je Suis Chez Moi.

As twilight began to spread over Paris, a tall, lean man who appeared to be in his thirties, with smooth, tanned skin and startling snow-white hair left the spa's side door, heading for a waiting limousine. Sarah felt a shock. She recognized him. She stared as he turned back to chat easily with someone inside. From where did she know him? The Ranch—? Yes, from something she'd read at the Ranch. A newspaper or magazine. He was an elegant man in a dark, expensive, conservative but stylish suit, and then she remembered—

He was Vincent Vauban, the Prime Minister of France.

She watched as he climbed into the back of the long, black limousine. It was amazing: He looked and moved like an athlete in his thirties, but she knew he had to be in his mid-fifties!

As the limo rolled away, she tried to figure it out. What connection could there be between the Prime Minister of France and Gordon Taite? Or Hughes Bremner?

She had to get inside Je Suis Chez Moi.

Thirty-five

After lunch with Bunny Bremner, Leslee Pousho drove her rented Ford Taurus up toward her remote cabin in Virginia's Blue Ridge Mountains. There was no point trying to sleep. She would get some work done on the second installment of her series before she headed back for her three o'clock appointment with Mrs. Bremner.

As she rode up through pines and sycamores, memories of yesterday morning chilled her. Yesterday she'd driven Lucas to the State department. Yesterday he'd been murdered.

Misery thickened her throat. When she wasn't writing, she felt miserable. She wondered how long before she'd get used to his never coming back.

She turned onto a blacktop mountain road and entered a forest of birch trees. Their chalk-white trunks reached straight up toward the luminous mountain sunshine. The glossy leaves trembled silver and white in a fine, clean breeze. She heard a blue jay give a raucous call, and another answer.

Just a few days ago she would have gloried in the verdant mountains. Now her mind could manage only the tasks at hand. She watched carefully, ahead and behind, for Hughes Bremner's men. She felt relatively safe, but she was no fool.

As she watched, she considered the next installment of the Sarah Walker series. This one would encompass the last four days before Sarah's final collapse. As she thought through the article, she noticed a big green Volvo behind her.

Instantly she was alert. It couldn't be—

The Volvo closed in. She stared back at the two men in the windshield behind her. They were dressed like locals. She could see their casual, Pendleton shirts. But they also wore black sunglasses like the men who'd attacked Lucas.

She hit her accelerator and surged ahead.

The big Volvo easily kept up.

She raced up the mountain road. The Volvo swung to the left and accelerated to come around her. They were going to try to push her over to the right, where the road dropped off in a sheer precipice.

She veered her car left, blocking the Volvo. The Volvo dropped back. Sweat bathed her face and saturated her sundress. Both cars were traveling nearly seventy miles an hour on a road designed for thirty-five.

Again the Volvo swung left. Trees whipped past in a blur. Again Leslee blocked the Volvo, but this time, before she could react, it dropped back and came up in her lane on the right. Now she was hurtling along on the wrong side of the mountain road.

She hit the brake. The Volvo slowed with her. She turned into it, tried to force it back. It was too big. It smashed heavily into her right fender. Sparks flew. Metal screamed. The jolt rocked her to her teeth. Fear clutched her heart.

The window on the Volvo's driver's side rolled down. "Pull over!" The driver rested a pistol across the window's lip. "Now!"

She accelerated, on the wrong side of the road. The Volvo kept up. A blast of gunfire strafed her back door.

As she floored her accelerator, she saw hope: A dirt truck ramp ahead, arrowing up the mountain on her right. The precipice was behind them now, and the two speeding cars were rounding a new mountain. The dirt ramp was intended to give trucks with failing brakes a way to stop at the bottom of a steep descent.

She plunged her car down. Near the base, she hit her brakes abruptly. Her tires screamed.

The Volvo hit its brakes, too. But the Volvo's speed was so great and its weight so massive that the time lapse between her action and its reaction gave her a few seconds.

She was out in the open! She swung onto the ramp. She'd make a 180-degree turn and reverse her course. She smiled grimly, preparing herself, then gunfire rang out again.

Her body slammed from side to side. The steering wheel spun

through her hands as if it were greased. The car whirled out of control. Dammit all to hell! They'd taken out her tires!

Leslee Pousho's face throbbed with pain. Her eyes were swollen. She lay with hands and feet tied to the iron bed in her one-room cabin, while her two captors tore it apart searching for Lucas's documentation. She'd been so close to accomplishing her vow to avenge him—

A tear slid down her cheek. She thought back to her disabled car and the forest of birches in which she'd tried to hide. The thin-trunked trees had provided little cover, and she'd had to keep moving, keep running. Fifteen years of heavy smoking had defeated her. She'd not had the lung power or energy to outrun these two cruel men.

Now the tall one strode toward her. He stood over her. There was blood on his hand. Her blood.

"Where is it?"

"Won't . . . tell." Her lips were bruised. She could hardly talk.

The hand bashed the right side of her face. She heard herself moan. Red lightning flashed behind her eyes.

The second one was locking her laptop, readying it to be stowed in the Volvo. With her box of back-up floppies in his hand, he gestured at the front door.

"Go check outside."

The tall one gave her a look of disappointment. He wanted to keep beating her. But he headed out.

Think, she told herself. Think!

The tall one reappeared in the doorway with the briefcase she'd hidden under the cabin in a shallow cellar. He dumped the Xeroxes onto the kitchen table.

"Now we'll pack her up and put her in her car—"

"It's got to look like an accident."

"There's that bad curve farther up the mountain—"

The shorter one nodded. "That'll work."

They walked toward her, anticipation in their icy eyes.

With tremendous effort, she said, "That not . . . only copy . . . Kill me. Won't stop this. World's going to know what Hughes Bremner did to Sarah Walker."

At 3:30 P.M. in the village café, Bunny Bremner finally ordered a double cappuccino. She was sitting at the table she'd shared with

Marilyn Michaels for lunch. She watched the door, hoping the pretty blond journalist would reappear.

The maître d' told her no one had left a message, and Bunny thought the young woman was the kind who would. She was a career person; perhaps a news emergency had sidetracked her.

Bunny liked Ms. Michaels, and she'd looked forward to meeting her again. It had been a long time since she'd looked forward to anything.

In the remote Virginia cabin, ice water splashed Leslee Pousho's face. Through a thick fog of pain, she gagged, coughed, and struggled toward consciousness.

She lay face down in a warm, sticky pool. She and the mattress were soaked. There was a terrible stench. It burned her nose and eyes. It was acidic, nauseating. She realized what it was. She'd vomited. She lay in a pool of her own sticky vomit.

"She's coming around again."

She kept her eyes closed and prayed they'd decide she was still unconscious. Somehow she could still make her mind work, even though her body screamed with pain. Lucas would be proud.

"Where'd you hide the copies?"

"Tell us and you can sleep."

She thought about Lucas. After seeing him die, she'd told herself she could endure anything.

"Where're the copies!"

The fist sank into her belly. Something seemed to rip inside.

"Tell us!"

The next blow hit higher. Pain knifed through her chest and her head exploded into blackness. The blackness collapsed around her, and she felt blessed nothing.

Hughes Bremner was back in his Langley office when the call came from Sid Williams. A few hours earlier Williams had reached the realtor, who'd given him the location of Leslee Pousho's cabin.

"Where are you?" Bremner demanded. "Is she dead?"

"I'm on the porch of Pousho's cabin out here in the sticks, Chief. I'm using my cell phone. Looks like we've got all Lucas's stuff. Xeroxes, like you said."

"Is she dead?" Bremner repeated.

Sid Williams cleared his throat. "Not yet, sir."

"Why not? You have the documents. I told you—"

"Chief?" Williams spoke in a rush. "She claims she made extra copies she sent to people. You know, more copies of what she had in the cabin. Maynard's stuff."

Goddamn Lucas Maynard and Leslee Pousho all to hell! It was the oldest ruse in the world, but Bremner could take no chance.

"Get it out of her. Now!"

"Yessir, but she's out cold. You know. And now she's not looking too good."

Bremner knew. Sid Williams was telling him she might die, and then they'd never learn a damn thing.

"Give her a few hours, then wake her up and convince her," Bremner said. "Sid? Really convince her. Everything you know, and worse."

Almost as soon as Hughes Bremner hung up, his buzzer sounded. It was his secretary. In a nervous voice, she announced: "The White House just called, sir. The President wants to see you immediately. The DCI will meet you there."

"Do you know what it's about?"

"No, sir. I asked, but no one seems to know. Or they're not telling me."

Hughes Bremner's work had put him through more scares than a whore off the pill. He'd taught himself to ride with problems, handle them, and move on. Which meant he seldom worried. But he'd never before been summoned abruptly to the President's office. He thought of the tens of millions of dollars he and his board had skimmed from BCCI deposits, and then he thought about Sterling-O'Keefe . . . MASQUERADE . . . Sarah Walker . . . Lucas Maynard . . . Leslee Pousho . . . and, finally, GRANDEUR. He was so close to fulfilling all his plans, creating the life he'd dreamed of, he was determined nothing would go wrong now.

The President of the United States and the director of U.S. Central Intelligence were waiting for Hughes Bremner in the Treaty Room, the President's home office. He was sitting behind the nineteenth-century table that served as his desk, while Arlene Debo stood nearby, gazing at titles in one of the massive bookcases. When Bremner walked in, she turned.

She didn't smile. Neither did the President.

"Sit down, Mr. Bremner."

"Thank you, Mr. President."

The wallpaper was dark-red simulated leather. Antiques from White House storage decorated the librarylike room, which had a feeling of masculinity that at another time would have set Bremner at ease.

There were no pleasantries, a bad sign. The President began curtly: "My press officer took a telephone call from Judith Zimmer an hour ago. You know her?"

"I know who she is. Editor of the *Washington Independent*." Bremner felt suddenly heavy, as if his chest and stomach had turned to stone. The *Independent* was the newspaper for which Leslee Pousho wrote.

"She knows the Carnivore is coming in." The President's voice was tight with fury. "She wants a quote from me about why we'd take in such a bloodthirsty ogre, because tomorrow she's going to publish a story that includes this fact. It will be the first of some series they're running about gross malfeasance in one of our agencies."

"Which agency?" Bremner's heart seemed to stop.

"It's not named, unfortunately. No way to fight it detail for detail until we know which one." He glared at Bremner and enunciated each word carefully: "I specifically required no one know about the Carnivore. *No one.* You're here because I'm ordering you to rescind our offer of asylum. He'll have to peddle his contemptible gore somewhere else. I'm going to give Ms. Zimmer a quote denying he's coming in, and then you're going to make damn sure he doesn't."

"Sir—" Bremner began.

"Don't bother, Bremner." The President raised his hand. "This administration must set an ethical tone in all matters. We need to turn this nation around. Plus, if the article in the *Independent* is accurate, we've got one hell of a mess on our hands anyway."

"Do you know what the story contains, Mr. President?" Arlene Debo's square face was pale.

"Ms. Zimmer has her own ethics. She refuses to let us see the story in advance. We'll have to wait until tomorrow, like the rest of her readers."

"Mr. President, I need to warn you about something." Hughes Bremner crossed his arms, leaned back. "The Carnivore performed some wet jobs for the United States back in the '60s and '70s when it was still legal. That won't look good, especially if another nation

with an agenda presents it to the world media. It would be very . . .
useful . . . for us to keep that information to ourselves, and also to
know exactly what other nations—as well as individuals—have been
up to through the Carnivore."

"And there's the Beni-Domo intelligence, too, sir," Arlene Debo
added. "Because of the Carnivore, we know that a man who is likely
to become Prime Minister of Japan is a murderer. As I'm sure you
recall, he hired the Carnivore to eliminate the founder of Beni-
Domo. And that's not all we know because of the Carnivore. Everything he's given us has been useful."

The President frowned, considering. At last he shook his head.
"No, I should never have let you talk me into bringing him in. It's
time we cut free of the past. Our nation has been responsible for
some reprehensible acts. Now let's own up and get on with making
this a better world. There'll be no more discussion on this issue. You
will inform the Carnivore he is no longer welcome in the United
States, Mr. Bremner. Arlene, you will glance over Mr. Bremner's
shoulder occasionally to make certain the Carnivore takes his dirty
business elsewhere. Thank you both for coming."

Thirty-six

In his austere Langley office, Hughes Bremner found a bottle of Jack Daniel's far at the back of his bottom desk drawer. Seldom did he drink at all, least of all here.

This afternoon was an exception.

He poured three fingers into a water glass, knocked back half, and on his secure line began to make urgent telephone calls. First he talked with his board members, Tad Gorman, Ernie Pinkerton, and Adam Risley at the FBI, NSC, and ATF. He gave each the bad news about the President's decision. Now they had to close ranks, cover, and give lip service. They'd have to hold off Arlene Debo until the coming-in tomorrow night. After that, the Carnivore would be dead, and the almighty President would be obeyed, but not the way he expected: There'd be no asylum for the notorious Carnivore in the United States, or anywhere.

In the den of her Virginia mansion, Bunny Bremner poured herself the first Scotch and water of the day. The trial was over, and she was celebrating. Also, she had to admit she was feeling sad, too. She'd wanted to chat more with Marilyn Michaels. Unfortunately she knew little about the woman, not even for which newspaper she worked. She could always ask Hughes, she supposed. He had people who could find out something simple like that.

Bunny dialed Hughes's office, but he'd left. His secretary said he was on his way home to pick up his bags for another overseas trip.

She looked at her glass and decided she'd better not drink anything until they'd talked.

As he expected, Hughes Bremner's bags were waiting inside the front door. He'd phoned ahead, and the butler had packed. Bremner was going to Paris. He'd told Arlene Debo it was for damage control, that he needed to make certain all details in the Carnivore operation were wound down completely, no slipups, nothing leaked to the press.

Thank God Lucas had never found out about GRANDEUR or Je Suis Chez Moi.

Now he stood in the doorway to the den. Bunny was leaning over her drink as if she wished she could fall in and drown. She was an ugly old drunk full of pretensions and lost glory, and under different circumstances he would have enjoyed contemplating her for an hour or two, much like an art lover contemplating his favorite still life at his favorite museum.

"I'm off," he told her. "Now, now. No tears. I know you'll miss me dreadfully."

She looked up, dry eyed. "Where are you going?"

"Paris. The City of Lights and Love. You remember the concept of love. I know you do, Bunny. It's what you've reserved for your money."

Once she'd had lovely violet eyes, but the more alcohol she'd consumed, the paler they'd become, until now they were a characterless, watery blue. She blinked. Her hands shook.

He strode into the room, removed the glass, and set it on the table.

"You're never coming back." Her voice was a tormented whisper. "I know you're not. You're going to meet friends over there. Some woman! You're leaving me."

She was half right. There was no other woman, but he'd never be back. But he lied easily with a bland smile:

"You're not that lucky, Bunny."

"I tried to get them to make you DCI," she went on, lost in misery. "Three years ago, the previous administration. I tried. Really I did, Hughes. I went to my cousin, the Vice-President, and he talked to the President." She wilted back into her chair. Her words slowed. "Don't look so upset, Hughes. Please. You're good. You should be head of Central Intelligence—"

"You fool! You meddling old bitch! That shows how little you know me. I turned them down. I *like* my situation now!"

He stalked away to the front door where his limo waited. He needed no promotion, no star in Langley's foyer, no more visits with the President. The last thing he wanted was visibility.

All he needed was the corpse of the Carnivore. Once that was accomplished, GRANDEUR was certain!

He left without a glance back at the imposing home he'd so angrily coveted for nearly forty years.

Bunny Bremner considered running after him. She could apologize, but then, apologies just made him nastier. She stared at her Scotch. She had a feeling he'd have been disappointed to know she hadn't had even a sip. She wondered why he took such pleasure in thinking her weak and stupid.

Restless, she stood. She was shaky, but more from fear of losing him than from yesterday's alcohol. She rang for the butler. She'd liked Marilyn Michaels. Marilyn had been nice to her. Marilyn had bought her lunch and listened with interest. Even respect. She ordered the Mercedes brought around.

She remembered the first time she'd seen Marilyn. It was in the little market in town. Marilyn had mentioned later she'd been sending a fax somewhere. Buddy was a careful young man, and she guessed he might keep records of such things. In any case, it was worth a try. Hughes wasn't going to help, so she'd just have to find Marilyn herself.

Bunny Bremner walked out of Carr's Real Estate Sales and Rentals. She'd had the most amazing time. From Buddy at the market, she'd learned the woman she knew as Marilyn Michaels had sent two faxes to the *Washington Independent*. But the name the woman had used to sign for them was Leslee Pousho. Then Bunny had found Jimmy Carr in his real estate office, working late. He liked to be called James, but she'd known his family far too long for that. With some prompting Jimmy had told her he'd rented a cabin to Ms. Pousho. Next she'd wormed out of him the address and directions.

Bunny was pleased. She stopped in the village café where she'd lunched with Marilyn. She forced herself to eat a toasted croissant stuffed with sautéed mushrooms and melted Gruyère cheese. She looked longingly at the bar, but something told her she'd better wait.

In the pastoral Virginia mountains, Leslee Pousho endured a world of pain. Colors melded into a vast sea of black. Sound and light were hard-edged acts of violence. She tried to concentrate on her memories of Lucas. She'd summon his image and hold on as if it were a life preserver.

Sometimes she heard herself crying. Sometimes she screamed.

They hadn't hit her in a long time. How long, she wasn't sure. But when she cracked open her eyes, she could see the long shadows of evening. Outdoors, birds sang. She could almost smell another beautiful day coming to a close among the bucolic trees and grasses beyond her personal hell.

Bremner's two men sat at her little wood table, drinking coffee in front of the kitchen window. The aroma drifted over to her, and she ached with every cell for a cup. For innocence. For a few days ago when she was just another reporter whose only problem was a lover who was blindly committed to the CIA.

She closed her eyes and found merciful sleep.

She hit the floor face down with a teeth-loosening thud. Pain radiated through her, echoed in a hundred places that already hurt terribly.

Someone grabbed her feet and dragged her toward the front door. The rough wood floor shot needlelike slivers into her belly and chest. At last she was on the porch. She gasped for air. Her body burned as if it were on fire. They turned her over and threw a bucket of icy water over her. She coughed and gagged.

More icy water. It burned down her nostrils and into her throat. She couldn't breathe! She sputtered and gagged. They turned her over again. Someone was tearing off her clothes.

And then suddenly they stopped. She lifted her swollen eyelids. A car had arrived. She could hear its powerful engine. The car was small, red, and sporty. One of the men dragged her back toward the cabin door, while the other trotted down the steps toward the figure who was emerging from it.

At the foot of the long driveway Bunny Bremner caught a glimpse of something pale and heavy being dragged from the porch into the rustic cabin. In the dusk, she couldn't see exactly what it was, but as she got out of her Mercedes she saw Marilyn Michaels'—Leslee Pousho's—Ford Taurus parked in the driveway above her. Next to it was a dark green Volvo.

She walked up the steep drive on her high heels, an awkward maneuver. She held her purse in both hands close to her chest, so she could watch her feet. She should have put on her Nikes, but then she couldn't have worn this chic new lavender dress with the wide belt and the cunning Peter Pan collar. Peter Pan collars were back, and she was glad.

A man of medium height with graying hair, an ordinary face, a few days of stubble, and a peculiar vacancy in his eyes came down the path toward her.

"I've come to see Marilyn," she announced.

"Who?" He looked puzzled. He stopped three feet above her, an obstacle between her and the cabin.

"Marilyn Michaels." She brushed past him and continued up the drive. "Perhaps you know her as Leslee Pousho."

"Whoa! Wait a minute, lady!" He held her arm firmly. "There's no one here by that name. This is private property. You'd better get back in that fancy car of yours and split before I call the cops."

She looked him up and down. There was a faint, unpleasant odor about him. Body odor, she decided. And his trousers and shirt were badly wrinkled, as if he'd slept in them.

"Young man," she said severely, "I happen to know that's Leslee Pousho's car. Also, this is the cabin Jimmy Carr rented to her. She and I had a coffee date this afternoon, which she wasn't able to attend. I want to arrange another appointment."

She tried to pull her arm free.

"You want to have a cup of coffee with her?" The man stared, astonished.

Perhaps he was hard of hearing. She repeated her intention. When he laughed, she suddenly understood. He considered the idea ludicrous. Well, he was ludicrous in his rumpled clothes, untidy stubble, and body odor.

"Release me!" she snapped and yanked on her arm.

He pulled her back down the hill toward her Mercedes. "Go home, lady. You've got the wrong place. There's no one here you want to see."

"Nonsense." She smacked her purse in his face and started back up the drive in her high heels.

"Marilyn!" she called to the cabin. "Marilyn! It's Bunny. I've come for a visit!"

Suddenly a small, hard, circular object rammed into her back. Her mind registered the information— Why, it was a pistol! The disgusting man had stuck a gun in her back! Then, before she could protest, he wrenched back her left arm and pinned it against her waist.

She stumbled forward. She managed to catch her purse in her free hand before it fell. He lifted her back up with her pinned left arm. Pain shot red hot into her brain.

"How dare you!" She was shocked. "Do you know who I am!"

"Honey, I don't care if you're the Tooth Fairy."

His laughter gave her chills. She had misjudged him and the situation. Marilyn must be in grave trouble. Then the unthinkable occurred to Bunny: Her own life could be in danger.

Thirty-seven

The sky was dark now, the hot summer air moist and soft. Sarah stood deep in the shadows of the massive stone building of Je Suis Chez Moi across from the brightly lighted Café Justine. The charcoal-colored gauze of the Paris night wrapped around her and sudden uncertainty drenched her with sweat.

She tugged on the straps of her day pack, felt the weight of the Beretta inside, and thought of the blond youth she'd killed in Denver. Had she gone mad? She was setting herself up to kill again, or even to die. She wanted to run away from her past and her future. Leave Paris now, get the help of friends in Europe to redo her face, and disappear until all this about the Carnivore had ended. Blount McCaw would help her. She had many old friends who'd help.

A trickle of sweat slid down the side of her face. The Carnivore was nothing to her. Hughes Bremner, Gordon Taite, and the Carnivore should be stopped by professionals.

She was just a profiler of celebrities, for God's sake, who happened to have had some tradecraft training. She didn't have the heart or the dedication of an Asher Flores or a Gordon Taite.

God forbid she ever enjoyed this awful work.

She should call Asher, tell him about Je Suis Chez Moi, rely on his experience to decide what to do.

She stared along the shadowed driveway to the stately Greco-Roman mansion. It was a solid stone fortress. She was crazy to even think of breaking into such a bastion.

And yet— She breathed deeply. Was retreating what she—Sarah Walker, not Liz Sansborough—always did?

Two years ago she'd walked out on her last lover. They'd lived together only a few months, but already she'd felt imprisoned. Her life with men had been one long series of honeymoons. No relationship ever evolved past that stage, and so she'd come to believe nothing but caged boredom lay beyond for her. Her parents' marriage mystified her. How could anyone stay in love that long? Stay excited and thrilled?

She'd left that last man, as she'd left the others, or she'd forced them to leave her. And as she'd walked out the door, this man, this enemy who'd once been her dear friend and lover, had cursed and blamed her: "The only real freedom is commitment to someone or something. To anything! What you're missing is inside you. Not me. Until you can make a real commitment, you're nothing!"

As if it had just happened, she felt the bite of his accusation and the pain of wondering whether it was true. There were advantages to having no memory—

And then she saw a large, black Cadillac turn into the spa's cobbled drive. She shrank back farther into the shadows. The Cadillac didn't stop at the side door, nor did it return there to wait for a client who was finished and ready to leave. This was the first time a vehicle had remained at the rear of the mansion. A vehicle under the cover of night.

Suddenly she felt impotent. Everything around her, her very life, had turned upside down. In a sense, she'd already died. They'd raped her mind. Stolen her identity. There was no greater crime than the destruction of a human identity. And without knowing who you were, you were dead. She could never be the old Sarah again. And with a sudden burst of clarity she realized she no longer wanted to be the old Sarah, the woman who abandoned relationships before they could grow. Who preferred being the interviewer so she had the illusion of control. A celebrity profiler whose most enduring accomplishment was to present gossip as news. Who had remained an observer because she'd always felt powerless to change the course of events—

With renewed determination, she took her Beretta from her backpack and slipped the small vial of delirium, still wrapped in a paper towel, into a pocket of her jeans. Hugging the mansion's wall so anyone looking out a window above would be less likely to see her, she moved lightly down the cobblestones of the drive. It angled left, and soon she saw the Cadillac again. It was parked near the double doors at the rear: Facing toward her, lights out, engine running, and trunk wide open.

The mansion's huge rear doors were open, spilling out yellow light in a rectangle next to the Cadillac, providing enough illumination for her to detect shadowy flower beds, bushes, trees, and cars parked at the edges of a grand turnaround.

No one was visible in the turnaround or inside the doorway. Sarah dashed toward the Cadillac, squatted at the side farthest from the doorway. She listened, but all she heard was the quiet growl of the idling engine. She lifted her eyes above the hood, still saw no one, and slid around to look inside the trunk.

Nausea swept over her. She swallowed and forced herself to look directly at the body. . . . *To see the blond youth's head explode into the bloody Denver night. . . . To feel the jolt of the Beretta's discharge in her arm and shoulder. . . . To know the pain . . . the awesome power . . . of taking a life—*

She fought down the nausea, shook her head to clear the unwanted, frightening visions. Liz Sansborough would never feel this way, would never allow herself to risk the loss of time, and the danger that could bring.

But Sarah Walker agonized and regretted.

She inhaled sharply, made herself focus on the bloody corpse in the trunk. It was a young woman, a brunette with upswept hair and pleading in her face. She'd been laid on a sheet of black plastic. Ruby blood and tissue formed a thick carpet in the center of her white T-shirt. She must have been an employee, because she wore an all-white uniform and a blood-coated name tag.

She had to be dead, but Sarah rested her fingers against the carotid artery in a kind of blind hope. Death wasn't something she'd ever accept easily. But there was no pulse, no life.

Fury engulfed her, violent and black. What was wrong with the world? How could butchery like this happen? She had no doubt the death of this woman was connected to whatever Bremner, Gordon, and whoever else it was at Langley were doing. And now, somehow, the Prime Minister of France might be involved! Her pulse hammered, and her breath came in rasps—

She heard voices! They were inside the mansion and coming

closer. She swiftly unpinned the name tag from the dead woman and melted back into the darkness between two parked cars.

Within seconds two muscular men wearing white T-shirts and trousers appeared, carrying out a small, limp man as bloody as the dead woman. They fitted him into the trunk next to her, careful to keep both corpses on the thick plastic lining. They slammed the trunk shut.

As soon as the men disappeared back inside, Sarah wiped off the name tag and angled it to pick up the light. It said the dead woman was Chantelle Joyeaux, Masseuse. Sarah didn't recognize the name. She shook her head sadly, put the tag in her pocket, and filed the face in her memory.

The two musclemen returned, this time in camouflage shirts and pants, accompanied by the driver in his chauffeur's uniform. All three jumped into the big Cadillac, the headlights turned on, and the machine rolled off down the cobblestones.

The mansion's doors remained open, and moths danced in the yellow light. Sarah's mind was clear as ice. Somehow she knew the answers she sought were inside that mansion.

The turnaround was empty and provided no cover, so she slipped through the bushes and trees around the periphery, heading indirectly toward the rear entrance. But then, with an abruptness that stunned her, massive floodlights blazed. She crouched. The turnaround was bright as day, and a van spun onto it from the driveway, its doors already swinging open. Before she could raise her Beretta, a half-dozen armed figures dressed in black jumped out and swarmed toward her. Two more burst from the mansion's doorway. In seconds, in a perfectly orchestrated ambush, she was ringed by assault rifles pointed at her head and heart.

Someone ripped away her Beretta. Hands dragged her through the mansion's rear doors. In a softly lighted corridor, four muscular attendants in white uniforms held Sarah. The group with assault rifles disappeared, and the floodlights blinked out. Behind her the night was dark and silent again, as if nothing had happened. The mansion's doors closed. Locks clicked.

She heard footsteps and turned. A towering, cadaverous man stepped into the corridor. Sickened, strangely exhilarated, she looked up into the gaunt face of Dr. Allan Levine.

"Well, well, Liz. Welcome to Je Suis Chez Moi."

Her whole body was numb. Even her lips felt paralyzed as she managed to say, "Sarah. I'm Sarah Walker."

"Ah?" Dr. Levine nodded slowly. "Then you do know. Well, we'll have to remedy that, won't we?"

She had never been so afraid.

Thirty-eight

Glittering stars spread across the black canopy of the Parisian night. Henri le Petit, the dynamic governor of the Banque de France, stood in the gardens of the magnificent Hotel Matignon at 57, rue de Varenne and admired the way the rising moon illuminated the villa's aged stone exterior in a radiant, candle-wax glow. This was the official residence and workplace of the Prime Minister of France. With a nod to himself, Henri next turned to survey with pride the twenty high officials and powerful business and civic leaders who had gathered here tonight without spouses or other companions for a very special, very private celebration.

"Where is he?" demanded a voice at Henri's elbow. It was René Christian Martin, the Minister of Finance. "We are here. Our host is not. Is there a problem?"

"Vincent was busy all day, *mon ami.* Running behind, as all of us have in our preparations for Monday. You know that firsthand." Henri chuckled. "His schedule forced him to attend Je Suis Chez Moi late today, and then he had yet another meeting. But at this moment he is upstairs in his rooms, dressing. Our patience will be rewarded." He smiled and watched the tiny worry line between the finance minister's eyebrows smooth and disappear. René was in superb condition now—muscular yet svelte. He no longer trembled with the nervous edge that had propelled him in his meteoric rise from Treasury to Finance, yet he was even more savvy and focused.

"Louise Dupuy is not here either," René observed.

"*Oui.* Vincent said she arrived at the spa shortly before he left. She is probably there still." Louise Dupuy was the most popular TV journalist in France. She would spend all of Monday broadcasting the bold, fresh direction their government would take.

"Ah, there is Martine!" René moved on, and Henri watched him bow over Martine Tisa's elegant, jeweled fingers. Martine must be eighty now, Henri reflected, but somehow thirty years had evaporated in the last eighteen months, and she easily looked a stylish, enviable fifty. She had a vigorous handshake, an aura of no-nonsense intensity, and platinum hair that curled coquettishly around her ears. Martine owned a publishing company that controlled some forty percent of newspapers and sixty percent of magazines in France, and she ran her empire with an iron will.

Nearby stood the oil magnate Jacques Mieux, looking sleek as a panther in his perfectly cut tuxedo. He was talking with Roger Cluny, who was in his twenties and used his unerring comprehension of youthful angst and life-styles to make himself the highest-paid, most sought-after consultant to companies targeting the lucrative French teen market. The third person in their little conversational group was Claudette Cochiti, the legendary movie star now also known for her good works benefiting children and animals. There was talk among Catholics she'd someday be made a saint.

Henri felt himself swell with respect for the luminaries gathered here in this lovely old courtyard under the stars. Surely that would be their destiny now, and France's—the stars!

He moved off among the throng, chatting, laughing, patting arms, reminiscing. It was a noble night, and the momentousness of the occasion was lost on no one.

When at last the Prime Minister stepped from the doorway of Matignon to greet them, there was a sudden hush. All turned to admire him, suave in his tailored tuxedo, his thick white hair stunning against the healthy glow of his tanned face. France was on the brink of her destined greatness, and their statesman–Prime Minister, Vincent Vauban, would lead them triumphantly forward.

The Prime Minister smiled. "My friends." He spread his arms expansively, affectionately. "We have traveled a long way, *non?* Once some of us were socialists, others conservatives. We remember 1968, when rebelling students and striking workers reduced France to anarchy. Today our glorious nation is again sick and injured, plummeting to depths that will show our fellow *citoyens* what the future would be without our stringent new plans. France will not give up its sovereignty to European technocrats; we will not allow industrial and agricultural ruin." He lifted his august chin, and his voice rang out across the courtyard as if it were all Europe. "Instead we unite for *La Grandeur!"*

As Sarah was marched along the silent corridors of Je Suis Chez Moi, her mind was clouded by fear and anger. Fear at being in the hellish hands of Levine again, and anger at being caught so easily. Liz Sansborough wouldn't have been so stupid, so unprepared. Sarah should have contacted Flores for backup. For a moment she realized how much she longed to see him, to warm herself in the glow of his zany kindness and intensity.

Dammit, she was still more Sarah than Liz, soft and distracted! She'd have to blend Liz into her identity if she was going to find out what had been done to her and why and get out alive. If it wasn't already too late.

The attendants opened a door and pushed her inside. Quickly she took in her surroundings: A large, sumptuous suite, decorated with eighteenth-century French, modern, and Oriental furnishings and art. Except for an ornate desk in front of its high windows and a row of polished-wood filing cabinets against one wall, it appeared to be some kind of elegant sitting room. Open double doors to her right revealed a dining room. A living suite and office combined.

As the towering doctor watched, the male attendant who held her pistol also took her day pack, and a woman searched her Western shirt and jeans. With a flash of fear, Sarah wanted to put a protective hand over the delirium in her jeans pocket, but that would only alert them. Her heart pounded against her ribs.

The attendant squeezed Sarah's jeans pocket. "Take it out."

Sarah pulled out Chantelle Joyeaux's name tag. The woman's face froze. She handed it to Dr. Levine.

"How did you get this, Sarah?"

Through a fog of fear she tried to calculate whether she would gain anything by lying. But the way the van had arrived to overwhelm her with an orchestrated attack told her time and planning had been necessary. They were undoubtedly Bremner's people from the Languedoc, and they must have known she'd been in the rear turnaround.

"I saw her body in the trunk of the Cadillac."

"Very good." Levine returned the name tag to the guard, who put it in her own pocket. "You've encouraged me that you're worth talking to. If you'd lied—" He shrugged, but the conclusion she was expected to draw was clear: Whatever fate they planned for her would have come more swiftly and cruelly.

"What did Chantelle Joyeaux do to make you kill her?" she asked, trying to distract the attendant from her search.

But almost immediately the woman found the bulge formed by the tiny vial of delirium with the paper towel wrapped around it. Blood throbbed at Sarah's temples. She didn't know exactly how, but she sensed if she were to have any hope of escaping from Levine, she had to have the delirium.

"Let's see that, too," the attendant ordered.

"My sinuses were bothering me on the flight," she lied as she pulled out the crumpled towel. She snuffled, blew her nose into it, then held it out to the attendant.

Stone-faced, the woman ignored the distasteful wad and glanced at Levine. "That's all she has on her, sir."

Sarah snuffled again and looked around. She saw the wastebasket beside the ornate desk. Her back to Levine and both attendants, she advanced on the wastebasket. Trying to appear calm, she pretended to blow her nose again, palmed the vial from the towel, and threw the wadded towel into the trash. At the same instant, with her hidden hand, she slipped the vial of delirium back into the pocket of her jeans. As she turned, a glint of silver on Levine's desk caught her eye. No surprise: It was a Cross pen, just like Gordon's.

She returned innocently to them.

The doctor nodded to the male attendant. "You can both leave and get on with your regular duties."

The two guards hesitated. The woman said, "I think we should stay with you, Doctor."

"I don't care what you think. Leave us."

The man said, "She's a trained agent. Bremner wouldn't—"

"She's a fictional agent created by me, and Bremner isn't here, I am. I'll take her gun. I assure you I know how to use it." Reluctantly the man handed Sarah's Beretta to the doctor. "Good. Get out."

The attendants left, and Levine dropped the gun into the pocket of his long white lab coat. He smiled at Sarah and said in a pleasant, almost eager, voice, "Sit wherever you like. You must be hungry after all your surveillance and exertion. We'll have dinner while we talk."

They'd been observing her the whole time. Inwardly she groaned. Liz Sansborough would have expected that. The *Herald Tribune* hadn't known she and Flores were in Paris yet, but Liz would have realized Bremner had alerted his people. Perhaps someone at the café had been Bremner's agent.

"Who was it?" she said bitterly. "The man in the straw Panama? The young couple holding hands, so much in love?"

He shook his head almost sadly. "Don't feel bad, Sarah. Hughes and his people are too experienced for you. After all, you're only a magazine writer." He sat in a damask chair in the middle of the room, relaxed and smiling. Somehow she had to get the delirium into him and soon. She could try to put it into his food, but dinner could be a long way away. She wanted the drug to begin working now, because it would take at least forty minutes to reach full effect. She had to find a way to do that immediately and get back her Beretta—

Casually she studied the two rooms. At the end of this one was a fully equipped bar with glasses hanging overhead. She saw the recessed, pencil-thin video cameras high on the walls.

The doctor watched her, and again his voice was gentle. "Don't bother considering escape, Sarah. This isn't the Ranch. All the doors have automated locks controlled from central security. The windows are a special glass compound that requires something on the level of a howitzer to break through. And our attendants are fully trained in martial arts."

He smiled his friendly smile. And, suddenly, a voice inside her said: *He wants something from you.* Not for Bremner, for himself. That was the reason for the amiable tone and the removal of the attendants and their implied threat. But Gordon had taught her well. She'd never again be duped by a disarming manner. With a rush of understanding, her mind cleared: When someone wants something, that person is vulnerable.

She had to divert his attention. "You haven't told me why you killed Chantelle Joyeaux and that man. Who were they?"

Levine sat straight, a lab-coated emperor on his damask throne, and he frowned. "Two people who made a mistake they won't make again." Then his smile returned. "Still asking questions. That's very good." He leaned forward, and suddenly his voice was again eager, almost trembling. "Tell me, Sarah, did your memory come back slowly or all at once?"

The question caught her by surprise. He didn't seem to notice. He was still leaning eagerly toward her, excited. "Did events trigger your memory, or was it spontaneous? Did you realize what was happening to you? Did you—?"

All at once she understood what he wanted: Scientific data! To Hughes Bremner and Gordon Taite she was part of a major operation against the Carnivore, but to Levine she was a research project, and he wanted what only she could tell him—her experiences. This was better than she'd dared hope. Nothing could distract a scientist as much as collecting research data from the guinea pig herself!

She said, "Why should I tell you anything? Are you going to let me walk out of here?"

"Of course! Once MASQUERADE is over, I'll simply—"

"What does Hughes Bremner want me for?"

Levine shook his head. "You know I can't tell you that."

"Then why should I tell you a damn thing?"

He leaned even closer. "For science, Sarah. For knowledge. For humanity and the future. Raise yourself above pettiness. I promise I'll make Hughes free you as soon as the operation is over." Again the smarmy smile. "Did your memory come back slowly, or all at once? Tell me, and you'll walk away."

She had to give him something, keep him interested. "A little of both. The first hint I had of returning memory was a single word. A name—Hamilton. That—" She looked toward the small bar. "I'm feeling a little shaky. Could I have a drink?"

"What?" Levine was totally involved in her story. He glanced toward his wet bar. "Oh, yes, of course."

A man with a fully stocked bar usually liked his liquor. With luck—

She saw him hesitate. She guessed he was considering whether to ring for an attendant.

"Hamilton," she went on. "The name came to me at the Ranch one day in cipher class. Then—"

She stopped and looked at the bar. Levine got the point. He stood and crossed toward it. She stood, too, following.

"You're not going to make me drink alone, I hope."

Levine glanced back at her, the gracious host. "Of course not," he said smoothly. As he moved behind the counter and took two glasses from the overhead rack, she leaned up against the front of the bar, where the cameras wouldn't be able to see, and slipped her fingers inside her jeans pocket. Feverishly she worked the vial of delirium out. A mist of sweat formed on her forehead. At last the vial slid into her palm.

He set two glasses onto the bar and reached for the bottle of Scotch. As he poured into the first glass, Sarah asked in her most composed voice, "Is there bourbon?"

"Bourbon?" He turned to search the rows of bottles. He was a Scotch drinker. It took him a while to locate the bourbon.

Meanwhile, barely moving her hand, her back to the video camera that monitored the bar area, she now worked frantically to get the stopper from the vial. A sigh of relief caught in her throat as the cork finally popped out into her hand. Quickly she dumped the golden liquid into the glass of Scotch. When Levine turned back with the bourbon, the empty vial was again in her pocket and she was suddenly drenched in sweat. He added water to both glasses and handed her the bourbon. As she followed him back to their chairs, she mopped her forehead with her sleeve.

His leg swung nervously. "Hamilton, yes. Your father's name. How did you feel when you thought of the name?"

He had all the advantages: Full security system, locked room, hellish drugs. Every advantage but one—he wanted data only she could give, scientific information he'd never get by force and still trust to be valid.

He took a long drink. "How long after you stopped taking the memory suppressant did you—?"

"I took a pill that suppressed memory?"

"Yes. Your last pill."

"You told me it was an antidepressant." She glared at him. "Then you *did* give me amnesia!"

"Yes." He smiled, thin lips over tombstone teeth. "I can tell you about that and a great deal more. Are you interested?"

"Obviously I was chosen because I could be made into Liz Sansborough's double, but was it more of your drugs that made me believe I was Liz?"

Levine nodded proudly, and Sarah saw he was as eager to brag about his work as he was to find out how she'd retrieved her past.

She suggested, "I'll tell you all about it in exchange for what I want to know."

"Agreed." He held his glass up in a toast.

They drank again as there was a knock on the door. Sarah's belly knotted. Had security seen her drug his drink after all?

"Come!" Levine snapped, annoyed by the interruption.

A waiter in a gold-trimmed white jacket and black trousers pushed a serving cart across the floor and into the dining room.

"Ah, dinner." Levine stood. "The usual 1,000 calories for me. Your fat-to-lean tissue rating at the Ranch was twenty-one percent, that means only 700 calories for you. But I guarantee the food is excellent. Our clients insist. Come."

With giddy relief, she watched him finish his Scotch and water in a single long drink. Then he marched into the dining room. She followed and took a seat at a small rococo table. The waiter served what looked like a gourmet casserole with chicken and many vegetables. Levine's plate contained nearly half again as much as hers. His fingers drummed on the table until the waiter had finished. Then he abruptly waved him out and leaned toward her again without touching his food.

"First tell me when you stopped taking your memory pill. What made you do it? Had your memory begun to return before?"

She ate. He waited, impatient, not looking at his food, and she finally began to reveal some of the timetable and details. She didn't let him know she still had little memory of the time between meeting Gordon and awaking as Liz Sansborough. That was one piece of information she needed to learn from him before the delirium took effect.

She had to keep him talking, eating, doing anything, for thirty more minutes. Each time she insisted she'd given him enough, he told her more of what she wanted to know, until, as the minutes passed slowly, she learned at last what they'd done to her.

Thirty-nine

It had all started in late spring with the Carnivore's offer to come in. What neither Arlene Debo, the President, nor the Carnivore himself had known was that the assassin had knowledge so threatening to the operations of Hughes Bremner and his board that they couldn't let him come in alive. Not ever, not anywhere.

Bremner had to silence the Carnivore. But the White House and half of Europe would be watching the coming-in, so he needed a plan involving minimal risk and maximum certainty. He'd gone to Dr. Allan Levine, one of the world's foremost brain scientists, who had long been on the CIA payroll. And on Bremner's secret payroll as well.

In his youth, Levine had been the protégé of the "godfather" of Canadian psychiatry—Dr. Ewen Cameron, who, in the 1950s and 1960s, had conducted CIA-funded experiments in brainwashing. The code name for that vast black project had been MK-ULTRA. Using a front called the Society for the Investigation of Human Ecology, MK-ULTRA had piped some $25 million through Cornell University to fifty universities in twenty-one countries.

The purpose of MK-ULTRA had been to discover how to control the mind, because the Soviets and the Chinese had been refining techniques in brainwashing and interrogation, and because Langley wanted more efficient ways to restore mental health than were offered by conventional psychiatry.

An obvious recipient of MK-ULTRA funding had been Montreal's

McGill University, where the renowned Dr. Cameron worked. While scientists in the United States conducted MK-ULTRA experiments on prisoners and prostitutes, Dr. Cameron used average Canadian citizens who came to his clinic with problems like anxiety and depression. None of the U.S. prostitutes and prisoners, nor the ordinary Canadians, was informed he or she was the subject of mind-altering experiments.

Dr. Cameron's treatments were intense, as extreme as the politics of the time. They included enormous amounts of drugs, including a then-brand-new hallucinogen, LSD. He conducted up to a hundred high-intensity electroshock treatments on patients, medicated them to sleep for up to eighty days, and played uninterrupted messages around the clock, often during drug-induced sleep.

The doctor worked directly on the central nervous system, and one of his findings was that this approach could go too far. One patient, who had sought treatment for mild anxiety, emerged six months later unable to recognize her husband or children, unable to read, write, cook, drive a car, or control her bladder. It was unfortunate, of course, but to Cameron and his protégé, Dr. Levine, it was an acceptable cost for scientific progress.

Eventually news of the experiments leaked out. Inquiries and lawsuits followed.

To protect everyone, Langley burned its MK-ULTRA files in 1973. Dr. Cameron had died in a mountaineering accident in 1967, and his family had the foresight to destroy his project records, too. MK-ULTRA was abandoned and destroyed.

But, at Hughes Bremner's urging, Langley secretly kept the sole link to MK-ULTRA—Cameron's brilliant assistant, Dr. Allan Levine.

They gave Dr. Levine his own secret lab in New Mexico to continue his search for biochemical solutions to psychoses. In furthering Dr. Cameron's dream of perfecting the mind, Levine developed a simple theory: In plumbing, when a pipe was badly broken, it must be replaced. So, too, the badly broken personality. He foresaw the future mental health of the world resting on its ability to redesign sick personalities.

And in total secrecy, with Hughes Bremner's encouragement and private financial support, he continued MK-ULTRA.

Every year his experiments on lab animals and the occasional human "volunteer" yielded impressive data. Then, two years ago, Bremner instructed the doctor to move his work, including the secret new MK-ULTRA experiments, to Paris. He would start a visionary "health" club and fulfill the promise of his research. Dr. Levine had leaped at the chance.

Thus MK-ULTRA continued. And, because Langley fostered a cult of protectiveness and deniability—the tendency to deny anyone was doing anything—Hughes Bremner and Dr. Levine had successfully kept the reborn MK-ULTRA and its unique spa/clinic under wraps. In any case, club members themselves required absolute secrecy. None wanted to be remade in the harsh glare of publicity or government rumor, and all wanted to keep this remarkable rejuvenation to themselves. There were only thirty members, each with his or her special attendants and masseuse.

Like his Canadian mentor, Levine focused on the brain, a three-pound galaxy with more nerve cells than the Milky Way had stars, some hundred billion of them. These nerve cells controlled all brain functions, including sensation, emotion, memory, and movement. In the early days of MK-ULTRA, Cameron had used a medical sledgehammer to attack all the nerve cells. Now his protégé took a far more refined approach. His new MK-ULTRA worked on the specific parts of the brain where modification was desired.

And then the Carnivore's decision to come in had jeopardized it all. The assassin could unmask and destroy everything. He had to be eliminated, and it had to be done without the faintest hint that Hughes Bremner, Mustang, or the CIA was involved. There could be no suspicion, no investigation. So Bremner had conceived MASQUER-ADE and delivered Sarah Walker to the doctor.

Dr. Levine claimed he could impose a range of changes on anyone—from a simple attitude to a whole new personality. He was particularly enthusiastic about Sarah Walker, because she provided a special challenge: Her type was the hardest to reprogram—she was young, resilient, optimistic, self-confident, held firm beliefs, had a strong sense of self, and had stable ties to family and friends.

He had begun by cutting her off from her family and friends. Then he'd provided a single surrogate "friend" on whom she could depend, a "friend" who would make her believe she needed psychiatric help, because cooperative subjects interacted more readily with the medication and more quickly and easily assumed new identities.

Sarah tried to get the details of how he and Bremner had manipulated her into cooperating, but his mind was so obsessed with his own theories she could learn no more without alarming him.

Once they'd convinced her to not only agree with but *want* treatment, Dr. Levine had put her on his state-of-the-art drugs. The various chemicals had affected two areas of her brain. The first was the hippocampus, where long-term memory was established. The second was the neocortex, where permanent memory accumulated. The drugs shut down the synapses of her fact-memory storage in both areas.

She lost her past, but her ability to function and perform most tasks soon returned. With new chemicals, she easily assumed a new identity.

But there was a problem. The human brain was so powerful, its ability to store and retrieve data so vast, that even the world's greatest supercomputers were no match for it. In fact, the brain was such a strong, resilient instrument, there was always the risk it might rebalance itself.

In other words, she might regain her memory on her own.

The doctor had forestalled that possibility by instructing Gordon Taite to feed her a daily pill that was a powerful fact-memory suppressor disguised as an antidepressant. As long as she took it, she'd never recall she was Sarah Walker. She would be Liz Sansborough, career CIA agent, recently retired.

When the Carnivore came in, Bremner would personally take the assassin to a safe house in France—not the United States—for the first debriefing. Experts from various Langley desks would be invited, all eager to pump the infamous killer. But before anyone could be alone with him, the assassin would die without any possibility of suspicion falling on Bremner, Mustang, or the CIA itself. An unforeseeable murder. Tragic, but unpreventable. MASQUERADE would fulfill its goals.

Dr. Allan Levine ran his fingers across the rococo dining table, his voice triumphant. "What I and other scientists have done with our subjects benefits the human race as a whole. Because of us, the species can surge forward in evolution. Already I have remedied weaknesses and enhanced strengths in my patients. I can enrich memory, enhance intellect, heighten concentration, and alter any subject's moods. Making Homo sapiens increasingly superior is my life's work, and soon I'll have all the money I need to continue into undreamed-of realms."

He was growing more flamboyant, and Sarah watched with an icy chill. He kept referring to the people he'd experimented on as "subjects" and "patients" and "the species." She'd read about the MK-ULTRA trials in Canada. His so-called patients were *victims*. He, a medical doctor who'd taken an oath to heal, damaged innocent people permanently in the name of science! She shivered. He could do it to her, too.

She said, "I've got my memory. What do you plan to do now? Are you going to make me believe I'm Liz Sansborough again?"

He seemed to be struggling to think. Then he smiled broadly. "Actually, no. Something quite different."

"No more drugs?"

"Chemicals will be involved, but—" The doctor stopped. He seemed confused, as if he couldn't remember what he'd been going to say. Then his gaunt face cleared. "Henrik Ibsen once wrote: 'To wish and to will. Our worst faults are the consequence of confusing the two things.' The will is our mightiest attribute—our mental and emotional steel. Full cooperation requires one's will, and the will is, as far as the electrochemical charges of neurotransmitters are concerned, vital to maximum functioning. It is your *will* I'll use this time, your cooperation! Your *will* . . . my genius . . . and Hughes will have all he needs to end the Carnivore and have millions to give my work!"

"If you think I'm going to cooperate, you'd better go take some of your own damn drugs, because you're crazy, Levine."

The doctor leaned back, spread his arms wide, and beamed euphorically at her. "Ah, it's not an expectation, it's a necessity. And I promise you, Sarah, you will do exactly what we want."

Forty

In Christine Robitaille's shop, Asher Flores leaned back in his chair and threw his arms above his head. He stretched, groaned, and glared at the glowing computer screen in front of him. God, what crappy luck. He'd tried all his tricks to find a link in ten different databases between Gold Star Rent-a-Car and Langley, Hughes Bremner, or Gordon Taite. All he'd come up with so far was a crummy backache and black dots dancing before his eyes.

He grumbled under his breath. Which gave him another idea—the Carnivore's dossier. Maybe the old bastard himself had some connection to Gold Star that Asher had missed.

He called up the assassin's file, but he found nothing new . . . until the end. What a bombshell: The President of the United States had canceled the assassin's ticket! The Carnivore had been told to take his business to some other country, because the United States refused to dirty its hands playing with him!

Asher turned the situation over in his mind and decided it didn't improve his and Walker's situation. Nope. In fact, if she wasn't necessary to Hughes Bremner anymore, they were decidedly worse off. As in "terminated."

The thought of losing Sarah disturbed Asher. She'd been on his mind ever since they'd parted that evening. It made him a little queasy to admit he actually missed her. He sighed. Neither would be alive to miss anyone if they didn't discover what that SOB Bremner was up to.

He signed off from Langley and accessed an international business data bank. There he found a profile of Gold Star. It appeared to be a huge, reputable international company, the biggest car-rental agency in the United States, with branches all over Europe and Asia. It was owned by Sterling-O'Keefe Enterprises, a colossal corporation of which even Asher had heard. He studied the screen and the long list of companies under the Sterling-O'Keefe umbrella. As he printed out the list, he rubbed his eyes. The name Sterling-O'Keefe kept clanging around in his brain, and he was wondering why.

Hughes Bremner settled back sleepily in his first-class seat, the *Washington Post* open on his chest. The gentle vibration of the great jet flying over the Atlantic was restful, lulling. Then the telephone jarred him awake.

It was his private Langley computer operator. "Sir, we've been accessed by Gordon Taite's old code. The access point's Paris, the Left Bank—"

Mentally Bremner rubbed his hands. Asher Flores!

With no show of emotion he told the operator, "Fine work, Ryan. Send the location to the Languedoc immediately." His people in Paris already had their instructions. "And Ryan, keep watching for anything more from over there."

He'd barely hung up and settled back to savor the news when his phone rang again. It was a patch-through from Paris—one of Allan Levine's assistants on a scrambled line: "Sir! The doctor wanted you to know we've got Sarah Walker. He expects to get her cooperation and begin her new program immediately!"

Bremner grinned a cold, wolfish grin. He had her. The key to MASQUERADE. Now the success of both MASQUERADE and GRANDEUR was assured. He kept his voice low, cool. "Tell the doctor to hold her in tight confinement. We can't be too careful."

"Yessir," the assistant said happily, "but, ah, there's been a slight problem."

Bremner frowned. The doctor had learned something from their years together. He'd no doubt told the assistant to relay the good news first, soften him up, so he wouldn't be as angry about the bad. "What's happened?"

"We found two of the masseuses going through the MK-ULTRA files. We could see no other solution than to eliminate them."

That irritated Bremner. He'd told Levine to hire only those who'd proved their curiosity could be bought. Instead the stupid idealist had gone his own way and hired for expertise. As soon as he arrived in Paris, Bremner would get rid of all the nonpros on Levine's staff.

He hung up and sat for a time, his anger smoldering. He hated incompetence. Then he forced himself to relax. He looked out the window as twilight spread lavender and black across the darkening ocean. Success was his. Triumph warmed him. He had Sarah Walker, and soon he'd have Asher Flores, too. Smiling broadly, he picked up his private phone once more. This time he dialed GRAN-DEUR's financial coordinator, Kit Crowther.

Asher Flores's joints ached. He stood and stretched. He picked up the *Herald Tribune* and strolled through the computer shop. Christine Robitaille was nowhere in sight. Her sales assistant was involved with a group of teen clients.

Outside, Asher looked up and down the dark Paris street. Then he leaned back against the shop and, under the overhead lights, opened his newspaper. At the back of the news section he came across a little two-paragraph story:

> Former U.S. intelligence official Lucas Maynard was killed yesterday by federal agents outside the U.S. State department. According to authorities, Maynard had been trying to escape with a kilo of cocaine hidden in a shopping bag. . . .

Asher couldn't believe it. Maynard had been many things, but a drug pusher? He was a true-blue, dedicated member of the old cold warriors. One of Hughes Bremner's deputies and closest associates. Maynard was the kind of gung-ho guy who'd work until he dropped or some retirement administrator had to kick his ass out the door. A pusher? No way.

Unless Maynard had been on an operation and the "federal agents" had made a terrible mistake.

Asher didn't believe that either. If Lucas Maynard was dead, who'd *really* killed him? And why?

Asher returned to the computer store and knocked on the door labeled OFFICE.

Christine Robitaille called, *"Entrez!"*

He stepped inside. "You remember Lucas Maynard?"

She stubbed out her cigarette in an overflowing ashtray. "I saw the item. Killed. He was a bad man to deal in drugs." She studied his face. "You do not believe it, eh? Listen to me, Asher, *mon cher.* The 'good' do evil for all the best reasons. Most often, so they can think they are still good." She shrugged and lit another cigarette.

He wanted to ask what she knew about Hughes Bremner. It would be a relief to tell her what had happened because he had helped Sarah Walker and because Bremner now was out to get them. But he didn't. It was unnecessary. He said good-bye. Her steely face was philosophical as she smoked like a diesel over her piles of papers and wished him *bon voyage.*

In the remote Virginia cabin Bunny Bremner refused to look again at the old iron bed where poor Marilyn lay. Because Marilyn was unconscious and unable to move, the two men hadn't bothered to tie her again, although bloodstained clothesline waited at each of the iron posters. The journalist was seminude, shivering in the night. Cuts and bruises covered her. Bunny decided Marilyn must have been lying in her own vomit and excrement. If she had no fever yet, she soon would. If she got no medical attention, she could die.

In her mind, Bunny could still see Marilyn's lovely heart-shaped face. Now it had swollen almost beyond recognition. For a beautiful woman, there was no worse punishment. Except growing old with a man who despised her.

Bunny sat tied to a straight-backed kitchen chair. The ropes cut into her wrists and ankles. She gritted her teeth and willed herself, the descendant of John Howland of the *Mayflower,* to not shame him and all her other illustrious forebears. She remembered the last time she'd felt physical pain. That was when she'd still ridden. A high-spirited Arabian of impeccable bloodlines had thrown her, breaking her arm. She'd driven to the village hospital, had the arm set, driven home, remounted the stallion, and finished the ride.

She tried to grasp what was happening. All her life she'd lived in the safety of family and name. Only deviant freaks could have done such evil as she saw here. She had no training to deal with depravity.

The one named Sid opened her wallet. "Jesus Christ. Mrs. Bremner, what's your husband's name?" Fear radiated from him like heat from an open fire.

She saw his fear and made her voice severe. "Hughes Bremner.
He'll see you go to prison for the way you've mistreated Ms. Michaels and me. It would be wise to release us. Ms. Michaels needs
medical treatment. If she dies, you'll be convicted of murder."

Sid and his partner went outside, and through the kitchen window she watched them. She could hear enough to know they were
arguing about whether to call Hughes. They knew Hughes?

She couldn't follow the logic farther. A connection among these
two heinous creatures, Hughes, and the CIA was unthinkable. She
wanted a drink. Scotch straight up. A double. But she fought the
terrible desire. She had to find a way to help Marilyn . . . and
herself.

As Hughes Bremner ate his dinner in the luxurious first-class
lounge, Sid Williams called to give him the news that not only did
they have Leslee Pousho, they also had his wife, Bunny Bremner.

He was actually speechless. What in hell did Bunny think she was
doing? The stupid, drunken bitch! He had no choice but to get rid
of her, he knew that instantly, and yet he still felt that old invisible
bond. She'd been the future of his youthful fantasies. He'd been
different then, an idealist who'd fawned over his wife. But reality
intervened when Bunny had betrayed him, and his government had
betrayed him. For an odd instant he had the feeling he'd always
known both would.

He'd expected never to see her again. After Monday, with the
fulfillment of his Faustian aspirations, he would disappear, and he'd
relished the image of Bunny left abandoned in the Virginia manor
that was far more important to her than he'd ever been. He'd
planned for her to grow decrepit alone, knowing she'd been discarded, no longer wanted even for her money.

But not now. Now she'd have to die.

He asked Sid, "Do you have any Scotch?"

"Not here, boss."

"Go buy a couple of bottles. Give Bunny all she wants. Then get
ready to burn down the cabin with the two women in it. Make it look
like an accident. Old wiring, whatever you can find. Do it tomorrow
morning. If the Xeroxes of Lucas's papers haven't appeared by
then, Pousho never made any."

"It's fire season, boss. The mountains are real dry."

"I know." A gaudy sendoff for the alcoholic old shrew. She was a
useless artifact from a dead dream.

In the cabin in the Blue Ridge Mountains, Bunny Bremner remained gagged and tied to the kitchen chair. She'd offered the men
a million dollars if they'd release her and Marilyn. The tall one,
Fess, had been tempted, but Sid had gagged her.

The men went outside, and she heard one of them talking on
what had to be a cellular phone. Then the Volvo drove away. The
leader, Sid, came back in, and Bunny watched him play solitaire,
drink coffee, and fiddle with the radio. Marilyn moaned from the
bed. He'd thrown a blanket over her, but now she was running
a fever. Her battered, swollen face was crimson and twisted with
pain.

The Volvo returned, and Fess carried in three bottles of Johnnie
Walker Black Label.

Bunny couldn't help staring. They noticed and exchanged cold
smiles.

"Take off her gag." At the kitchen table, Sid opened a bottle.
"Drag her chair over here and untie her hands."

The sweet smell of Scotch was intoxicating. Automatically she
reached for the bottle. Then she stopped. She looked up at the two
men. "How did you know?"

"A little bird told us. Come on, drink up."

She remembered the telephone call. "You talked to Hughes. You
work for Hughes."

Sid considered the question. "Yeah, he's my boss."

"You're going to kill us, aren't you?"

Fess said, "I guess he don't like you anymore."

"He's never liked me," she snapped. "He likes my money. But
why kill me now? And Marilyn?"

Sid sat at the kitchen table and pushed the open bottle to her. "I
don't know, Mrs. Bremner. We've just got our orders, that's all. He's
been my boss a long time, and he's taken real good care of me."

Bunny studied their expressionless faces. Two public employees
who, on her husband's orders, planned to kill her. Her husband,
the man she'd slept with and wept over for decades, had ordered
these degenerates to murder her.

She looked at the bottle as Sid picked it up. She clamped her hand over her mouth, but it was no use. Fess pulled her hand away and forced her mouth open. Sid poured the whisky down her throat. She gagged and coughed. Then the alcohol hit her bloodstream. Warmth and relaxation swept through her. She sobbed and reached for the bottle.

Forty-one

Dr. Levine gestured across the dining table, his eyes glowing. "Not long ago my scientific achievements would have seemed wizardry. Now they're merely part of biotechnology." His skull-head was thrown back, savoring his successes. If Sarah hadn't been so tense, she'd have enjoyed the irony—he'd used LSD to experiment on unknowing victims, and now he was an unknowing LSD victim himself.

"Today, DNA can decode the universe, babies start life in Petri dishes, and a synthetic human-growth hormone can reverse dwarfism," he continued. "Research was recently published claiming we'll soon know so much about replacing pieces of human chemistry we'll be able to slow aging and reverse some of its effects." He laughed too loudly. "I could've published that myself, because it's one of the tools I've developed and have been using extensively here at Je Suis Chez Moi!"

Listening to him, knowing what he'd done, nauseated Sarah. But she had to learn how and when she was supposed to help Hughes Bremner murder the Carnivore. "What's my role in MASQUERADE?"

He blinked at her, then smiled craftily. "Ah, that you'll find out soon, eh?" He laughed aloud, pleased with himself. Besides the excitement of gathering her data for his files, it seemed to her he was beginning to show the effects of the delirium. Soon the LSD hallucinations should begin, too. His symptoms could include spasms, choking, and massive psychedelic visions. Eventually he'd lose control and love it, and then she'd have to grab her Beretta from his coat pocket and escape before the video cameras alerted security to stop her.

She said, "Je Suis Chez Moi has to be very important to Bremner. All the money it must have cost. This suite, for example. Impeccable and extremely expensive."

Levine waved his hand dreamily. "All our suites are magnificent. Only the elite of Paris can come here."

"Like the Prime Minister?"

"Oh, yes, especially Prime Minister Vauban." He almost giggled. "Because of the great politician and his powerful friends, Hughes will soon give us permanent funding for a fully equipped lab in which I'll continue to push the envelope of modern science. And all because of my work with MK-ULTRA and you—my first complete identity transfer. Your redesign was a victory, until Gordon bungled the memory pill. But by Monday the Carnivore will be dead, and I'll never have to beg for money again!" He beamed at Sarah, on the edge of a complete ecstasy-LSD high. Maybe she could break through his defenses now.

"Monday? Is that when the Carnivore is coming in?"

"No. Eight o'clock Sunday night. *All* our worries—"

"That's tomorrow!"

"Plenty of time, now that you're here." He arose, swaying but unaware of it. "Come, there's something you should see."

She wanted to bash him against the wall, shatter every bone in his evil body. But she followed him out into the corridor. She looked for attendants, but there were none. Not twenty feet away she saw the massive double front doors. She had no time to see more before they turned down a side hallway.

Levine opened the first in a series of closed doors, and they entered a massage room scented with pungent eucalyptus oil. A young man was working the quadriceps of an attractive woman of about thirty. She lay beneath a sheet, and an IV dripped into her thigh. Her eyes were closed, and she appeared to be sleeping, yet there was a sunny smile on her face.

Sarah said, "I recognize her—"

Levine waved a hand smugly. "Louise Dupuy, France's most popular news anchor."

The young masseur stared at the doctor.

"And the most powerful," Sarah said quickly and stepped between Levine and the young man. "But she's got to be fifty years old, not thirty. And she used to have an enormous weight problem."

The doctor clasped his small hands. "She's also an alcoholic and has a history of drug abuse. But she's been coming to me for a year. At first it was four hours a day, because her problems were so vast. Now it's only one hour. She's had cosmetic surgery. She takes no more drugs or alcohol, and she eats and rests properly. That, plus our exercise, resistance, and chemical programs have resulted in this." He swept his hand grandly over her slender, still frame. "Now she no longer fears losing her job to a younger and more beautiful competitor, because she herself *is* young and extremely competitive."

"Amazing," Sarah said, taking Levine's arm as the masseur again stared. "There can't be more than this."

"More?" The doctor swayed, then laughed aloud. "I'll show you more. Come on."

They returned to the empty hall. He reached out to balance himself against the wall, his face puzzled.

"Did you change Louise Dupuy's personality?"

He pushed himself upright, nodded vigorously. "An attitude adjustment, you might say. I've discovered chemicals that cause certain personality traits, and from that I've developed drugs so I can perform mental makeovers. Each client gets a standard neural sculpting, which includes patterning them to return here daily and to feel robust and self-confident, plus whatever idiosyncratic changes they or we want. Not so difficult now."

He opened the next door, and they entered a twilight room of tubes, blinking lights, and the soft whoosh and click of various machines. The air smelled of antiseptic and soap. In the center was a cot on which lay a white-blanketed man with an IV dripping and various attachments to heart, forehead, wrists, and ankles.

There was no attendant in this room. The doctor's hand trembled as he touched the man's forehead, but the caress was so gentle it seemed almost loving. The man's eyes stared at the ceiling as if he were seeing a distant land.

"Gerard," Dr. Levine asked in French, "how do you feel?"

"Joyeux. Robuste. Intelligent. Constant. Vive La Grandeur!"

"You see, Sarah, our Gerard is a tycoon who owns many companies. His workers threaten to strike because of low wages, long hours, and poor working conditions. And of course there are the new, very high taxes." He translated for Gerard. "Correct?"

"Absolument!"

The doctor hesitated, trying to construct his next thought. Then: "But Gerard is aware of the greater good, and so he is holding steadfast—*constant*—and refusing to give them what they want. Therefore, most will surely strike on Monday, *non?*"

He again translated, and Gerard agreed.

"But why not give them something of what they need?"

"Some of our special clients are vital to Hughes. All had to learn certain 'attitudes.' The neural circuits responsible for ideas or attitudes are slow to act in the beginning, but once the idea is practiced over and over—much as you experienced as you assumed the identity of Liz Sansborough—the brain reorganizes itself and changes the neural circuitry to embed the idea. Aided by pharmacopeia, the process is infallible, and the payoff is, of course, *La Grandeur*—"

He froze. Sarah tensed. The doctor doubled over, head nearly at his knees. He made a hoarse sound in his chest, deep and painful, and straightened instantly upright. He swayed back and forth as if caught in an earthquake, then lurched around the dim room knocking down machines, smashing equipment, holding to anything he could. He turned his head to stare at Sarah, seeming to understand something was amiss. He whacked over the IV and crashed into the cot, throwing Gerard naked to the floor.

Sarah yelled up to a camera, "Medical emergency! Hurry! Medical emergency!" She grabbed a long white lab coat from a hook on the wall and quickly put it on, an impromptu disguise.

Levine lurched, stared at her. "What's wrong with me?" Bewilderment stretched his skull-face in a grimace. Then his features transformed: He grinned, happy, euphoric, and abruptly collapsed. Sarah grabbed him, turned his back to the cameras, and slipped her Beretta from his coat pocket. Then she let him fall to the floor and jumped behind the door.

She could hear feet pounding down the corridor. She steeled herself—she had to be tougher this time.

Six people burst in. Two, with stethoscopes jammed into the pockets of their white coats, ran to Levine and Gerard. Two more, who looked like nurses or orderlies, joined them. The fifth, a female attendant with a gun, stood over the others. The sixth held an automatic in front of him with both hands and swiveled all around the room. He saw Sarah and her Beretta. She felt herself hesitate.

"Who are you!" His finger tightened on his trigger.

She had no choice. She shot, and he slammed back against the female attendant with the gun. Sarah dashed into the corridor. She waited, nerves frayed. The female attendant ran out, gun up but off-balance. Sarah slammed her Beretta across the woman's face. The woman sprawled unconscious, and Sarah tore off toward the front corridor.

One of the front doors was open, and a voice spoke loudly from outside to an attendant who looked down from the doorway. "But my dear! No one refuses Blount McCaw. Tell your guru doctor he'll really, *really* want to talk to me!"

Oh, God! It was the unmistakable voice of her old friend and informant, Blount McCaw. He slid past the attendant and turned down the hall toward Sarah. He was wearing chinos and photographer's vest, no shirt, waving a tape recorder. Two more attendants ran past Sarah toward him. They were the young couple from the Café Justine! Bremner's people! Both had guns out, but in their haste they'd seen only the white lab coat Sarah wore and had not noticed who she was.

Blount saw their weapons and froze in terror.

Sarah yelled, "Blount! Get out of here!"

"Sarah? My God, Sarah, is that you? What have you done to yourself? You used to look so original, and now . . . your face! It's *ordinary!* You look like a *celebrity!*"

A mournful beep began to pulse all around them. It was the security alarm, rising and falling with the hypnotic insistence of "Bolero." For a split second, Bremner's agents were confused. The woman fired at Blount, who had turned to run.

Blount's head exploded. The shot had entered from behind and exited out his nose, taking off the top part of his face and leaving his lips peeled back in terror.

"Blount!" she screamed. But she knew he was dead, and she knew she had to save herself.

The man had seen her face and recognized her. His weapon focused on her heart. She didn't hesitate. She shot him three times. He fell, blood geysering from his chest. As she charged to the doorway she shot the woman's leg out from under her. The attendant at the door dove for cover.

Sarah sprinted past the unarmed attendant and the body of Blount McCaw and out into the warm night air, the "Bolero" alarm relentless and maniacal behind her. The long lab coat flapped against the backs of her legs as she picked up speed.

Then, a sudden, needle-sharp pain pierced her brain. A bullet had sliced across her left shoulder. Blood streamed out onto the white lab coat. Tears rose in her eyes, but they were more for Blount than for herself. She had no time for tears. She tore down the sidewalk as if all the hounds of hell chased her.

Within seconds a half-dozen Je Suis Chez Moi attendants cascaded through the door. She reached the rue Vivienne still holding her Beretta, with no money, no passport, no car, and too many trained killers in hot pursuit. She sprinted through traffic to the other side of the street. Horns blared. Drivers cursed. She pushed panic from her mind.

She saw the older gentleman with the straw Panama and red tartan band back at his outdoor table at the Café Justine. The hat was pulled low over his eyes, and the stem of his pipe was sticking up from his shirt pocket. In the haze of her mind it almost seemed he stood up and gestured to her.

Before she could sort it out, a huge force threw her explosively against a shop wall. A thunderous roar deafened her. She ducked and wrapped her arms over her head as bricks and stucco pelted down from the buildings above.

When at last it seemed safe, she stood and looked back. The front of the Greco-Roman mansion that housed Je Suis Chez Moi had disappeared behind a thick cloud. One stone column remained standing, rising above the smoke. Thick gray vapors billowed out into the street.

It had to have been a bomb. Did someone have some kind of vendetta against Je Suis Chez Moi? Or . . . another thought . . . perhaps it had been intended to kill her!

Forty-two

At the explosion, cars had slammed and crashed into each other all along the rue Vivienne. People shouted. Smoke spread. Residents ran out of apartments and cafés to see what had happened. Sarah noticed the man in the straw Panama strolling away, newspaper rolled under his arm, hands buried deep in his pockets as if nothing had happened. There was a jaunty air about him, and it seemed to her he was whistling.

Suddenly three bullets sang past her face so close she felt their hot draft, and a man in a white attendant's uniform limped toward her from out of the smoke and dust. She ran in a twisting course, around corners and along dark streets, for five full minutes before she glanced back over her shoulder. He was still chasing, and now there was a second one! A big man who appeared to be injured and a muscular, armed woman.

Sarah put on a burst of speed. Who'd set the bomb? And why? The man in the straw Panama might have had something to do with it. Otherwise he'd have stopped at the curb with the other gawkers to enjoy the thrill of the spectacle, or he'd have joined in the rescue operations. Had he gestured to her? Maybe tried to warn her? Or to point her closer so she'd die?

She angled up a flowered path. Her shoulder throbbed like hell. She felt light-headed. She had to hide. To her right stood a row of private houses with iron rails guarding their depressed basement areas. She leaped over a rail and landed quietly next to trash cans.

Dust rolled up, coating the lab coat dirty gray. She repressed a sneeze. The trash reminded her of Flores and their frantic escape from the Ranch in the garbage truck. It seemed like months had passed, but today was Saturday, and that must have happened on Thursday—only two days ago.

So many events . . . so much . . . everything! . . . had changed since then. And it seemed she was thinking more often of Asher, and how appealing she found his crazy, sweet, cocky self. What was wrong with her?

God, her shoulder hurt.

Then she heard footsteps on the sidewalk above. She'd have to move again.

Silently she melted back toward the dark house and felt her way around the side. That's when she got a glimpse of heaven: A flight of steps led to a high stone wall with a gate. She ran lightly up and opened it. Before her spread an eerie sight—a vast, old cemetery. A sea of bone-pale limestone and granite crosses and monuments stood as ghostly white as she must have been in her dusty lab coat.

She blessed her good fortune and hustled off, her shoulder burning terribly, scrapes and bruises aching. She was a weary, bloody wraith in clothes as chalky as the stone statues she hugged for cover.

Christine Robitaille's computer shop was about to close. Asher Flores nodded good-bye to her sales assistant and pushed out through the door into the gay *cité* evening. Without warning, three men emerged smoothly from the shadows and jammed shielded guns into his flesh. Like tourists they wore shorts and loose, open-necked shirts, and they jostled around pretending to be old friends in a partying mood who'd bumped into him unexpectedly.

"Good to see you, Asher, old pal!" The speaker removed Asher's Gunsite Service Pistol from beneath his arm, and, in a small, tight group, they pushed him down the sidewalk.

Bremner's men. How the hell had they found him so soon?

"Flores, you've fucked up big time," a second man advised in a low growl. "Only one thing's going to save your lying ass this time. Where's Sarah Walker?"

"Hey, when you guys find her, let me know," Asher said innocently. "That's what I've been doing myself. Looking for her. Tried everything. Hughes asked me to help out, you know."

"You never give up, do you, Flores?"

"Give up? I try to help, and all I get is guns in my ribs. What kind of thanks is that?" Sweat formed on Asher's forehead. Had Interpol alerted Christine Robitaille? When she'd gone into her office, had she reported him? Or had someone finally thought to track him through Gordon's code?

"In here, asshole." One of the men shoved Asher toward an alley. A dark-blue Renault was waiting next to a crumbling brick wall about twenty-five feet away. As one of the men unlocked the door, Asher coughed.

"Don't try it, Flores!"

"Jeez, you people are jumpy. So, tell me where you've been, and I'll tell you where I've been. We'll quit wasting time."

"Right." The first man swung open the door to the back seat. "Play dumb. You don't have a clue who nuked Matt Lister and the new kid, Beno Durante, in Denver, right?"

"Denver?" Asher waited for someone to push him toward the car door. He wanted that push. Wanted the momentum—

"Get in, chickenshit." It was the third man. His lips curled with revulsion. In their business a turned agent was more hated than a cop killer. To them, Asher had turned.

Asher stalled. "Not until you tell me what's going down."

There was no shove. They were too smart for that.

"Hey, come on, guys—" he tried again, but from behind a hard hand slammed down on the soft spot between Asher's shoulder and neck. A wave of pain engulfed him. He felt himself topple. Before he could recover, someone shoved him into the open car door. He flopped onto the seat. His legs sprawled out onto the alley's cobblestones. They weren't going to give him an opportunity to turn their momentum back on them. They—

"Don't move!" It was a woman's voice. "Any of you!"

Asher lifted his head. For a moment he didn't recognize her. "Walker! What in hell's happened to you? Watch these three clowns!" And then he saw she didn't need the advice. Her gaze never left Bremner's three men as she prowled warily down the dark alley toward them. She held her Beretta in both hands, cool and steady, ready for business. Christ, she'd been wounded: She'd got a

long dirty white coat from somewhere, and a lot of fresh red blood
plastered it to her left shoulder and chest! Her face was ashen and
filthy beneath wild black hair that stuck out all around her head.
She looked as if she'd just been in a fight to the death . . . and
won!

"That's Sarah Walker?" one of the trio asked, stunned.

The three men raised their eyebrows at each other, suddenly cautious. One remained where he was covering Asher. The other two
turned and moved toward her, aiming their weapons.

"Back up! Drop your guns!" She fired at their feet. The bullets
hit the cobblestones and whined.

"Our orders are to bring you—"

Before he could finish, Asher kicked the guy who was guarding
him so hard in the knees he heard a pop. The guy crashed back.

"Freeze, Flores!" It was one of the two men who'd been focused
on Sarah. "We don't have to bring *you* in alive!"

But Asher was lightning fast. The guy he'd kicked had dropped
Asher's pistol. Asher dove. The man raised himself up, while at the
same time the other two turned like vipers and hurtled down the
alley at Sarah.

"Stop!" Sarah yelled at the same time Asher rolled and fired. The
fallen man's temple erupted in blood and bone as he twisted sideways still kicking, trying to attack. Asher came up on his knees in
time to see the other two closing in on Sarah. A new, chilling look
flashed into her eyes. It was as if a huge floodlight had turned on in
her brain.

"Oh, shit!" She fired twice.

Instantly she realized all her questions about who and what she
was had vanished in the accuracy and dispassion of those two shots.
At such close range, the pair blasted back limp as straw men, blood
splattering across the dark cobblestones, bullets in their hearts.
She'd had no time for niceties like aiming for legs or shoulders.
There were two of them; one of her. It was their lives, or a date for
her with Bremner's satanic doctor.

Like the sudden release of an overinflated balloon, her fear of
incompetence evaporated. Her rage vaporized. What was left were
resolve and inevitability. Bremner had made a fatal mistake. She was
now Sarah Walker *and* Liz Sansborough. Both of them in one person, the union engraved on her cortex.

The alley was suddenly quiet. Traffic flowed normally on the street beyond. Asher took her arm. "Walker? Are you okay?"

She nodded. "I'm fine, Flores. Let's get out of here."

She made a vow to herself in that moment: She'd never let that bastard Bremner get away with anything again.

Forty-three

But Sarah and Asher didn't move. In the thin light of the Paris alley, they stared at each other across the three dead bodies.

"Christ," Asher breathed. He had that visceral sense he'd been waiting for her, and only her, all his life.

"Asher?" She had a sudden desire for marriage, and an instant jarring shock that such an idea could cross her mind. Permanence? Commitment? Her? Now?

"What?" he said.

In the distance a siren began to rise and fall, and what she'd been about to say was gone. She turned to the dead men's car. "You'd better drive," she said. She fell into the front seat of the dark-blue Renault, her Beretta on her lap, holding her throbbing shoulder.

He found car keys on one of the corpses, slid behind the wheel, and drove out of the alley.

"How bad's your wound?" Flores worried. "You need a doctor?"

"The bullet didn't go deep. Just across the top of my shoulder. I need antiseptic and some antibacterial cream. Aspirin for the pain. I had a tetanus shot at the Ranch." She dropped her head back, finally allowing herself to feel the depths of her weariness.

"Where's your day pack?"

"In Dr. Levine's office at Je Suis Chez Moi."

"Dr. Levine's—!" He glanced at her exhausted face. "No. You can tell me later. First we need to get you medical supplies, and then you've got to rest. I found a hotel as secure as we can get. I'll sneak you upstairs and go out for fresh clothes later. Okay?''

"Sounds good." Suddenly she picked up her Beretta and took out the clip. It was empty. She stared at it, then up at Asher. If she hadn't had that last bullet—? But she had, and she smiled at him.

Asher thought he'd never seen anything so beautiful, so exciting as that exhausted smile on that dirt-streaked face.

Her smile widened. "I drugged Dr. Levine. It was a real strong dose. I'll always treasure that moment."

At night Paris turned on the charm. Lamplight and music mingled in the boulevards. The aromas of cologne, full-bodied table wines, and exotic tobaccos drifted from doorways. Beneath the starry night sky, the helicopter carrying Gordon Taite landed atop the massive Tour Languedoc. He rode the elevator down one floor to France's secret heart of U.S. intelligence, and then from his temporary office he summoned the MASQUERADE team.

"Report."

They told him Sarah Walker had been captured trying to break into Je Suis Chez Moi.

Gordon's face darkened. "Where is she? Bremner'll want—"

"He's en route. He was told," the senior of the Paris team said. "But . . . she escaped again. She—"

"What!" Gordon glared at the Paris man. "How?"

"The doctor wanted to talk to her alone, so he dismissed her guards. She slipped some kind of street drug into his drink, got her gun away from him, and killed some of our people. She was hit but got away. Levine's out of it until tomorrow."

"When tomorrow? Once we repair his fucking damage and pick up Walker again, he's got a job to do."

"We don't know, sir. His assistant's with him. She's assured us he'll be fine. And if he isn't, she can take over."

Gordon crossed his arms over his muscled chest and frowned. He didn't much like that pompous dilettante Allan Levine, but Hughes Bremner—and MASQUERADE—needed him.

"What about Asher Flores?" he demanded.

The dozen men and women looked at one another.

"Tell me!" Gordon snapped.

"He got away, too, sir." The senior team member described what the backup crew had discovered when the original three-man team

had failed to report in. "The Paris cops were all over that alley like
pigeons on birdseed. We couldn't get a thing. All we know is our
car's gone, three of our people are dead, and the Frogs want to
know what in hell we're doing shooting up their country without
consulting them first. You'll be getting a call."

"I'm sure I will. Who'd we lose?" He listened to the dead men's
names and shook his head. "They were damn good people. So,
where does that leave us?"

The team took turns detailing the spreading of the web Gordon
had ordered earlier—two dozen regular agents on phones and visiting hotels throughout the city and suburbs asking for Asher Flores's
cover names. And if that failed, giving descriptions and showing
photos of both Flores and Walker. They also were conducting a
search for the missing Languedoc car and talking to pharmacies
and doctors who might have seen a woman with a gunshot wound
on the left shoulder.

"We have her day pack with all her identification and money,"
the team leader said. "If she gets stopped for anything, she'll be in
trouble with no passport. She was carrying a shit-load of dough in
cash and traveler's checks. We assume she'll join up with Flores
again, and that he has plenty more to give her. But where'd she get
so much in the first place, boss?"

"Flores, of course. The bastard embezzled one of our funds."
Gordon glared at them as if they were responsible for the humilia-
tion of Walker stealing his code and passing it to Flores. He lifted his
chin and gave them a cool gaze the way Bremner did. They were the
best, top operatives from all across Europe. "I've been authorized to
offer a $50,000 private reward to whoever finds Walker. You've got
only twenty hours." Sincerity flooded his voice. He was sharing with
them a sacred trust: "Hughes Bremner—and Langley—are counting on you!"

Each member of the team nodded soberly. They were the best,
and they knew it. They had ways to accomplish assignments no one
else could ever know. They'd find Sarah Walker.

Tall and brick, the classic Hotel Aphrodite had been built in the
nineteenth century. It was fringed by wood-shuttered double windows. Period florals papered the walls, and the gold-leafed public
rooms offered secretarial services, business machines, and elegant

carts selling everything from hand-painted flowerpots to peaches soaked in Armagnac.

As Asher sneaked her up a back staircase, Sarah tried to savor the luxury despite her throbbing shoulder, bruises, and exhaustion. In their room, she went straight to the bathroom. It boasted a bidet, hair dryer, and lotions, but she barely noticed as she took a double dose of aspirin, stripped painfully out of her clothes, and slipped into one of the hotel's soft, thick robes.

She emerged and sat at the table. Asher opened a bottle of antiseptic. She lowered the robe from her shoulder and told him about Je Suis Chez Moi. The wound was an angry raw channel across the top of her trapezius muscle. He pursed his lips, listened as she talked, and gently swabbed antiseptic into the open wound.

When she'd finished, he said, "So you have no idea how Bremner's going to make these billions Levine talked about?"

"Not yet." She held tight to the table as the antiseptic burned and the wound throbbed even more. "Levine's so immersed in his own work, he pays little attention to anything else. Bremner could've told him the whole deal, and he could've forgotten it all."

"What about that industrialist—the one getting drugged at Je Suis Chez Moi? Why isn't he giving his workers what they need, when he apparently seems to agree they need it?"

"For *La Grandeur,*" she gritted her teeth. "That's a Charles de Gaulle phrase. Back in the '50s, De Gaulle used it to fire up France's nationalist spirit. He wanted the country to return to the grand days when it considered itself ruler of the civilized world. In any case, this French operation of Bremner's has to be huge, and Levine's planning to build a private, permanently funded lab. It sounds as if the tycoon I saw there is somehow part of it. As we both know all too well, Bremner does nothing without reason. He has to be planning for a mighty big payoff to have gone to the trouble of setting up that extremely secret club for France's elite."

Asher retired the antiseptic and opened a tube of antibiotic cream. He squirted a thick line the length of the laceration.

The antibiotic was soothing. "At least that's what I figure," Sarah continued. "So—number one—we've got Levine's experiments on the brain and body, which are proving unnervingly successful. And —two—we've got some kind of huge operation happening on Monday that involves billions for Hughes Bremner and his people. And

—three—we've got an international assassin trying to come in, but Bremner wants him killed before he tells what he knows."

"I've got an addendum." Asher described his search through the various data banks at Christine Robitaille's shop. "There was a sentence at the end of the Carnivore's file that said the President had changed his mind and told the Carnivore to pack his toys and get the hell over to someone else's playpen."

She frowned. "That makes no sense. Why would Levine tell me the coming-in was set: Eight o'clock tomorrow night. He was very definite about it."

"That soon?"

She nodded.

He shook his head. "Somebody's either misinformed, or lying, or—"

"Or Bremner's out on his own, rogue all the way. My God, whatever he's got planned for Monday has to be damned big!"

"And there's more," Asher said. He told her about Lucas Maynard's death. "That makes no sense either. Unless Maynard knew something and Bremner had him killed."

While they thought of the enormity of Bremner's defying the President, Asher put a thick gauze bandage on her wound and taped it.

She smiled. "You're a tender doctor, Asher."

They exchanged a long look.

She broke away first. "How did the Languedoc locate you?"

"Could be they figured out about Gordon's code and traced me through that. It was only a matter of time." He paused. "Anyway, Gold Star Rent-a-Car turned out to be a dead end. It read like a textbook company. Nothing suspicious. I printed out the list of Sterling-O'Keefe companies, and I'll show it to you later. Maybe it'll give you some ideas."

She eased the robe up over her bandaged shoulder. It was time for Asher to sneak her bloody clothes out of the hotel and buy new ones in one of the local late-night stalls.

She wanted him to stay. He wanted to stay.

She said, "They killed Blount." She closed her eyes. "I still can't believe it. He was so sweet and honest and funny. He swore celebrities were the scum of the earth, and it was his personal quest to expose them all. He hated my new face." Two tears slid down her cheeks.

"You really liked him."

"Yes." She could hear Blount's impossibly bright voice: *My God, Sarah . . . you look like a CELEBRITY!* "Death is so damn final."

Asher said, "Lucas Maynard was one of Bremner's oldest associates. They'd worked together thirty years." He let the implication of that sink in for a moment before he went on. "You did a good job at Je Suis Chez Moi. It wasn't just luck that got you out alive. What made you buy the delirium?"

"I don't know. It was like a premonition. Or maybe it was just because I'm so aware of drugs, after my particularly intimate experience with them lately."

"In our business, that kind of instinct's called gut. You've got gut, Sarah, and that's something no amount of training can teach you." He waited for her to object, to tell him she was no spy and was never going to be.

She said, "I've changed."

"I know."

"I'm glad I've changed."

"Me, too." He wanted to hold her to him, tell her he realized how hard it had been and that she'd triumphed over the biggest adversary of all—herself. But he could delay no longer. She had to have a disguise. Tomorrow the Carnivore would come in. They had to find out where, and how Bremner planned to kill him, and how it all tied in to some billion-dollar operation on Monday.

Sarah locked the hallway door behind Asher. The aspirin had kicked in, and her shoulder felt better. The better the shoulder, the grimier the rest of her felt, and the more her bruises and battered bones ached. What she needed was a long, hot bath. Taking her reloaded Beretta, she filled the tub and crawled in, careful to keep her bandage dry. The water was hot and comforting.

She closed her eyes and tried not to think of anything. Neither the past nor the present. She tried, but Je Suis Chez Moi and her personal Doctor Frankenstein—Allan Levine—kept running through her mind. The crippling terror in Blount McCaw's eyes as he'd died. The night of horror replayed constantly. And then it was gone and she was thinking of Asher.

She could see him in her mind. Unconsciously she found herself undressing him. She smiled lazily.

Then her eyes snapped open. There was the sound of a key turning in a lock.

Besides the bathroom door, there were two other doors in the hotel room—one to the hall, and the other, locked, to the adjoining room. The sound was coming from the hallway door. She'd left the bathroom door open wide to give her a direct view.

Heart pounding, she picked up her gun from the floor beside the tub. She aimed at the door as it began to swing open.

A woman's voice called into the room, *"Bon soir! Bon soir! Pardon-nez-moi!"*

Sarah gazed grimly at the door. It could be one of Bremner's people. Or Dr. Levine's people. Or simply a maid.

She called disagreeably, "Go away. This room is occupied!"

The door inched open. *"Bon soir. Bon soir!"*

Sarah cocked the Beretta. Forced herself to exhale slowly. Lord, she hoped it was just a maid.

Suddenly Asher Flores's wide-planed, swarthy face appeared around the door. He was sporting a brand-new black beret. *"Bon soir, madame!"* He mimicked a woman's alto perfectly. He swaggered in, heeled the door closed, dumped his packages onto the nearest twin bed, and locked the door.

"Asher! Are you mad? I could've killed you!"

He started to grin. Then he really looked at her. He stared across the beds at her. And stared.

She saw her nakedness in his eyes. She lowered the Beretta.

For a long beat she stared back, feeling sudden heat in her groin. Desire flooded her, hot and insistent, and he was in her mind again, and she was undressing him, and—

He walked toward her, breathing heavily. She stood up, water sluicing off her body, and stepped from the tub. He enveloped her in his arms. His mouth fell upon hers, passionate and devouring. His salty tongue flicked the roof of her mouth. She felt the roughness of his jeans and shirt against her nakedness, teasing. Demanding. He shuddered and groaned. She unbuckled his pants, pulled, tugged, raised herself up on her toes.

"Oh, God," she moaned, as he slid hot and hard between her legs. "Oh, God."

Forty-four

The hotel room was dim now, lit by only one bedside lamp. The air smelled of musky sex and bath oils. Sarah and Asher lay entwined on one of the twin beds. Unless she really thought about it, she couldn't tell which legs were his and which hers. Her wound and bruises hurt dully, but she no longer cared.

"Are you purring?" he whispered in her ear.

"Maybe. I feel as if something's humming inside. A happy kind of humming."

"Well, not so long ago that was me. Inside you, I mean."

"Yes, but not purring or humming. More in the way of roaring."

"Noisy fucker, aren't I?"

She laughed and turned to face him, her nose touching the tip of his. "Breathe," she said. "I want to inhale you."

"I *am* breathing. Can't you tell?"

"I can tell. I want a commitment you'll continue." She inhaled the spiciness of his exhalation. "Delicious." She sighed. "God, I'm glad we're both alive."

"Yeah. Kind of makes you appreciate things." He ran his finger around the rim of her ear. "I think we should eat something now."

"Yes. Keep our strength up."

They'd have to stay in the room. The less they showed themselves, the better. He'd checked in under a name no one at the Languedoc knew, but still, they'd be idiots to take a chance.

He sat up on his elbow, peered down. His curly black hair and

beard made him look like a pirate. "The restaurant here is *superbe.*"
He got up, nude, long wiry muscles rippling. She loved the way his
chest tapered into his hips. So male.

She watched, feeling lazy and feline, as he wielded the phone like
a maestro and ordered in perfect, fluent French. She studied the
black triangle of hair between his legs, the way his cock seemed to
swell and relax, beckoning.

She got up, knelt beside his chair, and slid her fingertips across
his chest, through the soft curly hair, down over his belly.

"You're so incredibly sexy," she murmured, going lower.

He jumped, grinned, pushed her away. *"Merci beaucoup,"* he said
into the phone. He looked down at her. "God, you're distracting!"
"Merci beaucoup."

Still nude, they stood shoulder to shoulder at their tall window,
which overlooked the rue Bonaparte. Their arms encircled each
other as they peered down through a crack in the drapes at the
narrow street below.

Electricity crackled between them.

The rue Bonaparte was lined with chic art galleries and antique
shops. "That's one old street," he said. "Just think, peddlers and
princes were riding along it way back in 1250." He studied the
traffic, and she knew he was looking for more than thirteenth-century ghosts.

No one lingered on the sidewalk opposite, watching their hotel.
Without speaking, but understanding perfectly the importance of
that information, they left the window and sat across from each
other at the round table.

"We should put on robes," he said.

"Yes."

But they didn't. They pulled their chairs together, watching one
another's body, enjoying the exploration and knowledge. The risk
of intimacy.

She said, "I made some other telephone calls today I should tell
you about. One was to a colleague in London. He went back
through the microfilm of old issues of the *London Times* to when Liz
Sansborough's parents died. Sure enough, there was one of those
brief, official obituary notices. But there was something peculiar
about it. Remember how Gordon said they'd died when they were
mugged in New York?"

"I remember."

"Well, they died in New York, all right. And the police called it a mugging. But their bodies were found partially burned near Times Square. They had their wallets, but no jewelry or money."

"So?"

"In my experience, a thief takes everything. He doesn't stop to pull out cash and credit cards so he can leave the wallet. He doesn't stop to burn the bodies. All he can think about is getting away fast and clean."

"True. But what does that have to do with anything?"

"I don't know. Maybe nothing. But it's one more thing that makes sense, yet doesn't quite."

"Actually it does. What's in your Liz Sansborough memory is only what the files and Gordon told you. Was there any point to giving you any more specifics about the murders of your 'parents'? Remember, Gordon was intent on one thing—remaking you. At that point, the details didn't matter."

The food arrived, and they ran for their robes. He touched her breast as it flew by, and he thought he'd never seen anything more perfectly curved, more lovely.

Properly covered, they allowed the waiter in. With a flourish he removed silver lids and served their dishes at the table. For *monsieur* was *ravioli de langoustine au chou,* lobster ravioli on a bed of cabbage, and for *madame,* Challans *canard aux cerises,* Challans duck with cherries. *Monsieur* had ordered a red burgundy, an exemplary Morey-Saint-Denis Clos de Tart 1983, a very good year from a very fine winery owned by the Mommessin family.

As the white-aproned waiter bowed and left, Asher touched his glass to hers. "To a very fine vintage. Yours."

"Ours." She'd said it without thinking, without stumbling. Was that an omen?

"Ours." He grinned agreement, and his teeth flashed white inside the thickening black of his beard.

They picked up their forks and ate.

She said, "Your mother was a Jew from Poland, and your dad a Catholic from Mexico. So how come you speak French like a native and go on and on about all things Parisian, but I've never heard you once enthuse over the history of the Jews and Poland, or Mexico, Spain, and the Pope."

"Never thought about it much."

"Why?"

"Don't know." He chewed. "Does it matter?"

"It matters. It's important to have a life. Ask me, I'll tell you."

"It may be great to have *your* life, but mine, the verdict's still out."

This was a new side of Asher, and it struck her he was saying aloud thoughts he usually kept to himself. She asked, "You were that angry about going to both church and temple?"

"Actually I loved both religions. The ceremonies and the singing. The fathers and the nuns, and the rabbi and the minyan. The tales about noble deeds. On Saturday my mother and I walked to temple and did no work, because we observed Shabbos. On Sunday my father and I went to mass. Both ways seemed natural. Then one night I heard them fighting. They were fighting about God. Who had the real God? The Catholics or the Jews? Being an only child, which God I chose was important, because that would make one of them right. So what did that make the other one? Chopped liver? A chimichanga?"

He turned automatically to the window, as if he could see through the drapes to the thirteenth-century street below. As if he could see back in time to the logic of parents engaged in a religious war. He shook his head. He could see neither.

"It made you feel crazy, I'd guess." She studied the profile of his aristocratic nose. It could be straight off a Mayan hieroglyph or a Warsaw ghetto wall. He seemed to quiver in the lamplight.

"A little crazy, maybe." He turned to look at her, quizzical, surprised he'd revealed himself.

"Well, join the crowd. I don't have all my memories back. Maybe I'll feel even crazier when I know everything there is to know about me."

"On the other hand, maybe you'll like it."

For a moment she saw herself burying her face in his chest. Bathing herself naked in the electric intensity she found so magnetic about him. She picked up her glass. It was a fine wine, full-bodied. She wanted to stand naked with him again, tucked into his curves. She could smell him across the table, the scent of travel she'd washed off but he still carried.

He put down his fork and reached out to lay the palm of his hand alongside her cheek. She turned into it, kissed it. Saw the hunger in his eyes, soul-bared, vulnerable.

□   □   □   □

After dinner he showed her the clothes he'd bought her—a man's white shirt, black necktie, somber black suit with black socks and shoes, skullcap, broad-brimmed felt hat to go on top of the skullcap, a prayer shawl, and fake side locks that matched her dyed black hair.

She touched the satiny side locks. "My God, I'm going to a Jewish funeral."

"I hope not. These are your standard clothes for your standard young male Hasidic Jew. You'll need to add glasses—" he handed her wire-rimmed spectacles "—and *tefillin.*" He held out a little leather box with a long strap. *"Tefillin,"* he repeated, and she took it from him. "I'll show you how to wrap the strap around your arm. The box contains Holy Scripture. See, *Hasidim* means 'the pious ones,' and they're serious about it. They believe in trusting God, preaching joyous worship, and praying a lot. They pray a whole lot."

"I'll look like a student, won't I?"

"Yep. A young male yeshiva student, very beardless. No one will recognize you."

She chuckled. "Brilliant."

Then he showed her his new clothes—a businessman's leisure apparel—and the long list of Sterling-O'Keefe companies. She read some of the names aloud: OMNI-American Savings & Loan, located mostly in the western and southwestern United States. Presidents' Palace hotel-casinos in Las Vegas and Atlantic City. Gold Star Credit Resources, America's biggest credit-check company. Gold Star Rent-a-Car, an enormous international company. She studied the list. "I don't get it. Is there a connection between Sterling-O'Keefe and Gordon and Bremner, or even Langley?"

Flores had been pacing back and forth across the room, his long bathrobe flopping against his bare legs.

"Langley!" He snapped his fingers.

"What?"

"I should've thought of it before. Who was a 'founder' of Langley? One of the leading visionaries who turned the OSS into today's CIA?"

She stared at him. "John O'Keefe. 'Red Jack' O'Keefe."

"Sterling-*O'Keefe.*"

"O'Keefe's a common name, Asher."

"Maybe, but Jack O'Keefe was Bremner's mentor. If Bremner's part of Sterling-O'Keefe, Jack O'Keefe could be, too."

"But is O'Keefe still alive?"

"If he were dead, I'd have heard about it. There would've been tributes everywhere. He was the emperor of U.S. espionage, for Chrissakes. If we can find him—"

"We'll find him."

"Christine Robitaille." He resumed pacing. "He and Christine were lovers years ago. She told me about it once. Maybe she'll know where to find him."

"The Languedoc must be watching her shop."

"Yup. They'll know it's only a remote possibility I'll show up again, but they won't take any chances. Tomorrow I'll try to get a message to her and convince her to meet me somewhere. She's already saved my life once, years ago. I've got to trust someone to find O'Keefe. It's not like I can waltz up to the Languedoc and ask. She's my best bet. I won't talk to her unless she's clean."

"Good. But if she didn't turn you in, how did those three goons find you at her shop?"

"My guess is Bremner. They had to have found out I tapped into the Denver slush fund to finance our trip over here, and that I used Gordon's code to do it. Bremner would have put a tracer on the code to see if I'd use it again. I pressed my luck too long." He shrugged.

She told him her plans. "Tomorrow I'm going back to Café Justine. It's a long shot, but maybe somebody there can tell me who that guy with the straw Panama is and where I can find him."

"All right." He stood behind her, put his hands on her shoulders, and grimaced to himself. He couldn't stop her from going out just to keep him from losing her. "But if they expect to bring in the Carnivore tomorrow night, they're sweating nails trying to figure out how to get you back so they can put you on whatever diabolical program that ghoul Levine has prepared."

She lifted her face. "Kiss me."

He kissed her upside down.

"*Merci beaucoup.* Kiss me again." She stood, letting her robe fall open.

He slid his hands inside, up the long hips, the willowy waist, to her heavy breasts.

"Ummmm," she hummed. "Ummmm. Ummmm."

He bent her back, his robe fell open, and she felt the full length and heat of his male body like an intense sweet pain. He kissed her long and deep, and the ache, the need, within her spread hotter and hotter.

"This isn't what I'd planned," he whispered hoarsely. He was caught, trapped in his own new future. There was no turning back.

"I know what you mean." She panted, melted into him.

He pulled her back up, and his mouth fell on her throat.

She inhaled him, drew his scent, his essence deep into her soul. "Bed," she said.

Tomorrow they could worry about tomorrow.

Forty-five

There was something wrong about the pitch-black hotel room. Sarah glanced at the illuminated dial on the alarm: 5:00 A.M. Asher lay on his side facing her, his arm across her chest. Her breasts were naked. She felt like exposed prey.

Where was her Beretta?

Then she heard the sound again. It was a doorknob, soft, like the sound of Asher coming in while she was in the bathtub. She turned her head, whispered in his ear.

Instantly he was on his feet.

She stood close beside him so they could almost see one another in the inky night. "Let's try to get one alive."

He pressed her Beretta into her hand and motioned her to take the closed, locked door that separated them from the adjoining room.

Naked, he padded to the hall door.

Asher Flores glanced only once in Sarah's direction. The room was so dark he couldn't see her. But he could imagine her, legs apart, solidly balanced, the Beretta ready. There was something enormously sexy about a competent female. Especially a bare-ass-naked female.

He felt around until he knew he was behind the door, where the hall light wouldn't reveal him when it opened.

All his senses were alert. The initial rush of fear had come and gone, and now he waited calmly. He always felt excitement, too. Only a fool or a masochist did this kind of work without liking the excitement.

At last the door cracked open. The way the attack came would tell Asher whether the Carnivore was still coming in, whether Bremner still needed Sarah alive.

He could hear clicks at Sarah's door. Bremner's people were co-ordinated.

And then a figure dressed completely in black slipped inside Asher's door. Asher could hear the soft sounds of activity across the room where Sarah waited.

The hall light had shown the figure briefly, and Asher had frozen the image in his mind. The door sealed shut. Asher slammed the figure back against the wall and jammed his fist into the guy's gut so hard he could almost feel backbone.

The intruder doubled over and vomited, helpless. Asher gripped the back of his neck with one hand, marking the spot, and crashed his gun down with the other. The guy dropped to the floor and was silent. Next Asher pictured the arrangement of the room's furniture. He ran through the blackness toward Sarah's door. It was a mistake. He crashed heavily into someone.

"One got away!" Sarah's voice was clear but soft. She'd had two intruders, had taken out one, but not the other.

Asher wrestled with the one who'd gotten away. The guy was strong as a Caterpillar backhoe. Asher could hold onto no limb long enough to find purchase.

Suddenly the overhead light blazed on.

Sarah stood by the switch, nude and haughty. Instantly, Asher executed a *tai otoshi* body drop. As the man fell, Sarah ran to him and pointed her Beretta down at his nose.

"Where are your backups? Now!" she demanded.

The guy wore a black ski mask along with a black, skin-tight body suit. Even through the ski mask Asher could see his shock at the beautiful, nude woman who stood over him. For some guys it would be a sexual fantasy come true. But for this one, it was nothing but trouble.

Sarah moved her Beretta to the guy's groin and shoved. "I said *now.*" The intruder talked so fast his words spilled on top of each other. He described the positions of the four backups who waited outside: One in the corridor, one in the lobby, and two in the street. As Asher tied him, the agent snarled, "Bremner'll be in from D.C. soon, Flores, then you're fucking finished."

"Keep talking, Howells," Asher said. "How'd you find us?"

The guy lifted his head and looked left and right. Sarah was stripping the other two intruders, and the stench of vomit from the one Asher had knocked out permeated the room. As Asher and Sarah put on the black body suits of the other two agents, the one named Howells told them Languedoc personnel had been calling Paris hotels, examining guest-registration books, showing photos, and giving physical descriptions until sometime around 3:00 A.M., when the desk man at the Hotel Aphrodite had recognized Asher.

"Old-fashioned police work," Sarah said as they tied the intruders.

"You bastard, Flores." The guy on the floor glared up at him. "Fucking murderer. How could you kill your own people?"

"Bremner's the 'fucking murderer.' " Asher was throwing things into his old gym bag. "What's going down Monday, Howells?"

"I'll tell you shit." But his eyes reacted, puzzled.

Sarah went into the closet and grabbed the sacks containing their new clothes.

Asher said, "You don't know about Monday, do you? Bremner's big operation? I'll bet Langley doesn't know either."

"Bullshit." Tied up like a pig at slaughter, the guy on the floor refused to believe anything bad of Hughes Bremner. "The Carnivore comes in tonight. Nothing's happening Monday. You're all bullshit and a goddamn murderer."

Asher zipped his gym bag. "Hughes and Gordon set me up. Tell that to my old buddies at the Company. You want to do our country a favor? Stop Hughes Bremner."

Sarah moved to the door. "Bremner's up to something so critical, so horrible, he's willing to sacrifice and murder his own people. We're trying to find out what in hell's going on."

Before the guy could respond, Asher gagged him. They surveyed the room one last time. Sarah turned off the light and cracked open the door. The hall was deserted.

Dressed in the intruders' black body suits, carrying their things, they slipped out, two smoothly moving shadows.

They found Bremner's backup man unconscious inside the stairwell. They looked at each other, but didn't stop to ask questions as they hurried down the stairs.

The older gentleman strolled down the hall of the Hotel Aphrodite in his bathrobe, rubbing his eyes, apparently too restless to sleep. He'd heard the scuffling in the young couple's room, just as earlier he'd heard several rounds of noisy sex. He'd enjoyed the vicarious sex thoroughly.

Now, if he wasn't mistaken—

Yes. The fire door was swinging shut. He counted to twenty, then silently opened it and peered over the unconscious agent and down the stairwell. The young pair, in black body suits, were tearing down the steps. Both carried weapons, and one hauled a battered gym bag.

He grinned. Whistling quietly, hands deep in his bathrobe pockets, he ambled back to his room. Last night he'd tried to get Sarah out of Je Suis Chez Moi before the bomb exploded, but she'd been too suspicious. Fortunately she'd moved fast enough to be thrown by the blast, not seriously hurt. His *compadres* had tracked her through the old cemetery, where she'd lost Dr. Levine's men, to Christine Robitaille's computer shop, and then here. Dear Christine. He remembered her with great affection. Once she'd been an extraordinarily lovely woman, but time, and her line of work, had not been kind.

In his room, he picked up the phone. At 4:00 A.M. in Paris, it would be 10:00 P.M. in Washington, D.C., six hours earlier. He dialed Langley. If he gave his name, they'd patch him through instantly to Arlene Debo. He didn't want that. Instead he gave the operator an anonymous message. "Write it down exactly," he warned sternly. "Don't miss a word: Hughes Bremner is bringing in the Carnivore 8:00 P.M. Sunday. Arlene, you'd better get your butt over here pronto if you want to stop it."

Finally he gave the operator a top-priority code that guaranteed the message would go instantly to Debo at whatever Foggy Bottom party she was being bored by.

As he hung up, he grinned to himself, charming and conceited as ever. He was seventy-five years old, and he'd never felt healthier, smarter, or more in control. He dressed, packed up, and checked out.

Back in his shabby rented room on the opposite side of the city—

temporary but necessary digs—there was a message on his answering machine from one of the people he'd assigned to watch the
strange mansion on the rue Vivienne. The fire fighters and bomb
squad had come and gone, and all was now quiet.

He went out once more to leave a message for Quill at their drop.
Then he returned to his bed to rest. He'd need it. Tomorrow would
be a big day. As always, he drifted off as soon as his head touched
the pillow. He slept like a baby.

There was a single, muffled shot from Sarah and Asher's former
room in the Hotel Aphrodite. Gordon Taite opened the door and
returned to the corridor where four of his people waited. He carried a Beretta with a sound suppressor.

"Bill Howells just tried to kill me, poor bastard," he told them.
"Flores got to him." He let the news sink in, hardening their resolve
to be better than that. "Okay, let's search it."

"What about Bill?" asked one of his people.

Gordon told them sadly, "Dead." Flores had filled the poor jerk's
head with information he shouldn't have had, so Gordon had been
forced to kill him. His people wouldn't understand that, so he'd
invented the attack.

They swore.

"Goddamn that fucking Sarah Walker and Asher Flores."

When the night clerk had gone into the back office, Sarah and
Asher knocked out the lobby backup man and left him in a broom
closet. They dodged through the hotel alley and stopped behind the
cardboard shanty of some homeless person to strip, dress, and decide where to meet.

As dawn spread across the city, religious music and radio news
began to float from Paris's open windows. Church bells chimed.
Birds sang. The inviting aromas of espresso and fresh croissants
drifted from cafés. The sun climbed into the pastel August sky, and
the ancient city shrugged itself awake.

Within an hour, as Sarah and Asher had planned, they were
breakfasting in a café far from the Hotel Aphrodite, sharing an
International Herald Tribune, and smiling across the booth at one
another. She was in her side locks, spectacles, plain black suit, and
wide-brimmed Hasidic hat.

He was in gray summer trousers, Bally loafers with no socks, and a cream-white linen, open-necked shirt. The shirt was loose, blousy, so he could hide his Gunsite pistol in his armpit. With his dark good looks and thickening black beard, he cut a striking figure. The one interesting eccentricity was the black beret, which didn't belong, yet somehow did. A statement of individuality. Asher, Sarah decided, was gorgeous.

She said, "You did a pretty accurate job guessing my size for these clothes."

"I'm good, even if I do say so myself."

"Yeah," she said dryly. "You memorize women's bodies real well."

He laughed. "Only yours."

The waitress gave the young Hasidic Jew a curious glance, then took their order.

Asher grumbled about the Dodgers. Apparently they had no games that day. Sarah scanned the front page and turned inside. A headline on page three caught her attention:

DON'T COME HOME, SARAH

Her chest contracted.

That headlined name, so bold and black, *Sarah,* held all the intimacy of her only "old" memories. Her mother calling her to dinner. At bedtime her mother would brush her silky woman's lips against Sarah's cheek.

"I love you, Sarah."

Her father, red faced and worried, shouting, "Sarah! Come down off that roof!"

She was sure the article was just a coincidence, but still she read on—

Forty-six

DON'T COME HOME, SARAH

By MARILYN MICHAELS
Special to the Herald Tribune

WASHINGTON, D.C.—Most of us live lives of routine and responsibility. Jobs, family, friends. Our very ordinariness is a comfort. From that solid foundation, we enjoy the triumphs and solve the problems of everyday life.

But what happens if we begin to doubt our sanity?

Meet Sarah, 32, intelligent, attractive, and ambitious. In six short days her world turned upside down.

What happened to her is a lesson in trust. If we can't trust our government, whom can we trust? And it's a lesson in the imagination. What most of us find unimaginable is the fuel that powers geniuses . . . and monsters.

I'm not allowed to use Sarah's last name or the real names of those who appear in this series, but be assured they all exist. I have the transcripts, notes, and paper trail to prove it.

>Because I'm in danger, my byline is a
>pseudonym. Because you're in danger
>from the mentality that allows self-in-
>terest to thrive among those in power, I
>write this series. . . .

In the Paris café, Sarah Walker handed the newspaper across to
Asher. "Take a look at this."

Asher frowned when he saw the headline. He began to read.

She turned to gaze out the window at the pale blue sky, hazy with
thin morning clouds. Her only movement was her eyelids. She
blinked periodically.

The newspaper story had described her cosmetic surgery at the
hands of a Beverly Hills plastic surgeon, now disappeared. Then it
had recounted her meeting with a certain man who was obviously
Gordon. Although the carefully detailed article promised the next
installment tomorrow, her memory continued on its own. At first it
came in pieces, and then in large, graphic scenes, until it all made
sense.

Her mind focused on the new pair of Levi's she'd bought back
then. At home in her Santa Barbara condo, she'd taken the jeans
from the Nordstrom's bag and found them slashed to ribbons. She
remembered being terrified. Who? . . . How? . . . Then she remembered . . . Thiel—her best friend—had come over to tell her
something important—

"You first," Thiel had commanded. "Men before careers for a
change. Who's the new guy?"

Thiel had curly yellow hair, wide green eyes, and an abundance of
energy. A reporter for the *Santa Barbara News-Press,* she was a Botti-
celli beauty traipsing with a tape recorder through politics, the
ghetto, and Santa Barbara's grand University Club, where only a few
years ago women, no matter their credentials, had to enter through
the side door.

As they'd sat before her fireplace, Sarah had described her meeting with Gordon Taite.

"How sure are we about him?" Thiel's pale eyebrows raised in
mock seriousness. "Can he put a safety pin inside where it doesn't
show? Is he sensitive, generous, nurturing? In other words, is he
female?"

"Thiel!"

"I know how it is. I want to meet someone, too. Someone I can take for granted."

Sarah laughed. "Why do we bother? They don't remember anniversaries or birthdays, but they know basketball scores from twenty years ago."

"The one good thing about Monday Night Football is the knit pants. Mighty good booty!"

"Put two men, perfect strangers, in a room with a case of beer, two bags of potato chips, and ESPN, and they bond faster than Krazy Glue. Football season, and we never see them again!"

They slapped hands and laughed.

"Oh, lord. If only it weren't so true!" Thiel wiped tears from her eyes.

"Do you think we'll ever meet guys we can settle down with?"

Thiel was shocked. "You mean *marry?* Have you seen the divorce statistics lately?"

"I've seen them. But think of the gene pool. Don't you feel guilty not making a contribution?"

"Children? Sarah, wash your mouth!" Thiel ate a carrot.

Sarah ate a carrot. "Okay, so how about telling me why you called this meeting?"

Thiel was silent. Whatever it was, it was hard to say. "Well, see, I got the job at the *Chicago Tribune.*"

"Thiel! Congratulations!"

"But they need me now. And that means we're not going to have any good-bye lunches. I won't even get to meet this Gordon of yours until I come back for my furniture. I have to fly out tomorrow. I start the next day. Somebody died on them."

It was Sarah's turn to be silent. "Have I got herpes, AIDS, the plague? Is it my new face? Why is everyone deserting me?"

Thiel hugged Sarah. "I'm sorry."

"No, don't be. This is great for you."

They smiled at each other. Sarah touched her friend's arm. "It's okay, Thiel, really. But now I'd like you to come into my bedroom. I want to show you something." They went in, and she pulled the Nordstrom's bag from under her bed. Inside were the slashed jeans. She handed the bag to Thiel.

"Tell me what you think."

Thiel took them out. "Hey, these are great. Just my size—" She glanced up, stopped speaking, grabbed Sarah's arm. "Why are you looking like that? Sarah? Here, sit down. Are you sick? Sarah! What's wrong!"

The jeans were perfect.

Yes, Sarah remembered everything, from the slashed, then un-slashed, jeans all the way to the horror of thinking she'd poisoned the puppy Gordon had given her. A devastating act of carelessness on her part. Except . . . she was sure now—Gordon had to have done it himself. He'd killed the dog he gave her just to undermine her belief in her own sanity.

All for Monday. They'd kill a dog, a friend, an assassin, or an innocent bystander for whatever Monday was bringing Bremner.

Meeting Gordon had been the beginning of her nightmare. She'd blown two easy magazine assignments. Been fired from her job at *Talk*. She'd supposedly had a one-night stand with a Las Vegas bell-boy. She recalled heading upstairs in the hotel that night to tran-scribe a taped interview she'd just conducted. But during the inter-view she'd had a drink. It could've been drugged, which would explain why she knew nothing of the so-called night of lust . . . nor how she'd managed to break her little finger during it . . . nor how she'd managed to erase the entire interview from her recorder.

She shook her head. God, no wonder she'd thought she was los-ing her mind. No wonder she'd agreed to see Gordon's friend, the psychiatrist, Allan Levine. No wonder she'd been willing to take his medication.

Now she remembered something else. After she'd started the medication her furniture—her old, thrift-store furniture—had dis-appeared. One of those first mornings she'd awakened to find Dan-ish-modern furniture filling her condo.

But Gordon had said, "It's all yours. Don't you remember?"

She hadn't remembered, but it had been too much effort to say so. After a while, she'd been unsure where she was. Then she forgot her name.

"What's my name?" she'd asked.

"You don't know?"

"No."

"You will. Soon, I promise. Just rest, my beautiful darling."

At the end she'd emerged Liz Sansborough. Liz Sansborough,

whose Danish-modern furniture from her London flat had taken over Sarah Walker's Santa Barbara condo.

The writer of the article said there'd be five more parts to the series. She hinted that behind Sarah's transformation was an operation whose roots lay within the U.S. government. She named no agency, and she listed no one responsible. Those, she wrote, would be revealed in the last article in the series.

Sarah sat for some time, oblivious to the Parisians strolling down the sidewalk just beyond the café window. Her hot croissant grew cold. When Asher finished the story, she asked to see the list of Sterling-O'Keefe companies again.

She studied it, tapping her growing memory bank. "I got fired because a movie star I was supposed to interview tanked on me at the last minute. He was a spokesman for *Nonpareil International Insurance.* My parents' prize, the fabulous retirement home, was awarded by *OMNI-American Savings & Loan.* The *Presidents' Palace* in Vegas was where I went to do another interview, and the next morning the bellboy told me I'd seduced him and then broken my finger screwing around with him. The bastard." She held up the crooked little finger. "It was all fabricated, except the broken finger. That's real, because Liz Sansborough has a broken finger. They had to break mine and give me a story I'd believe."

He nodded. "Gold Star, Nonpareil International Insurance, OMNI-American Savings & Loan, and the Presidents' Palace are all part of Sterling-O'Keefe. Hard to believe that's a coincidence." There was fire behind Asher's coal-black eyes. "One way or another, I'll bet Sterling-O'Keefe's one of the keys to what's going on. I'd better see what I can find out about Jack O'Keefe."

He dropped the newspaper, and it fell open to another page. They stared at each other, then down at their photos—mug shots, with a large headline warning that two killers were on the loose in Paris and extremely dangerous. They'd expected it, and yet it was still shocking. One more card from Hughes Bremner's deadly deck stacked against them.

Forty-seven

Inside a windowless, air-conditioned room in his safe house near Montmartre, Quill deciphered a warning he'd just picked up at a dead drop. He read the message twice, then sank back in his chair, his cosmetically adjusted face puzzled. The U.S. President had changed his mind and ordered Hughes Bremner to turn away the Carnivore, yet he had heard none of it, and apparently neither had Liz. Instead, Bremner's people had left confirmation at the agreed dead drop that the coming-in was set for 8:00 P.M. Sunday, this very night.

Bremner was the kind you never turned your back on. What was he up to?

Quill prowled the room, flicked on the oversized television, then flicked it off. He paused to stare unseeing at his free weights and Nordic Track. At the jar of steroids. Then he returned to the message: The Languedoc was on the alert, looking all over Paris for Liz's cousin, Sarah Walker. What in hell was Sarah doing here? Some celebrity assignment for *Talk*? Or was Bremner using her somehow?

Then there was that mansion on the rue Vivienne. It appeared to be a place where some kind of cultlike activities took place, involving some of France's top leaders in business, communications, and government. And Quill's informants had recently heard hints of a connection between the mansion and a highly placed CIA chief. Was that chief perhaps Hughes Bremner? Did he have some private agenda of his own? And if so, did it involve the Carnivore?

Quill paced. He knotted and unknotted his hands. He stared at his fingertips, where the special acid had burned away the prints. He stretched his arms back and forth over his muscular pectorals. To an outsider, he'd look as restless as a caged wild cat, but all he felt was his usual heavy sense of waiting. He'd felt this enormous sense of waiting every day, day after day, from the moment the Carnivore had agreed to come in and Quill's life had been radically curtailed by that decision.

He hated it. The Carnivore should be free.

But the decision had been made, and now his one motivation was Liz. She wanted to live a normal life.

He went to change into a disguise.

The helicopter carrying Hughes Bremner landed atop the Langue-doc in golden August light. The pilot killed the engine, and Brem-ner jumped out, head low beneath the whipping blades. Gordon Taite was waiting, his square face grave. Hell and damnation! What else had gone wrong? Had he made a mistake putting Gordon in charge of MASQUERADE?

As Bremner walked Gordon over to the low wall that rimmed the Languedoc's roof where they could talk privately, he reflected on how his twenty-year relationship with Gordon had changed. It had started simply enough, when he had identified Gordon as a patho-logical liar, and that trait, in combination with certain others, had indicated he might find the young man useful.

Gordon lied that he'd been an excellent college student, re-cruited into the CIA by his favorite history professor. Not true. Gordon had been a Ku Klux Klan member who'd carried an illegal pistol, and a loner often on academic probation. But in those days Langley could still order legal assassinations, and so, when a campus recruiter had interviewed and researched Gordon, he'd judged the youth correctly—trainable as a killer.

Like serial murderers Ted Bundy and Jeffrey Dahmer, Gordon was not only a pathological liar, he was highly intelligent and, when it suited his purposes, smooth and charming. Parents tended to trust him. But their daughters, if he was seeking excitement, quickly discovered his need for blood.

Bremner had analyzed the youthful Gordon shrewdly: He had an overinflated sense of confidence, with little self-esteem to back it up. He also had such a low level of excitability that, when Bremner first met him, Gordon was having to search harder, work harder, and tread perilously close to murder to get the exhilaration he craved. He had become ruthless.

Bremner prized ruthlessness and intelligence. He needed a man with a great deal of charm and a low level of excitability. He wanted all that, and he wanted it in someone whose desperate needs could no longer be met within the law.

Gordon didn't even try to understand Hughes Bremner, because what was vital to him was that Bremner understood him and, knowing the worst, still give him authority, respect, and a place in the world. Gordon killed for Bremner and thanked him for it. If he had one unfulfilled dream, it was to somehow become Hughes Bremner's son. They both knew that. And after twenty years, Gordon sensed Bremner occasionally did think of him that way.

And so they stopped together on the rooftop, two tall, polished men, athletic beneath tailored suits, each powerful in a different way. Fearless, bold, they gazed down the sheer face of the Languedoc, a seventy-story drop straight to the concrete street, and then out across the vast, undulating city. The boulevards and avenues were quiet. Then church bells rang from every corner. It was eight o'clock.

Bremner said, "Tell me."

Gordon handed him the *Herald Tribune*. "I'm in this article. The writer, Marilyn Michaels, didn't use my real name, but it's me. Anyone who knows anything will know it's me."

"It can't be that bad." Hughes Bremner read. It was that bad. He repressed rage and panic.

Gordon asked, "Who's Marilyn Michaels?"

Bremner said, "It's a pseudonym for Leslee Pousho. Lucas's bitch. She made copies of his documents. But we've got her and the documents. There'll be no more in this series."

He didn't tell Gordon the woman was alive and might have another copy of the documents. It was immaterial. She'd be dead soon, and so would Bunny. And in two days, after GRANDEUR rocked Europe and made him rich beyond imagining, he'd be untouchable in his stronghold—Indigo Reef, his lush atoll south of Pago Pago in the South Seas. Far from Washington, Langley, Arlene Debo, and that yellow turncoat, the President of the United States.

"What if someone finds out?" Gordon asked.

Bremner clapped him on the back, squeezed his shoulder. "They

won't. Now fill me in on Sarah Walker." Behind them, the pilot had
finished his work and joined the helipad crew in their office. Bremner's suitcases would be waiting there.

Gordon described Walker's escape from Je Suis Chez Moi, Asher
Flores's escape from the alley near the computer shop, and the
near-miss early that morning when the pair had almost been captured at the Hotel Aphrodite. "Someone set off an explosion at Je
Suis Chez Moi and helped her escape, and someone was in that alley
with Flores. We're not sure who it was either time, but it almost
looks like it was Walker in the alley. If it was, she's the one who got
our agents. Maybe all three of them."

"You may have taught her too well," Bremner said dryly. Then
softened it: "But perhaps that will help tonight."

"Yes, it could," Gordon agreed. "Our people are covering the
city. Everyone's out there. We've found her twice, we'll find her
again, and this time she won't get away."

"It's got to be by 6:00 P.M. Levine needs two hours to get her
ready for the coming-in."

"Everyone knows the time problem, sir. It's made them even
more determined, and they're taking Bill Howells's death at the
hotel personally. It was unfortunate I had to eliminate him."

Bremner nodded once. "Unavoidable."

"Yes. And after Flores and Walker murdered Ed, Steve, and Jasper
in the alley last night, our team's blood is really up. Nothing will
stop them from getting the woman."

"Good." Emotional commitment was the strongest motivation of
all. But Bremner frowned. "You haven't found any indication who
set the bomb at Je Suis Chez Moi?"

"We're still looking into it."

"What about the police?"

Gordon grinned. "Taken care of. I had one of our agents make
an anonymous call claiming she represented one of the Basque terrorist groups. She told them a rival clan had done it."

Bremner smiled his chilly smile, and Gordon felt a surge of pride.
"Let's walk."

Bremner moved off, and within a step Gordon was again at his
side. They strolled along the ramparts, each lost in his private
thoughts. Gordon felt peace, undisturbed by the usual nagging
need for the next thrill. Bremner's presence did that for him.

Halfway around the building, Bremner judged the direction of the wind was right. They stopped. Hughes Bremner climbed up on the wall, balanced above certain death. Gordon hesitated, then did the same. They stood defiant against normal fear. Bremner felt as if he were on top of the highest peak in the world. The blue sky stretched endlessly. Below, the people hurrying to church were the size of ants. He looked up and out and down with the calm certainty of ownership. He understood to his marrow that no cost was too high, no deed too violent to acquire what he wanted. He would always do what was necessary.

"Look at them, Gordon. So content to pass from birth to grave nothing more than ants. Insects. Unseen and unknown in their miserable petty lives."

Suddenly he reached down and unzipped his pants. With the wind behind him, he urinated in a long yellow stream out past the Languedoc's sharp drop. Bremner laughed into the wind high atop his own mountain. Gordon stared in awe, then followed his master. They watched their urine shatter into drops and fall upon the world of insects far below.

"As you know," Bremner said, zipping his trousers, "I'm moving permanently to Indigo Reef right after GRANDEUR is over. You'll be a rich man, too. Would you like to come with me, Gordon? Would you like to be my number one?"

Gordon's heart seemed to stop. Joy flooded him with the greatest rush he'd ever felt. He would be Bremner's heir, his son in all but name. And, someday, perhaps that, too.

"I'd like that very much, sir." There was sincere affection in his voice.

Hughes Bremner looked at him with calculating eyes. "Then I must have Sarah Walker by 6:00 P.M. today."

Forty-eight

Sarah missed Asher already. If she allowed herself, she could feel him wrapped around her, his warm breath against her ear. As she walked down the street in her Hasidic clothes, wire-rimmed spectacles on her nose, she felt more female than at any time in her life. It was ironic she'd not only become an agent, she was in love with one, too. She remembered an old Chinese curse: "May you live in interesting times." She felt cursed, but with Asher she was also blessed.

As she turned onto the rue Vivienne, she slowed, wiping from her mind this newfound experience, this love. She thickened her jaw, sobered her face, walked with her shoulders rather than her hips, and felt herself grow heavier, more masculine.

She looked ahead and inhaled sharply, stunned.

The stately Greco-Roman mansion that had been Je Suis Chez Moi was gone. All that remained was smoking rubble. Fire-blackened stones, soot, and ash lay heaped across the property. The conflagration must have been horrible, enormous.

Two fire trucks were still parked in the street. Firemen were retracting ladders and rewinding hoses. On the other side, onlookers filled the outside tables of Café Justine, watching the show. A hundred other spectators lined the rue Vivienne.

Sarah pretended ignorance. She asked a young man with a lion's mane of hair what had happened. He was straddling his bicycle, watching. All he knew was that no bodies had been discovered. Two older men sat on a bus bench, Gauloises cigarettes drooping from

the corners of their mouths. They were arguing about who could
have created such a disaster.

A nanny was rocking a baby carriage at Café Justine, observing
not only the smoking ruins but the variety of people there to enjoy
the show. She was stout, with one of those little white caps pinned to
her salt-and-pepper curls, a serviceable dress, thick cotton stockings,
and heavy shoes. A classic, no-nonsense nanny straight from the
pages of a European photo album. When Sarah asked, she knew no
more than the boy on the bicycle.

Sarah turned and pushed into the café. She had an odd feeling
she'd seen the nanny somewhere before. Inside, a few heads turned,
but there were no significant stares. The man in the straw Panama
was nowhere in sight, nor were any of the people she'd seen last
night at Je Suis Chez Moi.

She took a seat at the coffee bar and ordered a glass of hot tea in
a low voice in her halting French.

"Americain?" the woman behind the counter asked curiously.

Sarah nodded. *"Oui. Étudiant* from California.'' She fingered her
prayer shawl as the woman struck up a conversation. In between
waiting on other customers, the woman told Sarah the fire had
started just before daybreak, but because of the bombing, the ten-
ants—whoever they were—had already moved out. And, of course, it
was all the doing of the Basques. All that isolation and thin mountain air. The woman twirled her index around her ear, indicating
her belief in their madness.

Sarah was surprised. So there were two incidents—the bombing
last night and a fire this morning. She pondered both as she drank
tea and answered the woman's questions about Israel and California. At last she was able to ask about the man in the straw Panama
with the red tartan band. But the woman reminded her it was summer and many men wore straw hats. Alas, she had no memory of
this one, but that was not to say he didn't come in periodically. She
gave a classic Gallic shrug.

Sarah took her tea outside and drank standing up. The youth on
the bicycle had gone, but the two men smoking Gauloises cigarettes
were still there. The old-fashioned nanny was still in her chair, still
gently rocking the baby carriage. Sarah continued to look for faces
from last night—attendants, the masseuse, café patrons, anyone at
all. But she recognized none. She thought briefly of Dr. Levine and

hoped he was still hallucinating, or if not, at least suffering a severe hangover.

She still had three hours until her noon meeting with Asher. In a nearby phone booth she found a directory and looked up Chantelle Joyeaux. She smiled as she read the address. She'd passed that block this morning. She strode off down the street.

As she turned the corner, leaving behind the crowds and confusion on the rue Vivienne, her gut kicked in—Liz Sansborough's gut: She sensed two men coming up behind her. A door was open to her left. Without consciously thinking about it, she darted inside and along a dim corridor. There was light at the end.

She burst out into a tiny patio ringed by geraniums, jumped over a stone wall, and dropped down into a basement-level passage. As she landed, she could feel her bandage tear loose. Hot blood spread under her black jacket.

She ignored her shoulder, which was beginning to throb again, as she caught the sounds of cursing voices and heavy feet running toward her. Instantly she hurried up ten stone steps and out onto another narrow street dim between high old walls. The feet still pounded somewhere back among the buildings. She paused and listened to the silence on the street. Beretta in hand, she trotted toward the far corner, which would intersect with the street she'd just left.

Three feet away, she sensed someone waiting, probably left behind to guard against her doubling back.

Beretta in both hands, she swung around the corner. He was crouched and rose up under the sweep of her gun. She slammed the muzzle across his sweating face, smashing blood from his nose. He stumbled back, reached out, grabbed her jacket, and pulled her down on top of him. She saw the shine of a knife in his free hand. Her Beretta was jammed against him. She fired. He grunted, coughed, and rolled over on his back, mouth open, eyes glaring at nothing.

Holding tight to her nerves, she grasped her painful shoulder as she walked swiftly toward the corner and the congestion of the rue Vivienne.

She had almost reached the busy intersection when a tan Renault pulled up alongside. She saw the man inside. *Gordon!*

The hatred in his eyes told her what he could, and would, do to her. He rolled down his window and called out, "Right to me, guys. Bring her!"

She whirled. Four men were spread out behind her. In the Renault, Gordon sat between her and the relative safety of the rue Vivienne. They wouldn't kill her, but they'd wound and take her. There were enough of them, and probably more on the way, but she'd make the bastards pay. One bastard in particular.

She fired straight at the Renault. Gordon dodged, flung open the driver's door, and dove out the far side unharmed. She spun, shot the leg of the man nearest her. As he fell, she started to fire at the second, but he was too quick. With a flash of his foot, he kicked the gun out of her hand.

From somewhere there was a long tattoo of automatic gunfire. The man who'd kicked her collapsed beside her. A bullet creased her skull. The two remaining men flew back, torsos riddled with blood.

Sarah looked around, confused. It was the nanny! The baby carriage lay fallen on its side, and the gray-haired woman held an Uzi in her hands. Sarah's head swam. Vaguely she realized the "baby" in the carriage must have been the Uzi.

A siren wailed in the distance. Sarah fought, tried to stay conscious, and pitched forward into a black, cold abyss.

Part Four

The Carnivore

Forty-nine

Through the fog of her mind, Sarah heard the low hum of a window air conditioner. She opened her eyes. She was lying on a sofa in a small, shabby living room. The blinds were closed against the world, or the morning's heat, or both. Exercise equipment stood in the corner. A worn recliner faced a new wide-screen television. A scarred table with piecrust molding stood next to the chair. The mantle displayed the only merry spots in the drab room—a gaily decorated jester's hat, china poodles in pink tutus, and a photo of a cavorting clown.

"How are you feeling, Liz?"

A muscular man of medium height with a gray crew cut stood in the kitchen doorway and gazed worriedly at her. He appeared to be somewhere around fifty years old. He was drying a cup with a dishtowel. His makeup had been wiped away, but he still wore his nanny's dress, the thick stockings, and the sensible shoes.

"I don't know." She felt the ache. "My head and jaw hurt." She recalled grappling with the man who'd tried to knife her, and her head being creased by a bullet in the fight near Gordon's Renault. She touched her head and found a fresh bandage.

"I changed the one on your shoulder, too. You didn't tell me you'd been shot." There was a question in his voice. He knew Liz Sansborough; she had to be careful.

"It was nothing worth talking about."

She sat up. The man in the nanny's dress made no move to help.

But once she was upright, he disappeared back into the kitchen. She looked around, considering where she was and who he was. He thought she was Liz Sansborough. She doubted this was the Languedoc, so he had to be one of the Carnivore's people. Unless there were other players she knew nothing about.

He returned with a tray and sat in the recliner. He poured tea and added milk and sugar. That must be the way Liz Sansborough liked it. He handed her the cup.

She drank. It was too sweet for her taste, but good.

"Take these." He spoke English like an American.

He handed her two white tablets. His hands were huge and appeared very strong. He wasn't particularly tall, but he was broad and muscled. Maybe a former football player or wrestler, who'd kept in shape. Automatically she smelled the pills and touched her tongue to them. Aspirin. She saw him staring at her, realized she'd made a mistake.

She'd indicated she didn't trust him.

She laughed. "I must be in shock. I forgot where I was."

He shook his head. "You scared the hell out of me. What did you think you were doing?" His voice radiated barely controlled anger, kept in check until he was sure she was all right. He cared about Liz.

"I surprised you," she said. "Sorry."

He smiled, and in the smile she saw a photo in her mind. It was a black-and-white photo of a man with an identically smiling mouth. The rest of the features were different, and the man in the picture had been much younger. Who was he?

His mood changed. "You could've ruined everything. They're searching for us everywhere. Especially you, because they know what you look like. Your disguise is good, but obviously not good enough."

If he demanded details she would be in trouble. She needed to change the subject. "How did you get me out of there? The last I remember was your shooting those men. And what happened to Gordon Taite? Did you kill him, too?"

He coughed into his napkin, and it vanished. He pulled it from the throat of his nanny's dress. He was a specialist in sleight of hand. "Arrogant asses. A couple of them had been watching you while you were hanging around the Café Justine, then more arrived. I couldn't contact you. So I waited until they made their move. Taite decided retreat was wisest, and he was goddamn right. I had the firepower."

Her voice was casual. "Anything new on the coming-in?"

"All the arrangements are in place. But is that the kind of life you really want? You may be making an enormous mistake."

"It's no mistake. It's time to go in."

Bingo. This man was part of the Carnivore's team. How could she find out his real name and where Liz Sansborough and the Carnivore were?

He drank tea. "You haven't told me yet, Liz, what you wanted there." He leveled his gaze at her, and she knew what it must be like to be a Protozoa beneath a microscope.

She had to say something. "Why were you there?"

The broad features stiffened. The eyes grew flinty, detached. A Walther appeared in his big hand. "My Liz gives direct answers to my questions. And she hasn't carried a Beretta in years. Who are you?"

She was trapped. She sipped her tea, lifted her gaze, and looked steadily into his eyes. "You care about Liz. I'm her cousin, Sarah Walker. I'm looking for her. We need to talk."

Astonishment lighted his face for a moment. Then the Walther moved closer to her head. "Don't lie. Sarah Walker and Liz aren't twins. And you don't act like Walker. A celebrity profiler?" He sneered. "Hughes Bremner would eat her alive, bones and all, and still be hungry."

She was stunned. How did he know what Sarah Walker had looked like? How did he know her work? But she had no time to think about that now. His fingers were white on the Walther.

"Tell me who you really are and why you've been surgically made to look like my Liz!"

She kept her gaze steady on his cold face. "I am Sarah Walker, and I don't know why. Except it has something to do with the Carnivore's coming-in."

"How would Sarah Walker know about the coming-in?"

"Because it was Hughes Bremner who had my face changed and then ordered me trained to act like Liz."

He studied her. "Prove you're Sarah Walker."

"My mother is Jane Sansborough Walker. Liz's father was Harold Sansborough, her brother. My father, Hamilton Walker, is a college professor. I—"

"You could have been told all that."

"Okay, you seem to know Liz well. If you do, you'll know she had a grandmother who often made a special Italian bread flavored with rosemary. Her name was Firenze."

"Grandmother Firenze?" His eyes probed. "But she wasn't your or Liz's grandmother at all, was she?"

Sarah frowned. "No. She was our *great*-grandmother."

He sat for a moment, then lowered the Walther, and he smiled that smile she'd seen before. Somewhere—

He asked, "What do you want with Liz?"

"I have reason to believe Hughes Bremner's going to pull some kind of trick and try to kill the Carnivore."

He leaned forward, thick shoulders and barrel chest incongruous in the bogus nanny dress. "Tell me everything you know."

"I can't give the information to just anyone. I need to know who you are."

His muscled body adjusted itself into the recliner as if he'd never be quite used to it or any other comfort. "I work for the Carnivore. They call me Quill." He passed his palm an inch over his short, gray crew cut. "My history is unimportant."

"Then tell me about the Carnivore and Liz. Something so I know I can trust my information to you."

"I could make you tell."

"If you did, you'd never be sure it was the truth. I don't want Bremner to have the Carnivore killed. Do you?"

He gave a hollow chuckle. "Tidy reasoning." He considered her. "I've been with the Carnivore a long time. He'll understand if I reveal a little, especially since many will hear soon enough." He sipped tea. "You might be interested to know he's an American. In fact, he grew up in Beverly Hills, a rich kid, wild and unmanageable. By the early '50s he was smoking grass and stealing cars. He was in and out of jail. His father was a big society lawyer who finally got tired of the kid's problems. He threw him out. So the kid went to live with his mother's relative in Vegas, an Italian uncle named Bosa."

Bosa! She remembered the Langley dossier on the Carnivore: His name was believed to be Alex Bosa!

Quill stood and paced. "In Vegas my friend got a job in his uncle's casino, and he married and tried to settle down. But he was still restless. So he picked up a couple of girl friends. His wife found out, and she took a boyfriend in revenge." Quill paused, not happy with what he was about to say. "His wife got beaten to death by her boyfriend. The cops did nothing. They said they had no evidence. After the funeral the boyfriend got a new girl. But the boyfriend was a maniac, and he beat her, too. My friend, who in a few years would be called the Carnivore . . . he couldn't stand it. The boyfriend was a bastard, and the bastard was getting away with it. Sure as hell he'd murder this new girl friend, too. So the Carnivore killed him.''

Quill shrugged. "Of course, my friend had to skip town. His father refused to see him. His Italian uncle—he was La Cosa Nostra, you know—got my friend enforcement work with his New York family. That's when my friend took the name Alex Bosa, his uncle's name." Quill smiled, thinking about what came next: "When he got a contract, Alex spent weeks on the details. He got so good, the family lent him to other families who needed out-of-town enforcement. You see, he had an analytical mind like his father's. He liked that link to the old man, especially doing work the self-righteous old prick would hate.

"Then, after a couple of years, Alex got a really tough assignment: Take out a Cuban general who'd refused to pay his gambling debts. But the guy was President Batista's best general, and his death just then was a big help to Fidel Castro when he was trying to capture Havana." Quill's grin was wintry. "In international circles this impossible hit made Alex Bosa a respected man."

So Langley's file on the Carnivore had been accurate: A mob hit had helped Castro take power, the Carnivore was born in the late 1930s, had at least one U.S. parent, and was heterosexual.

"Why the name *Carnivore?*" she asked.

"The godfather felt Alex deserved a name to reflect his talent, so he called him Il Carnivoro. The Carnivore." Quill stroked his Walther and looked up. "After the Cuban job, Alex asked to go private. He promised the godfather he would still do any 'special' work the family needed. This was an honorable request, so the godfather agreed, and the Carnivore was in business."

Quill set the Walther on the piecrust table and poured himself another cup of tea.

"I'd like more, too."

He took her cup. She felt another moment of admiration from him. For her coolness, perhaps. She had her training at the Ranch to thank for that. The training and psychological makeup that were now integral to her.

He watched as she took her brimming cup. Her hand showed not a tremor. She said, "How did you happen to be at the Café Justine this morning?"

"A note from a contact to let me know Bremner was doing some strange things at a health spa on the rue Vivienne," Quill said. "I'd say you were lucky. Now, tell me about Bremner."

"But I need to see Liz! This isn't idle curiosity. How can I prevent him—" She stopped, aware of his sudden wolfish grin.

A wave of menace swept hot and violent from him. "*I* will take care of Hughes Bremner. You will tell me what he's been doing. Everything! Begin with your face. When—"

The rapid beeping of a digital alarm filled the apartment. Quill pressed a small button on his watch, and his oversized TV screen flashed on to show a long hall filled with armed men moving stealthily toward the camera. Sarah saw Gordon's determined face as he urged the others on.

She turned. The Walther was in Quill's hand, aimed at her heart. With the other hand, he reached down the far side of his chair and pulled up his Uzi.

"You brought them!" he growled.

She knew instantly he must be right. "Not intentionally."

Think!, she told herself. She grabbed her Hasidic jacket from the end of the sofa and frantically searched the pockets.

She spoke rapidly. "The one who had the knife. He must've dropped a homing device somewhere in my clothes!"

"I have no more time." Quill stood, aimed at her temple.

"Here it is! A nickel, in the pocket!" Her heart pounded. The "nickel" was like those she'd seen at the Ranch, and it held a tracking device. She threw it away.

"I should've searched you, dammit! Getting old." He tossed her the Walther. "This way. Move!"

She followed him down a dark passageway. Of course, Quill would have another way out. There was an enormous explosion behind them. The floor shook. Quill knew it had to be the heavy steel door to his apartment. They'd blasted it open. In seconds Gordon and his people would be after them.

Quill jumped out a window and onto an asphalt roof. Sarah followed. Hunched low, they tore along the roofline. He stopped at padlocked shutters. Behind them feet thundered but were still not in sight. He unlocked the shutters, opened the tall roof window, and they leaped into a dusty storage room touched with the stale odors of long-ago garlic and onions. He unlocked another door, and now they were in another dimly lit corridor.

They turned right, ran down rickety stairs and through another doorway into a single-car garage. He closed and padlocked that door. The lock wouldn't stop their pursuers, but it would slow them. At this point, that could be enough.

They climbed into a sleek MG and, with a flick of his hand, the engine growled with power. Quill pressed a button, and the garage door opened.

He zoomed out into the quiet street.

Gunfire erupted on Quill's side of the car. A man and a woman with M-16s ran toward them. Gordon's people. Of course, once Gordon had tracked them to this block, he'd ordered the block surrounded. Quill propped his Uzi on his windowsill and fired round after round into them. They erupted in brilliant red tissue and peach-colored bone.

"Quill! They're dead!" She shook his shoulder. "Stop it!"

He grunted and dropped the Uzi to his lap. He drove swiftly out into the street, and as they skidded around a corner, she saw a strange site—a clown, holding a bouquet of balloons, seemed to be running toward them. Quill floored the accelerator.

She sat unmoving, the stench of death in her nostrils. It wasn't a real smell, she realized. They were too far from the corpses for that. It was her past. The blond boy in Denver. The couple in the trunk of the Cadillac. The guard-attendants at Je Suis Chez Moi. Blount Mc-Caw. The three men in the alley. And now this couple. So many dead.

The MG slowed and weaved erratically. They were a few blocks from the apartment, and Quill's gaze was locked on the quiet street ahead. The car decelerated, veered wildly.

"Sorry, Sarah. Tried to—" His voice was so thick he could hardly talk.

He angled the MG into an empty spot at the curb. In slow motion he gripped his heart, leaned forward onto the steering wheel, gave a huge sigh, and collapsed.

She pulled him back and saw the red river spreading across his chest. One or more of the couple's shots had gotten him. Maybe that's why he'd kept firing until the pair exploded.

He smiled, and the smile was strangely kind, as if from a forgotten past. "Guess my luck finally ran out."

From where did she know that smile? She searched her memory. The smile was recent— And then it came to her.

It was the smile of Hal Sansborough!

Liz's father, in the Sansborough photo albums. Those albums she'd studied and studied when she'd believed *she* was Liz Sansborough. But Hal Sansborough was dead, killed with his wife in New York City by a mugger—

How could Quill be Harold Sansborough?

"Quill!" She grabbed his chin, made him look at her. He was still smiling. "Quill! Are you Hal Sansborough? Are you my uncle?"

The smile seemed to stretch wider. "Janie's daughter. Tell her I'm proud of you."

He grimaced and his chest contracted in a sudden spasm of pain. Air gusted from his lungs.

"And tell Liz . . . I love her."

She put her cheek to his mouth. There was no breath, no life. Without warning, tears rushed down her cheeks.

Fifty

The glass-domed tourist boat was one of the many *bateaux-mouches* that cruised the Seine between the Pont de l'Alma and the Pont de Sully. On Sunday mornings, the boat offered oven-hot *brioche*, perfectly aged *fromage*, and sun-ripened *fruit*.

Hughes Bremner stood alone, eating from his plate and gazing out at the quay. He pretended to enjoy the sights, but he was really visualizing the triumphant completion on Monday of his two-year, multibillion-dollar operation: GRANDEUR. It would crown his career and make a legend of Hughes Bremner. Except no one would ever know.

Before anyone could comprehend what had really happened, he would slip away to the South Seas paradise that awaited him on Indigo Reef. For two years he'd been collecting paintings, ceramics, and sculptures for it. His office there, so very different from his puritanical seventh-floor aerie at Langley, would be richly appointed, with paintings by Braque, Kandinsky, and Soulages. The villa's stonework was by the finest Italian craftsmen. His wine cellar was already filled with the best bottles from France and California. He had a state-of-the-art computerized security system and a communications network that would keep him in touch with the world to whatever degree he wished—

"A Sunday morning in Paris," said a voice at his elbow. "Nothing quite like it."

Bremner didn't turn. He continued to survey the riverbank. A mother with two children was buying balloons. Next they'd parade along the quay. He could think of nothing more boring.

Bremner said, "Report."

Kit Crowther talked in a low, steady tone. He was orchestrating the financial part of GRANDEUR, and he stood to make a fortune for his trouble. But he wouldn't live long enough to acquire it. As soon as the transaction was completed, Gordon would eliminate him.

"This is what will happen," Crowther told him. "When the announcement is made, there'll be a major realignment of European currencies. Interest rates will drop, and so will stock markets. I've shorted the franc and bet that interest rates and securities will be hit by the realignments. I've sold francs short about $10 billion, bought the U.S. dollar, which is very strong right now, for $8 billion. I've also bought nearly $1 billion in French stocks, because equities rise when a currency devalues. With Sterling-O'Keefe's credit, I've been able to maintain these positions with just $1 billion in collateral. You're margined to your Adam's apple. I hope you know what you're doing, or Sterling-O'Keefe could be wiped out."

Bremner only smiled and watched the river pass.

Crowther had borrowed money in francs and converted the francs into U.S. dollars at the fixed rates. As soon as the franc made its sharp dive, Crowther would buy in the far-cheaper franc to repay the debt, and Hughes Bremner would pocket the rest, as well as the additional profits—after he'd paid off Gordon Taite, Allan Levine, and a few others. His profits would make him the multibillionaire he'd made up his mind to become the moment he'd turned his back on an immoral and ungrateful country and started Sterling-O'Keefe.

Crowther ate from his plate, his gaze safely on the quay. "I'd like to know what information you're working this on."

"No you wouldn't. You want to make a clean $5 million."

From the corners of his eyes, Bremner saw Crowther smile and give a slight nod of agreement. For $5 million, he could live without knowing. Except, of course, he wouldn't live long.

"Daddy! Daddy!"

The international currency expert turned and carried his plate away without another word to Bremner. "Coming, honey. Did you lose Mommy?"

Bremner gave a final glance out toward the quay, and for an instant of pure joy he again saw Indigo Reef in his mind. A palm-fringed jewel in an aquamarine sea. Soon he'd be able to tell the whole world to fuck off. He'd walk out of the CIA, disappear, and live life as he'd always dreamed it. Gentle trade winds. Warm nights. Wealth beyond the fantasies of mere kings.

Back in his Languedoc office, Bremner's visions of Shangri-la collapsed into nightmare.

A message from Arlene Debo was waiting on his desk:

I'm flying over, Hughes. Arrive around five o'clock your time. I have a report the Carnivore is coming in to you this evening.

Bremner's chest contracted. Goddamn that woman! What had gotten into her? Had someone warned her—! No. Impossible. No one who knew of the coming-in would tell her. They were *his* people. Loyal to him alone!

With rigorous discipline, he forced himself to calm. Then he turned the problem over in his mind. Had someone betrayed him? He had only a few hours to find out and plan how to handle Arlene. And he still had all the arrangements for the Carnivore's coming-in to deal with.

He needed Sarah Walker, and he needed her *now*.

Bremner reached for his private phone.

Sarah Walker closed her uncle's eyes and wiped tears from her face. He was still smiling. Blood oozed from his chest, down his side, and into the front seat. She remembered those photo albums as if they were open before her now. She'd lived and breathed them until they'd become the past she'd lost. His nose was flatter, and his chin was smaller, but take off twenty-five years and thirty pounds, and he was Liz's father, Hal Sansborough, as he'd looked in that photo taken outside the house in Chelsea, holding his daughter's hand.

His last words had been, "Tell Liz I love her."

She jumped out of the MG and looked carefully around. No one was on the street, and no one seemed to be watching from the buildings. She retrieved Quill's Walther and checked the clip. She walked toward the nearest *métro* stop. She was sad and confused and worried. A man she'd never known, but for a while had believed to be her father, was dead. She knew she ought to be furious. She ought to want revenge, but what she longed for was an end to the murders. She wanted to lay it all to rest as permanently as death itself.

And finally, there was one inescapable fact: She was the blood niece of an accomplished, ruthless killer.

Who had said he was proud of her.

It chilled her. She didn't want a killer to be proud of her. Without realizing it, she walked faster, as if by force alone she could speed herself toward resolution.

When Sarah reached the bistro where they had agreed to meet, Asher was waiting at the curb on a low-slung BMW motorcycle. "My God, your head!" He touched the bandage above her temple. "What happened?"

"I'll fill you in later. You look anxious to leave."

"Right." He glanced up and down the street. "The photos and story about us have done a good job. I got stopped twice. Third time might not be so lucky." He handed her a black leather jacket and a helmet with a darkened visor identical to his. "Think you can put this on over your bandage?"

"Sure." She grimaced at the fast, sharp pain as she eased it down. "Where are we going?"

"That's the good news. Jack O'Keefe's. Christine Robitaille told me where he lives."

"At last! Now maybe we'll find out what Bremner's up to!"

As she pulled on the leather motorcycle jacket, her white shirt rode up, and he spotted the Walther in her waistband. "What's happened? Where's your Beretta?"

"It's a long story, Asher. Let's get out of here."

Christine Robitaille sat on her filigreed balcony in Les Halles and looked out over the bright noontime glow of Paris. Down the center of the great city wove the wide, silvered ribbon of the Seine, glorious at any hour. She smoked her gold-tipped cigarettes and thought about the river, about the past, about history. And about herself.

She knew where she'd come from. Now she wondered whether she was doomed to repeat old mistakes. She'd had a good beginning, growing up among the florists of Paris. In this romantic city, where the three staples were bread, wine, and flowers, she'd loved and understood the importance of the work from a very early age. How better to introduce *amour* than with sixty ruby-red roses? What better gift than a Chinese bowl filled with snowy lilies, satin-white hydrangeas, green artichokes, and emerald ferns and mosses?

In Paris even the poorest areas had their own florists, but the Robitaille shop was in an elite section. The family's ivory-columned store faced the National Assembly on the Place du Palais Bourbon, where nearby embassies and ministries had a great need for fine flowers. The Robitailles were renowned for their elegant, witty, fresh arrangements.

Christine had two brothers and two sisters. As the baby, she was indulged. As the prettiest girl, she was fawned over, clothed in delicate net stockings and frilly dresses, and shown off as yet another exquisite Robitaille creation. She went to school and worked in the shop. She had a flair for arrangement, but her real love was the counter. There she could flirt with the young government clerks and the distinguished gentlemen of state who came by to select a flawless blossom for their latest love.

She was pregnant at fourteen. Her lover was an arranger at a popular artificial-flower shop. Not only her youth, but the work of her young man, caused an uproar in her family. He was the greater problem. As an arranger of fraudulent flowers, he could have no appreciation for the beauty, fragility, and impermanence of God's own blossoms. Still, he offered to marry her. He was that kind of honorable young man, although both knew theirs was earthy lust, not heavenly *amour*.

Her Catholic family saw no other solution. She must marry.

She ran away, found an abortionist, and went to work in the clubs in Montmartre. Soon she was on stage, dancing and singing in fewer and fewer clothes. When her father found her there at last, he left in tears. He would tell her mother she was dead. She promised never to return home.

There were more men, more *amours,* but when she turned thirty, she knew her nude dancing days were coming to an end. That's when her lover at the time, a dark charmer from Marseille, suggested she speak to his friend, Jean.

Jean had been the only name by which she'd known her new boss, and their professional association had lasted twenty years.

Thus she went to work for Interpol, and *amour* became her career. It was a good career, working for the government, selling something she'd never run out of. But now she was past fifty. She had gray hair, which, six months ago, she'd abruptly quit coloring. With the years, her soft, sweet face had grown steely. Now she smoked too much, drank too much, and was weary of *amour*. She'd learned that for men, power was sex. But for women, sex was a poor substitute for power.

She liked Asher Flores, not only because he was a darling man who'd always treated her with respect, but because his last name was Spanish for flowers. It seemed destined they should meet, become friends, and she would be able to give him information that would save his life. Afterward she'd bedded him. Not for love, but so he could thank her properly.

This morning he'd phoned the computer shop. She'd told her assistant to say she was not at work. She'd needed time to think, because she'd had a message from her new boss, Jean's replacement. "Guy." Guy had told her Interpol was looking for Asher Flores and, in fact, three Languedoc men had died in an attempt to capture him outside her shop. Of course, she knew about the murders, but she'd not known they were Asher's work. Also, she'd read that Asher and some young woman were being hunted for murders they'd supposedly committed in Denver.

This unsettled her. She trusted Asher. She knew he wouldn't have killed unless he had to. He was no traitor. But Guy said that was indeed what Langley claimed.

Asher Flores had turned. He'd gone rogue.

She must help take him out.

Sarah Walker, however, must be captured alive and turned over to the Languedoc.

She'd met Asher anyway, nearly two hours ago. Even the condemned deserved a hearing, although she didn't tell him that was why she'd finally agreed to see him. He'd explained about his young woman, Sarah Walker, and what Hughes Bremner had supposedly done to her. He'd also told her the Carnivore was coming in after all these years.

She'd believed Asher. What a child he was. Also an excellent lover. He'd wanted to know where Jack O'Keefe lived. She'd made a few calls and tracked him to Burgundy. Jack O'Keefe had also been her lover. But that was years ago, when she was still competitive and Jack was a silver-haired legend, about to retire. Too bad. She'd liked to have known him before, when he'd had the red hair. All over, she'd heard. Red Jack O'Keefe.

In her belly she knew it was time to retire herself. Everywhere she turned she saw the shades of long-ago men whose names she no longer recalled. *Merde!* She could no longer remember even the name of that first one who would have married her so many years ago. She had no regrets about the abortion. Secretly she'd always known she was the only child who mattered.

Some five years ago, after her parents died, she'd recontacted her family. She'd made friends with a nephew who'd recently moved to Seattle, where he'd opened his own Robitaille floral boutique. Outside Seattle, he'd written her, the trees grew so lush, the area was a vast northern jungle. She would like to see that. But even more, she would like to live in Seattle, where no one would know her and she would see no ghosts. She needed someone in the United States government to cut through the bureaucracy, give her resident alien status, and award her a pension.

Guy and Asher Flores had just opened the door for that. With one telephone call she could buy a one-way ticket to Seattle. Was that what she really wanted?

And what about Asher? Could she live with herself if she were the instrument of his death?

She stubbed out her cigarette and strode into her apartment, stripping off clothes as she went. She dressed in her chaste nightgown, brushed her teeth, gargled, and climbed between the sheets as if it were bedtime. It had been many months since she'd had a man, and she cherished her celibacy. Still, there was the yearning between the legs. The body had its own memory.

She rolled over and pounded her pillow. What should she do?

The bottom line, as the Yanks liked to say, was a choice between Asher's life . . . and her own.

Christine Robitaille did not sleep. In an hour she was up again. She made a phone call. Within thirty minutes she was marching down the rue de Rivoli.

She passed perfume stores, boutiques, souvenir shops, and bookstores, noticing business was slow. The wretched recession again. At last she stepped under the arcade of the Café Madeleine. She selected a table outdoors, where she could watch.

She ordered *café*. She noticed a tall and austerely handsome man, who looked in need of lunch. He'd paused in the entryway and was surveying the tables. Perhaps he was the one.

She took out one of her signature gold-tipped cigarettes, and paused.

He saw it . . . and her.

"Allow me, *madame.*"

His lighter clicked beneath her cigarette. She inhaled and looked into his chilly eyes. He had the face and heart of a hawk, she decided. As she had heard, he was a predator. She was glad she'd taken precautions.

"Hughes Bremner?" she murmured.

"Oui."

"Sit down, *monsieur.* We have a large matter to discuss."

Fifty-one

The tinted motorcycle visors completely hid their faces, but Sarah's eyes watched everywhere, acutely aware the hunt had intensified and Hughes Bremner never quit.

Over the roar of the BMW, Asher shouted, "Your Beretta?"

She talked against his helmet. "Probably at the Languedoc. Gordon almost got me again." She told him about the attack in the street near Je Suis Chez Moi and how the "nanny"—Quill—had saved her. Then she described the second CIA assault, Quill's death, and his admission of who he was.

"He's your uncle? You mean Liz's father?" Asher yelled back at her. "But didn't he and your aunt die in New York?"

"Their deaths must've been faked. Or at least his was. Remember, there was identification in their wallets. No one would have done too much checking. After all, they were 'only' a salesman and his wife. No one special."

They were out of Paris at last. Asher pulled off the road, let the engine drop into idle, and hitched himself around on the seat.

"But why go to that much trouble?"

She took a deep breath. "Bear with me, Asher. I think Uncle Hal had a very compelling reason. First, he was supposedly a salesman, but the man I just met was a skilled, ruthless killer, great at disguise and sleight of hand. And he knew so much about the world's most mysterious, most enigmatic assassin he could describe the guy's family, his mafia ties, and his first hit."

"Liz could've told him that."

"Okay, then look at the coincidence: The Carnivore's father was an asshole Beverly Hills lawyer who sent the Carnivore away when he was a teenager. My uncle's father—my grandfather—was an asshole Beverly Hills lawyer, too."

"The two fathers do sound suspiciously alike."

"The Carnivore and Uncle Hal are about the same age. My Grandma Firenze, actually Uncle Hal's grandmother, was Italian. The uncle in Vegas who took in the Carnivore when he was a screwed-up teenager was Italian. Then there was the godfather in New York. Grandma Firenze had lots of relatives who came from Sicily—"

They were silent. Time seemed to stand still.

She continued: "Being a traveling salesman gave Uncle Hal cover to do the hits. His wife and daughter gave him more cover: Who'd suspect a hard-working, middle-class guy with a lovely wife and an adorable little girl of being a professional assassin?"

Asher nodded. "The mafia godfather in New York would've expected the Carnivore to pay respects once a year, which would explain the annual 'sales' meetings in New York."

"When Mom wrote Uncle Harold, she probably sent photos and told him about Michael and me. That's how he knew what I looked like before my cosmetic surgery. After he 'died,' he probably kept up with what we were all doing, so he'd know where we were and that we wouldn't inadvertently cause him trouble. That's how he knew what kind of work I did. I always thought it weird Mom talked so little about him and his family. For obvious reasons he must've kept her at a distance. He probably didn't write much or send photos for Mom to show around. Then, of course, he 'died.' " She shook her head. "God, I can't believe I may be the Carnivore's niece!"

Asher absorbed the shock. "It makes me wonder whether he planted Liz inside Langley as his spy."

They sat in silence, considering the Carnivore, Liz Sansborough, and Hughes Bremner.

At last Asher said, "It's over. The whole thing. If the Carnivore's dead, Bremner's got nothing to fear."

"It's not over for us. Bremner still can't let us live. We know too much."

"We've got to find out more about Sterling-O'Keefe and also

about this mysterious operation of Bremner's that's going down Monday. Somehow the Carnivore, dead or alive, has to be a danger to one or both.''

"Don't forget Liz. She's obviously smart and tough, and she may know plenty about the Carnivore's business. Bremner has to eliminate her, too.''

"True.''

"Maybe she'll try to come in anyway.''

He looked off into the distance, where cattle grazed in the lacy shade of a stand of sycamores. "If she tells what she knows, at least she won't be hunted anymore. She could get asylum and have a regular life—marry, have a family, a new career, whatever she wanted.'' He nodded to himself. "Yeah, she's got every reason to come in. So it looks to me like Bremner's in the same spot: He won't be able to take a chance on what the Carnivore might have told her.''

"The situation's changed, yet it hasn't. Even if the Carnivore's dead, Bremner's still got to eliminate us. He might not even find out the Carnivore's dead by eight o'clock tonight.''

"It's tough to identify a man whose face you've never seen, even for Bremner.'' He paused. "Maybe we're the only ones who know. We could turn that into an advantage.''

"And I could be wrong.'' She touched his chin. "Quill was my uncle, but maybe he was just what he seemed—an assistant trained to be like his boss. The rest could be sheer coincidence—or a lie Quill made up. Quill could have fabricated the whole story about how the Carnivore got started. In any case, the Carnivore's fooled the world before. Often. My uncle is dead, but the Carnivore could still be very much alive!''

At the Café Madeleine on the rue de Rivoli, Christine Robitaille drank not a sip of *café*, but she enjoyed Hughes Bremner. Even though she didn't trust him, she could appreciate him. *Un homme galant.* Charming enough to be French.

She also admired his ability to use a compliment and set the tone for negotiations. He offered champagne. Alas, she had to refuse that, too. Being charmed had not softened her brain.

"You have information for me about Sarah Walker and Asher Flores?'' Bremner smiled his hollow smile.

She liked the predatoriness of him, the savvy hawk face, the sunken eyes, the aristocratic gestures. He was a man of the world.

She said, "I can tell you where they're going right now. Where they will be this afternoon."

He cocked his head and nodded, impressed. "Do go on."

"But first, I, too, have certain needs."

He listened attentively as she explained her desire to move to Seattle with money in the bank. "Hmmm. I see no problem. A modest request."

"I cannot tell you about Asher and the woman," she explained, "until I see my new documents. You understand."

"Of course. But alas, dear lady, I'm in a bit of a rush."

She smiled. She was flexible. She sat back, held out a cigarette for another light. "How long will you need?"

Bremner seemed to consider. "An hour. No more."

"I will return here in an hour."

Bremner left.

Christine was hungry, but she would not eat here. She put out her cigarette and walked for some time to be sure Bremner had no one following her. Then she picked a *bistro* she'd never patronized. She ate a good lunch, and was back at the Café Madeleine in precisely an hour.

Bremner was waiting. He showed her a new U.S. passport, filled out with her name and information. All that was missing was her photograph. Then he returned the passport to his pocket. He showed her a fat envelope filled with hundred-dollar bills. Then he returned the envelope to his pocket also.

"And the pension?" she demanded.

"It's being established now." He shrugged. "You'll have to trust me on that. I won't have the paperwork until tomorrow."

"Hmmmm." Her gaze scanned the street. "Then I must give you the information tomorrow."

"That will do me no good, since you know where Flores and Walker are *today*."

"True. *Quel dommage*. What a pity." If he was bluffing, she'd discover it now. If he was telling the truth, she'd have to find another way to get her documents, because she believed a predator like Bremner would never be trustworthy.

Resolute, she stood.

He raised his brows, impressed. "My apologies, *madame*. I see I have misjudged you." From another pocket he handed her the document. She sat and read it carefully. She was to receive a generous pension, beginning the first of next month, from the U.S. Department of the Treasury.

She gave him her most charming smile. *"Excellent.* Now I will have the passport and the cash, and then I will tell you what I know." She held out her hand.

Bremner put one then the other in her palm. She stood again.

His face darkened. He rose, towered over her. "Your information, *madame!"*

She savored the thrill. "Here, *monsieur.* Enjoy." She took a small piece of paper from her purse, laid it on the table, and walked briskly away.

Fifty-two

Christine Robitaille exited the back door of a bookstore, strode down an alley, and emerged onto the busy street where she had parked her car. She looked at it, and suddenly she felt apprehensive. She had a new U.S. passport, an envelope filled with cash, a pension . . . and a sudden sense of unease.

She marched along the street in the opposite direction. What should she do? She tried to hail a taxi, but dozens whipped past, carrying church-dressed passengers home to Sunday dinners. She hated the *métro*. She wanted her car. Tomorrow she'd have a friend inspect it, make sure it wasn't wired for sound or with plastic. Meanwhile she could simply rent one. There was a car-rental agency down the block. Gold Star Rent-a-Car. She turned toward it, and again she changed her mind.

There was someone following her.

She hurried back toward the rue de Rivoli, which would take her to the intricacies of the Louvre. For the first time she had a sense of terrible dread. She was certain at least one man was following her. He was dressed in light summer trousers, a blousy shirt, and sunglasses. For a while he'd been on the same side of the street as she, but now he'd crossed over.

He was pretending to look in a store window, but her years working for Interpol told her he was watching her.

And following her.

She wanted to reach the Louvre. There she could hide. *Mon dieu!*

The Louvre could hide all the spies of France, England, and Germany combined!

Just let her reach the Louvre, and—

Now she spotted a woman behind her, too. On her side of the street. An attractive woman in shorts and a tank top, a large bag held close to her side.

Large enough for a pistol.

Christine was sweating now. She increased her speed. Then, as she rushed past the mouth of an alley, a man hurried out.

They collided.

"Pardonnez-moi!" he exclaimed, holding her in his arms to balance her.

She needed no help! She pushed away. *"Ca m'est égal!"*

"Christine, *ma chérie!"* the woman behind her waved.

At the sound of her name, Christine shoved with all the force of her small, hard muscles. She had to get away!

And almost immediately she knew she was too late.

She felt a sting in her *derrière*. A sharp sting, like a needle. Weakness flooded her. Her knees buckled.

Christine wanted to scream. She wanted to fight. She wanted to run. But her muscles and intentions failed. Someone took her purse. She felt a moment of fury. Inside the purse were the money and papers that guaranteed her new future. Too late. *De par le roi, defense à Dieu, de faire miracle en ce lieu.* She collapsed into cold, silent death.

That morning in Virginia, an irritating noise awoke Bunny Bremner. Her mouth was dry, her eyes itched, and she wanted to brush her teeth. She heard the noise again. It was a scratching sound, and it seemed to come from under the mountain cabin. A steady scratching and men's voices. She recognized the muffled voices of her captors but not what they were saying.

The noise grated on her alcohol-inflamed nerves. She looked at the clock on the kitchen stove: 9:00 A.M. She'd fallen asleep sometime after midnight, after she'd persuaded both men to drink with her. But by then she'd been too drunk to escape, even though they'd become careless. She needed her Scotch too damn much, and, suddenly, in her mind she heard Hughes's mocking voice:

Have more, Bunny dearest! Can't stop, can you, you disgusting old drunk? The Lord God above never made anyone as revolting as you, and that, Bunny dearest, is why I love you so!

With rare insight, she realized her alcoholism had let him feel better about himself. No matter how bad he was, he could always tell himself he wasn't as bad as "that disgusting old drunk he'd married." And now—

She looked at the iron bed. Marilyn was motionless. She studied the crumpled form until she saw the blanket rise and fall over her chest. Marilyn was still alive. For all the good that did either of them. Suddenly the comforting voice of her aristocratic father seemed to speak to her:

As long as we're alive, we can win, Bunny. The Hartfords never give up. Never. It's time you quit letting Hughes humiliate you. You're better than that.

She paused, furious and suddenly determined. Papa was right. She shook her head to clear last night's Scotch and listened carefully to the strange scratching sounds. Like metal being scraped. Echoing faintly into the kitchen. The pipes? The two men scraping at the water pipes under the house? Why would they care about water pipes?

Bunny studied the cabin. Everything the men had brought into it was gone, except for their jackets. The jackets hung just inside the door. Through the front window she could see her Mercedes and Marilyn's car parked close to the porch. The green Volvo was now in the driveway with its trunk open as if waiting for a last item before driving away.

She heard the men crawling down beneath the floorboards again, and then the voice of the leader, Sid: "That ought to do it. One more good nick, we light the stove, and *boom,* that's all she wrote."

Bunny looked at the gas stove in the little kitchen. They were scraping a hole in the gas line under the house! They would light the stove, make one last nick in the gas line, run for their car, and—

She blinked slowly, allowing herself time to absorb the shock of what would happen next: Gas would seep into the cabin. When it reached the flame, the cabin would explode. There would be an inferno. Marilyn and she would be either asphyxiated or burned to death.

Sid spoke near the front door, "Take the tools down to the car. As soon as we get the call, we'll be out of here in five minutes."

He stepped into the room and sat at the table across from Bunny.

He smiled, a mortician taking the measurements of the not-yet-dead.

She felt strangely calm. *The Hartfords never give up,* she reminded herself.

"Want a drink?" He opened the last bottle of Scotch and pushed it toward her.

She stared at the bottle, and an idea began to form in her mind.

"Well?" he demanded.

She nodded.

He laughed, untied her hands, and sat back down facing her.

If she did everything exactly right, Bunny thought, Marilyn and she might survive. For a moment she had a sense of utter dread. This might be her only opportunity. And she had to do it before fear immobilized her—

"What's wrong, Mrs. Bremner? Change your mind?"

"No." Heart pounding, she quickly grabbed the Scotch bottle by its neck, leaned forward, and slammed it against his forehead.

Blood poured down his face and into his startled mouth.

"Cunt!" Stunned, he lunged for her.

But he was too late. She crashed the bottle against his forehead again. The bottle shattered. Blood sprayed. His eyes closed, and he started to topple. She reached across the table and tugged on his shoulders until his torso slumped quietly before her.

She was breathing hard. Now she had to figure out what to do about the other one. She didn't try to untie the rope that bound her legs. She already knew the knots were too tight. She lifted her chair around to where she could take his knife from his pocket.

She cut herself free, wriggled her toes and feet, and stood. She looked out the window.

The tall one was at their Volvo, talking on the cellular phone. As she watched, he punched a button on the phone, ending the conversation. He started toward the cabin. He was in his shirt sleeves, and the gun in his shoulder holster was clearly visible.

She needed a weapon. She looked at the man she'd hit. He wasn't wearing his gun!

Frantic, she hurried to the jackets hanging next to the door. The gun was in its holster under his jacket. Swiftly she pulled it out. Her father had taught her all about hunting rifles and a moderate amount about hand guns. She was a fine shot. Even Hughes admitted that. She inhaled, trying to keep calm. A rifle or side arm was a woman's equalizer, her father had told her.

The gun had a silencer. She checked the chamber and clip, released the safety, and moved to the cabin's front door. Trying to keep calm, she glanced out the window next to the door and saw the tall man had just ambled up onto the porch.

She steeled herself. He was a torturer and killer. She opened the door and fired. Immediately she realized she'd made a terrible mistake by not moving Sid out of view. Fess was rushing across the porch to the door, his gaze on Sid's slumped form in the kitchen window.

Her bullet missed. It bit into the floorboards behind him. Sudden sweat drenched her.

He grabbed for the gun in his shoulder holster.

She was paralyzed. Couldn't breathe. Couldn't think.

The instant seemed to stretch into an hour as she forced an old, rusty switch to turn itself on inside her brain. Still, she was too shocked to aim. So she pumped out bullets as fast as she could. For a long beat she thought his gun was going to complete its arc toward her chest and shoot her point-blank in the heart.

Instead, he screamed, spun back, and sprawled flat across the porch. His right shoulder and chest erupted in blood. His fingers convulsively released his gun and the cellular phone.

Shaking, she kicked his gun away and stood over him, her pistol pointed down. Spittle appeared at the corner of his slack mouth. His eyes were closed. She poked him with the toe of her tennis shoe.

"Get up!" she ordered. His body undulated with the increased pressure of her foot.

Breathing hard, she looked around and saw clothesline strung across the yard. She ran into the cabin, picked up Sid's pocket knife, and ran out. With the clothesline, she tied Sid to the chair in which he sat. She dragged Fess into the cabin and tied him to the foot of Marilyn's cot.

"Marilyn?"

She spoke the injured woman's name urgently and touched her arm. Marilyn—Leslee Pousho—made no response. Her eyes remained closed. Her skin was gray. There was something sepulchral about her, Bunny decided. The poor woman must have medical treatment immediately.

Somehow Bunny got Marilyn to her feet and half carried, half dragged her to the red Mercedes outside the cabin.

Bunny shot holes in the tires of Leslee's rental car and the men's Volvo. She returned to the cabin, found her purse with her car keys inside, found Marilyn's purse, then hurried back out. Even though it appeared they were safe, sweat still bathed her and fear had left a dry, bitter taste in her mouth.

She got into her luxury sports car, symbol of all she loved and believed in, and gripped its steering wheel. She made herself breathe deeply. Then she hit the accelerator and sped down the steep drive. Her tires squealed as they gripped blacktop and shot the car forward.

Suddenly she smiled.

Marilyn moaned in the bucket seat next to her.

"Now, now, dear." She patted Marilyn's arm. "You'll be all right very soon."

Marilyn opened her eyes. Bunny was astonished she had the strength. "Where going?" Marilyn's swollen lips hardly moved.

"I'm taking you to the hospital, dear. I'm sure you want to know how we got away from those sadists, but you're much too ill to have to listen to all that. When you're better, we'll have lunch. I'll buy this time, and I'll explain—"

"Must . . . tell . . ." Marilyn swallowed.

"Of course, dear. Go ahead."

"Made . . . documents . . ." But the effort was too much. Marilyn slumped in the seat, unconscious again.

Bunny rushed down through the Blue Ridge Mountains, into the foothills, and then through the rolling vineyards and Arabian estates of the flatlands. At last she arrived at the village hospital. Fortunately, Charlie Smithdeal was on duty in the emergency room and took charge immediately. He sent Marilyn straight to ICU while he himself treated Bunny's welts and bruises. She smiled again, remembering his grandfather, who had delivered her at a time when doctors came when they were called.

When he released her, Bunny took the elevator up to check on Marilyn. The young journalist looked much better now that she was clean and her wounds were bandaged, even with all those tubes in her.

"You must rest, dear."

Marilyn clutched Bunny's arm. ". . . documents . . . copies

. . . mailed   to . . . myself . . . P.O.   box . . . must . . . stop
. . . Bremner . . .''

Bunny froze. "You may be absolutely sure of that. *I* will expose
Hughes and deal with him personally.''

"No . . . now . . . now . . .'' The hand fell away.

Bunny called the nurse, who came quickly. She bent over Marilyn,
then nodded to Bunny. "She'll be fine, Mrs. Bremner. But she really
must rest.''

"Of course. Tell her I'll return tomorrow. Here's my card in case
she asks for me.''

Bunny rode down to the lobby, which, on a Sunday afternoon,
was full of visiting families. She wondered what Marilyn had wanted
to tell her. She must remember to ask tomorrow. After she contacted Senator Joe Allen, and Philip Shelton at the White House, to
demand Hughes be arrested immediately.

She considered trying to reach them at once, but it was Sunday,
and August, and it would be extremely difficult to get through to
anyone. Suddenly she felt weary to the bone. What should she do?
But before her brain had finished the question, she knew. If ever
she deserved to have a few quiet drinks, this was the time.

Fifty-three

SUNDAY, 3:45 P.M.

Asher Flores turned the motorcycle off the highway onto a paved road that rolled up and down the undulating hills like a shipping lane in a high sea. The August sun beat steadily down, and the warm wind flowed across their skin. Behind him, Sarah adjusted her weight. For a moment her legs tightened around him. With a thrill, his mind returned to last night. To Sarah and heated relief. To the issue of love.

Was it love to want her all to himself? To see her come through doorways when she wasn't there? To be unable to imagine ever being bored with her?

She squeezed him tenderly. He held her hand against his heart, savoring her smooth skin and the confidence, the belief, she had in him, while he worried about Hughes Bremner and what they might find at Jack O'Keefe's estate.

After another ten miles, just as Christine Robitaille had said, a castlelike tower appeared above the tops of a forest. Then, around a curve, they saw the rest of the grand Château de la Vere. It arose from manicured grounds, a yellow-brick fortress with a round tower and a conical roof.

He turned the motorcycle up the gravel drive and stopped in front of an imposing single door with huge wrought-iron hinges.

But before they could disembark, the door swung open, and a beefy man leaped out, waving a musket over his white powdered wig.

From his powdered face to his white-silk stockings and shiny black slippers, he appeared to have stepped right from the eighteenth century. But he wore sunglasses. And his wig was crooked, his face powder was blotched, and the black slippers were on the wrong feet.

"Liberté! Egalité! Fraternité! To arms. To arms!'' The man pointed his musket at Asher and Sarah. "The prisons are full of conspirators. Have you escaped, *citoyens? Zut! Zut!* I will send you to your graves!'' He cocked the musket.

Sarah pulled out her Walther.

Asher said, "Hello, Jack. We've come for a visit.''

Sarah glanced from Asher to the older man, then she put away her weapon. Dammit, this sorry fellow with his crooked wig and reversed slippers was the legendary spymaster himself, Red Jack O'Keefe. But there was something very wrong with him, maybe wrong enough for him to drop out of sight.

Asher introduced himself and Sarah. Then: "Christine Robitaille sends her regards.''

Red Jack O'Keefe recognized the name. "Christine?''

A voice rang out from the château. *"Monsieur Jack! Monsieur Jack! S'il vous plaît!''*

Jack O'Keefe lifted his head. A puzzled expression came over his powdered face, and he lowered his musket as the man's voice continued to demand to know the location of Monsieur Jack.

"Me voici!'' he called back at last into the marble foyer. Nervously he ran a hand down his ruffled shirt.

A bald man appeared in the doorway. He was of medium height and build, but heavy in the shoulders. He wore thick-lensed eyeglasses, a precisely trimmed mustache, a snooty expression, and butler's clothes. With a glance he took in the scene. He rested his hands on his hips, shook his head, and tut-tutted. Then he led Jack O'Keefe up the château's steps.

Sarah and Asher quickly popped off their motorcycle helmets. While Asher tended to the BMW, Sarah tested her wounds. Her shoulder was sore, but no longer painful. She unwrapped the bandage from her head. The bullet had cut through her scalp just above her ear. It was sore, too, but not enough to bother about. She pulled her hair down over it.

She and Asher exchanged a look, and they followed Jack O'Keefe into his château.

□   □   □   □

The butler was settling the old spy at a table in a grassy courtyard at the back. Asher stayed, chatting to a blank-faced O'Keefe, while Sarah followed the butler back into the château.

"Schizophrenia?" she asked.

"Monsieur has the Alzheimer's, *hélas."*

Sarah had once done a magazine piece on Alzheimer's, and she knew it was the single most common cause of dementia. Sufferers often had hallucinations and paranoid delusions. If the disease was far advanced, they'd get nothing from O'Keefe.

She asked, "How long has he been sick?"

The butler peered through his glasses at her. "Who knows? The doctors cannot say from exactly what moment. But the last two years have been bad, *très* bad." In a modern, spotless kitchen he arranged a tray of little crustless sandwiches, raw vegetables, and Oreo cookies. "He's always hungry after an *épisode,"* he explained. "Perhaps you will join him? He has few *visiteurs.* They find him, ah—"

"Of course." She forced a cheerful smile. "Does Jack know who he is? Where he is?"

"Occasionally."

Occasionally was a lousy prognosis, but they had few options. And there was one sign of hope: O'Keefe had recognized Christine Robitaille's name.

The butler picked up the tray. Sarah followed him back to the grassy courtyard. A large pond glistened beyond the thick, green lawn. Snow-white swans floated across its smooth surface. Her gaze casually swept the landscape and met Asher's. He nodded slightly, just enough to tell her he'd been watching.

The butler laid the tray on the glass-topped table, while Sarah took a seat across from O'Keefe. Asher was struggling to talk with him about the weather, the château, France's recession, anything that might capture the old spy's interest.

Sarah knew one of the characteristics of Alzheimer's sufferers was they often recalled the past as clearly as if it had happened yesterday, while the morning's bath was lost in degenerating brain cells. Which meant Jack O'Keefe's memory might still hold what they needed. But even if it did, would they be able to get to it?

Sarah wanted to settle him down and engage him. "I've heard you worked for Wild Bill Donovan back in the old OSS days."

O'Keefe looked up. A smile spread across his powdered face. This was a subject he cared about. "Ah, Bill! The best. . . . Did you know . . . he got more decorations in the First World War than any U.S. soldier? . . . Ike called him the Last Hero. Then during the second war Bill ran intelligence. Damn, he was good. He turned the OSS into a private club." He twisted his hands with excitement. "Talk about a hard one, Bill was hard as boar's teeth. But we loved him. Yes, we did. When he said we'd done a good job, we knew it. He didn't give a damn for flattery."

Asher was playing along. "Hughes Bremner was one of your boys, wasn't he?"

"Taught him everything I could." O'Keefe beamed again.

"He's my boss." Asher stuffed his sandwich into his mouth. "Gives me some real interesting assignments."

O'Keefe chuckled. "And you've got the scars to prove it."

Asher laughed and nodded.

Sarah was encouraged to try another tack. "Asher, I'll bet we can tell Jack. I'll bet he's still got security clearance."

Asher nodded. "Yeah. Jack would get a kick out of it."

"What?" O'Keefe's powdered face was eager. For him, lack of work was a disease worse than Alzheimer's.

She said, "The Carnivore's coming in."

O'Keefe's dark glasses trained on Sarah. "After all this time. Good lord. What that killer knows—"

"Bremner's bringing him in," Asher said. "But there's something we don't understand. Perhaps you can explain it."

"See what I can do." O'Keefe patted his lips with his napkin. He enjoyed being back in the role of mentor.

"What would be the point of Hughes grabbing the Carnivore for himself?" Sarah watched the old cold warrior as he frowned first at her and then at Asher. His powder-splashed, beefy face seemed to close down behind his glasses. He knew something, and he wasn't going to reveal it . . . or was he about to drift off again?

Fifty-four

Sarah had an idea, but it was a gamble. O'Keefe was shaky, and she might trigger a full-blown Alzheimer's episode. Still, she felt there was little choice. Time was passing too swiftly. She spoke casually:

"You've got a magnificent château here, Jack. Very expensive. Your shares in Sterling-O'Keefe must be paying off."

He looked shocked, then confused.

She'd hit close. No Langley salary could have bought the Château de la Vere, and neither could a Langley pension have maintained it. O'Keefe was getting money somewhere else.

"Didn't know you were a businessman, Jack." Asher had caught on. "Pretty smart, eh?"

But they'd gone too far.

Jack O'Keefe jumped up. "Damn you all to hell! I have nothing to do with Sterling-O'Keefe! I won't have my reputation ruined. I've got nothing else left!" With a swipe of his arm, O'Keefe crashed the food-laden tray to the grass. Another episode was beginning, and if it were a long one, it could be days before his mind would be sound enough to hold another conversation.

Sarah used her calmest voice. "We'll protect your reputation, Jack. It's important to all of us at Langley."

"That's what we're here for." Asher's tones were soothing.

O'Keefe's splotched, powdered face was pathetic, lily white

against his black glasses. His voice dropped. "All I've got now is the legend. My mind's going. This hellish disease—"

Asher urged him into his chair. "We're here to help."

"It's a dicey situation, and we need you." Then Sarah lied: "We've learned Hughes is walking into a trap. Someone's planning to kill him and the Carnivore, too. If we don't know why Hughes is worried about the Carnivore, we can't stop it."

"We'll take care of everything," Asher promised, "but we have to know enough to save Hughes!"

They waited nervously. Would O'Keefe tell them what he knew? Could he? The old spy's hand trembled as he picked up an Oreo cookie that had miraculously remained on the table. He seemed to be deep inside himself, concentrating.

His hand steadied. His face cleared. His mouth stopped twitching. A few years ago he would have questioned them closely before believing them. Now his reasoning powers had deteriorated. But had his memory?

He spoke slowly at first, and then with gradually increasing assurance—

CUBA, CHRISTMAS, 1958

Music, laughter, and sporadic gunfire resounded throughout downtown Havana. Armored vehicles shared the palm-lined streets with mule carts and Cadillacs. At the hotels, security officers patrolled with machine guns, while glamorous women slung mink coats over their swim suits as they crossed lobbies on their way to sapphire-blue swimming pools.

The city never slept. Encircling it was the ragtag guerrilla army of Fidel Castro, which in a few days would sweep President Fulgencio Batista y Zaldívar from office.

La Cosa Nostra—the mafia, the mob—guarded its Havana casinos, brothels, and bars. It stayed, believing with Sicilian wisdom that, peace or war, someone had to do business—and take the profits. Sensing change, foreign agents prowled the tropical nights, buying favors and information to ensure their nations a say in the future of this strategically located island.

Hughes Bremner was there undercover, tracking the political cyclone that was about to land. Bremner was blessed with "gut," that sixth sense with which the best operatives were born. For this reason, Red Jack O'Keefe had taken the young man under his wing.

But Jack O'Keefe had been sent to Nuremberg on emergency business, and Bremner was left alone, in charge.

One night Bremner met a young American salesman, Alex Bosa, with whom he went drinking and whoring. They got together often after that. Gut told Bremner to keep an eye on Bosa.

On New Year's Eve the two young men met for drinks. Bosa took several telephone calls, and after midnight he left with a mambo dancer. Bremner followed. Around one o'clock in the morning Bosa left the dancer's apartment. Bremner tailed him to the plantation of General Geraldo Ocho. There Bosa left his brand-new Chevrolet hidden in a tangle of vegetation. He stripped down to some kind of dark clothing. He took out a rifle with a telescopic sight, a knife, and a rope, and he vanished into a field of sugarcane.

Batista's army was all around. It was safe for no one, so Bremner returned to Havana. That night Castro captured the capital. Word spread like wildfire—Fidel Castro had won because a guerrilla had killed Batista's best commander, General Geraldo Ocho. People said Castro's guerrillas had shot the general in a daring raid. But Bremner knew better.

Bremner knew General Ocho had huge gambling debts, which he'd refused to pay. A mafia sniper—Alex Bosa—had killed him. Not for political reasons, but because the mafia could allow no defiance, not even from a great general in the middle of war.

The assassin, Alex Bosa, hired a private yacht to take him back to Miami. Bremner found him on the yacht with two of Batista's supporters holding cane knives to his throat. Alex Bosa had cost them the war, their country, their little fortunes, and, unless they could get off the island, their lives.

Bremner knew that Alex Bosa might prove important to the United States; the two Cubans wouldn't. Even at such an early age, the young CIA man knew how to take the long view. He surprised the two Cubans, and he shot and killed them. He and Bosa dumped them overboard.

Now Bremner had a mafia assassin who owed him. Bosa was no fool either. Bremner was CIA. It was good for a professional killer like Bosa to have a "friend" in the CIA. Life was one long business transaction. The two understood that. They understood each other.

Three weeks later Alex Bosa told his new CIA friend he'd taken the name *Carnivore* and was for hire. In turn, Bremner told Langley he'd heard rumors about a first-rate new assassin. Only Red Jack O'Keefe knew Bremner's personal connection to him.

To further hide his identity, the Carnivore resumed his birth name, Hal Sansborough, a step which only Bremner, O'Keefe, and his mob family knew. For additional cover, Sansborough decided to marry a London girl. He chose her carefully.

Her name was Melanie Childs, the daughter of a British colonel. While her mother was busy with social engagements, Melanie had raised her three younger brothers. Like her father, she was a firm disciplinarian. Hard rules, high expectations, and no excuses. But there was a sweetness to Melanie that covered her toughness like velvet over an iron fist, and that combination was what Hal Sansborough needed.

When the colonel was assigned to Whitehall, Melanie was delighted. After years in foreign outposts around the world, they were stationed back in England at last. That's when Sansborough met her. She was seventeen. The colonel was impressed by Hal's obvious success as a salesman of U.S. products. Hal Sansborough drove a Daimler, wore classic clothes, and had good manners. Also, he was ten years older than Melanie, mature enough to accept a husband's responsibility for a wife. His long sales trips were worrisome, but Melanie was used to the head of the household being gone. And she was in love.

Hal and Melanie married, he bought her a place in Chelsea, and Elizabeth was born. Like most military brats, Melanie had always done what she was supposed to. Rules were inflexible, there was little chance for personal choices, and the needs of others came first. Hal was first, Liz second, her parents third, herself last. She was a housewife, unimportant. A cipher.

The Carnivore's business flourished. Through Hughes Bremner, he occasionally served Langley and the intelligence agencies of other friendly nations. This enhanced Bremner's reputation as a man who could walk in all worlds. The Carnivore also worked for Iron Curtain countries. That was a fact of life, and all sides accepted it even while they tried to take him.

After twenty years the Carnivore's involvement with Hughes Bremner and Jack O'Keefe shifted radically because of his daughter, Liz. She had no idea her father was the Carnivore. His haven was his family, but that was threatened when Liz went up to Cambridge.

Hired to assassinate a prominent Pakistani dissident, the Carnivore met the dissident's son, a student at Cambridge. The son was Liz's friend. When the Carnivore killed the father, the boy spotted a connection between the "accidental" death and the actions of Hal Sansborough. The son told everyone he could think of—Liz, the KGB, British intelligence, Langley.

Liz didn't believe him. She told her father.

Hal Sansborough pretended shock. He denied everything.

Liz trusted him, but the son had raised such a stink that Hal Sansborough's cover was in danger. And so was his relationship with his innocent daughter, because she'd fallen for the boy.

The Carnivore called on his friend Hughes Bremner to eliminate the son. He himself could have no ties to the Pakistani boy's death.

Afterward, the Carnivore set about erasing all questions about his now-shaky identity. He asked his mafia family in New York to arrange the "deaths" of Harold and Melanie Sansborough. Both hated to let their daughter think them dead, Melanie most of all, but Melanie was a good wife. This was the only way they could keep the secret of Hal Sansborough's hidden life.

And so they "died," and the Carnivore resumed his work.

After that Liz seemed to recover and do well. She met and married Garrick Richmond. But he turned out to be like the boyfriend of the Carnivore's first wife—an abuser. He beat Liz.

All this time the Carnivore had been watching over his daughter. When he could stand it no more, he again called on Bremner, this time to demand he eliminate one of his own people. Richmond had to die, and, again, with no connection to the Carnivore.

Bremner sent the abusive husband to Lebanon, then tipped the Shiite Jihad. The Jihad did as expected, and the Carnivore's goal was achieved.

After her husband's death, Liz joined Langley. Bremner and O'Keefe watched her closely. She no longer seemed to wonder whether her father had been the Carnivore. Then, three years ago, she was sent to pull a message in Lisbon. But her father had a contract on the courier. When Liz got to the intercept, he'd killed the courier. He'd been so fast, Liz had no time to interfere.

But she'd recognized him. He was her "dead" father.

That night she crossed over.

Alarmed, Bremner scrambled to cover himself. He fabricated the girl-friend story for Liz's Langley file and declared her a rogue agent. Since then, no murders had been attributed to the Carnivore. Was that because of the new world order? The aging of the Carnivore? Or had it been Liz's influence?

Fifty-five

The odor of sawdust drifted on the hot air in the circus tent north of Paris. Poodles pranced around the center ring to merry calliope music. A middle-aged Frenchwoman gripping a shabby Samaritaine shopping bag paused beneath the bleachers.

Soon a dozen clowns tumbled out of the side exits, heading toward the rings. One knelt next to the Frenchwoman to retie a shoelace.

"Well?" the clown whispered in English.

"I'll be at the Languedoc at eight o'clock tonight, as scheduled. All my arrangements are made. Are yours?"

"Of course. The contingencies have been covered."

"Are you worried?" the Frenchwoman asked.

"Worry's not a word I understand."

The shabby Frenchwoman hesitated. "Quill's dead. One of our most trusted contacts passed the news. Maybe we should worry."

"I heard, too." The clown glanced around the colorful tent. "We were together a long time, but that doesn't change anything."

"No," the Frenchwoman said, "but I'll miss him very much."

"I will, too, Liz." The clown stood, waggled gloved hands high as if it were all part of the act. Then, in a loud, guttural voice in French: *"Pardon, madame!* Enjoy the show!"

The clown did a back flip onto buffoon feet and dashed off to join the others in the ring. Wearily the Frenchwoman climbed the

bleachers. She watched and clapped appropriately. Never did she
show how distracted she was. At intermission she left.

4:36 P.M.

In the courtyard of the Château de la Vere, Sarah Walker had
watched a metamorphosis take place, and she'd lost an uncle she'd
never really found.

As he told the story of Hughes Bremner and the Carnivore, Jack
O'Keefe had become robust and lucid. He'd reveled in his knowledge, the spymaster once more. When he finished, he ordered aper-
itifs for everyone, his face shrewd behind the sunglasses.

Now Sarah had more evidence the Carnivore was dead. Unless
Quill had not been Hal Sansborough. The smile in the photo had
been the same, but not the face. He'd said he was her uncle, but
smiles could be imitated and people could lie. Especially loyal assistants. She remembered reading that in medieval battles squires wore
armor and livery identical to their king's.

Perhaps Quill hadn't been her uncle, but it made no difference,
because they still had to stop Bremner. They had to get answers, get
out of here, and get back to Paris.

"We're really worried about Hughes and the coming-in," she reminded O'Keefe. "Why would Hughes want to kill the Carnivore?"

O'Keefe grinned. This was his favorite game. "Because Hughes
and his group inside Langley and a few other agencies own Sterling-
O'Keefe, and the Carnivore has information that would destroy
them and it. Kill the billion-dollar goose *and* its golden eggs."

Sterling-O'Keefe was owned by Hughes and others inside the government, and maybe funded by stolen government money. Now
Sarah understood, and with a glance at Asher, she saw he did, too.
No wonder Bremner's name was associated nowhere in the public
record with Sterling-O'Keefe Enterprises. It was the same way the
byzantine and rogue BCCI had used fronts to acquire, control, and
operate businesses secretly all over the world.

Sarah kept her face impassive. "We guessed that much, Jack.
What are the specifics? What does the Carnivore know?"

O'Keefe paused, enjoying his knowledge and his game. "Back in
the early days when Sterling-O'Keefe was struggling, Hughes had
two obstacles. One was the CEO of a rival S&L. You see, OMNI-
American Savings & Loan is one of Sterling-O'Keefe's largest enterprises, and OMNI-American needed to buy that competing S&L.

But the CEO had the clout to block it." O'Keefe leaned back. "The second obstacle was a deputy in the French finance ministry. Good family, right schools. He'd just been invited to be treasurer of a hotshot French insurance company. The last thing he wanted was competition to slow him down. So he blocked Sterling-O'Keefe's insurance company from coming into France."

Sarah could compute the rest. "Hughes wanted the CEO and the finance deputy eliminated. And the deaths had to look like accidents. He could afford no mistakes."

"Which meant he hired the Carnivore," Asher said. "But the Carnivore's smart, Jack. He's not going to rat on Hughes."

O'Keefe's grin held something like childish delight. Was he slipping back into the darkness of his disease, or challenging them to follow the twists and turns to the right conclusion?

It was Sarah who saw the truth. "The Carnivore doesn't realize Hughes—Sterling-O'Keefe—hired him!"

Jack O'Keefe nodded his wigged head. "Hughes went to the Carnivore directly, told him the jobs were for Langley. After he comes in, at his debriefing, the Carnivore will give a list of his work for Langley, and when Langley records show it didn't authorize the hits, they'll dig until they discover Sterling-O'Keefe. Boom! Hughes and his secret board are unmasked!"

"But Bremner could warn him, tell him to keep quiet—" Then Sarah saw the ramifications. "No. Bremner would never trust someone who's used to working all sides. The Carnivore would have too much power over him."

Langley could absorb peccadillos, infractions, even Bill Casey's violations in Central America. But it couldn't tolerate massive theft, fraud, and personally arranged executions on the scale of Hughes Bremner's.

If the revelations leaked, the entire U.S. intelligence complex would be involved in a scandal worse than Watergate, Iran-contra, or Iraqgate. But why the urgent need to silence the Carnivore *tonight*, in total defiance of the President? Why not wait, stall, talk to the President again?

Sarah heard Dr. Allan Levine's triumphant voice at Je Suis Chez Moi, euphoric with the delirium: *By Monday the Carnivore will be dead and I'll never have to beg for money again . . . he'll have millions to give my work . . .*

She studied O'Keefe's face behind the sunglasses. "There's some-

thing else, Jack. Something more urgent, maybe bigger than anything Sterling-O'Keefe and Hughes have ever done. Something that
will make billions. And it happens tomorrow.''

Jack O'Keefe's shoulders suddenly trembled. He shook his head,
his face clouded. "What? What did you say?''

Sarah and Asher exchanged glances.

Sarah tried again. "An operation here in Paris vital to Hughes.
One that's going to make him enormously rich.''

But Jack O'Keefe said nothing. He smiled a distant smile, started
to sing the "Marseillaise." He swung his arms in time to the music.
His white wig fell off to the side and over his ear.

Asher frowned. "Looks like that's all we're going to get.''

It was time to leave. They stood up. The rest of the answers would
have to be found in Paris . . . somewhere.

Abruptly Jack trotted off toward the château. They followed him
to a door, not the one Sarah had used when she'd accompanied the
butler in and out. Inside was a seventeenth-century hat rack. And
hanging from it among the other hats was a straw Panama with the
red tartan band.

In one smooth, expert motion, she pulled the Walther from her
belt, slammed Jack O'Keefe against the wall, and shoved the muzzle
up under his chin.

"Sarah!" Asher was stunned.

"Take off his sunglasses!''

Asher glanced at her, then pulled the glasses from O'Keefe's face.
The old spymaster was rigid, his hands low, palms pressed into the
wall. She looked into his eyes. It was he all right, the man with whom
she'd exchanged an unguarded look as they'd both sat watching Je
Suis Chez Moi.

"You bastard!" she snarled and pushed the muzzle deep into his
throat. "You tell me what the hell's going on, or I'm going to pull
this trigger.''

Fifty-six

4:50 P.M.

Jack O'Keefe froze against the château wall. His voice was suddenly clear and firm. "Careless of me to leave my hat at the door."

Sarah kept the Walther firmly imbedded in his neck. His silver head leaned back against the old stone wall, and he gazed down at her with weathered blue eyes.

"Talk, Jack."

"Hard to do that with my larynx squeezing shut." He gasped for effect. "Be a dear and give an old man a break."

Sarah almost smiled. He was so obviously trying to con her. But he'd been among the best, and from all signs he was still a force to be reckoned with. "Just like you gave the people in Je Suis Chez Moi a break. You're lucky none of the clients died from your bomb."

"No, my dear. *They're* lucky. Not like those poor slobs in the alley you and Asher so viciously did in."

He waited for her to react, but she ignored his bait. "I saw you sneak into Je Suis Chez Moi, and decided to give you a hand breaking out, for all the good it's doing me now. A small bit of plastic explosive to rattle the mansion's façade, and I cut the army on your heels to a battered pair, and you did just fine."

Asher swore, "You wily old bastard, you don't have Alzheimer's!"

"Not so old." He grinned. "Had you fooled, didn't I?"

"Why?" Sarah asked. "If you were working for Hughes you wouldn't have told us anything about—"

She stopped and listened. Asher swung around, pistol in hand, eyes searching. There were footsteps.

Four men and a woman emerged like shadows from the doorways around the large rear entrance hall. Each had to be well over sixty, and all carried weapons as if they knew exactly how to use them—the butler, three men in summer trousers and shirts, and a woman wearing a dress, a pocketbook over her arm.

"Compadres," O'Keefe greeted them. Their weapons were trained on Asher and Sarah. "Looks like the tables have turned." His hand rose to take Sarah's Walther from his neck.

She shoved deeper. "Not friendly, Jack. Back off."

His throat constricted. His hand slowly lowered.

"Drop them," Asher told the five newcomers.

But their weapons remained on Asher and Sarah. They looked at O'Keefe.

"I think not," the legendary spymaster said.

It was a standoff.

"Perhaps we could help one another," Sarah suggested.

"Ah, a compromise! We're peaceable, aren't we, *compadres?"*

"Then tell us what's going to happen tomorrow that's so damn important to Hughes Bremner and Sterling-O'Keefe."

Jack's lips twitched. "Hughes's private operation? Well, perhaps I could be of help there. What do you offer in return?"

"How about an improvement in my mood?" Sarah said. "Make it good, because you might say my mood's a real killer."

From her peripheral vision, she took in the tableau the eight of them formed. Her Walther pinning Red Jack O'Keefe to one wall. Asher standing with his back to them, rotating his pistol to keep the outside five from closing in. All this among fine antiques, irreplaceable art, and a beautifully restored medieval château. There was irony in this somewhere.

There was also irony in Red Jack O'Keefe's sad sigh as his face sagged. "Actually, Sarah, I know regrettably little. I've been fishing around trying to find out, just as you have. I'd hoped you might lead me to some answers, which, fortunately for you, put me in a position to help you out from time to time."

He paused, waiting for her appreciation.

"We both thank you, Jack. Now tell us what you learned."

"Alas, I know the vague outline, but none of the details."

"We'll take the vague outline."

"Very well, but compromise works two ways. I really must insist you give me some room to use my vocal cords."

Sarah glanced around at Asher. His back was to her as he watched O'Keefe's five *compadres*. He gave a faint nod.

She lowered her Walther to Jack's heart.

"Much better." He made a show of painful swallowing. "Sadly, all we could dig up about tomorrow is that Hughes is involved in a large currency transaction with some financial bean counter, and he's using Sterling-O'Keefe to finance it without bothering to tell his old friends on the secret board."

Sarah raised her brows, excited. "Of course! A currency transaction. That's where Levine's money'll come from!"

"Don't know about Levine, but the deal's hush-hush and apparently quite dicey. Kit Crowther—he's the bean counter—has sold francs short about $10 billion U.S. and bought the U.S. dollar, which is very strong right now. He's also bought over $1 billion U.S. in French stocks and various other surefire investments. With Sterling-O'Keefe's credit, he's maintained these positions on margins so thin that if the franc moves the wrong way Sterling-O'Keefe could do more than take a bath. It could drown."

"What's the wrong way?" Asher asked over his shoulder.

"Up," Jack said.

Sarah remembered writing an in-depth article about an international financial wizard. "If the franc goes up, Bremner has to spend more to deliver the francs he's sold short. If it stays the same, nothing happens. But if the franc drops, he repays his debt in francs with fewer dollars and makes a profit." Her eyes flashed. "Levine expects millions for his lab. That could translate into a billion or more for Bremner, which means he's betting the franc's going down a hell of a long way. And he's betting it happens tomorrow."

O'Keefe nodded. "That's how we figured it, too. But it looks like a dangerously large gamble to us, and—"

"And Hughes Bremner doesn't gamble," Sarah said. "He's a man who trusts nothing to chance." Her mind raced. "How much value would the franc have to lose to make him a billion or two?"

"A bit of a whopper, I'm afraid." O'Keefe paused for effect. Then, "Twenty percent."

"Twenty percent!" She was shocked, and stared at O'Keefe. "My God, that would rock financial markets around the world! The damage in France and the rest of Europe alone could be devastating!"

Asher half turned. "Devastating how, Sarah? Why?"

"France is Europe's second-largest economy," she explained. "Such a huge devaluation in the franc would mean France was tubing the European Exchange Rate Mechanism, and the other countries' exchange rates would swing wide and maybe wild. The costs companies use for their cross-border business would be distorted, and European business could end in financial chaos!"

Jack nodded in somber agreement. "To stay competitive, other European nations would have to pull out of the ERM and devalue, too. That would hit the United States and Japan hard. Europe needs exchange-rate stability if it wants maximum benefits from the free movement of goods, labor, and capital. Europeans would likely retreat into protectionism, and the single market they've worked so long and hard for would be destroyed—"

"Doesn't Bremner realize all this?" Asher said.

"Hughes doesn't give a damn." Jack's eyes were hard. "In '92, George Soros made the biggest financial killing in history when he bet Britain would have to devalue. Hughes has a big ego, has to be tops in everything. He's going to double Soros."

"Who's George Soros?" Asher asked.

" 'The Man Who Broke the Bank of England,' " Sarah remembered, "and walked away with $1 billion."

"A billion dollars?" Asher's back was suddenly very straight. "Are you saying Hughes Bremner expects to make at least $2 *billion* and maybe take Europe down at the same time?"

O'Keefe nodded. "That's exactly what we're saying, my boy. If Hughes wasn't keeping his transactions so very, very secret, he'd be known as 'The Man Who Broke the Bank of France *and* Beat Currency King George Soros' . . . if he pulls it off."

"But how," Sarah said, frustrated, "*does* he expect to pull it off? A plunge like that would never happen on a specific day without advance warning. Bremner's got to *know* something! What haven't you told us, Jack? Anything!"

O'Keefe shook his head. "Not a thing, I'm afraid, Sarah. Except the grandiose name he put on the operation: GRANDEUR, for God's sake. Histrionic as—"

"Levine!" Sarah cried. "That's it!"

Suddenly it all made sense: The elite clientele at Je Suis Chez Moi. The daily "treatments." The tycoon on the health spa table whose actions were contributing to the unrest among workers for the "glory" of France: *La Grandeur.* The announcement on Friday from the Banque de France that interest rates were once again raised. The demonstrations, strikes, increasing unemployment, higher taxes, bigger deficit, massive layoffs . . . all under the leadership of the new Prime Minister who was a "client" at Je Suis Chez Moi.

Excited, Sarah swung around to face Asher. "Bremner's going to *make* the franc fall. That's the operation. And it's brilliant!"

"How?" Asher turned to stare at her.

O'Keefe spoke behind Sarah. "Yes, you can tell us all, Sarah. But you'll have to wait just a moment. *Compadres!*"

Sarah stiffened. In their excitement, they had forgotten the delicate balance of power in the room. With Sarah's pistol no longer against his heart, O'Keefe's colleagues had spread out behind both Sarah and Asher. They were caught!

"Put your weapons on the floor," Red Jack O'Keefe ordered. "Gently, please."

Fifty-seven

4:58 P.M.

Jack O'Keefe nodded. "George."

The muscular "butler" with the heavy shoulders picked up Sarah's and Asher's weapons. He backed away holding both in one meaty hand, while his other held a Smith & Wesson steady on them.

Sarah's eyes narrowed. "You've been stalling, Jack—keeping us here for Bremner."

O'Keefe sighed. "Hughes called and asked a favor. He knew you were coming here, and he wanted you kept busy until his people arrived. I couldn't refuse, and they'll appear soon. We won't really be able to hold them off, so we need to trust each other and talk fast." He nodded again to the butler. "Give them their guns back, George, and everyone put your pistols away." He smiled his most charming smile. "Sorry about this, but I didn't want to mention the arrival of Hughes's people while you had deadly weapons in your hands, eh?"

"Who's coming for us, and what's their plan?" Asher demanded.

"Gordon Taite and some others. I don't know how many or exactly how they expect to do it. Did you know Gordon hates you, Sarah?"

"I did get that impression."

"He's a dangerous man. I wouldn't want to be in your spot."

"You're comforting, Jack."

The butler, George, said, "I think we can keep watch better from the tower, Chief."

"So we can. And we can all use a drink. Good for the cardiovascular system, you know."

O'Keefe led them to a stone stairway that rose inside the château's tower. As they climbed, O'Keefe explained that after he'd bombed Je Suis Chez Moi, Bremner's people had moved the entire spa to a backup location in the Eighteenth Arrondisement.

"The fire started moments after the building was empty. I have no idea how."

"But we know why," Sarah said. "They wanted nothing left for the police to find."

"Yes, and by 6:00 A.M. the spa was open again at its new location." O'Keefe pushed through a heavy wood door into a luxurious den. "Do come in."

Ten black-and-white photos of the celebrated spymaster with various U.S. Presidents decorated one wall. Mementoes adorned the room—a gold perfume bottle from Macedonia, framed beadwork from Lapland, a beer stein from East Germany, a ship's clock from Portugal.

As O'Keefe wiped the white makeup from his face, he quickly introduced his colleagues. All were retired, but intelligence work was still as integral to their systems as veins and tendons. When he'd summoned them to help discover what Hughes Bremner was up to, they'd joined eagerly.

George went to the bar to get drinks, and the others took up posts at the high tower windows. Asher walked from window to window, watching and listening. O'Keefe and Sarah sat. George passed around beaded glasses of good Chimay ale.

Jack took a long drink. "All right, Sarah, what about Allan Levine and tomorrow?"

She drank, leaned toward him, intense. "He's developed a new form of mind control that works on specific parts of the brain. He told me he's discovered the chemicals that cause specific personality traits, and he's developed drugs to perform mental makeovers, attitude adjustments, whatever. He calls it neural sculpting. He says he can get any idiosyncratic change he wants. Or Bremner wants. Compliance, suggestion, the works."

Jack pursed his lips. "Sounds like a black program we had at

Langley years ago—MK-ULTRA. The public got wind of it and came after our hide. We had to tube it permanently."

"It *is* MK-ULTRA. New and improved. It was never terminated, it went underground. Bremner set Levine up to continue and develop a far more advanced and more dangerous MK-ULTRA, then brought it to Je Suis Chez Moi. The only difference is, the new MK-ULTRA is completely successful. Levine can actually reprogram individuals to do whatever he wants."

"Or Bremner wants," Asher reminded them from a window.

"Especially Bremner," Sarah agreed. "I'm certain now he brought Levine over here specifically for GRANDEUR. Which means he's been planning tomorrow's bombshell for at least two years."

"But why are you so sure Levine and MK-ULTRA are involved?"

"You gave me the clue, Jack," Sarah told him. "While I was at the spa, one of the clients used a particular phrase, and later so did Levine. *La Grandeur*. It refers to the good old days of the mighty French empire."

"And a favorite idea of the right wing," O'Keefe said. "But no politician in his or her right mind would—"

"No, but how about a politician without a mind? At least a mind of his or her own?" Sarah watched them all. "While I was observing Je Suis Chez Moi, I recognized a man who was leaving—Vincent Vauban, the Prime Minister. When I mentioned his name, Levine said, 'Hughes and the good Prime Minister will soon give us our permanent funding. A fully equipped laboratory where I'll continue to push the envelope of modern science.' "

She hunched over. "Bremner has to be using the spa and MK-ULTRA to program certain government, business, and civic leaders. And the first thing he had those people do was create economic upheaval in France to legitimize devaluing the franc."

O'Keefe stood. "The governor of the Banque de France and the Minister of Finance are also clients at the spa."

They were all watching her now.

"Yes," she said, "that would have to be." She looked up at them. "The Prime Minister, the governor of the Banque de France, and the French finance minister have been reprogrammed to make a joint announcement some time tomorrow that France will devalue the franc twenty percent!"

"Good God!" O'Keefe looked in shock. "And they have the power to do it!"

"Jesus," George turned from his post at the window. "The bastards!"

"Not a good time to be in France or Europe, I'd say," his wife, Elaine, observed quietly.

Sarah continued, "I can just see Louise Dupuy. She's another Je Suis Chez Moi patron, and I'll bet she'll be on TV all day tomorrow interviewing Bremner-programmed business people and economists who support the move. There'll be other important civic and government leaders from the spa who'll rally around, and France will be on a course of economic disaster—"

"And while Europe rocks, Hughes gets out with his billions," O'Keefe growled. "His resignation is probably all typed up, ready to be dropped into the mail on Monday. And you can bet he's got some fabulous hideout set up and waiting—"

"Unless we stop him," Sarah said.

"It's after five o'clock already," Asher said impatiently. "The Carnivore, Liz, or someone else comes in at eight—"

"Wait a minute." Jack O'Keefe frowned. "What are you talking about?"

Sarah told him about meeting Quill, the attack by Bremner's people, and Quill's death.

The old spymaster chuckled. "You think the Carnivore's actually dead? Has anybody reported the body? No, he's survived so long because he knows more tricks than anyone!" His grin grew sly. "Except for me, of course."

"Good thing we're on the same team then, Jack," Sarah said. "But it doesn't matter at this point if the Carnivore's alive or dead. Someone's coming in, even if it's only Liz."

"We've got less than three hours," Asher reminded them. "There's damn little time. If we're going to stop Bremner, we better make some plans."

"No one at Langley or in the States would believe us," Sarah decided.

O'Keefe crossed to his desk. "I think I can get to the French President. He has the authority to stop all this. I have an old friend on his staff." He opened a thick black address book and reached for his telephone.

"It's Sunday, Jack," Elaine reminded him. "And August."

"Oh, hell, yes. Everyone's probably out of the city." He looked up another number and dialed. "Andre? Jack O'Keefe. Listen, I have to talk to the President. It's a matter of life and—! There has to be a way. Dammit, it's urgent! What?" He listened, his foot tapping. "No. Okay, sure. Never mind."

He hung up. "The President's incommunicado. A top-level 're-treat' at some industrialist's fishing lodge in the Pyrénées. No doubt another one of Levine's clients. And according to Andre, quite a bit of the government is there, too. Unreachable. He thinks it's an odd coincidence."

The telephone rang. Everyone jumped. Nerves were growing raw in the old tower room.

Jack picked up the phone. "Good work, *compadre*. Gracias." He hung up. "I sent Arlene Debo a message last night suggesting she might want to check whether Hughes had really dumped the Carni-vore, as per the President's orders. Now she's landed at the Langue-doc, pissed as hell. She'll give Hughes the devil. Maybe he'll have a stroke and we can all walk away clean."

"Arlene's at least a good diversion," said Asher.

Sarah had been standing quietly, looking out at the forest. Now she said, "Why is the Carnivore dangerous to GRANDEUR? We know what he can do to Sterling-O'Keefe. But how can he sabotage Hughes tomorrow?"

O'Keefe's cool eyes appraised her. "I've been wondering about that, too. There's only one thing it could be. Do you recall how Vincent Vauban got to be Prime Minister?"

Asher said, "Didn't something happen to his major rival?"

"He died," Sarah recalled. "Only a few weeks before last spring's election, the leading candidate for Prime Minister died suddenly, and Vincent Vauban was his logical replacement."

"Exactly." Jack drained his glass of Chimay. "The rival was Phil-lipe Paquin, victim of an unexpected heart attack during a volleyball game on the beach at Cannes. Only it wasn't a heart attack. He was assassinated by a new gas derivative of Rauwolfia serpentina."

Sarah frowned, and Asher explained, "Rauwolfia serpentina is related to common tranquilizers and damn near undetectable. In-haled or sprayed on the skin, it depresses the central nervous system and can kill in seconds, depending on the conditions."

Sarah digested this information, but what really mattered was: "The Carnivore assassinated him? For Hughes Bremner?"

Jack nodded. "I was the go-between. I never knew why Hughes set up the hit, but now it makes sense: Vincent Vauban had accepted Dr. Levine's invitation to join Je Suis Chez Moi, but Phillipe Paquin probably hadn't. Paquin's 'heart attack' is the most critical reason Hughes Bremner must eliminate the Carnivore. No one knows Paquin was assassinated. It's not in any Langley file. But it's the Carnivore's most recent kill, and the first he'll reveal. That's the way debriefings go, start with the latest and work backward chronologically."

"Then that's the way we stop Bremner," Sarah realized. "We save the Carnivore ourselves. If he's still alive."

They were silent, nervous. The idea of going against Hughes Bremner, his army of CIA agents, and the MK-ULTRA program didn't thrill O'Keefe's *compadres*. They knew what Bremner could do. So did Sarah and Asher.

"It's me they're coming for, isn't it?" Sarah asked.

O'Keefe nodded. "I've never been able to pinpoint exactly why they need you so badly, but Gordon plans to grab you here and fly you to the Languedoc. Levine's going to put you on some drug called LP48. I didn't know why LP48 was significant, until you told us about Levine and MK-ULTRA." He looked across the room. "Dirk, my boy?"

The man he called Dirk was no boy. Close to eighty, he was of medium height and weight, and disarmingly ordinary looking. He limped forward, took a pillbox from his pocket, popped it open, and set it on O'Keefe's antique desk.

Inside were three gray tablets. "I made friends with a little fellow at Je Suis Chez Moi named Maurice Arl, The Mouse. I told him I was Interpol, that Levine was illegal, and I asked him to find out about MASQUERADE. He didn't discover much more than we already knew, except that Levine was rushing to prepare a new drug for a 'client' he expected to arrive soon. I asked for more details, but Maurice and the young woman he was lusting after ended up dead yesterday before they could get back to me."

"Chantelle Joyeaux," Sarah said. In a flash, she saw the woman's body in the Cadillac's trunk, the terrible death wound on her chest, and the body of a small man with a similar chest wound being fitted in beside her.

"Was that her name?" Dirk seemed to inscribe it on some memorial in his mind. "All I ended up with was the name of the drug—

LP48—and these pills Maurice said would block its effects. It seems Levine always prepares an antidote in case anything goes wrong with his clients.''

"It wouldn't do to have someone famous die in their hands," O'Keefe said in disgust. "Set back the whole operation.''

Sarah took the pillbox. "It blocks the drug Levine's going to use on me?''

"Yes, Sarah," O'Keefe told her quietly.

"No!" Asher hurried from the tower window and grabbed her arms. He looked grimly into her eyes. "It's too damn dangerous! Once you're in the Languedoc, we won't be able to get to you. What happens if the antidote doesn't work? If you think they'll let you live afterward, you're nuts!''

Sarah took his hands and smiled. "We don't have much choice, darling. We don't know where the coming-in's going to be, so we can't stake it out beforehand. We don't know exactly how Bremner plans to use me. All we know is that he needs me a lot. This is our only way to reach Bremner, preserve the Carnivore's information, and stop GRANDEUR from shattering Europe.''

"No!" His grip was like steel on her hands. "I won't—''

Her eyes hardened. "Bremner and his gang stole my memory, my identity, and my life. They stole *me*. For money! They robbed me of everything that makes me a person, just to eliminate a threat to the enjoyment of their millions, and I'm not going to let them get away with it!''

"But—''

"Chief!" George was staring out his tower window, his glass halfway to his lips. "They're here. In the woods!''

Asher hurried to his side. "I don't see anything.''

"They're there. Believe me.''

Jack O'Keefe sat on the edge of his antique desk and swung a leg. "You have a better plan, Asher?''

Sarah said, "Europe's got enough problems without economic anarchy, darling. There's no one who can stop Bremner in time except us.''

"Except you, you mean," Asher said bitterly. He looked at Jack O'Keefe. "How do we get her out alive?''

"We do our best," O'Keefe replied steadily.

Fifty-eight

As Arlene Debo's chopper touched down on the Languedoc's helipad, Hughes Bremner ducked and ran toward it. He'd seen Gordon and his people off to collect Sarah Walker just minutes before, and he expected their return at about six o'clock. Allan Levine had already arrived and was making arrangements. At eight o'clock, the coming-in would begin with the appearance of the real Liz Sansborough.

Everything seemed to be happening at once, and Bremner felt time speeding much too fast. Yet he had it all under control—all but the most unpredictable element:

The director of Central Intelligence herself, Arlene Debo.

Bremner swung open the helicopter's door. The blades whipped overhead, and his hair rose with the gale. Impeccably dressed as usual in an expensive business suit, Arlene Debo stepped down, lowered her gray head, and hurried toward the elevator. The pilot handed Bremner her heavy briefcase.

Bremner strode after her, his patrician face appropriately solemn.

"Hughes!" Arlene's ample chest heaved as she waited at the elevator. "The President's going to have your ass on a platter! You'd better have one hell of a good explanation—"

"The situation's changed, Arlene." He pushed the elevator button. "Good thing you're here. The Carnivore claims Phillipe Paquin was murdered. You remember, he was the front-runner for Prime Minister. Vauban was his challenger. The Carnivore says he can tell us the group that did it. They're an exceptionally dangerous cabal, so extreme they've also put out a contract on Vauban himself. I think we'd better bring the Carnivore in and find out what the hell he knows, before the Prime Minister of France is assassinated!''

As the elevator door opened, he watched shock turn to worry on her round face. They stepped inside, and he considered his options. The most extreme would be her death. But killing her would focus extraordinary attention on Languedoc personnel, which could endanger GRANDEUR. After tomorrow, there would be far too much on France's, Europe's, and the United States's collective mind to notice the sudden retirement of one career CIA man.

"Hughes! You'd better have some damn compelling evidence to back up your allegations!''

On the château's front drive, Sarah and Asher bid Red Jack O'Keefe a swift good-bye. The old spymaster was back in costume and in character, trembling as if in the beginning stages of another Alzheimer's episode. He gave them a wink as they jumped onto the big BMW motorcycle.

Sarah surveyed the front lawns and distant forest, but she saw nothing. Asher stomped the starter. Just as the cycle rolled forward, bullets exploded its tires. Black rubber shredded up before their eyes. The heavy motorcycle shuddered and toppled.

Instantly they shoulder-rolled to the ground and yanked out their weapons. As more bullets whistled past, they scrambled behind the downed bike. On the steps the bald "butler" hustled a confused Jack O'Keefe inside the château. The massive door with the huge iron hinges slammed.

"Where are they?'' Asher's dark eyes were black points of fury.

"Can't tell. We'd better make it look good.''

They waited for a pause in the hail of bullets. Then they ran around the side of the château and toward the garage. Vehicles would be stored there. Gordon would expect them to try to escape.

As they ran, bullets peppered the drive. None even came near them.

"Oh, my God,'' Sarah breathed.

From the beeches and poplars that surrounded the château's parklike grounds emerged a dozen armed men and women. They were running, too, converging on Sarah and Asher. In the distance, a helicopter chopped toward them from the direction of Paris.

Asher and Sarah put on a burst of speed and closed in on the potential safety of the garage. The helicopter flew directly over the château and hovered above them. A bullhorn bellowed: "Walker! Flores! Stop! Raise your hands. You won't be hurt!"

"They're taking no chance we'll get away this time." Asher yanked open the side door of the garage.

Sarah jumped first into the gloom, Walther ready.

"Ah, Sarah. How nice to see you again. You, too, Asher." Gordon smiled a sinister, hate-filled smile.

He and the woman who had been with him at the Denver airport stood seven feet inside the door, Berettas trained and ready to fire. They were positioned at least ten feet apart. No way could Sarah spin off to the side or hope to shoot both before one got her or Asher. But if Sarah was going to go, she'd like to leave Gordon with a souvenir.

She said, "Okay, I guess you've got us, Gordon. Very clever to have your people herd us to the garage."

"Everyone's predictable under pressure." His sense of triumph made his Rock-of-Gibraltar face seem more solid than ever. Certainty was a drug. "People try to escape a trap. The only way for you, once we shot out your tires, was the garage."

"How'd you know we were at Jack O'Keefe's?" Asher was playing the act out.

"No games, Flores. Drop your guns and lie face down."

Asher's voice whispered, "Door."

"I said drop those guns! Janet, take—"

Asher kicked the garage door behind him. It slammed shut. Gordon and the woman, Janet, tensed. Sarah made a move as if to drop her gun, then she pitched forward on her good shoulder and rolled right down the middle between Gordon and the woman.

Bullets ripped the ground after her, but none hit. They weren't making it easy to fake resistance. Then Sarah looked up into Gordon's granite face. His lips had stretched back across his teeth as if he were a wild animal in the midst of a good kill. His gun was aimed straight at her. Was his hate going to blind him to his goal of taking her in alive?

His gun swung away and aimed directly at Asher.

She fired.

Gordon's right side spurted blood. He spun back and fell.

Asher shot the woman. She arched up and then collapsed in a pool of crimson.

Behind them, the side door of the garage slammed open, but no one came in. The attackers were being cautious.

"We can't look as if we gave up," Sarah whispered.

"Let's try for the cars," Asher said softly. They ran to inspect the line of four. "The Peugeot has keys in the ignition."

"How careless of Jack," Sarah said. "A Gordon trap."

"Let's be dumb."

They jumped into the Peugeot. Asher started the engine. The garage door was closed, but the heavy sports car would have the power and weight to crash through and keep on going. Instantly attackers swarmed in through the open side door. Gordon was up, his face twisted in rage, holding his bloody side as he shouted orders.

Asher put the car in gear—and nothing happened! The Peugeot moved not an inch.

"Surprise," Sarah said quietly.

Then there was no more time to talk.

They jumped out, guns raised, but it was like jumping into the center of a tornado. A dozen men and women converged, guns aimed directly at Sarah and Asher. They froze. She looked at him and tried to smile. He took her hand and squeezed it. She memorized his angular face, the black beard, the black curly hair, the smoldering dark eyes that could be so tender. She touched his cheek. It was over.

Gordon barked an order, and the Languedoc people stripped away their guns.

"On the car. Lean and spread your legs."

"Hughes Bremner's gone bad—" Asher began, his hands on top of the Peugeot's hood, his legs spread.

"I'm Sarah from the *Herald Tribune* story," Sarah tried. She looked back as a tall woman patted her down. "Bremner's using you. He's out for himself—"

"I know all the tricks, so stow it."

Gordon moved in front of Sarah, holding a hand over the wound on his right side. She looked into his narrow, enraged eyes and realized only Bremner's need for her was saving her life. Without Bremner, he would kill her instantly.

He said, "I have an offer to make."

"Since when does Bremner negotiate with words?" Asher's voice was sarcastic.

Gordon ignored him. "I've been instructed to let Flores go free."

"No! Not without Sarah!" Asher was furious.

Sarah said, "What's the condition?"

"You come with us voluntarily and cooperate fully." His harsh, enraged face softened into the kind smile Sarah remembered from Santa Barbara and the early days at the Ranch. "It's really all been a mistake, dar . . . Sarah." He stopped, and his smile became sad. "I wanted to call you darling, didn't I? But I know I'll have to earn that right again. It really is all a mistake on your part, Sarah. Come with us and we'll prove it to you."

Asher was beside himself. "Don't do it, Sarah! We'll go in together. There's got to be somebody at the Languedoc who'll listen—"

Gordon nodded. Two men grabbed Asher, and in an instant a woman knocked him unconscious with a hard karate chop. The men dropped Asher unconscious at Sarah's feet. The woman pointed her pistol down at his temple.

Gordon told Sarah, "If you don't come willingly, she'll shoot him. It makes no difference to her, Sarah. Asher's turned, and she sees no reason to let him live."

Sarah inhaled. "How do I know you won't kill him later?"

"We'll leave him here. You'll see he's alive. What more do you need?"

Outside the helicopter chopped to a landing near the garage. It was there to take her to Paris, where Dr. Levine would put her on LP48. She'd already taken the blocking antidote, but still she shuddered as she listened to the thundering chop of the blades. The garage walls seemed to vibrate with the noise. She thought of the tiny tracking device Dirk had surgically planted beneath her scalp, the fresh stitches hidden by her hair.

"I'll go with you, Gordon."

She refused to go until she saw everyone else vacate the garage, leaving Asher alone. Then she went outdoors, the armed woman on one side, Gordon on the other. She watched them lock the garage to make sure Asher didn't escape right away. Two men loaded the body of the woman Asher had killed into a dark-windowed van and drove away.

That was it. Asher was alive. She boarded the helicopter.

□ □ □ □

In the garage, Asher Flores awoke to a throbbing headache. God. Lights streaked through his brain. He lay in a fetal position on the cold stone floor and tried to understand the chopping roar he heard.

A helicopter. It was taking off. Sarah was on it!

He noticed muffled sounds from somewhere in the back of the garage. He opened his eyes.

He heard the sound again. He rolled under the Peugeot and on under the next car until he could see the recesses of the dusky garage. There were two pairs of feet. Male. The feet moved toward him.

His smile was that of a fox. Two people left behind by Hughes Bremner and Gordon Taite, liars to the end. They would handle the final detail: Killing him.

Asher searched the shadows, spotted a workbench, and crawled silently toward it. He picked up a heavy wrench and an axe.

The feet were closing in. He raised the axe, when suddenly the garage door burst open. Jack O'Keefe and four *compadres* rushed forward, weapons drawn. The explosion of their gunfire was atomic.

Then there was silence. Dust and the stench of gunfire filled the air. Asher walked over to Jack O'Keefe. He was staring down at two bullet-riddled corpses on the floor in front of him.

"Had to let that chopper get out of sight, Jack?"

O'Keefe nodded his silver head. "I was certain you could handle yourself until then." He gave Asher a wicked grin. "Bremner trained you well, my boy."

Jack O'Keefe turned and walked nimbly out through the side door, followed by his cavalcade of fellow spies. George was waiting for them in a light plane in a field on the other side of the forest. The plane would fly the group to Paris. To Sarah.

Fifty-nine

Arlene Debo sat at Hughes Bremner's Languedoc desk, holding his private telephone to her ear. Her heavy cheeks trembled with outrage and worry as she reported to the President: "Yes, sir. The problem is the Carnivore claims the French Prime Minister's slated to be assassinated tomorrow, and our assets have confirmed the plan. The economy over here is deteriorating, and there's a group of knee-jerk reactionaries that believes the only way the country can be saved is to eliminate him."

She listened, then: "The reports from our assets are very definite about the day. Tomorrow for sure. Fortunately, Hughes has worked fast. He offered the Carnivore a coming-in tonight, and the Carnivore's accepted. The show starts at eight o'clock. We can turn the Carnivore over to the French government as soon as we get him—"

Handing the assassin immediately to the French had been Bremner's idea, but Arlene Debo was presenting it as her own. Silently Bremner sneered at her vanity. And her blindness: The reports from assets were fake. The Carnivore would be dead before anyone could ask any questions about Bremner's story that Vincent Vauban was to be assassinated.

Arlene hung up. "The President doesn't like it, but it's a go. France gets the Carnivore." She leaned back, crossed her arms over her ample chest, and mused, "When I think back to my predecessors, Bill Casey stands out. He was a hands-on DCI. Legendary, really. None of his people could figure out how to bug the Soviet ambassador's private apartment, so Casey invited himself to dinner. He sat on the sofa, and when no one was looking he stuck an over-sized 'needle' into a cushion. Of course, it was a miniaturized, long-stemmed mike and transmitting device." Debo chuckled at the former DCI's audacity.

Bremner chuckled right along with her. He said smoothly, "Yes, Bill Casey was one of the absolute best. But you're certainly in his league, Arlene, if not better."

Arlene Debo's savvy gaze leveled on Hughes Bremner. Her voice was sharp: "The President wants the public to find no fault later with what we're doing about this matter, and I want to see for myself the Carnivore's immediately turned over to the French. Therefore I'll be accompanying you to the Carnivore's coming-in tonight. I'm sure that will cause you no problems, Hughes."

6:01 P.M.

"Of course, the Carnivore's alive." Hughes Bremner glanced at Walker as she lay strapped to the table in the Languedoc. He was pacing the room, full of nervous energy, as he coped with Arlene Debo's announcement that she'd be at his side during the coming-in.

The stark-white infirmary was devoid of color or compassion. With Sarah were Hughes Bremner and a seething, waxen-faced Al-lan Levine, who was preparing the intravenous drip for her arm. She thought of the antidote to the LP48 she'd taken and silently thanked Jack's friend Dirk for his thoroughness.

She tried again. "My uncle was the Carnivore."

"Yes," Bremner agreed impatiently.

"I saw him die."

He dismissed her with a gesture. "If you saw someone die this morning, it wasn't the Carnivore. My people picked up a message from Liz this afternoon. She and the Carnivore are coming in at eight o'clock tonight, as scheduled." He glared at the doctor. "Aren't you ready to start yet, Allan? I got you the two hours you said you needed, and now you're fussing around and wasting them."

"No one told me she was injured!" Levine snapped. "Trauma could cause problems. I'm trying to deal with that."

"Dammit, stop making excuses. Get on with it!"

"What's going to happen in two hours?" Sarah demanded.

Bremner moved to the foot of the bed. "You have no need to know that, and remember our bargain. Your cooperation in exchange for Asher's life. We've done what we agreed. You're an honorable woman. I know I can trust you to keep your word, too."

She didn't for a second trust Bremner to keep his word, but if Bremner was going to be stopped, she had no choice but to cooperate.

In his Languedoc office, Hughes Bremner finished instructing the agents who would accompany him to the coming-in. He watched them file out. They were his people, loyal and eager. They'd do exactly what he ordered.

Two doors down the hall, Arlene Debo was occupied with individual briefings from Mustang agents assigned to other tasks throughout Europe. Bremner had arranged their arrival earlier.

Now he sat back in his chair, his high-boned face immobile as he considered the curve Arlene had thrown him. Damn her and her ambitions! She wanted to leave a mark as big as Wild Bill Donovan's. He closed his eyes and pressed the heels of his hands against them, willing his fatigue to vanish. With his usual self-discipline he concentrated on the problem of Arlene. He turned it over in his mind.

Suddenly a rare smile creased his severe, patrician features. Of course. He should have seen it before: The bitch had actually done him a favor. She—Arlene Debo—the powerful Director of Central Intelligence—was the best cover he could ask for himself, for Sterling-O'Keefe, and ultimately for GRANDEUR.

She'd be an unimpeachable eyewitness.

No one would question her personal report that "Liz Sansborough," the Carnivore's "girl friend," had gone mad and shot the Carnivore, and that he, Bremner, had been forced to eliminate her before she murdered anyone else.

Yes. If the Carnivore came in exactly, precisely, as planned . . . if Arlene were convinced of the legitimacy of the Carnivore's death . . . then there'd be no investigation.

Tomorrow GRANDEUR would proceed unimpeded.

And whatever mark DCI Arlene Debo left on history would be

microscopic compared to the mark Hughes Bremner was about to make.

Dr. Allan Levine was an arrogant man, and he enjoyed it. After all, intellect was what separated the elite from the stupid, owners from employees, mankind from monkeys. He was unusually gifted, with an I.Q. near 200 and a photographic memory. As he stood over Sarah Walker, he relished the fear in her too-lovely face. The dark mole above the right corner of her lip was darker, even more beguiling, against the sudden paleness of her skin.

"You enjoyed drugging me last night, didn't you?" he said icily. "I wonder how you're going to enjoy what happens next."

She refused to give him the satisfaction of a response. All she had to do was stay alive long enough for Asher, Jack O'Keefe, and his colleagues to track her to the coming-in.

The doctor brought an intravenous needle to a vein on her wrist. He jabbed it in, far more roughly than necessary, and he watched her face for a reaction.

"You have a gentle touch," she said acidly.

His skull-head smiled, leaf-dry lips over tombstone teeth.

He started the IV. "This contains a substance I created—a synthetic brain hormone in combination with certain folded proteins. You know what neurotransmitters are? They're the brain chemicals that send signals between neurons. My compound attacks the neurotransmitters in your frontal and temporal lobes. Those lobes control your judgment and emotions. There your neurotransmitters will make a startling readjustment—erasing your judgment, sensitizing your emotions to a sharp pitch, and making you highly suggestible. You'll forget your past and bond to the first person you set eyes on. You'll enter a kind of dissociative catatonia and rigidly follow commands."

She inhaled sharply, stunned. He was going to destroy her personality. Thank God she'd taken the antidote!

"Sound entertaining?" The doctor gave a nasty laugh. "The advantage of this compound is its speed and near infallibility. The disadvantage is you'll follow orders blindly and have no individuality."

"You're a paragon—"

He slapped her. And then she felt a sudden wave of something

warm and sickeningly sweet. Whatever was in the IV had hit her
system. She waited for the antidote to fight back—

Allan Levine's attention had shifted. His last important task was to
make certain Sarah Walker bonded to Hughes. That way Hughes
himself could instruct her, and he'd have only himself to blame if
his directions went awry.

Sarah abruptly demanded, "What have you given me?"

He looked down on her, a gaunt pillar. "Q101."

She couldn't keep the panic from her voice. "Not LP48?"

He frowned. "I'd planned to use LP48 last night, when I had a
full twenty-four hours to get you ready. But I had to switch to Q101
today, because your escape gave me too little time. The big disadvantage to Q101 is that it has no subtleties, which forced Hughes to
redesign his plan again—" He gazed intently at her, as if trying to
penetrate her brain. "How did you know about LP48?"

She moaned. The poison was spreading, and she couldn't stop it.
She pulled against her restraints. She couldn't move, couldn't save
herself. And Dr. Levine's Q101 would turn her into a robot—an
unfeeling, nonthinking mechanical woman who looked like Liz
Sansborough and would follow orders without question. She wanted
her memories, her identity, her life!

And this time it could be worse—This time the drugs could permanently destroy her mind!

She stared at the tube that dripped Q101 into her system and told
herself she had no time to be angry . . . or to feel sorry for herself.

But what could she do? She was tied up, helpless—

Think!

She summoned all her newly acquired powers. She focused.
Bremner needed her because she was Liz Sansborough's double. He
would replace Liz Sansborough with her. Somehow, somewhere.
But she was Sarah Walker. She wasn't Liz Sansborough.

She concentrated on that one single thought. No matter what
they did to her, she had to remember she was Sarah Walker.

I'm Sarah Walker. I'm Sarah Walker.

Silently she repeated the phrase over and over. *I'm Sarah Walker.
I'm Sarah Walker . . .*

The drug was rushing through her veins with terrifying speed.
She kept her eyes open and struggled to make the words throb with
her heartbeat.

Resonate with her breathing.

Burn themselves forever into her brain: *I'm Sarah Walker.*

Allan Levine returned to work. He could see she was succumbing to the potent drug. Through her, he expected to gain more knowledge about Q101. There were side effects to study, of course. Q101 caused cell degeneration. He was keeping strict records, and he'd conduct an autopsy as soon as her corpse arrived back at the Languedoc. Hughes planned to eliminate her immediately after she killed the Carnivore. If all went well, he'd shoot her in the heart. That way her head—particularly her brain—would be undamaged.

6:18 P.M.

"I trust you, Allan," Hughes Bremner said in his most sincere voice. "You understand, it's not you. It's the circumstances. If anything goes wrong—"

"Of course," the doctor said.

Bremner had returned to the infirmary and now stood at the foot of Sarah Walker's cot. The doctor again checked the needle and then the drip through the line of clear tubing.

Her eyes remained eerily open, watching.

"Is everything all right?" Bremner asked.

"Perfect." Satisfied, the doctor gestured, and a male nurse approached with a cart of shiny, sterilized instruments. The doctor swabbed the skin above Walker's carotid artery. She moved slightly, and he stopped. She was mumbling the same unintelligible phrase over and over. Her eyes were glazed and there was no way she could fight the drug, but still—

Dr. Levine waited, kept his face calm. What was she doing? Then he decided it didn't matter. It was nothing.

Soon she lay quiet again. He gave her another few seconds, then made a tiny incision in her neck. He slipped the microscopic explosive device under her skin, closed the incision, and carefully applied skin-toned tape over it. By 8:00 P.M., the incision would be invisible.

"All I have to do is press this button," Bremner said with satisfaction. In his hand he held what looked like a gold cigarette lighter. He flipped open the cap and inspected the brown plastic button.

Dr. Levine said, "The button triggers the explosive device, and—"

"I know how it works!" Bremner snapped. "It will shatter her carotid artery. She'll die instantly. Just the kind of fail-safe I need in case anything goes wrong and I have no other way to eliminate her."

The doctor nodded and glanced down. The woman was mumbling again. Her eyes were open and staring. Unnerved, he closed the lids.

Sixty

The mammoth Tour Languedoc filled a full Paris block and rose so high it seemed to fade into the summer sky. Asher Flores and Red Jack O'Keefe stood anxiously in a doorway across the street. The offices in the Languedoc skyscraper and neighboring buildings were closed, but, even on a Sunday night, the street was full of cars and pedestrians heading for cafés, cabarets, and cinemas.

Nearby in a delivery van, O'Keefe's comrades waited. It was a specially equipped surveillance vehicle, and they expected to use it to track Sarah. In the French manner, it sat with two wheels up on the sidewalk in a line of other similarly parked vehicles. From that location, the van could slip into traffic and tail any car leaving the Languedoc.

Asher and Jack had been studying the Languedoc for an hour. Marble steps led up to the foyer, clearly visible through floor-to-ceiling glass windows. A well-lit parking garage had been built only a few feet below street level. The garage entrance was patrolled by a sharp-eyed pair of attendants waiting to park or retrieve cars. The Company's overwhelming security left no need for visible muscle.

There were only three entrances to the Company's secret floor. One was from the helipad atop the building. Another was from the special elevator in the foyer. And the third was from this parking garage, where the same elevator also opened next to the bank of regular elevators clearly visible from where Asher and Jack O'Keefe watched. At all three, cameras performed sentry duty, and the high-security elevator would open only for someone with a numeric code, fingerprints, or a face filed in the computer's data bank.

Asher and Jack O'Keefe walked around the block studying the layout, but learned nothing new—the Company's architects had created an invincible fortress. They saw no Company personnel. Bremner's people would be holed up on the top floor, no one getting in, no one leaving.

No way could Asher sneak onto the elevator or rent a helicopter to land on the roof. Company security would pick him up in an instant. If he tried to break in, he'd be sighted too swiftly by too much security for him to survive, much less help Sarah.

Their best choice, the most nerve-wracking choice, was to wait. To pray the antidote worked and Sarah would survive. Since Bremner wanted Sarah somehow to help murder the Carnivore, he'd keep her alive at least until then. Asher tried not to think about her condition, or what would happen to her later.

Instead he thought about the coming-in.

Obviously Bremner believed someone was coming in. But no way would the Carnivore ever let the Company preselect the spot, since then the Company could throw up a net, a terrible disadvantage if something went wrong and Liz and the Carnivore needed to escape. No, Liz would wait as long as possible and then lead Bremner and his people to a location of the Carnivore's choosing.

If Asher were right, she should arrive soon. If Bremner were going to use Sarah to make the hit at the coming-in point, Sarah would go with them. And if Bremner planned not to use her, Asher and some of O'Keefe's comrades would try to sneak into the Languedoc with the group when they returned with the Carnivore.

In or out, the action would be through one of the three entrances —the garage, the foyer, or the helipad. If it turned out to be the helipad, they were screwed, unless the van could keep up with the tracking device from the streets below. But with the foyer or the garage, they had a better chance. At least, a chance.

Whenever Asher thought about losing Sarah, his gut knotted and his head hammered. Was this love? This overwhelming desire to protect? The fear she might experience more pain? The wrenching sense of loss when he allowed himself to consider she might die?

He wanted to spend the rest of his life with Sarah.

He had to save her. He'd do anything!

When he thought about all the lousy relationships he'd seen, and how he'd always successfully avoided any that might get serious, he figured this must be love.

He refused to think about losing her, yet the worry lived in the back of his mind like a demon.

He pushed away the fear and returned to logistics. Was the Carnivore alive after all? Perhaps Liz was coming in alone but wanted to put Bremner through his paces to make certain no tricks awaited her surrender. Or . . . did she want Bremner to sit up there in his Languedoc aerie waiting all night? Her idea of a grim joke, making Bremner figure out for himself the Carnivore was never coming in? A small revenge?

He fervently hoped not. That would be the worst scenario of all for Sarah. Hughes Bremner would no longer need her alive.

7:40 P.M.

Dr. Allan Levine removed the intravenous tube from Sarah Walker's right arm. Next he removed the monitors from her forehead. As he'd expected, the tiny incision above her carotid artery was invisible. He studied her waxy, unconscious face. Her vibrancy had disappeared, a good sign.

"Well, Allan?" Hughes Bremner stepped into the stark-white infirmary.

"She's doing very well. Remember what to expect: Judgment erased and emotions sensitized to a high pitch." Dr. Levine pointed. "Stand there. She bonds to the first person she sees."

"She'll do what I say?" Bremner moved to the spot beside the hospital bed.

"Rigidly." Dr. Levine turned Walker's head so Hughes Bremner would be first in her line of sight.

Bremner asked, "When will the drugs wear off?"

The doctor hesitated. He'd experimented on primates with substance Q101, and the only glitch he'd found was with those who'd taken the drug short term: Less than two hours. Once off Q101, about a third exhibited hazy recognition when shown a once-loved object like a ball or a stuffed animal. Autopsies on their brains had disclosed less cell degeneration than in the brains of those who'd been on Q101 longer. Since Walker would be on the drug less than two hours, he'd increased her dose to compensate. In any case, hazy recognition shouldn't break her trance short-term.

"Allan?" Bremner was staring at him.

"Relax, Hughes. The drugs will hold as long as you need. I was thinking of something else. Such as when I'll get my private lab and permanent funding."

Bremner laughed. This he understood. "By tomorrow night, you'll have fortune enough to build a dozen labs."

"I'll hold you to that."

Sarah Walker's eyelids fluttered.

"She's waking up." The doctor took her pulse, listened to her lungs, checked the whites of her eyes.

At last her lids opened.

Her gaze locked instantly onto Hughes Bremner. She blinked infrequently. Drool slid onto her chin. She stared at Bremner adoringly, a china-eyed, ashen-faced doll.

Bremner said, "Close your mouth."

She blinked and closed it.

Bremner smiled. "Very good. Get up."

Dr. Levine helped her. Her gaze still riveted to Bremner, she sat on the edge of the hospital bed, then slid down until her feet touched the floor. The doctor supported her while she balanced herself.

Her gaze never left Bremner. He ordered her to walk to the door. She did. He told her to sit. She did. He asked her who he was.

"The Man," she said.

"Do you know who you are?"

"No." She showed no interest in knowing.

He smiled. "Come here."

She came.

"I'm going to hurt you, but you won't mind." He punched her in the kidneys.

She grunted and doubled over. Urine dribbled onto the floor. Then she stood straight again.

"You did very well," Bremner told her.

The corners of her mouth turned up slightly in as much of a smile as her stiff lips could manage. Her eyes glowed with devotion for the Man and gratitude for his praise.

Dr. Levine rubbed his small, knobby hands up and down his sunken chest, elated. "Well, Hughes. Well, well." He'd give a lot if his old mentor—his surrogate father, Dr. Cameron—could see what he'd accomplished with MK-ULTRA.

Bremner nodded. "Very good."

He called in two female nurses, who dressed Walker in a sexy black linen sheath with a T back and black high-heeled sandals. They added a long auburn wig and carefully applied makeup. He'd gone to a great deal of trouble to duplicate the outfit the Sansborough woman always wore for her meetings at the Languedoc.

Bremner sent the nurses away. "Looks identical to Liz Sansborough, doesn't she?" he remarked, putting oversized black sunglasses on her face.

"The resemblance is amazing," Dr. Levine agreed, although privately he found her too taut and bloodless for his taste. And, for a moment, he could have sworn she mumbled something. But he had more sense than to mention either thought.

Bremner told Walker to sit. He handed her a black cloth purse. "Open it. Take out what's inside."

She did. She extended the pistol in front of her. The muscles in her arms corded with the weight. Automatically she held it correctly, one hand gripping the butt and trigger, the other hand supporting the first. The pistol was an old, heavy Colt .45. It would be impossible to trace.

"Return it to the purse," Bremner instructed. She did, and he described her assignment in precise detail.

Sixty-one

Asher Flores, Jack O'Keefe, and their small band were sweating in the parked van when they saw the woman.

Asher was behind the wheel. "It's her. The real Liz Sansborough!"

She had the same long, elegant build as Sarah's. The slim hips and large breasts, the long, thick auburn hair that glinted gold and red in the evening sun. She wore oversized black sunglasses and a black sheath dress with a T of material across the low back. On her feet were black high-heeled sandals. She carried a black-cloth purse. As she passed down the street, one man after another turned to stare.

The assassin's daughter.

As she disappeared into the Languedoc's foyer, Asher said, "This means either the Carnivore *is* still alive, or Liz is up to something else."

"Not exactly a big surprise," O'Keefe said. "Now the next question: Where will Hughes and his people come out? You better pray it isn't the helipad."

"It can't be," Asher realized abruptly. "The Carnivore wouldn't allow it. Too easy to follow on radar, too easy to track him from the air if he senses a trap and has to abort the coming-in. No, he'd have specifically said no helicopters."

"By God, I think you're right."

"I *hope* I'm right," Asher said.

He wanted to start up the van, as if revving the engine would force Bremner and Liz Sansborough to speed up their last-minute fencing for small advantage. He wanted them to come out.

Instead he rolled down his window to get some air in the stifling early evening. The August sun was beating down in long, slanting shafts. The odors of hot concrete and exhaust hung in the Paris air.

The minutes ticked slowly.

8:00 P.M.

Asher looked at his watch. "Eight o'clock! Where are—"

"There they are!"

An automatic metal-mesh gate had emerged from hidden slots at the entry to the parking lot and was closing. The two attendants vanished, and six men in light summer suits and sunglasses stepped out from the Languedoc's elevator. Two took up posts near the gate as it rolled shut. They locked it and watched the street. Three prowled back into the garage. The last stood sentry next to the Company elevator.

Then, like two black ghosts, a pair of limousines emerged from the bowels of the garage. They would be Languedoc limos with full high-security equipment. The long vehicles stopped one behind the other, engines running, in front of the Company elevator. The first limo was near the mouth of the garage, while the second was directly in front of the elevator. The windows of both were darkly tinted.

Asher inhaled. "This is it."

He started the van's engine. Next, the Company elevator opened. It looked as if he'd guessed correctly, because out stepped Liz Sansborough, Hughes Bremner, and—

"Arlene Debo!" Jack O'Keefe's eyebrows shot up. "So Hughes convinced her and the President to change their minds again. I'd love to hear what cock-and-bull yarn he concocted this time."

Asher was uneasy. "Hughes must be feeling damn sure his plan is foolproof to give the DCI a ticket to the actual coming-in."

"She probably invited herself," O'Keefe decided. "She's no shrinking violet, our Arlene."

The elevator returned upstairs as Bremner, Liz Sansborough, and Arlene Debo walked rapidly to the lead limo. Bremner put Sansborough into the back seat. Arlene Debo took the front passenger seat. Bremner himself got behind the wheel.

In two minutes the elevator opened once more. Through the mesh gate Asher watched a second Liz Sansborough step into the parking garage. A twin in every detail from hair to sandals.

"Lordy, lordy," Jack O'Keefe breathed.

Immediately she crawled into the second limo's back seat.

"The resemblance is uncanny," Asher said worriedly. "Which is Liz, and which is Sarah?" He replayed in his mind the way the second Liz had walked. "No, the second one's all wrong. She's stiff. Despite the makeup and huge sunglasses, you could see her face was pasty. There was something almost sickly about her. Sarah is the second 'Liz,' and she's on Levine's chemicals."

O'Keefe said quietly, "But the antidote pills should have blocked the drug's effect. She shouldn't look so rigid, so pale, so ill—"

"I know it was the antidote," Dirk insisted.

"I'm probably wrong," O'Keefe said. "She's probably acting it out to convince them."

They had no time to discuss it further.

Ten men in tan summer suits, one of whom was Gordon, had instantly followed Sarah from the elevator and into the second limo. Another was Allan Levine with his doctor's bag. Three sat in front, and seven in back. Gordon took the wheel. It was a lot of manpower. So many people even for a stretch limo that two in the back would have to sit on the floor. Bremner was prepared.

He was also clever. The way the two limos were positioned—with the first idling ahead of the elevator, nose angled up the drive, and the second at the elevator door—Arlene Debo and the real Liz Sansborough would have had to turn their heads at the precise moment to see Sarah slip into the limo behind them. Even then, they wouldn't have seen her clearly, and Bremner was probably distracting them with his Prince Charming act anyway. Still, Bremner had to be sweating blood right now.

One good look at the second Liz Sansborough by either Arlene Debo or the real Liz would blow his whole plan.

Apparently he'd gotten away with it, because the garage's mesh security gate retracted. The two limos rolled up the driveway ramp. They paused at the top while the two Languedoc men surveyed the street. One made a swift motion, and the limos sped onto the boulevard.

Asher let three cars feed in behind, then pulled the van into traffic after them. He resisted the desire to floor the accelerator and grab his Gunsite pistol. But the truth was, he would be willing to kill all of them, even Arlene Debo, if that's what it took to get back Sarah.

Then cold fear and a wave of nausea hit his stomach in a rush. "Jack?" He was in a kind of shock. "Maybe it was the wrong chemical. Maybe Levine used a different drug on her!"

Inside the van, everyone fell silent as they followed the government limousines through the evening streets. If the doctor had used a different drug, they all knew, Sarah's situation was desperate.

Sixty-two

"Is the tracking device working?" Asher asked tensely as he glanced at the two men hunched over a computer screen in back.

"We've got an excellent reading."

In tandem the two high-security limousines crisscrossed Paris. They circled blocks, sped in and out of alleys, and made dramatic U-turns. Hughes Bremner's limo was always first. Bremner was an excellent driver, devious and daring.

Asher Flores could have written a book on the art of surveillance. He stayed back and was patient. Finally the two limousines swung west out of downtown Paris on the Avenue de la Reine. With the tracking device pointing the way, Asher followed. A few miles later they turned into a private, gated estate behind high, thick walls. With razor-sharp concertina wire topping the walls, the estate looked as forbidding and isolated as the Bastille.

Bremner's limo paused at the security check. His window lowered. The guard asked questions, listened to responses, made a call, and finally waved both vehicles through.

Asher drove around to the employees' entrance, where the van would attract less notice. The guard at the employees' gate studied the expensive vehicle with respect.

"You like my baby, *bon ami?*" Asher got out, closed the door.

He and the guard discussed the splendid vehicle. Then Asher scratched his head and pretended to remember he had business. He explained he needed to show his card, and carefully he reached inside his jacket.

Instead he brought out the Beretta. Apologizing, he tied and gagged the guard, while Jack O'Keefe and George jumped out, cut the phone line, and locked the gate. Asher drove them on inside the high walls, following the signals of the tracking device planted on Sarah.

The estate was densely wooded, and after a half mile Asher stopped behind a stand of trees. He cut the engine as he peered at the two Languedoc limousines. They were parked on the entry drive, at an angle to a grand stone villa with Doric columns. In front of the villa a children's party was busily in progress.

Gordon and six of Bremner's men loosely ringed the two Languedoc limousines. Their sunglasses constantly surveyed the trees, the lush lawn, and the house itself. They were vigilant, conscious of being on the Carnivore's turf.

Liz Sansborough—animated, real—stood between Hughes Bremner and Arlene Debo outside the lead limo. The doctor and one of Bremner's tan-suited men stood outside the second.

Sarah was nowhere in sight.

The five with Bremner formed a ragged row, backs to the limos, watching the party. Ponies trotted laughing youngsters around a temporary ring. A tiny man in a pink frock coat led an elephant on whose back rode a pink satin box full of more laughing children. A carousel rang with lively calliope music. Clowns capered and juggled across the thick, rolling lawn.

If this was the coming-in, the Carnivore couldn't have picked a better spot. Outside observation and interference would be minimal. A contained environment. And what Langley shooter, no matter how hardened, would fire into a group of families with children?

Then Asher spotted the last of Bremner's men. He'd joined the party and was eating cookies. As if he were a guest.

Asher let the van roll backward and put it in park. He, O'Keefe, and O'Keefe's comrades returned to watch from among the horse chestnut trees.

Liz Sansborough was speaking into Hughes Bremner's ear.

Bremner nodded, and the beautiful former agent looked out across the verdant lawn and waved. Asher could see no one respond in any way.

Then a clown cartwheeled from the crowd and, juggling three

colorful balls, approached the three men and two women. Dressed from head to toe in the costume of a plump French sailor from the days of Napoleon, the grease-painted clown tossed the balls to the men.

They were taken aback. The doctor caught his ball, but Bremner and his man slid their hands inside their jackets, reaching for their weapons.

The clown doubled over in exaggerated glee.

Liz Sansborough walked forward. The clown waved, and the two rapidly exchanged whispers.

Events speeded up. Bremner said something and opened the back door to the first limo. The clown got in. Immediately Arlene Debo got into the front seat. Bremner slammed the two doors shut.

"Jesus," Jack O'Keefe whispered to Asher.

"Yeah. The clown's got to be the Carnivore!" Using a clown's makeup and clothing to hide a face—and an identity—was an old trick, but it sure as hell still worked.

The Carnivore was alive. He'd fooled everyone again.

Then, as Asher watched, Liz Sansborough, escorted by Gordon, walked toward the rear of the lead limousine in her tight black dress and heeled sandals. She was going around the limo to get in next to the Carnivore. She looked tired and relieved.

At that instant four ponies broke free and thundered across the lawn. Children squealed. Adults shouted. Bremner's man, who had been amiably enjoying the party, appeared to try to catch them. But it was clear to Asher that the agent had created this diversion— parents running helter-skelter after their children.

The panic drew everyone's attention from the limos.

Yes. The second limo's back door opened, and Sarah Walker emerged!

Asher's temples throbbed. Sarah!

Behind the lead limo, the real Liz Sansborough stopped in her tracks, astonished, as Sarah closed in.

Sarah hesitated.

The two beautiful women in sunglasses and identical black dresses stared at each other, face to face, no more than a foot apart. They were mirrored reflections of one another, although to anyone who studied them closely, one appeared slightly smaller, weaker, thinner than the other.

□   □   □   □

Sarah's mind was a haze of gray. Colorless, shapeless. She felt nothing, knew nothing, except the Man. He stood close by, observing, as she circled the limousine. That was what he had instructed her to do. Walk around the limousine. She would always do exactly as he directed. She desired only that.

And then she saw the woman's face.

Her mind seemed to split in a jagged, painful tear. Her hand rose from nowhere, reached out to touch the mole above the woman's mouth. *A beauty mark,* some distant voice in her brain announced. A beauty mark?

And then the voice inside her mind said, *"I'm Sarah Walker."*

Who was Sarah Walker?

Her hand moved to her own mouth, to her own . . . beauty mark.

Before Sarah could touch Liz Sansborough's face, Gordon clamped a hand over Liz's mouth and the doctor injected her arm. Liz struggled briefly and collapsed, limp, unconscious. Gordon carried her back to the second limo and shoved her inside. The doctor followed.

Bremner nodded briskly to Sarah, and like a robot, she resumed Liz's path around the lead limo. Sarah climbed into the back seat next to the clown, the Carnivore. Bremner slammed the passenger door, stepped into the driver's seat, and slammed his door. He was sitting directly in front of Sarah.

The substitution had taken maybe fifteen seconds. Unseen by anyone.

Except Asher Flores and his little group.

Cursing, Asher lunged from the forest. The others followed. The first of Bremner's men turned in alarm. Asher smashed his pistol across the startled man's face and raced on shouting:

"Sarah! Sarah!"

In the limo she again touched her beauty mark. *I'm Sarah Walker.*

Then she dropped her hand, because she heard other words in her mind—the Man's orders: *"Remember, he will be sitting beside you. You must shoot him and only him. Is that clear?"* The Man hadn't said she had to kill a clown, so she was surprised to find a clown sitting in the seat beside her. The clown must be the man she was supposed to kill.

The purse was on her lap. As soon as the car moved forward, that was her signal. Not when the Man started the engine, but only when the car actually rolled. Then she was to shoot instantly. Use all the bullets in the gun to kill him. The man on her right. Kill him dead. The clown.

She liked the way the gun had felt in her hand.

The way the beauty mark had looked on the other woman's face.

Why was there another woman with her same beauty mark? She struggled to understand. *I'm Sarah Walker.*

The Man got in behind the steering wheel. He spoke to the female in the front seat next to him, and then he spoke to the clown in the back seat next to her. As the three talked, she looked out the darkened limousine window. She stared, saw . . . *I'm Sarah Walker.*

A man was out there—short black beard, black curly hair. A man with a gun, running toward the limousine and shouting . . . shouting . . . faint . . . "Sarah! . . . Sarah! . . ." Other men and a woman—all older—came after him.

The gray-haired woman in the front seat rumbled, "Hughes, what the hell's going on!"

The clown demanded, "You'd better have an explanation, Bremner. Fast!"

I'm Sarah Walker! The fog in her mind fought to form shapes, colors, memories.

The Man behind the steering wheel spoke to the woman and the clown, and then into a telephone, his mouth twisted in rage.

"It's Asher Flores and Jack O'Keefe . . . stop them . . ."

Asher ran toward the lead limousine, where Sarah sat in the back seat next to the Carnivore. Bremner would've sealed the doors with the master lock on the steering wheel. How in hell was he going to break in? Christ, all the Languedoc limos had full armor plating and every anti-bomb device known to modern science. He'd need a nuclear warhead—

Another of Bremner's men ran toward him, firing as he came.

Asher squeezed off two shots.

The Langley agent flung backward to sprawl on the grass.

Two more men came from behind the limousines and converged on Asher. Asher fired.

Behind him, O'Keefe's people spread out, firing.

A bullet burned past Asher's cheek.

He dropped to his belly, making himself a smaller target. Three of Bremner's people were converging on him. Their shots chewed up the lawn. But the arrogant idiots were running straight at him, figuring their numbers would overwhelm him.

He picked off two, and then came the surprise bullet. It slammed across the side of his left arm. He was stunned just long enough to take a second bullet across his gun hand.

Jesus! He let out a volley, and the remaining man reeled and pitched over dead.

Behind him the engine to Bremner's limo purred to life.

They were about to drive off!

But some of Bremner's men remained. If he didn't take care of them first, he'd be dead before he could reach Sarah. Where in hell were they?

Inside the limousine, the Man's voice was grim, tense, as he explained rapidly to the woman and clown: "There's a secret plot to kill you, Carnivore. Our men are taking care of it. No one can get to us in here. In a moment we'll be moving—"

The clown was staring at her. *I'm Sarah Walker*

"Liz, what's wrong with you?" the clown asked.

Liz? Liz . . . *Sansborough?* Surgical bolts of lightning attacked her mind. She closed her eyes with the pain. Still, she made herself think the words:

I'm Sarah Walker. I'm Sarah Walker! I'M SARAH WALKER!

Dizziness swept over her. And as if a raging storm had passed, her mind cleared. With fear and then elation, she remembered—

That bastard Gordon Taite.

The secret training camp high in the Colorado mountains.

Hughes Bremner's treachery. Sterling-O'Keefe. GRANDEUR!

Dear Asher—

Asher ignored the blood and pain of his hand, the blood running down from his upper arm. The last of the entertainers and partygoers had disappeared into the trees on the far side of the villa. Even the ponies and elephant had vanished.

It was ominously quiet. Jack O'Keefe and his people prowled, looking for more of Bremner's men.

Asher scrambled to improve his angle. There they were behind the second limo. Gordon and one other. Low to the ground, watch-

ful, guarding the second limo in which the doctor and the anesthe-
tized Liz Sansborough waited. Doing their job no matter what happened. Idiots!

"There they are!" Asher shouted and jumped up. O'Keefe's
group raced toward the remaining men while Asher focused on one
goal: Get Sarah!

The lead limousine rolled forward

Sarah told the clown, "I'm Sarah Walker." Shocked, she glanced
down as her hand, holding the gun inside the cloth purse, rose
anyway.

"You're Sarah Walker?" A gun appeared in the clown's hand.
"You bastard, Bremner! Where's Liz? Where's my daughter!"

Sarah tried to fight off the uncontrollable need to kill the clown,
to force her finger off the trigger, to force her hand down, but still
she gripped the Colt, preparing to fire—

Somewhere, vague understanding penetrated: If she killed the
Clown, she'd let GRANDEUR succeed!

"It's all right," the Man said sharply and glanced back at the
clown, his aristocratic face intent, sincere. "In a few minutes we'll be
safely in the Languedoc. You *and* Liz."

Sarah noticed the clown's hands, in skin-tight, white clown gloves,
gripping the pistol. She frowned. The hands were narrow, slender
hands.

Delicate hands.

Sarah lunged and yanked off the clown's wig.

A woman's light-brown hair tumbled down to the clown's shoulders. Angry shock spread across the clown-woman's face, and she
flung Sarah back across the seat.

But Sarah was supposed to kill a man, *not a woman!* With that
realization, the irresistible need programmed into her brain evaporated. The gun inside her purse stopped moving up.

She inhaled sharply. She had no need to kill anyone.

But then she saw Hughes Bremner's hand move on the steering
wheel. She saw a flicker of gold. A gold cigarette lighter. She'd seen
it in the infirmary—

No!

What?

Not a cigarette lighter. Her *neck!*

She reached up, felt her skin. Something hard. Something . . .
the doctor . . . had implanted!

In a split second Sarah fired through the handbag.

She fired again. And again.

Skin, bone, and hair erupted from the back of the Mustang
chief's head. A chunk of his forehead hit the windshield and splattered down to the dashboard. His body pitched forward and fell,
grotesquely twisted, against the steering wheel.

In the limousine there was total silence. A vacuum of silence like a
vast emptiness filled with the acrid stench of gunfire as Arlene Debo
and the Carnivore stared at Sarah and the bloody corpse of Hughes
Bremner.

Sixty-three

Asher Flores shot out the lock of the limousine and ripped open the door.

In the front seat Arlene Debo was staring blankly at Hughes Bremner's corpse. Blood drenched her face and stylish business suit.

In the back seat Sarah held the big Colt .45 limp on her lap, the burned remains of her handbag beside her. Asher studied her, afraid. Had her brain—?

"Sarah?"

"I finally killed him. That asshole Bremner." She gazed up. "My mind kept telling me I was Sarah Walker, but knowing it wasn't enough to stop me from killing the clown. The Carnivore. But then I saw her hands. The Carnivore's a woman." She looked quickly around.

The seat beside her was empty.

"Asher! She's got to be Liz's mother. Melanie Sansborough! We forgot all about her. Where is she? We have to—"

A voice spoke behind Asher: "I'm here, Sarah."

Melanie Sansborough held her Walther against the cheek of a trembling Dr. Allan Levine, who carried a drugged Liz Sansborough in his arms. Melanie's light-brown hair hung loose around her face, her red clown nose was gone, and her white grease paint was partially rubbed away. She had the lovely, delicate features Sarah remembered from the photos in the Sansborough family album, now hardened by time and experience.

Sarah went to her aunt, suddenly understanding. "You were *both* the Carnivore," she said. "Uncle Hal *and* you!"

"Of course. Partners. It was good business."

"But what about all this? The circus people? The 'guests' at the party?"

"Longtime associates. They put on a good show, didn't they? The police will never find them, and neither will the Languedoc."

The party had been a con. "But why—?"

"Hal and I decided to live apart until the actual coming-in. When you finally make the decision to ask for asylum, you take no chances. So they've been my cover for months. Off and on for years before that." Melanie Sansborough's eyes narrowed on Allan Levine, who was still holding the unconscious Liz but edging away toward the second limousine. "Forget it, Doctor! One more step, and it will be my pleasure to kill you!"

Allan Levine's pasty skull-face seemed to collapse in on itself. His feeble attempt at escape ended abruptly. His big feet stopped, paralyzed.

Sarah had to ask: "Did Uncle Hal really die?"

Melanie nodded. "Some hoodlums stole the MG and dumped his body. The police haven't found it yet, but there was so much blood in the driver's seat, no one could've survived—"

Melanie stopped and stared. Arlene Debo jerked out of her trance in the bloody front seat. She jumped out of the big vehicle in horror. Back in the trees, an engine roared to life.

Sarah looked at Asher.

"Jack O'Keefe and his *compadres,*" he said in a low voice and shrugged. Sarah looked around, could see none of them. They'd finished their job and vanished. She wondered why they hadn't come forward to take credit for their work.

"JesusfuckingChrist." Arlene Debo stared at them all, and then back at Hughes Bremner's slumped body. "What happened here? Has the whole world gone mad? Who are you? What is—?"

Melanie Sansborough's voice turned flinty. The voice of the Carnivore. "You were here to see the Carnivore come in, the hands-on DCI. You've seen that. You also saw an attempt to kill the Carnivore by the man you trusted to bring him in. Why, I don't know. But I expect my niece and that young man with the beard and blood all over him can tell us."

Arlene Debo glowered at Sarah and Asher. "Who *are* you two?

What the hell was Hughes doing? *Why*, for God's sake?" Her face darkened. "Is the French Prime Minister going to be assassinated tomorrow or not? Start talking!"

Sarah spoke rapidly, explaining who she was and the story of MASQUERADE—the plastic surgery, the switched identities, and the secret board of Sterling-O'Keefe. Asher added the details of Bremner's murders and his betrayal of Langley.

"You've got to reach the French government immediately," Sarah insisted. "Tell our President to contact the French President, because—" She explained the byzantine plot of GRANDEUR as briefly as she could. "With MK-ULTRA and Je Suis Chez Moi exposed, I doubt the Prime Minister and the others will go through with tomorrow's devaluation, but we'd better take no chances. Please believe me: You *must* alert the French President and the National Assembly at once!"

Melanie Sansborough said, "I guarantee you I know nothing about any assassination attempt on Vincent Vauban. A Bremner lie, I expect."

"If I could suggest, Chief, maybe you should get on the radio and alert everyone," Asher told the DCI. "It's only a matter of time before the French cops show up anyway. This is a secluded estate, but someone's got to have heard all the gunfire."

Arlene Debo shook her head, uncertain. "How do I know any of this is true?"

"Because I'm here," Melanie Sansborough said, "and you're still alive. Do you want me or not?"

The DCI pursed her lips. "I'll talk to the President." Then she brushed at the blood on her expensive gray suit and glared at Asher. "You! Agent Flores, is it? All right, Flores, get on the pipe to the Languedoc. Blue code urgent. Tell them to prepare a priority patch through to Washington. Do it!"

"You'll have to use the one in the rear limo," Sarah said. "I shot out the phone here."

Asher trotted off into the deepening twilight.

And then she saw movement in the dusk around the rear limousine.

"Asher!" she shouted frantically. Her chest contracted with fear.

She saw the movement before she saw Asher fall backward and before she heard the sharp retort of gunfire. In an instant she was across the lawn and on her knees at his side. His handsome, swarthy face grimaced in pain. Blood poured from a new wound on his leg.

"I—" he tried. And his eyes closed, unconscious.

"No!" she shouted. And then she looked wildly around.

"That fucking bitch." The hoarse voice came from the other side of the limo. Gordon's contorted face rose above the hood, and he stepped out, swaying toward her.

He held his Beretta in both bloody hands, staggering as he walked, looking for a target. For her. For "that fucking bitch." He weaved as if he'd been on a week-long drunk. But it was his face that held Sarah's shocked attention. The Fourth-of-July mask had vanished, and what remained was pure viciousness and a spirit warped by a lifetime of evil. Sarah had never seen such hate.

"You bitch! You murdered him. My . . . *father!*"

She slid Asher's Gunsite Service Pistol from its holster. As her hands moved, she felt the reassuring beat of his heart. He was alive, and they were both going to stay that way—

Gordon's Beretta was pointed directly at her. "You stupid, filthy bitch!"

She swung the Gunsite pistol up and shot him. And shot him again. This time she knew exactly what she was doing.

Sixty-four

By the time the French police arrived twenty minutes later, the Languedoc helicopters had landed and taken off again. Arlene Debo and the chief of liaison would stonewall and demand the police call in their security and intelligence agencies. The French and American spooks would negotiate for advantage and then quietly bury everything.

They would especially bury GRANDEUR, and Europe's narrow escape from disaster. At that very moment, the French President was hearing the bare facts on a hot line from the White House. He would instantly alert the secret agencies and the police. They would fan out to locate and shut down Je Suis Chez Moi and to isolate Vincent Vauban and the head of the Banque de France.

Twilight had turned to night, and the helicopter bearing Melanie Sansborough, with Liz still unconscious against her shoulder, neared the Languedoc. Also in the helicopter, a doctor tended Asher's wounds. Sarah sat with him, directly behind the pilot. She touched Asher's black hair and beard, now streaked with blood. Blood also oozed, red and fresh, from his wounded arm and the leg where one of Gordon's bullets had grazed it. There was blood all over his hand, too. But he held her to him and smiled.

"It's over, Sarah. It's all over!"

She kissed him and smiled back. "Not quite."

MONDAY

The round, golden tower of the Château de la Vere rose above the treetops. At last the entire building came into view, medieval and imposing in the late morning light. White geese waddled across the grounds. The only other movement was a gentle wind rustling the sycamores and oaks. Sarah and Asher were cleaned, detoxified, and bandaged. They parked out of sight of the château itself and moved silently through the shadows until they spotted Red Jack O'Keefe at the back. He was dressed in beige linen trousers and a loose yellow silk shirt. His once-red hair gleamed thick and ivory. There was no sign of George, Elaine, or the other *compadres*. A distinct lump showed under O'Keefe's armpit.

"You see the gun?" Asher said.

"Couldn't miss it."

The retired spymaster was carrying two leather suitcases to the battered old Peugeot parked at a back door to the south wing. He heaved the suitcases into the trunk, and stared into the woods where Sarah and Asher hid, but gave no indication he'd seen them.

He returned to the doorstep and picked up the last two suitcases and a slim leather briefcase. He lowered the suitcases into the trunk and closed it. He tossed the briefcase onto the front seat, headed back to the château, and went inside.

"Looks like you were right," Asher said.

They melted through the trees until they reached the point closest to the Peugeot. Then they ran to the stone garage and hugged it around to the car. The briefcase lay on the front seat. Sarah grabbed it. Inside was a white business envelope, which contained the documents for three numbered accounts in three different Swiss banks.

Sarah read the numbers, nodded to Asher.

"My papers, please." The voice was behind Sarah. Jack O'Keefe had come the long way around the château. He smiled affably, but his gun was in his hand and aimed at her back.

Asher reached for his weapon—

"I wouldn't, Asher." O'Keefe's eyebrows raised. "My finger's pressing the trigger of this toy, and even if you managed to kill me instantly with one of your well-placed bullets, I'd fire reflexively. We both know what that means."

"I doubt you'd do it, Jack," Sarah said quietly.

O'Keefe considered. "Perhaps not, but it's not worth the risk to

Asher. She's the love of your life, isn't she, Asher? All I want is to leave in peace with a little money in the bank. I intend to live long and comfortably, and to indulge my *compadres*." He gestured with the gun. "Come here where I can see you, Asher. Stand close to Sarah. Not that close. There, that's right. Turn around, and I'll take those papers, Sarah."

Sarah waved them at O'Keefe. "Stolen money, Jack? You've been part of Sterling-O'Keefe all along, and now you're running with the loot?"

He smiled, cocked his head. "Filthy lucre. But I've earned it a thousand times over."

"Just like Hughes Bremner," Asher said.

"You never know, do you, in our business?"

Sarah shook her head. "No one's going to believe that, Jack. You've got nothing to do with Sterling-O'Keefe. Bunny Bremner's confirmed that."

He raised his eyebrows. "I doubt Hughes ever told Bunny a damn thing about Sterling-O'Keefe."

"No, but a journalist named Leslee Pousho did." Sarah related the story of Lucas Maynard, Leslee Pousho, and Bunny Bremner. "When Ms. Pousho could talk, she called Mrs. Bremner and told her everything. That was late last night. Mrs. Bremner immediately called the White House. The Chief of Staff himself picked up Leslee's second set of copies from the post office box where she'd mailed them."

O'Keefe was surprised. "Christ, Hughes really was a pig. His own wife! But she ended up turning the tables, did she? Too bad the bastard didn't live to be made miserable by it."

Sarah waved the papers at him again. "Come on, Jack. These are Hughes's accounts. Arlene Debo has his inventory, and these three are listed."

"Really?" He held the gun steady on them. "Well, then, I suppose you can add stealing to my crimes. Now hand over—"

"In a minute." Sarah slid the papers back into the envelope. "I'd like your help on one little matter. You acted Brutus to Bremner's Caesar and told us the truth about Bremner and why he'd decided to kill the Carnivore. You didn't have to reveal that, did you? So why did you do it?" She studied his sun-bleached eyes and twisted the knife: "Getting tired of Hughes paying your bills, 'keeping' you?"

The pistol in Red Jack O'Keefe's hand stayed true on its mark—

her heart. They stood that way, watching each other in the luminous French sunshine.

At last he said, "When they forced me to retire, I had nothing but a lifetime of service and a room full of awards. My pension couldn't buy a third of what I was accustomed to, much less a place like this. I'd always wanted this château. Hughes knew it. He bought it for me. Gave me a monthly stipend. At first I thought it was gratitude for all I'd done for him, pure generosity." He paused. "Then I learned better."

"He rubbed your nose in it," Asher guessed. "Kept you on a leash. You'd been his mentor, now *he* gave the orders."

"And he used your name for his illegal empire," Sarah added. "Sterling-*O'Keefe*. The ultimate insult. He—"

An angry flush rose up Jack O'Keefe's neck. He exploded: "How goddamn dare he use *my* name for his illicit, greedy business! He was a dog peeing on a tree, using my name to prove he owned me. All I have is my reputation!" He paused, blinked furiously. "When he phoned to tell me to stall you two, I saw my chance. I couldn't risk going against him directly, but maybe I could destroy the son of a bitch and keep what I had if I filled you in and helped out. If he killed you and the Carnivore, I was still safe. But if you killed him, Sterling-O'Keefe would end, I'd be free of Hughes, *and* I'd still have what I wanted!"

Asher nodded. "So you kept us here for him, but you also gave him to us. You planted your hat by the door, knowing Sarah would spot it. I guess you never forget how to play all sides?"

"Which means," Sarah said, "you already had the numbers to Bremner's Swiss accounts. You just couldn't use them while he was alive. With him dead, you had your revenge, your freedom from his 'generosity,' and his money."

O'Keefe gave her a shrewd look. "Someone always 'owes,' Sarah. I have contacts in Swiss banking circles. Some of them 'owe' me a great deal. It was child's play to get Hughes's so-called secret numbers."

"It wasn't Hughes's money, Jack, and it's not yours," Asher reminded him.

Sarah nodded. "I guess Hughes forgot your rule."

"And what's that, Sarah?"

" 'The speed of the leader determines the speed of the pack.'

Ultimately you ran a faster, smarter race than Hughes. Sadly for you, you weren't quite fast enough to get away with it.''

The spymaster looked from one to the other. Slowly a grin spread across his weathered face. "Too bad you're too young to have known Wild Bill Donovan. Even he would've been impressed.''

"Never mind the flattery, Jack.'' Sarah held out her hand. "Give me the gun. Arlene Debo wants to talk to you. It seems that when the French police arrived at Je Suis Chez Moi last night, the whole thing had been bombed to smithereens. We heard your van take off early from the coming-in—that wouldn't have been you going off to take care of that rather large detail?''

"As a matter of fact, I believe some of my *compadres* might have been responsible for that. Did seem a little stupid to let biotechnology like Levine's continue in an irresponsible world like ours, don't you think?''

"Now we'll never know. All Levine's records are gone.''

"That was the idea.'' O'Keefe hesitated. He pointed the gun at her heart again. "No one's going to miss these three little accounts, Sarah. There's hardly $5 million in them. The great U.S. government can have all the rest.''

"No.''

"Perhaps a split?'' he offered.

"The gun, Jack,'' Asher said.

"And we keep the papers,'' Sarah added.

"Perhaps *one* account?'' Red Jack asked hopefully.

"All the papers,'' Sarah said.

The old spymaster sighed, lowered his weapon, and handed it to Asher. "I never was any good at looking out for myself.''

"Maybe Arlene Debo can arrange something,'' Asher suggested.

"After all, you helped expose Hughes, Sterling-O'Keefe, and GRANDEUR,'' Sarah said. "You cleared your name.''

A flicker in O'Keefe's eyes told them that's the way he viewed it, too, and if he couldn't be rich and keep his château, at least he'd remain an untarnished living legend.

"I suppose that's what's important,'' he said. "And I'm sure something will turn up, some way for an old man to make a few francs, eh? I believe I'd rather not talk to Arlene just now. George and Elaine Russell are waiting on the Côte d'Or. Can't disappoint them, can I? Their pensions are even less than mine. I can't say exactly where we'll be down the road, you understand. But I'll be available anytime Arlene cares to offer that reward."

"Jack—" Sarah said.

He stepped toward the Peugeot. "I really have nothing else to tell Langley, Sarah. What I know is ancient history, Asher. You'll get along fine without me. I pass the torch to you."

He flashed them his best smile.

Sarah and Asher laughed.

"All right, go on," Asher said. "Meet your friends. But check in with Langley soon. I'm serious about that reward. You did give us the last piece we needed to stop Hughes Bremner."

"Even if you had an ulterior motive," Sarah added.

O'Keefe nodded, climbed into the sporty Peugeot, and drove off down the long, stately drive. He was whistling "God Bless America."

Sarah and Asher laughed and turned toward the forest where their Languedoc car waited. Suddenly she stopped and stared at Asher. "We never searched the Peugeot. The glove compartment. Under the carpet. The floorboards."

"And there were those suitcases in the trunk." Asher stared back, stunned. "We never even looked!"

"No, we didn't. Do you think he could already have withdrawn some of Bremner's money? An odd million or two?"

"Those three accounts were awfully easy to pick up on," Asher said. "The way he flung the briefcase into the car and walked away long enough for us to find the papers. Very careless of Jack. Kind of like his leaving his straw Panama by the door yesterday."

They gazed down the drive. Without looking back, Red Jack O'Keefe gave a jaunty wave and vanished onto the main road. They looked at each other again. They shrugged, and then they began to laugh.

Sixty-five

JANUARY
It was winter in Santa Barbara, and a cold ocean storm was drumming the roof and pounding the beach. The two cousins—Sarah Walker and Liz Sansborough—stood shoulder to shoulder in Sarah's bungalow and stared into the hall mirror.

At each other. At themselves.

At the pair of them.

"It's eerie," Sarah said. "We're eerie."

"Almost as if I'm two people," Liz decided.

They returned to the oolong tea on the coffee table. Sarah poured. "When your father thought I was you, he put in milk and sugar. Is that right?"

Liz nodded and sat back, relaxed in gray wool trousers and a pale blue turtleneck sweater. Her thick auburn hair cascaded to her shoulders, catching the lamplight in rich golds and reds. Sarah's own hair was that color again and growing out into a glossy mass that fell in ringlets around her high-planed face.

"Do you miss your original face?" Liz wondered.

"Sometimes. But I must've been ready for a change, or I never would've agreed to cosmetic surgery." Sarah handed Liz her cup. "I've been thinking about getting some adjustments so I'd look less like you. But truthfully . . . the ensemble seems to suit me. I haven't figured out quite how or why."

Liz smiled. "I thought you'd be sick of looking like me, especially after all the trouble it's caused you." She sipped tea, studied Sarah. "Do you miss your fling in the business?"

Sarah shook her head. She was relaxed, wearing sweats and slippers. A fragrant oak fire burned in her fireplace. There was still a part of her that was dissatisfied, that felt somehow the whole thing still wasn't over, but she'd gone on and rebuilt her life anyway. "I'm doing investigative pieces now. My most recent is a big environmental article about the Diablo Canyon nuclear power plant north of here. It was built on an earthquake fault, can you believe that?" She sipped her tea. "What about you?"

"The desk boys have finished debriefing me, and I'm back on the payroll. I'm considered a risk because of my parents, so Langley will give me only contract work. I think that'll satisfy me. For a while I considered dropping out. Climb a couple of mountains. Take up deep-sea diving. Hang gliding. Maybe go back for a graduate degree in something." She shrugged.

As a fresh blast of rain thrummed the windows, Sarah watched the conflict in her cousin's face. Liz no longer wanted to be who and what she was.

Sarah said, "I can understand why you'd miss it. It's addictive somehow. But you figure out really fast that if you want to exit intact, you have to compromise. I'll never feel easy about the people I killed, because I'll never know for sure whether I could've found a better way. But I think I was right, and I've had to learn to live with that."

"That's because you're marching in the parade. Mother says, 'Some people march in the parade of life, some people stand on the curb and watch, and others don't even know the damn thing's going on.' " Liz looked down at her teacup. Her voice was low, sad, as she confessed, "Papa let himself be killed, Sarah." She raised her dark-brown gaze. "He knew better than to stop outside that garage long enough to take out the couple that was firing on you. He should've driven the hell out of there. He seldom made mistakes, and never anything as basic or stupid as that. I'm sure it was because he never really wanted to come in at all. For him, death was better than retirement."

Sarah nodded. She'd never thought about why he'd stopped, and Liz was right. It had been a mistake. But there was something else that had happened right afterward. . . . And then it came to her. She recalled seeing a clown— Or had that been an illusion? The adrenaline of the violent action and the photos she'd noticed on Quill's fireplace mantle?

Liz gave a small smile and continued, "Mother, however, is in her element. Now that the President's relented, they'll be debriefing her for at least another year. She feels as if she's making amends, making a contribution, and that's what convinced the President. I wish you could see her and Arlene Debo." She gave a dry chuckle. "They dislike each other, but they understand each other, too. Makes for some interesting fireworks."

Sarah and Liz discussed the secret hearings the House and Senate intelligence committees had conducted into MASQUERADE, MK-ULTRA, Sterling-O'Keefe, and GRANDEUR. They'd testified at both.

"I'd like to write a book about the Carnivore," Sarah said, "maybe with Leslee Pousho. We talked about it when I visited her in the hospital. Her face was almost repaired. Talk about courage—" She paused, recalled Leslee's suffering. "The problem is the government won't declassify the files for twenty years. I'd need information from other sources."

"I'd like to help, but I know only what was in the messages I was ferrying into the Languedoc. Papa told me nothing. Neither did Mother, and now she won't talk because her deal with the U.S. government is that they get it all."

Sarah poured more tea. "It was a shock to realize I was the Carnivore's niece." She handed Liz her cup and looked into her dark eyes. Not Sarah's eyes, but somehow connected. "How was it being their daughter?"

Liz held the cup as steadily as her father had held his back in the dingy safe house in Paris. "When I was growing up, Papa was away on business a lot. That's all I knew. After a while Mother traveled with him, and eventually on her own. Later I learned he'd been training her then. My grandparents took care of me."

Liz shrugged. "It all seemed normal. They were good parents, and we had great times together. But I knew only part of who they were. I'd always sensed there was some huge secret, but I couldn't figure it out. Maybe it was because of that I started having nightmares when I was little. I used to scream myself awake. I had those nightmares until three years ago when I saw Papa on that job in Lisbon. Suddenly everything made sense. The big secret was my parents were assassins. I was stunned. Horrified."

"You talked them into quitting?"

"Into taking time out. And then we fought a lot. Fighting is one hell of a lot better than silence. From the beginning, Mother made it clear she'd never loved or needed the work. In fact, Papa had tricked her into it by telling her it was for England. Since she was raised in a military family, she knew her duty. By the time she figured out he wasn't on staff with MI5 or MI6, she was in too deeply to quit." Liz looked down at the floor. "I think she almost got to enjoy the work, too. The danger, the matching of wits, the thrill."

"I'll bet she was protecting you, too, Liz."

"Yes. Neither one of them wanted me to know. But when I joined them, she realized what it was doing to all of us, and then she desperately wanted to quit. Papa wanted to keep working. He was damaged, Sarah. Something was broken inside. In the end I think the only reason he agreed to come in was he was afraid of losing us. He always said I was his weakness. I loved him, too, until I saw his eyes that night in Lisbon when he killed the courier. His eyes were so deadly, so sick. The courier was just a boy—" She bowed her head. "I hated Papa after that."

They continued to talk until nearly midnight, when Liz announced she had to leave. She was driving south to Los Angeles International to catch the red-eye back to Washington. She crossed the room with the elegance of a cheetah, all athletic rhythm and body-joy.

She put on a trench coat, tied the belt, and went to the door, fidgety. They kissed cheeks.

"When will I see you again?"

"Who knows?" Liz cocked her head, pursed her lips. "You know, there's talk at Langley about hiring you. Interested?"

Sarah felt a flash of panic, then curiosity. What would it mean? She shook her head, certain. "My mother has a saying, too: 'Never fight with a pig. You both get dirty, and the pig loves it.' " She smiled. "Now I'm fighting for causes I choose. I don't mind the dirt nearly as much. Keep your eye out for more investigative pieces from me."

"I will. Oh, and one more thing. When you see Asher, remind him to forget he knows me." She gave a cheery wave, ran lightly through the rain, and disappeared into her car.

They had lived together, Sarah and Asher, in the bungalow on the beach since their releases from the Languedoc's infirmary. While he

was away on assignments she met with editors, researched, interviewed, and wrote. Her probing articles appeared in major magazines across the nation.

Each day that winter she walked on the beach beneath the gray,
heavy sky. The ocean crashed and pounded the sand. Seagulls gathered in large flocks, beaks pointed into the wind, taught by nature
to prepare in this way for a storm.

One day she returned from her beach walk to find the light on in
the bedroom. Asher was home! She ran up the steps, flung open the
door, and rushed into his arms.

"You're so cold." He kissed her cheeks, her throat, her mouth.
"God, it's so good to see you—"

"Did you get an address for Jack O'Keefe?"

"Of course. But I don't know why you want it."

"Tell you later." She smiled mysteriously, kissed him deeply.
"How long will you be able to stay?"

"A month. And this time you'll damn well marry me."

She thought about Liz, about how much distance there could be
between two identical women joined by blood and fate.

"I might want to have children," she warned.

"That's good, because I might want to, too."

They tore off each other's clothes, panting, smiling, whispering
secret love words. She couldn't get enough of his wild black hair, his
snow-white teeth, his feral eyes. When they were both naked, he
spun her around, her back to his front, and they fit together tightly.
It made her ache, the old need renewed each time. He buried his
mouth in her hair, his breath warm and spicy against her throat. She
inhaled and arched back into him, her spirit soaring, healing, with
love.

She wrote the letter in late January and began her wait.

It went first to a post office drop in London, then was forwarded
to Amsterdam, and finally found Red Jack O'Keefe on Majorca.
From there, he sent it on to Madrid, where it was forwarded to
Algiers, and then mailed one last time, to Palermo, Sicily. All in all,
it took six weeks.

Don Alessandro Firenze received the letter at his villa outside the
beautiful resort of Cefalù, halfway between Palermo and Messina. A
small town of some 12,000, Cefalù had been his occasional home
for some forty years. It was the family seat of the Firenzes and the

Bosas. No longer the young firebrand who'd rejoined his heritage as a teenager, then whored all night and drunk all day, Don Alessandro now sought the education he'd passed over as a youth. He was systematically reading through the eclectic library he'd collected. He still took a job periodically, just often enough to quench the fire that otherwise would blaze out of control and make him destructively restless.

Besides his books, the don enjoyed Cefalù's white-sand beaches, the rocky coves, and the dramatic backdrop of sheer rock that towered above the old fishing village. He liked the fresh grapes and olives, and the unsophisticated life-style; Sicilians were mostly a primitive farming people. Over the last two thousand years in this difficult arid climate, they'd learned to mind their own business. Thus, Cefalù—and Sicily—were congenial to him in all ways.

The don looked first at the signature on the letter. A lump formed in his throat. It was her handwriting: "Liz." He glanced around. Nothing but the winter wind moved amid the olive trees that dotted his vast mountainside estate.

Lo leggo subito. He would read it immediately. He took the letter to his chair beneath a cork tree in his large garden and began—

Dear Papa,
I thought you'd like to know Langley is giving me some
contract work. I suspect I'll be bored, and I'll have to look for
something else to do with my life. I'm telling you this because
you probably haven't heard from Mother, and you won't for at
least another year. That's how much longer Langley will keep
her on a short leash, in safe houses, debriefing her. . . .

He waved for the maid. *"Signorina, vorrei tè subito per favore."* The winter day was chill, and he wanted his hot tea with milk. Also he asked for his radio. He moved his simple wood chair and little side table out into the Mediterranean sun, and he held up the envelope to gaze at it in the light. He next held up the letter, scrutinizing it closely, too.

Off in the distance, three vultures caught his eye. They were circling lower and lower. Some carrion must be waiting beneath. This was another thing he liked about Sicily: Few wild animals were native here, except several varieties of vulture. The vulture was an elegant bird, great, patient, and it performed a useful service, ridding the scrub of rotting flesh and maggots.

His tea and radio arrived on a tray. He told the maid she and the other staff could have the rest of the day off. She bowed herself back to the villa, and he added milk and sugar to the tea, then a little packet of something else. He touched several buttons on the "radio." He resumed reading.

> You must be wondering how I know you're alive, Papa. I saw Sarah recently. She told me when you and she were in the MG leaving your safe house, she saw Mother on the corner in her clown disguise. I now know Mother was there because she and I were coming in that night, and she was going to help you fake your death again. Later Jack O'Keefe told Sarah you had to be playing one of your tricks, pretending to have died. I imagine he's regretted his slip. . . .

The don took a long drink of the hot tea—assam, his favorite. He looked off down the slope toward the turquoise Tyrrhenian Sea. He stood, beat his arms against his chest, warming himself. They'd be here soon.

Even as the words entered his mind, he saw shadows dart among the trees, swift and elusive, but still he saw them. He could smell them, too, as a vulture smelled prey. As a dog smelled a bone he'd buried a lifetime ago. The sea breeze and the experience of years carried their scent. He felt his heart squeeze, and then the sudden rush of adrenaline that made life worth continuing.

Again, he read.

> Once more, you've lied to me. You said you'd come in, and now you haven't. I want to see you. Come in, Papa.

It was signed, "Love, Liz."

Hal Sansborough raised his chin and bellowed, "Sarah!"

The sound reverberated across the dry Sicilian slope.

The wily cold-war assassin turned, shaded his eyes with the letter Sarah had faked. "I know you're here! Show yourself!"

He was alone, arrogant and sure on the mountainside. Beside him stood his chair and side table. Behind him spread his elegant pink stone villa and the grove of olive trees.

As Sarah and Asher left the trees and walked toward him, the first explosion jolted the ground like an earthquake. A brown-gray cloud erupted behind the villa.

"What the hell was that?" Asher said.

A helicopter appeared from over the mountain to their left. It was their backup. They ran toward Hal Sansborough. Men and women in camouflage melted out from the olive trees and converged from all sides on the killer. This time they'd get him.

"It's over, Hal," Sarah said as they approached. "No fake blood this time. A systemic depressor to make your heartbeat and pulse so faint only a doctor's instruments could detect them. No more tricks of a master. The Carnivore is going to come in this time. It's over."

The assassin smiled. "Stay back from the villa unless you plan to come with me." And Sarah saw in his eyes what Liz had described. It was as if she were peering down a dark, cold well of evil.

Two explosions erupted on either side of the villa.

"The villa's sinking!" Asher's gaze swept the shifting land.

"We're above old subterranean caves." Hal Sansborough picked up his tea, finished it. "Does Liz know you're here?"

"No," Sarah told him, anxiously watching the trembling land. "We used a computer scan to fake her signature."

"Does the laser-jet ink contain some kind of homing device?"

"One of R&D's new toys," Asher admitted.

Hal Sansborough lifted his head, savoring the sea air and his memories. "The explosions are automatic now. Set off with my 'radio.' No way you or I can stop them." He gave no glance to the sinking villa behind him, nor to the wary troops whose circle was tightening. "The world's changed too much. It's all fucking technology and disposable governments."

And then two more blasts thundered on either side of Sarah and Asher. Shock waves knocked them flat. The Carnivore dropped to his knees. The troops fell, struggled up shouting, and scrambled back. The helicopter closed in, blowing up a tornado of dry Sicilian soil.

"Uncle Hal!" Sarah crawled to him.

The land beneath them suddenly dropped a half foot.

"Go away!" he yelled. "I can't live like you!"

Asher grabbed her around the waist and pulled. The earth split and plunged. Hal Sansborough heaved himself up onto his chair. His gaze was clear. His short crew cut glistened salt-and-pepper in the sunlight.

"Hal, you bastard!" she shouted. "You've lost!"

He laughed as if he'd just heard the biggest joke in the world, and he closed his eyes. He mouthed, "No! I've won!"

Trees toppled. Behind him the villa sank from view, and a mushroom cloud of dust and smoke rolled across the slope. Sarah and Asher jumped up and ran, leaping widening cracks and tilting slabs of hardpan. Sarah glanced back just in time to see Hal Sansborough, unconscious and slumped in his chair, drop with startling suddenness into the bowels of the earth.

At last Sarah and Asher stopped on a distant ridge. The ground that had supported the Carnivore's lovely villa had collapsed into a giant crater. Dust hung above, caught the sun, and sparkled. She watched the sight, awed and sad. The first part of her plan had worked: She'd guessed correctly that Red Jack O'Keefe had maintained contact with the still-active Hal Sansborough, but she hadn't been certain until he'd received her faked letter and forwarded it on through various drops and it had reached the Carnivore's last lair.

But—dammit!—she'd wanted *him*, not his death.

"Did you see that packet he put into his tea?" Asher asked, his face gentle.

"Probably some kind of poison."

"I agree. But if the mop-up crew can't find his body, we'll never know. Or whether he's really dead."

Sarah gazed across the forbidding, windswept land. "That's probably the way he wanted it."

Asher took her hand, and they turned away. She looked up at the blue sky. Energy coursed through her, and hope. If she didn't have complete resolution, she now knew she had something far more important—Asher and life.